- Colleen -

Dark Woods

Sammy Jones

First Edition: October 2020

Cover photography by Filip Zrnzević
Design by Sammy Jones

ISBN 978-1-7357385-0-5 (ebook)
ISBN 978-1-7357385-1-2 (paperback)
ISBN 978-1-7357385-2-9 (hardcover)

Published by Whimsical Gnome Press
www.authorsammyjones.com

Dedication

To my awesome little family–

My loving husband, Greg,

My wonderful children, Scarlett and Elliott,

Your patience and support have been indescribable. I am so grateful that my dream has come true with you by my side. I love you all so much.

Chapter 1

"Carter, your dad's home!" Alison said, viciously scrubbing a casserole dish.

The front mahogany door slammed shut while angry footsteps echoed throughout the foyer.

"Hi, honey! How was work? Hope you had a good day," she shouted from the kitchen.

The deep, grouchy voice barely uttered an audible word as he trudged up the stairs.

Attempting to spark a conversation with her husband, Alison asked, "Richard, are you hungry? Dinner will be ready soon!"

As the words left her mouth, his office door closed.

Resting his head on the table, Carter scribbled the answers to his algebra homework, ignoring his mother's excitement. Carter had no energy to waste on his miserable father. He wanted to speed through his math problems, so he could try to piece together his beloved model ship.

His mother saw the crushed look on his face. Brushing her blonde hair out of her face, she sighed. "I bet if anyone can fix it, it'd be you, honey."

"Mom, Sadie's teeth popped holes in the mast," he explained. Glancing down, his six-month-old golden retriever wagged her soft, feathery tail. Carter's gray eyes darted over towards the heaping pile of wood and string. He couldn't believe she chewed his intricate model ship into pieces.

Trying to offer a new perspective, she shrugged. "Well, maybe it'd make it look more rugged or authentic?"

Looking at his mother, Carter forced out a half-smile while running his hand through his thick, dark hair. She would say anything to raise his spirits. He knew he was lucky to have her. Who else uses all of their vacation time to go out-of-town so their son could learn how to drive a boat? Or come down the stairs at two o'clock in the morning to sit and talk with hot cocoa after he wakes up from one of his recurring nightmares? Despite being fourteen, she always treated him as a person—not just a kid.

"Right?" she said with a chuckle. "Maybe pirates attacked them."

"Pirates?" Carter rolled his eyes.

"Well, hey, it's a beautiful ship! They probably have something valuable on it. Next thing you know, pirates come sailing by and boom! A cannonball gets shot through the mast," she described, drying her hands with a dishtowel.

Attempting to humor her, he said, "Mom, I don't know who the bigger kid is."

"Carter, if you can hold on to anything in life, let it be your imagination," she explained with a glimmer in her eyes. "You can travel anywhere, do anything, be anyone; and no one can tell you otherwise."

After a few moments passed, he sat back to think about what she said. The more he thought about it, the more he realized it was true. He was happier when he thought Santa was squeezing down his chimney or when the Easter Bunny was plopping candy into his basket. Heck, even the Tooth Fairy got him excited about making money after losing his teeth. Sadly, life seemed to lack that extra sprinkle of imagination or magic anymore. Even his friends at school seemed duller once they lost the passion and excitement of childhood.

As Alison studied his face, she noticed how stubbles of dark facial hair were poking out from under his soft skin. A bittersweet tear formed in her eye. It felt like yesterday when she couldn't wait to bring home her precious bundle of joy. Despite missing her little, chunky baby, she was beyond grateful for their relationship now. Their deep bond and openness made communication easier over the years. Luckily, it even assisted through gloomy times.

Although it was long ago, the wounds still felt fresh. It was several years ago when Richard and Alison were simultaneously at the height of their careers. Since their schedules were intense, they decided it was best to hire a babysitter for just a few hours a day. The only family member close by was Richard's father, who was completely out of the question because of his abusive history. With that being said, they were very picky about who they wanted as their sitter. After many interviews, they hired the smart, cute, and outgoing Bethany. She was perfect—or so they thought.

When Alison got home one night, Carter was fast asleep in his room. She wanted to catch up on her emails, so she headed over to the couch.

"Mommy," five-year-old Carter whispered, wandering towards her.

"Hey, babe! What's the matter?" she asked as she looked up from her laptop.

"My head hurts," he whined while holding the back of his head.

Jumping up to console him, she blurted out, "What happened? Did you fall?"

"No, Mommy," he said with his eyes to the ground.

Goosebumps spiked up her neck. "What happened then?"

Carter's eyes remained glued to the floor as he rubbed his wound. While Alison waited for a response, a tear fell from his eye and rolled down his cheek. Her heart tightened as she tried to understand what was going on. Sliding off the couch, Alison picked Carter's chin up to raise his eyes to meet hers.

"Babe, you can tell me anything. We can work out whatever happened. Was it an accident?" she asked, attributing his shyness to something that went wrong.

He shook his head no.

"Did someone do this to you?" she demanded.

He remained silent.

"Look, if someone hurt you, you can tell me. You can tell Mommy anything. I'll always be here to protect you," Alison desperately explained.

Carter looked at her with red, teary eyes. "Beth got mad and hit me."

She wanted to scream at the top of her lungs but didn't want to upset him even more. Alison darted for her phone to check the memory card footage from the hidden nanny cam. Her arms pulsated and tunnel vision set in as her shaky hands scrolled through her phone. Once she found it, Alison took a deep breath and began shaking her leg uncontrollably as she watched the video.

Carter crawled on Alison's lap and buried his head into her chest. The sound of her heart beating was almost deafening. Even so, she was his rock, and instantaneously his pain melted away. She rested her lips on his head, and his mouth curled up into a tiny smile.

Scanning through the footage, she glanced at random images from the night. From Carter sitting on the couch to running around with his toy airplane, Alison couldn't tell what happened. Would he lie about something so serious? Could it have been an accident or just a dream? Right when she had the hope it was a misunderstanding—there it was.

There it was! Right there, no way, rewind!

She screamed in her mind while she brought her hand to her mouth. Carter was swirling his plane in the air. While spinning in a circle, he accidentally stepped on Bethany's foot. Without thinking, she grabbed the remote from the arm of the sofa. With a swift, hard swing, she backhanded him over the head with the edge of the remote. Immediately, Carter dropped to the floor, crying.

Looking down on Carter's little mop of hair innocently propped against her, Alison sobbed. How could a person be so cruel to a child? They are so vulnerable and just want to enjoy life. Her heart tore apart. Immediately, she called Richard and notified the police.

No matter how many years passed by, that night always had a way of coming back to haunt her. Alison blinked her eyes and took a deep breath as she tried to bring herself back to the present moment. She couldn't let herself go down that road in her mind. Alison was grateful that she had footage to share in court, leading the jury to convict Beth on child abuse charges. Richard and Alison immediately placed Carter in self-defense classes, and she left the company to be home with him. Luckily, he enjoyed fencing and grew to respect karate. She would do anything for her son. If only Richard could have that relationship with Carter.

A perfect thought popped into her head. She dropped the soapy sponge into the sink and darted up the stairs. Slowly walking towards their home office, Alison cracked the door open.

"Hey, how was work?" Alison asked, popping her head around the corner of their study.

A slow, perturbed sigh exited Richard's nostrils as he typed on his laptop. "Fantastic."

With his hair slicked back, Alison noticed the silver strands poking through his natural dark color. Trying to be sympathetic, she uttered, "I'm sorry to hear that, honey. It seems like work has been unforgiving lately."

"Yep."

The staleness in the air could turn the sweetest fruit sour. These repetitively draining conversations took a toll on Alison's patience.

"Well—" she suggested, "Carter had a rough day too. Sadie used his model ship as a chew toy, and now it's sitting on the table in pieces."

Richard didn't respond. Either his work emails had his attention or he didn't care. Regardless, Alison felt determined to make Richard hear her out.

"I figured this would be the perfect opportunity for you to pick out a new one with him. I know he has been secretly hoping to save for the—" Alison described with a fading smile.

"Sorry, Alie, but he'll get over his little boat breaking. In the meantime, I'm trying to work on important problems," he sneered while shaking his head. He quickly unbuttoned his sleeves to roll over his tanned forearms.

"Look, Richard," she scoffed. "I'm done trying to help you."

"Help me?" he yelled. "Help me with what? When I come home from work, you'd think I could unwind or be able to tie up loose ends. But no, I'm being constantly badgered with nonsense," he aggressively refuted.

"That's great! This whole time, I've been trying to help you maintain a healthy relationship with your son. You know, the one who may not get over his little boat breaking after saving up for two years to buy it? You never try to be a father to him. It's like you can't be bothered to bond with him. Well, Richard, I'm done trying to help you. I'm done trying to help you salvage whatever connection you might've wanted. He'll grow up to hate you, and there'll be nothing more I can do to change that if you aren't willing to yourself," Alison blurted out as she swiftly left the room.

Richard let out a grateful sigh, reaching for his glass of scotch. After a heavy gulp, he continued typing.

Even though an internal rage burned, Alison flew down the stairs with a forced smile.

"Let me guess, too busy to come down to eat?" Carter asked, shaking his head.

"Don't worry about him," she said, shutting off the stove. "I have a surprise for you."

"A surprise?" His eyes lit up. "What did you get me?"

"You and I will pick out a new ship and work on it together!"

"Are you serious, Mom? That's awesome! Are you sure, though? They are so expensive," he anxiously said.

"Honey, you don't worry about a thing. It's my treat. Now, grab your coat," she mentioned, swinging her purse over her shoulder.

Closing the front door behind them, a bitter gust of Alaskan wind slapped them across their faces. They quickly darted to the car, minimizing their exposure to the cold. As they hopped inside Alison's car and buckled their seat belts, she looked over to him. "Carter?"

"Yeah, Mom?"

"I love you. I've always loved you, and you'll always mean the world to me. I just never want you to forget that." She smiled warmly.

"I love you too, Mom."

After Carter reclined his seat in his mother's red sedan, he glanced up at the window in their study. He never understood why his father was so miserable. Carter could understand why being a lawyer would overwhelm someone, but he didn't know why he took out all of his frustration on them. Looking over at his mother, she saw his concern.

"Carter, which hobby store would you like to go to?" Alison asked with smiling eyes.

"It doesn't matter."

Patting his knee, Alison suggested, "Let's go to Red's. We should make it before they close. In the meantime, we can listen to some music."

Carter zoned out, pressing his forehead against the cold passenger window. The trees and signs zipped by as they drove down the empty road. Before he knew it, they were pulling into the parking lot of Red's Ships, Trains, & Planes. The street lights blinked on one after another, quickly lighting up the parking lot.

Hopping out of the car, Carter wore a giant smile on his face. He still couldn't believe he was getting a replacement so soon. After all, everything here was a couple hundred dollars up to a few thousand. As he reached the store, he held the door for his mother.

They carefully walked through several aisles before Carter settled on the model ship he loved the most. There were pieces of rosewood, mahogany, and western cedar included in the box. The model had three decks with numerous metal canons on each side.

The metal anchor, linen sails, and miniature lifeboats were so intricately designed that Carter couldn't wait to bring it home.

With a nervous grin, Carter peered down at the price tag. His jaw dropped once he realized the ship was almost five-hundred dollars. Knowing it was too much, he gently slid the box back on its shelf.

"Honey, if you want it, we can get it." Alison rubbed the back of her neck.

"No way. It's beautiful, but it's too much." Carter nervously grinned.

Nodding in agreement, she explained, "Look, it's more than what we'd normally spend, but I really want you to have something special. Not to mention, you've worked so hard in school and are always helping."

"Wow! Thanks, Mom!" he exclaimed. "I have money that I can put towards it, too!"

"You're welcome, honey. Don't worry about it." She gently smiled.

Driving back from the store, the heavy winds forcefully pushed against the side of the car. Carter always found it eerie how he could barely see into the woods when the sun would go down. The shadows from the tree branches danced in the stream of light while the remaining trees faded into the black abyss.

As Carter read every word on the package, Alison joyously mentioned, "I'm so excited you found the one you liked!"

"Mom, you're the best!" Carter raved, smiling ear to ear.

She'd find a way for Richard to bond with him. *Carter deserved more than just a man living with him. He deserved a present father,* she thought to herself. Her eyes turned from Carter back to the road. The Alaskan winds viciously pushed snow off of neighboring tree branches and slammed into the windshield. As they continued to drive, the snow and winds formed a thick wall in front of the car, obstructing her visibility. Alison took a deep breath, hoping the snow would lighten up a bit. Luckily, a swirl of wind cracked an opening through the whiteout so Alison could see. Right as a sigh of relief was about to escape her lungs, the car hit a slick patch of black ice and spun towards the edge of the road.

"Ahh! Hold on tight, baby!" Alison screamed.

Pins and needles covered her throat from screaming while gripping fear of consumed her. She attempted to regain control over herself and the car, but the little red car slid off the road and crashed into a large tree.

Pressure surged through Carter's ear canals, causing his head to throb, as he awoke to a blaring horn echoing in the woods. He fought to peel open his eyes. What happened? He looked over to see his mother lifelessly hugging the airbag. Although it was so dark, the contrast of her hair draping over the white airbag was clear as day.

Shaking her shoulders, tears streamed down his face. "Mom! Answer me! Mom! Mom! No!"

Carter frantically searched for his cell phone to call for help. The darkness from the black interior and deep shadows made it impossible to find. Thick tears blocked his vision as his hands desperately slapped around the car to find his familiar ribbed cell phone case. Chilly air seeped into the car from the cracked windshield. It cupped his face while grazing the back of his neck.

"Where's my phone? Where's my phone? I need help! I need help," he screamed so hard his throat burned. "Mom, please, wake up!"

His breathing continued to increase as he stressed about what to do. Just as hyperventilation was about to overcome him, Carter felt someone watching him. He glanced up from the floor to see dark eyes staring at him, challenging him to come outside. Why was an arctic fox here? The last time he saw one in the wild was years ago when they took a special trip through the Alaskan tundra. His mom was ecstatic to see nature and the wilderness in its raw form.

Its pure white coat glowed from the headlights beaming through the trees. Carter slowly opened the door to crawl out of the car, but the interior lights turned on, temporarily distracting him.

"My phone!" He quickly snatched it from the passenger seat.

Carter immediately dialed 911 with unstable hands. Despite being terrified he would drop his phone, Carter could still dial and click the bright green phone icon.

"911, what's your emergency?" asked a female voice.

"My mom—" Carter whispered as his voice trailed off. The sight of his mother's arm dangling from her body seared his mind.

"Hello? I'm having trouble hearing you. Are you or your mother in danger?" asked the female voice.

He broke down with his hand on his forehead. "I think she's dead."

"What's your location?"

"I don't know. We were driving home, and then—we crashed into a tree," Carter said, trying to catch his breath.

The woman continued with questions, but his brain switched to autopilot as he answered. His focus was back on her helpless body. She wore her gray winter coat that they had picked out during one of their shopping trips together. Fear prevented him from touching her. As long as he didn't touch her, she was alive.

"Emergency crews are on their way," the voice calmly explained. "Do you want me to wait on the phone with you?"

"No, I have to call my dad," he replied as he hung up the phone.

Scrolling through recent calls, Carter realized he couldn't remember the last time he had been on the phone with his father. *Screw it,* he thought as he opened up his full list of contacts. A sense of dread poured through his veins as he tapped on the call button. Conflicted, he didn't know if he wanted his father to answer the phone or not. What was he going to say? Would he even pick up the call?

"Hi, Carter. Look, I'm sorry about—" Richard apologized.

"I think Mom's dead," Carter blurted out before breaking down in a waterfall of tears.

"What?"

"Mom's dead. I mean—I think she is, but I can't tell for sure. I won't be able to tell unless I touch her, but I don't want to touch her. I *can't* touch her. What if she's dead, Dad? I can't lose her, I can't lose her. This can't be real," Carter rambled, pacing back and forth in the snow.

"CARTER!" Richard yelled.

"Yeah, Dad?"

"WHERE ARE YOU?"

"I . . . we were coming home from the store. We are near the thick patch of trees on the windy road," he blurted out.

"Call 911. I'm on my way."

"Dad?"

"Yes, Carter?"

"Please hurry. I'm scared."

As he hung up the phone, Carter exhaled and chills crawled over every inch of his body. He never felt so alone.

Chapter 2

Grabbing his coat and keys, Richard almost left without his shoes as he raced to get to Alison. If anything happened to them, if anything happened to her, he could never forgive himself. He was so busy with his job, and she was adamant about going to the store just for a stupid boat. His body was already teetering on the verge of a heart attack because of the never-ending emails and phone calls from work, and now this might put him over the edge.

He slammed the gas pedal to the floor as he whipped around each slick bend in the road. His eyes intently scanned from the left side of the road to the right and back to the left. Although the wind was now calm and the snow finally at rest, he couldn't locate Alison's car. *Where are they?*

As he rounded the bend, bright flashing lights bounced off a cluster of trees. Richard's heart jumped up to his throat, and then it sunk in a deep pit within his stomach. Suddenly, he spotted Carter standing next to what appeared to be the back of Alie's car. His white face indented with bright red bags under his eyes. He looked visibly distraught and lost. Despite regularly acting older than his age, it was no misunderstanding that he was fourteen now.

Richard clicked on his hazard lights and sharply pulled up alongside the scene of the accident. He stumbled out of the running car as the door lamely attempted to shut. His eyes glanced into the car that resembled a red accordion glued to the tree. As his vision adjusted, a dried blood drip faded into the airbag, and then distant yelling grabbed his attention. *She's in the ambulance,* he whispered in his head. Richard darted past Carter with a grazing shoulder pat as his consolation.

By the time he reached the ambulance, an emergency responder was closing the doors in front of him. Distressed, Richard tried pulling it open.

"Sir, we need to get to a hospital now," the responder said.

"That's my wife in there!" he yelled.

"I understand that. We just resuscitated her, but she's not doing well. We need to go now. Your son seems to be physically okay, but he is in severe shock," she relayed before closing the door behind her.

Carter watched his Dad desperately trying to barge his way into the ambulance. Turning to look back at his mom's car, he had an overwhelming sense that someone was watching him. Once Carter was facing the car, his eyes met two dark orbs protruding from the petite arctic fox's face again. The fox eerily sat next to the driver's side of the vehicle. The fierce winds gracefully caressed its ghost-white fur as the creature sat and watched the commotion at-hand.

"Dad," his quiet, timid voice muttered.

While facing the ambulance, Richard directed, "Get in the car now."

"Dad—" Carter repeated, hoping to gain his father's attention.

Without acknowledging Carter, Richard hopped back into his car. Unsure if it was out of fear of the fox or fear of being left behind, Carter quickly followed his father. He immediately buckled his seatbelt without breaking eye contact with the little visitor. As they drove off, he couldn't understand how his father didn't see the bright, furry animal watching them. When they took the turn around the mountain, Carter saw the fox slowly disappear into the darkness.

The silence was deafening as they drove to the hospital. Distracted by the accident, Richard only thought of ways how Alison could've prevented this from happening. In the passenger's seat, Carter sat with lonely, weak knees. He didn't know if it was even worth mentioning the fox at this point. *Honestly, it doesn't even matter,* he said to himself. *Mom is dying, but I can't get my mind off of how creepy that fox was.*

"Dad," Carter began, " . . . do you think she'll be okay?"

"I—I don't know, Carter," he barked. "I wish she wasn't so gung-ho about getting another dumb boat. It could've waited for another day, for God's sake. You have twenty of them, but now—"

His words were like sharp daggers stabbing into a bag of grain. Instantly, Carter began crying. He hated how his father always called his ships . . . *stupid boats.* Nevertheless, he was right. It was his fault. If it wasn't for him complaining about his broken ship, his mom would be alive—in their kitchen—rinsing dinner dishes while asking if anyone wanted some dessert that she perfected. He hated himself, and he could never forgive himself if his mother died.

"I'm sorry, Dad."

Richard continued to drive in silence for the rest of the ride. Carter's sobs soon quieted as he sat in shame while the bright street lights flashed by. He wondered how the city could feel so different, so much colder, knowing that he could lose his mother. He envied the random cars as they passed by. People drove home without a care in the world as his mother was battling for her life. Did everyone experience this pain?

A thick wall of fresh tears glazed his eyes as his throat tightened. Carter desperately needed the comfort of warm arms to wrap around him, but he was afraid that feeling of security would never come again. After what felt like a lifetime, they eventually pulled into the hospital.

Sadly, even when the nurses examined Carter for potential injuries, Richard failed to acknowledge Carter's presence. Knowing his father wouldn't humor small talk, Carter paced the hallway alone after the nurses said he had no serious injuries. His fingertips gently slid across the ridges on the walls as thoughts raced in his head. His mind brought delusions that maybe he was dreaming. Maybe when he woke up, she would be there with her giant beautiful smile asking, *How'd you sleep, sweetie? I hope that you had wonderful dreams!*

Tears puddled in his burning eyes again. Pain and sadness filled his heart. Carter feared it would burst and black blood would pour over the floor. He begged himself to wake up from this nightmare. *Please wake up,* he screamed in his mind.

After the longest hour of his life, Carter finally saw his father making his way towards him.

"Get all of your stuff together. I'm taking you home," Richard thundered.

"Is—is she okay?" he curiously asked with an active teardrop waiting to fall from his eye.

"I don't know. I know nothing except that they had to resuscitate her again in the ambulance. You're going home though and going to bed. You have school in the morning."

Carter's mouth dropped as pins and needles covered his body. "I want to stay. I want to make sure Mom is okay."

"You need to go home. I'll come back, and I'll let you know if anything happens," Richard coldly directed.

Without a doubt, Carter didn't believe him. If anything happened to his mom, he would probably be the last person to know. That would mean his dad would actually have to call and have a conversation with him, something that hasn't happened in a long time.

"Can I at least see her before I go? What if something happens while I'm gone?" Carter demanded.

"Go ask the nurse over there." Richard waved his hand toward a blonde nurse with bright green eyes.

Carter uncomfortably walked himself to the nurse's station. "Hi. I, um, my Dad wants to take me home, but I was hoping I could see my Mom before I go. Am I allowed to?"

"Oh, sweetie," the gentle voice answered with a compassionate smile. "Of course, you can see her. Just give me one moment."

The nurse finished typing something into her computer and ushered Carter into a nearby room. As Carter followed her, his body started trembling.

"Did your Dad explain what's going on with her?" the nurse asked, effortlessly pulling new gloves over her delicate fingers.

Embarrassed he had to reveal how dysfunctional his relationship was, he shook his head. "No, he didn't tell me much of anything."

"Okay. Well, your mother had a brain hemorrhage, so she has a lot of bleeding coming from her head. The doctors think they've located where it's coming from, but we'll prep her for surgery soon. Her face may look a little different because of the trauma from the accident," she warned while pulling back the curtains.

As the nurse stepped out of the way, Carter's eyes looked at the foot of the hospital bed. Terrified of what he was about to see, he found the courage to look at her hand lying softly on the white bedsheet.

Carter's stomach turned as he noticed many wires and IVs connecting to his mother's body. After he took a deep breath, he forced his eyes to look up at her face. A waterfall of tears cascaded down his cheeks as he saw her eyes swollen shut on her puffy face. What once was porcelain skin was now a mixture of dark shades of blue, purple, and red. A giant gash across her forehead quickly reminded Carter of the sound from her head smashing against the windshield. She was barely recognizable as blood even tinted her hair color. He hesitantly walked over by her side and reached his hand up to hold hers.

Carter gulped air into his upper chest as he continued to cry. "I love you so much, Mom. You'll make it through this! You have to. We didn't get to build my new ship yet together. You promised me we would. Please, Mom, please don't leave me."

After a few minutes, Carter kissed his mother's lukewarm forehead, whispering his love for her repeatedly. When he heard his father's throat clear, he turned around to see Richard standing in the doorway.

"We should go. You need rest. You have school in the morning," he awkwardly fumbled.

Carter's face twisted out of rage. "School? You're worried about me getting enough sleep for school? Since when do you care about what time I go to bed?"

"Get in the car now," Richard demanded with authority.

"I don't know what Mom ever saw in you," Carter mumbled, walking around him.

On the ride home, the mood in the car was awkward and tense. Carter was furious that his father forced him to go home while his mother could take her last breath without him. *I don't know what I'll do if I lose Mom,* he thought. *She loved me no matter what. I'm not sure he even cares if I exist. I wonder if he wishes it was me instead.* Carter's mind spiraled down a dangerous path as he sat in his father's car. All the noise from Carter's thoughts and emotions made him feel nauseous, so he closed his eyes. When they pulled into the driveway, Richard handed Carter his house key, and Carter looked up at his father.

"Here. I'll let you know if anything changes. Make yourself a sandwich if you're hungry," he blandly murmured.

Shocked by the lack of empathy or compassion, Carter was motionless for two seconds before realizing his father wasn't getting out of the car with him.

"I . . . have to go in the house . . . by myself?" Carter stuttered.

Slamming his hands on the steering wheel, Richard argued, "Carter, you're not a child. I need to go back and watch over your mother. Don't be ridiculous. You can handle being in the house, can't you?"

Saddened by what his reality was becoming, Carter hung his head as he pushed open the car door, which almost seemed heavier than him. Right as his father was about to say bye, Carter just closed the door. *I don't need him,* he thought to himself as he climbed the brick porch steps. How he envied those kids who got to sit on the porch steps with their dads while overlooking the front lawn after a playful game of catch.

Was that a real thing I missed out on? Or was it a legendary movie myth? Whatever.

A shallow breath slowly entered his nostrils, filling his lungs as he unlocked the front door. It felt like he was entering a foreign house in a dream, one that seemed so familiar yet not home. Luckily, Sadie was patiently sitting at the front door. At this point, if she couldn't make him happy, no one could. She jumped up and gently placed her paws on his chest to greet him hello. Despite her poor behavior earlier, she was the perfect puppy. He couldn't stay mad at her. She loved sinking her teeth into anything that might resemble a toy.

He massaged her smooth head and kissed her ear. A warm tear delicately rolled off Carter's face and spattered on her neck.

"I feel so alone. I miss Mom already," he lightly cried. "She can't die. She just can't."

Sadie gracefully licked his cheek as he slowly sat down on the off-white tile floor. With his back resting against the wall, he looked over towards his favorite picture sitting on the coffee table. Both Carter and his mom wore an enormous smile as they stood in front of the lake at the state park. Vivid sounds and smells entered his mind as he felt the warmth of that summer sun prickle his neck. Snuggling into his warm coat, the sound of waves splashing the water's edge slowly put him to sleep.

Roughly two-and-a-half hours had passed when Carter awoke to the slamming of his front door. He jumped up as the vibration pulsated through his back. Alarmed by the noise, he shook his head several times to wake out of his deep sleep. When his eyes could focus, he noticed his father's eyes were bloodshot and glazed. As Richard walked by without a word, the smell of cigarettes and alcohol infiltrated Carter's nostrils.

"Where were you, Dad? Is Mom okay?" Carter questioned. His gut immediately answered all of his questions, but Carter wanted to hear the answers from his father's mouth.

Richard paused as he let the interrogatory judgment sink in. "She's dead. She died on the operating table before I even made it back to the hospital. I didn't get to kiss her and say goodbye. The last interaction we had was an argument about you and your ridiculous boat. Now—now she's dead. So yes, I went to the bar to clear my mind and get a moment to myself!"

The aggression and hostility toward Carter caught him off-guard. He knew nothing about his mother's plans to get a new ship. He barely said anything to her about it that he could recall. He didn't know how to respond since he was so upset. Was it his fault she died?

Overcome with grief mixed with guilt, he bolted out of the house. By no surprise, his father didn't follow as Carter sprinted across their front lawn and into the darkness behind their house.

The destination was unknown, but he knew the path was leading him into the woods that lined the back of his yard. Growing up, he would always visit the woods when he needed to escape his father's toxic presence. Carter felt oddly safe and calm when surrounded by the protective arms of the maple, birch, and oak giants. The fluttering of leaves lifted his spirits while the cold rushing water gave him a refreshing perspective on his current problems. When he encountered his favorite spot at the stream, he decided it'd be the perfect place to sit and think. Once he began positioning himself to sit on the edge of a large boulder, he felt someone watching him. Nervous that it was a bear or wolf, he slowly turned his head.

To Carter's surprise, a familiar face greeted his eyes—two small dark orbs he had met earlier. The wise fox sat quietly in the distance, observing Carter's every move. Despite the instant shock to his heart, Carter felt oddly comforted by the pearl white fox. He searched the forest floor to find berries to toss to his new friend. After grabbing a few frozen blackberries, he tiptoed towards where the fox was resting. As he stepped onto one of three rocks in the middle of the stream, the fox sat unfazed, yet inviting. Maybe he could get close enough to caress its soft fur.

Carter balanced on his right foot as he tried to find the proper placement for his left. Once he felt grounded, he placed all of his weight onto his left foot. Within a matter of seconds, his sneakers slid on the wet rocks. Still holding onto the berries, he tried catching his fall with his left hand and right forearm. As he splashed into the stream, Carter hit the right side of his head, and his face sunk into a cold blanket of water.

Chapter 3

Carter's arms flapped in the water, desperately reaching out for a nearby rock. The water felt deeper, warmer, and more active than he remembered. Exhausted, he flipped his body over, attempting to stand up in the stream. Unable to reach any ground, he opened his eyes. The blinding sunlight bounced off of violent waves.

Despite being able to swim, he flailed his arms from panic and confusion. How did he get here? How was it daytime? Nothing made sense. Carter looked down into his hands to see if he was still clutching the frozen blackberries, but all he could see was water everywhere.

Just as he went to rotate his left arm in the water to turn his body around, a smooth and slimy sensation pressed against his back. What was that? Was it a big fish, whale, or shark? When Carter turned his head, a giant serpent was swimming through the water. It appeared the creature would have no problem swallowing three people at once. As Carter's eyes scanned the beast, he noticed its aquamarine scales and sharp spines set on the top of its back. All of Carter's courage sank to his feet.

The strength of this sea serpent was remarkable. With a whip of the tail, the water formed a demonizing wave that threatened to drown Carter. What was he to do? He might die!

Thinking quickly, he inhaled a deep breath and dove under the gigantic wave. Terrified it would eat him, Carter desperately searched for something to swim towards. His only option was a massive, wooden ship rocking in the distance. Carter couldn't believe how old it looked. Torn, dirtied sails slowly flapped, then rolled in the sky as he admired the rust-covered cannons below. Although the ship looked less-than-friendly, he hoped there were helpful sailors aboard. If he wanted to get out the water alive, this was his chance.

Despite being on a swim team for several years, he never was in life-threatening danger to test his skills, so fear tightened his throat and squeezed his heart. Inhaling another deep breath, he dipped down into the water and swam for his life. As he forcefully slipped his right arm into the water then the left, he heard a screeching noise that jolted his heart into overdrive. Forcing himself to focus, he counted each stroke before he let fear take over.

One, two, three, four—five, six, seven, eight.

If he did one more repetition, he should make it.

Carter felt the vibration of the screech grow closer. The noise pierced his ears as he wanted to cry in his mind.

Focus! Almost there!

He knew his life was over if he didn't keep his mind on a short leash. Any slip-up would cause an unfavorable demise. To his dismay, Carter noticed that he had miscounted the strokes needed to reach the floating haven.

Two more to go! One, two!

"Help!" he choked with all the strength in his lungs.

He couldn't see anyone, and no one responded.

"Help! Help!" he screamed, slapping the side of the ship.

Not a single person came to his aid. When Carter swam towards the stern, he noticed barnacles clinging to the dark, wooden planks. Swaying in the water's current, hundreds of squiggly shipworms layered the ship's underside.

Once on the other side, he encountered a rope ladder. Reaching up to clutch it, he wrapped his hands around the sides of the ladder to hoist himself up. One by one, he weakly, yet swiftly, dragged himself to safety. As he crawled onto the ship, he flung himself onto the floor, gasping for air. When he regained himself, it surprised Carter to see no one was there to greet him.

As he stood up and ran his hands through his drenched hair, he looked around. "Hello? Anyone there?"

To his surprise, not one person was visible. *Who leaves a ship in the middle of the sea? Was it left stranded? Did someone fall overboard?*

Baffled, he walked towards the edge of the deck to analyze the water. The vibrant blue water sat rather still as the sea-salted breeze caressed his face. Strange. Where were the waves and the terrifying sea serpent? He snooped around the enormous deck and found some pouches of water and old bread. Although he was appreciative for safety, he didn't understand how the serpent just disappeared. Did it just get bored? Maybe it found something else to torment or eat? Whatever the reason, he was safe—for now.

Carter poked around, hoping to find some clue about what was going on. He stumbled across ropes, black powder for the cannons, and some wooden boxes filled with herbs and spices. Walking over the creaking boards on the deck, his eyes gazed over the old yet marvelous ship. The hand-carved railings had detailed female figures for each baluster throughout the ship.

Looking up into the sky, the giant mast appeared to touch the clouds. While he explored, Carter saw that even the crow's nest appeared empty above. Unsure of what to do, he ventured down the stairs of the ship. As he explored, the inside glimmered with decorations ranging in size, shape, and shades of blue and green. The shine reflecting off of the walls drew him in closer. Once he got close enough, Carter could see that the bigger shapes were seashells. Running his hand across the surface, each finger massaged a different colored shell. *What a clever idea,* he thought.

While his hands studied the walls, he noticed sharp pieces jutting out from between the shells. He wondered what they were. Maybe they were tiny shells or pieces of rock. Looking closer, he realized they weren't rocks—they were teeth and shards of bones.

Instantly, he yelled and started scraping his hands all over his clothes in hopes to shave a layer of skin off. *Who decorates a ship with teeth and bones?* Fear dripped down his neck and back as he thought about whose vessel he had stumbled upon. He quickly darted up the stairs towards the main deck of the ship. Stepping on the main floorboards, Carter shuffled his way over to the edge of the ship.

"Going so soon?" a seductively sweet voice asked from behind.

About to jump out of his skin, Carter spun around to see an enchanting woman wearing sleek aquamarine breeches with a form-fitting trench coat, draping to the floor. A large, dark captain's hat sat gracefully on her long, golden blonde hair. She had welcoming blue eyes that made him feel strangely safe and calm.

"Uh, uh . . ." Carter stuttered.

Tilting her head to the side, the woman chuckled in a high pitch tone. "Cat got your tongue?"

"Um, no." Carter nervously laughed. "I didn't see anyone here. Where'd you come from?"

Looking deep into his eyes, she giggled. "My dear, you're on my ship. I should ask where you came from."

"Oh! Um, well—" he said. "Honestly, I don't know."

As she stared with her entrancing blue eyes, she asked, "You don't know?"

Carter rubbed the back of his neck. "This might sound weird. The last thing I remember was looking into the eyes of a fox. When I woke up, I was in the middle of the sea being chased by a serpent-like beast."

"Well 'beast' is a bit much, don't you think? Seems to me the fox is the one you shouldn't be trusting." She sweetly wrinkled her nose.

"Huh?" Carter scratched his head.

Her golden locks tousled as she spun around to go towards the ship's wheel. Her heels clicked as she walked forward. "Sorry, I'm not a fan of foxes. Wretched little creatures."

Following behind her, he analyzed the impressive vessel. Unsure of what to say, Carter responded, "Anyway, I have no idea what brought me here."

Climbing up a set of stairs to the helm of the ship, the captivating woman asked, "Well, if you don't know where you came from, where are you headed?"

Carter remained quiet as he tried to think. Where was he headed? All he could remember was the petite fox's face with the two dark orbs studying him. The image of the fox staring at him permanently seared his mind.

"You mean to tell me you have no destination?" she asked as her hand gracefully gripped the ship's wheel.

"I guess not," he whispered to himself.

A smile grew on her face as she waved to her crew to set sail. Carter looked behind to see roughly ten women working on the ship. Some were stacking boxes, one was sweeping, and others were preparing for the ship's next journey.

"How—" His jaw dropped, trying to think how these women got on the ship. "Where'd they come from?"

She chuckled. "Maybe you should go sit down and get something to eat."

"Okay," Carter answered quietly, rubbing his face.

"By the way, I didn't get your name. I'm Elena." She warmly smiled.

"C-Carter," he stuttered.

"Ah, nice to meet you!"

"Likewise."

"Don't you worry. We'll take care of you, Carter. Let me get one of my girls to help you to your room." Elena winked as she turned away. "Linx!"

A petite girl, around Carter's age, dropped some rope into a pile, and then she ran up the stairs. Her pointed ears pushed through her golden hair, and her eyes resembled sparkling green gems. With attitude, she blurted, "Aye aye, Captain."

"Please take our guest here to the private quarters. Make sure he gets food and dry clothes," Elena sharply ordered. "And send me Qita."

"Aye aye, Captain," Linx obeyed without further question. Her bright green eyes shifted to Carter. "Follow me."

Carter trailed behind Linx, who almost floated across the deck of the ship. Her hair gently pushed to the side from the light breeze that passed by. Everything appeared calm compared to just moments before. *Where was that serpent? It couldn't just disappear,* he thought.

As they approached a woman sharpening a harpoon, Linx whispered, "Qita, Captain requested to speak with you."

The woman's deep brown skin glistened in the sun as dark elegant braids rested over her shoulder. She gracefully swiped her blade two more times before looking up to meet eyes with Linx and then with Carter. His heart dropped as her piercing cinnamon-brown eyes locked on his. Carter was taken aback by her beauty.

Qita slightly nodded her head as she stood up. With quick strides, she walked over to meet Elena.

Once she was close enough to Elena, Qita quietly mumbled, "Do you think he knows?"

"That you wish to eat him? No, but I just found out something else," Elena whispered as her eyes lit up.

Qita crossed her arms. "What'd you find out?"

"We'll be able to afford anything we've ever wanted! Send word! We've got the queen's son," Elena said with a sneer.

"I see! So that means we won't feast? I'll tell the girls that this one is off the table. They won't be happy. They're craving human meat. They've only been living off puny shrimp and potatoes."

"Not this one. Trust me, sister, we'll have enough gems to buy us food to feast on for eternity. No more hunting. We'll bleed the queen dry."

Qita sighed, looking towards Carter. "Unless she bleeds us."

"Nonsense. Now go! Tell—I don't care who. Just make sure they go straight to the castle and don't leak our location!" Elena demanded.

Despite her concern, Qita nodded. "Aye aye, Cap'n."

Chapter 4

Letting out a sigh, Linx hustled Carter across the deck towards the steps. "Right this way."

When they descended the stairway, Carter glanced again at the creepy teeth intricately decorating the wall. He wondered how he could bring up his concern without sounding judgmental or putting himself in harm's way.

"This ship is exquisite," he said.

Linx sighed. "Yeah."

"What's it made from?" he nonchalantly asked.

"Um—I don't know. Wood?" Linx rolled her wide green eyes.

Carter laughed at how weird it came off. "I meant what's on the walls? It's very vibrant and shiny."

Linx wasn't interested in conversation with him. She knew Elena had intentions of selling Carter for a pretty penny or offering him up as their next meal. In the meantime, the girls would pamper him until they decided his fate. She dully ushered him into a large room filled with a buffet table of food.

In the center of the table, cuts of fish rested while bread and fruit neatly decorated the table. Carter couldn't believe how prepared they were for a visitor. Did he show up right before their meal?

Carter looked towards Linx. "There's so much food here! I'm assuming everyone will be down soon? Where should I sit?"

"No, eat as much as you wish. Personally, I prefer boar. When you want to rest and change your clothes, there's a bed and some clothes in the next room." Linx pointed to a connecting room. Without another word, she closed the door as she left.

Carter's mouth dropped. He attempted to make sense of everything, but his head continued to spin. Was he supposed to eat all of this food himself? Maybe their custom was to allow guests to eat first? Either way, Carter wouldn't complain about getting first dibs on the food. His father would've reprimanded him for heaping piles of food on his plate, but he couldn't help it. His stomach was guiding his eyes across the table from the steaming plate of roasted potatoes to fresh fish that he never tried before.

Grabbing a plate, he walked around the table scooping at least two spoonfuls of everything on his plate, maybe three. How did they cook all of this food today? Maybe that's what they were doing when he first came aboard. Right when he was about to shovel a mountainous spoon of mixed vegetables in his mouth, the door swiftly opened.

Elena walked in with a breathtaking smile on her face. "Ahoy, love! I see that you're enjoying your meal!" Her rosy lips curved ever so slightly to reveal white, perfect teeth.

Carter wondered to himself how they looked like models while braving the sea. Instantly, he felt the blood rush to his face as he looked down at his gluttonous plate of food. Now was the first time he wished that his father was here. He would've told him to reel back the enthusiasm for food and saved him a lifetime of embarrassment.

"Uh, um—" he stuttered while looking at his dish. "Sorry. I don't know the last time I ate anything."

"No need to apologize! I'm just thrilled that you're content. If you need anything, please let me or the girls know," Elena explained, beaming another warm smile.

Nervously rubbing his hands together, Carter inquired, "Oh, thanks! I don't need anything else. Uh, will you be joining me?"

"Oh, no. I'm saving my appetite," she whispered with a wink and left the room.

Carter opened his mouth to respond, but he couldn't think of anything to say. Was it strange that he was falling for her? She had to be in her mid to late twenties. Any relationship would be illegal—if anyone found out. He laughed to himself as he thought about his mind going from zero to one hundred. For all he knew, she could have a significant other. Regardless, she was pure perfection. And then there was Qita. All the gorgeous women intimidated him. To his surprise, many appeared to appreciate his presence. They had smiles on their faces except for Linx. Did he upset her somehow? He slowly began eating his meal fit for a king.

"Wow, this is delicious! This food is almost like Mom's—" Instantly feeling nauseous, he placed his fork on the table. "I need to go see her. Where is she? Where am I?"

Right when pieces of his memory started to return, the door opened again. This time it was Qita. Her black hair swung from side to side as she made her way to the table. She pulled out a chair that sat directly in front of Carter.

"I hope you don't mind me joining you," Qita sensually growled as she crossed her legs.

Coughing up food, he forced out, "I, uh, no. Please don't let me interrupt your dinner. I—I'm sure that you're starving from all the work you do."

There was a spark of yellow in Qita's cinnamon-brown eyes as she looked deep into Carter's. Any attention from girls made him somewhat nervous, but Carter hoped he didn't appear immature or awkward. His attention dropped from her ethereal eyes to her beautiful nose down to her perfect lips. Suddenly, he couldn't believe his eyes. As he continued to gaze at her, Qita's lips curled into a smile revealing sharp pointed teeth. His heart shot straight to his throat.

As Carter assessed his surroundings, in case she attacked him, a figure dove past the outside of his window and dropped into the water.

"Qita! What was that? Was that a person?" Carter yelled.

"Oh, it was probably a rope or something," Qita responded, without skipping a beat.

"No way. Are you sure? That looked like a person diving into the water. Are they okay? It's dangerous in there! I was almost killed by a hideous—" he began.

"A serpent? A beautiful serpent almost killed you?" she eerily mocked. "They are far from hideous and not the biggest monster that you'll see here."

What was she talking about? What was scarier than a twenty-foot snake in the water? Not to mention, one that could swallow a dolphin without hesitation. How did she know about that? Did Elena tell her? And who fell overboard? That was definitely a person.

With each question popping into his head, Qita's smile grew larger until it seemed almost unnatural. Immediately, he felt that he was in danger. If it wasn't Qita, she knew that something or someone wanted to harm him. Carter's chest dispersed warm prickles that evenly covered his body.

"Qita . . . " Carter began, "where is this ship headed? I'm kind of lost, and I didn't know how to find my way back home."

"Child, we set sail for a long voyage at sea. We rarely visit land, maybe a couple weeks a year. It just isn't in our blood to be confined to such a *boring* prison," she emphasized, swaying her shoulders.

"Not to be rude, but isn't it more confining to live on a ship rather than being on land? At least you can move around or go places. Don't get me wrong, though, I love being on the water. It just seems less than enjoyable if it's all the time," he lightly stated.

Qita glared at him. "We are freer here than you'll ever know."

"How do you afford to live out here for so long?" Carter wondered.

"I didn't realize I would be interrogated," Qita laughed. "We manage just fine."

Her lack of response confused Carter. Maybe he could try asking Elena. She appeared to fancy him more than Qita.

"I have a question for you, Carter," she said with a slight roll of the tongue.

"Uh, sure. Shoot."

"Shoot what?" Qita questioned with eyebrows twisting high onto her forehead.

"Oh, I just meant ask me whatever you want," he clarified.

She stared at him for a moment. "Where are you from?"

Tapping his fingers on the table, his gaze fell to the floor. "Alaska. Where are we here?"

"We are on the Ong Sea near Nuary. Alaska? What's Alaska?" Qita questioned, pushing her braids behind her shoulder.

"Wait, what? Where are we?" Carter stammered.

"We are on the Ong Sea. The closest city is Nuary," Qita hissed.

"I'm sorry. I just—" Carter paused. "What other countries are we near?"

"I'm not playing your games. I answered your question, answer mine. Where is Alaska?" She growled.

"You never heard of Alaska? It's near Canada. Part of the United States . . . " he continued.

Qita looked Carter up and down as if he was spewing witchcraft.

"Well—how did you get here from *Alaska*?" Qita laughed.

"I really don't know," Carter mumbled. He sat back for a moment, trying to think again. He could only recall the fox's dark orbs staring back at him. But how did he get here? Wherever *here* is.

"You don't know? You're telling me you're from a place called—" Qita began waving her hand in the air.

Confused, Carter interjected, "Alaska."

"But you have no explanation for how you got to our ship," she finished without acknowledging Carter's comment.

"I told Elena that I only remember looking into a fox's eyes as I fell into water, and then I woke up here. My eyes opened as a terrifying serpent almost ate me!"

Qita rolled her eyes. "I'd be more suspicious of the fox. They are the ones who shouldn't be trusted."

"I'm supposed to be more afraid of a tiny, cute fox compared to an enormous water dragon?" Carter retaliated.

"It's easy to see you aren't from around here. Serpents and dragons are not the same. Dragons will never be as elegant as sea serpents." Her cinnamon eyes sizzled.

"Look, I'm just as confused about this as you. I don't know what's going on and why everyone here is afraid of foxes over massive sea serpents," Carter blurted out, running his fingers through the front of his hair.

"We are not *afraid* of any *fox*," she theatrically enunciated. "Unlike you, we know they cannot be trusted. As I have said to Elena, I wouldn't be surprised if there's some kind of deal with the fairies. Sly creatures."

"Did you say fairies?"

"What world are you from?" Qita joked. "Aye, fairies. They are little evil things. Can't trust 'em."

"Fairies are real?" Carter questioned with wide eyes.

Qita stared at him in disbelief. She attempted to understand how he never saw fairies before. She contemplated on whether he was deceiving her. He appeared genuinely confused, so she opted to play along. "Aye, they are real."

"This is crazy. Do they fly around and grant wishes?"

"Many use wands to funnel magic, but for a price. More often than not, it's not worth it. The strongest of fairies can use their hands," Qita warned as she sat back in her chair.

"What do they look like, in case I ever encounter one?" he prodded.

"As they teach us from a wee age:

Skin is fair,
Golden hair,
With ears pointed high.

"Some say they'll turn you into pixie dust, others say worse. We have learned to contain some of them, but fairies can never be trusted," Qita said with bright eyes glistening in a stream of sunlight.

Needing a moment to process everything, he motioned towards the connecting room. "My clothes are a little wet. I'm going to change into something dry. Linx said there were some extra clothes I could use."

Standing up from her chair, Qita tauntingly replied, "Ah. Well, don't let me interrupt you. I just wanted to check to see if you needed anything."

"I appreciate everything, Qita. I really do. It was nice of you to check on me. None of this makes sense, I just need some time to process," Carter awkwardly confessed.

Qita lightly chuckled as she opened the door, "Well, I know nothing about Alaska or however you say it. Don't worry though. We'll take care of you."

As the door closed, Carter slumped into his chair out of relief. Qita was beautifully intimidating. As much as he would like to trust her, something didn't feel right. His stomach did three somersaults before tying itself in a knot. Since he didn't want to make himself out to be a liar, he walked into the connecting bedroom to see what dry clothes he could find.

His feet dragged across the creaky floorboards as he attempted to keep his balance. Either he wasn't feeling well, or the ship was coming across powerful waves. Once he finally reached the bed, he flopped down on the old, firm mattress. Carter closed his eyes for several seconds to take a deep breath. When he opened his eyes, he glanced around to see where the clothes would be. The room appeared very outdated, with walls stained from something brown. Looking down at the bed, he wanted to gag, looking at the comforter covered in stains and random sprinkles of hair and dirt. It seemed like the guests didn't occupy the room for long. Next to the bed was a nightstand that held an old cup of water. After a moment, he gathered some strength to stand up and walk over to the closet.

When he opened the closet door, roughly fifteen shirts and ten pants in all different sizes hung inside. The clothing had no rhyme or reason. Why? Why on a ship with only women would there be a closet full of random men's clothing? Where did they come from?

Carter opted to stay in his damp clothes as he shut the closet door. Getting dirty never bothered him, but his skin crawled at the thought about the unknown history of his room. Even the air held a heavy musk reminiscent of his grandmother's moldy basement. His mind was screaming for him to leave, so he went on deck for some fresh air.

As he climbed the stairs, all Carter could think about was the dialog with Qita. *How were fairies real? And should they be feared?* He thought about her description . . . fair skin, light hair, and pointed ears. Walking across the deck to the starboard of the ship, he wondered where the fairies lived. *Were they in woodlands or in a castle? This is ridiculous,* he thought. Qita had to be toying with him. The stories were probably nonsense to freak him out.

Arguing in his mind between Qita being a potential friend or foe, he strolled towards a few women who were stacking boxes. They glanced over to see their new guest. One girl with dark, braided hair and ocean-blue eyes giggled to another as she whispered in her friend's ear. He didn't know if they were making fun of him or were happy to see another person's presence, so he politely smiled as he passed by. Part of him still wondered if this was all a dream, but it felt different—it felt real. A powerful gust of sea-salted wind slapped his face as the cool air spiraled through his nostrils.

Right as he was about to continue forward, something caught his eye. It was Linx. She was standing over a giant wooden box used as a table with a tattered map rolled across the top. Two bottles held each side in place. Despite the wind pouring over the ship, it stayed put. While Linx pointed her delicate finger adamantly towards the upper part of the map, he noticed her hand scoop her golden hair over her ear while she bickered with Qita. Although she didn't acknowledge his presence, it appeared Qita knew he was there.

Going over his head for a moment, it finally hit Carter like a ton of bricks. He could see it — *golden hair* and *pointed ears! Wait, this made little sense. Was Linx a fairy? Qita clarified that fairies could not be trusted, so why would they have Linx, a fairy, on board their ship?*

Carter didn't know what to think. Maybe he just misinterpreted her story. Maybe numerous creatures had pointed ears — and her golden hair was a coincidence? Either way, he had no way to find out for now.

Boots clicked in his direction. "Back so soon? I thought you surely would have taken a nap after eating all of that food," Elena joked, descending a set of steps connecting to the upper deck.

"I—uh, yeah, I needed some fresh air," Carter shyly responded while scratching the side of his head.

Raising her eyebrows, Elena offered, "Well, you're more than welcome to join me. I need to speak with Qita and Linx. They were figuring out the best route to pick up some of my favorite tea."

Despite being on the ship for mere hours, Carter appreciated the relationship he had with Elena. She was a woman of power, but in her presence, she covered him in a blanket of warmth and happiness. Though they were strangers to one another, Carter believed he might trust her. After all, she trusted him enough to be her shadow.

Carter gleefully agreed, "Okay!"

Approaching Qita and Linx, Elena's tone grew more serious. "Ladies, have we figured out the best route to take? I want a solid plan of attack before the winds pick up speed."

"Not yet, Cap'n," Qita grunted as she glared at Linx in disapproval.

With authority, Elena asked, "Oh, no?"

"Captain, I explained to Qita that we should take this shortcut. It'll save us time and energy—" Linx elaborated, pointing her finger from one direction on the map to another. Her porcelain skin started tinting pink out of a mix of frustration and extensive sunlight.

"There's no way we can trust her when we are so close to the Violet Woods. I would rather spend two more days on sea than chance an opportunity for her to put us in danger." Qita slammed her dagger through the wood next to the map.

Elena studied Linx's eyes and shifted her gaze to Qita before turning around.

"Qita, lead us through your route. Tell the women to get ready. I sense a storm is on its way," Elena foretold with a solid stance.

She motioned for Carter to follow her back up the stairs. The ship was already remarkable, but truly breathtaking once he turned his head to look down towards the main deck. Excited to be aboard an actual ship on the sea, Carter thought he could only dream of such an experience.

"Please dismiss the commotion," Elena informed Carter. "There's a little tension between the two of them sometimes."

"I know it isn't my business, but is there a reason Qita doesn't like Linx?" Carter innocently pried.

"Simply put, Linx is rather new here. Mixing that with the fact Qita doesn't trust anyone easily, it can become slightly hostile. Nevertheless, Qita is a strong quartermaster, so she is a valuable partner," Elena explained.

With a gulp of embarrassment, Carter impulsively asked, "Is Linx a fairy?"

"What do you know about fairies, boy?" She lightly laughed, tilting her head to the side.

"Nothing at all. I thought they were a myth until Qita mentioned something about pointy ears and golden hair. Linx seemed to fit the description," he confided, watching Linx hang her head in disappointment from a distance.

"Aye, she is a fairy, but you have nothing to worry about. She is under control," Elena bragged, patting her embroidered pocket.

Unsure what she meant, Carter noticed something shiny on Linx's outfit. A thin chain wrapped around her chest. It almost went unnoticed had he not looked at the right time. A square lock attached to her back, which must have been what Elena was referring to.

Before he could ask anything else, Qita darted up the stairs to discuss other matters with Elena. Her eyes glaring with urgency, Elena excused herself for a moment to allow for some privacy. Carter couldn't make out any words, just heightened mumbles accompanied by animated arm movements.

"They know we have him," Qita uneasily reported.

"Great! Now, let's wait to see what they do for our precious gem!" Elena clapped her hands together. "Qita, you don't seem happy! We can finally make some life-changing money, rather than just selling them as targets to Donem."

"Look, Elena, I look up to you. I respect your decisions. You have never steered us wrong, but there's something about this plan. It's not sitting right with me," Qita expressed.

"All right. We'll take caution with this one then. I didn't realize you were adamantly against it."

"There's something different about this voyage. Linx is hard to control, the waves are intense, and now we have the queen's son on our ship with zero knowledge of our world. What's going on, Cap'n?" Qita mumbled in disbelief, glancing over Elena's shoulder towards Carter.

"We shall sell him to Donem for double then. He'll be his problem, and then our hands will be clean of the queen's wrath," Elena declared with a sigh.

"You're doing the right thing for the girls, Elena. The last thing you want would be for a war against the queen. Right now, she minds her business as we mind ours. That's best for everyone." Qita nodded.

"Tell our fairy we want to go see Donem," Elena demanded, raising her eyebrow. Although she received money to feed her girls and improve her ship, visiting Donem wasn't an activity Elena looked forward to. He was too dangerous, but as long as she had a man to sell, she had nothing to worry about.

"Will do," Qita agreed. She walked towards Carter before making her way down the stairs.

Looking him up and down, she said, "I thought you wanted to change your clothes? I don't remember having another outfit like yours."

"Uh, yeah. I was going to change, but then—uh, I don't know. I just needed fresh air," Carter fumbled. He took a step back, unsure of what Qita's intentions were.

Passing him by, she laughed. "Relax, I'm won't hurt you."

What was she talking about? Carter wondered. He thought they were on good terms from the last time they spoke. Maybe she overheard the conversation with Elena about the fairies? To ease his nerves, he walked over towards Elena.

"So, are we far from where you get your tea?"

"Carter, you can sit tight. We'll take an alternative route. We have another destination to visit first," Elena announced without going into detail.

"Oh, okay. Well, I wanted to thank you for being so gracious and welcoming. I've been a little confused by whatever happened that brought me here, but you have been very kind."

Elena glanced over at Carter with a fading smile and whispered, "Of course."

Chapter 5

Awkward silence pushed Carter back down the stairs that were once so welcoming. What was just an astonishing sight, quickly became a daunting experience. The ship seemed larger than before. Even the path back to his room felt like a long walk. While trying to reach the main deck, he noticed several women were staring at him. He felt so uncomfortable that he sharply turned his head away. At that moment, the roaring waters and vicious waves slapped the ship, almost tossing Carter to the floor.

"Didn't grow yer sea legs yet, eh?" a pirate yelled, with bright red hair curled to perfection.

Attempting to save his ego in front of the audience, he refuted, "Believe it or not, I've been on a ship before."

"Ha! Sure you have," the pirate teased as she sloshed a swig down her throat from a canteen.

Ignoring her jeers, Carter didn't say another word and walked past her. Once he reached the staircase, he took a deep breath and filled his lungs to capacity. As he approached his room, he noticed someone sitting in the buffet area. He curiously walked into the room, unaware of what their motive was. When he got close, Carter noticed that it was Linx sitting in the chair.

Noting that nothing was on her plate, Carter figured she was waiting for someone. "Hello, Linx."

Staring directly into Carter's eyes, Linx blurted, "What questions do you have for me?"

"I'm sorry," Carter responded, somewhat confused. "What are you talking about?"

"I heard you talking to Elena. You were asking if I was a fairy. What's it to you?" Linx defensively snapped.

"I never saw fairies or knew that they—you—existed. My apologies for the rudeness, but someone made a comment that got me thinking. I honestly didn't know you could hear me. I'm sorry," Carter confessed.

"Look, I'm not seeking an explanation of why you were talking about fairies. I just wanted to educate you. Too many people misjudge fairies as little demons because we react to our environment."

Intrigued, Carter asked, "What do you mean?"

"Many say how wicked fairies are. It's interesting because the ones who claim we are evil creatures are, in fact, the evil ones themselves. Everyone is so blinded by the niceties; they don't see the truth of what's right in front of them." Linx growled.

"I'm sorry. I don't understand."

Linx sighed while rubbing her face. "Look, I'll only tell you this because I know that you're a good person, but you have to promise to keep it to yourself."

"How do you know that? I'm flattered, but—"

She shrugged. "Let's just say I'm a good judge of character, most of the time. I've misjudged some, but I know you're different. I can see it in your soul."

Carter uncomfortably chuckled. "Well, thanks. I hope I don't disappoint you. But I promise I won't tell anyone anything. I mean that."

"I wanted to warn you. I see you're getting close to Elena and possibly Qita, but you need to be careful. Beware, they're not as nice as they appear to be. They kidnapped me, stole my ability to fly, and use me as their compass and guide. Yet fairies are the evil ones," Linx began with a tone of resentment.

Chills ran up his neck. "Wait, what? Did you say they kidnapped you? Are you serious? When was this?"

"They came to my island searching for pixie dust. When they were told we didn't have any to give, they terrorized us. On a normal day, we would've been able to pulverize them." She raged with red eyes. "But they caught us off guard in the middle of the night. After we tried defending ourselves, the pirates kidnapped me. They bound me, took my wand, and held me as a prisoner ever since."

Carter stared in disbelief. "I'm so sorry that happened to you."

He didn't know what else to say. What was he supposed to do? The thought flashed through his mind of helping her escape. Was that even possible or smart, though? Carter barely knew anything about this new world. Not to mention, he hardly knew Linx. The only interactions he had with her were less than favorable, but now he knew why. Why would someone be pleasant if they were kidnapped and held as a working prisoner?

After a moment of silence, Carter asked, "What can I do to help?"

Rolling her eyes, Linx chuckled, "Are you actually going to help me? How can you possibly help me?"

Carter beamed with hope. "I have absolutely no idea, but I'm willing to. You and I have at least one thing in common."

"Oh yeah? And what's that?" Linx scoffed.

"We're here, against our will, far from our homes. That's reason enough for me to help you. If you can help me get home, that'll be a bonus."

"Well, I think I might have an idea," Linx revealed with a dangerous grin.

Carter's eyes lit up. "Oh, yeah? What can I do?"

"We need to get my wand," she ordered. "We can do it tomorrow. We'll be sailing very close to my home, so they'll keep an eye on me. However, they won't be paying attention to the kid that didn't know fairies were real. They'll never see it coming."

"Well, where's your wand? How do I get it?"

"There's a compartment under the ship—" Linx began.

"Wait, under the ship? How the heck am I supposed to get under there?" Carter asked with disbelief.

"I saw how well you swam in the water. If you can hold your breath long enough, you should be able to access it," she explained, lowering her gaze to the ground.

Carter sensed pain in her presence, but he didn't understand why Linx couldn't leave the ship for months despite knowing where her wand was. Thoughts ran through his head. Maybe she didn't know how to swim or was afraid of the sea serpents, but what if she was setting him up to make a fool of himself? He didn't know what to think.

"I'm not trying to trick you," Linx eagerly stressed.

"What? I didn't say anything." Carter jumped from the eeriness of her statement.

"I know. All fairies have telepathy, plus some other beings including your beloved sirens and their friends, the serpents. But I bet they didn't tell you that! Why would they expose something that doesn't benefit them?" Linx disclosed.

"Siren pirates and their serpent friends?" Carter repeated as his head spun. "Well, that makes sense. They were rather defensive when I mentioned any comments about the serpent. It must've been one of the girls that jumped into the water earlier! But why'd they lie about it?"

"Why'd they lie? Well, why are they going to tell you the truth? Do you even know where we're going?" Linx whispered, tucking her legs beneath her body on the chair.

"Um, I have no idea. Elena mentioned getting tea, but now she said that we're headed to another destination."

Linx shook her head. "Did she say anything else?"

"Well, no—"

"Of course not. How do I put this? She's going to sell you to an evil creature named Donem. Let's just say that if you ever find yourself in his presence, you'll never get out. He's powerful and thrives off of inflicting pain."

"What? Are you serious? They're planning on selling me? Why? I don't understand," yelled Carter.

"Shh! You don't want them to hear you! My friend, you're the next prized pig. You're very valuable. Now that the word is out you're here, everyone wants you."

"Why does anyone care that I'm here?" Carter sat back in his chair.

"You're the son of the most powerful woman in the land, aren't you?" Linx asked, dumbfounded that he was so disconnected.

This moment was the first that he had time to think about his mother. Possibly because he was so out of his element, along with the commotion, he didn't have time to think. Or maybe it was deeper than that. Haunting screams filled his head. The noise rose to an overwhelming level and then ceased with a bang. Dead. She was dead. His heart tightened to a level that made it difficult to breathe.

"No, you must have me mistaken for someone else," Carter murmured, turning his head in a different direction.

Linx stared through Carter's eyes and into his thoughts. As she saw him dive deeper and deeper into his memory, her eyes widened then closed as she saw his car smash into a giant tree. A rush of pain and loss flooded her body. She waited for him to gain his strength to face her again. He turned back with bloodshot eyes.

"I'm sorr—" Linx started to say.

Her eyes locked onto his. Carter reflected on seeing his mother's lifeless body hugging the steering wheel. He pictured her hair and her jacket; but then, he glanced out his window and saw this vibrant creature. The white arctic fox just sat watching, protecting.

"Carter!" Linx whispered in a high-pitched tone.

He shifted his attention to focus on Linx.

"The fox, that white fox—"

"Wha—" he gasped. "How?"

"That fox was your mother," she blurted out of excitement.

"You can see my thoughts too? Knock it off!" he asserted. He turned away, holding his hands over his head in hopes to protect his mind from being invaded. Finally realizing what she said, he dropped his hands and spun back around. "What'd you say?"

"I said the fox who was watching you, that was your mother. And your mother isn't dead. She might be dead in your world, but she is very much alive here. She is actually a queen here," Linx explained with hopeful eyes.

"How does that make sense? Impossible," Carter argued.

"Simple. Her spirit moved here, but it may not be the same as you remember. She seems kind and sweet there. Here, she's— well, powerful and—angry."

Carter's face shifted into a heavy frown. "I don't understand. If it's her, why would she be angry?"

"Unfinished business normally makes creatures angry. I assume since she died leaving you behind, that would have had something to do with it. I'm not sure, though. I've never spoken to her before, but her power is remarkable. She overthrew the previous queen," Linx cautiously replied.

"That's horrible! It doesn't sound like her at all. How can I see her? I need to see her and talk to her—if it's her," Carter begged.

"You help me, and I'll help you," she demanded with her emerald eyes staring into his. "Trust me, you don't want everyone knowing who you are. It'll be a dark bidding war just to be the one to take your head."

Carter's knees felt weak and heavy. Who could he trust? Elena seemed so warm and inviting to him, but she developed a weird temper about her after speaking to Qita. And then there was Linx. She was the only one who explained that his mother was still alive, but Linx was a fairy. According to Qita, that wasn't a good thing. But what if Qita was wrong or if she was the bad guy? What had she done to warrant Carter's loyalty?

Linx sat still on the chair, amused by the conversation in Carter's head. He debated back and forth, slightly favoring Linx. She felt if she waited it out, he would align with her.

"Look, I'll let you figure out what you want to do. In the meantime, I'll fix up your room so it's more comfortable. I'm expecting someone to pop in shortly. If I were you, I'd probably refrain from giving them details about your other world." She hopped up from the chair. "Also, start meditating to control your thoughts. You're an open book, and that's dangerous."

Embarrassed she has listened to too much, Carter thanked her and walked over to the table to pour a glass of water. His thoughts shifted to the idea that his mother was alive in this world. To think she was furious and dangerous was unfathomable, and it saddened him. Is it safe to see her? There was a real possibility she wouldn't be the same person he once knew.

"Linx—" Carter urged.

"What do you need?" Linx yelled while popping her head out of the bedroom.

"Let's do this," Carter agreed with an unsure, half-smile.

"Fantastic! I'll be back in a half-hour with a plan. Until then, say nothing and maybe take a nap. That way no one will find out." Linx jumped out of excitement.

After two minutes, Linx walked out of the room and headed for the door. She looked over at Carter and winked. "You won't regret this."

Linx quickly closed the door behind her, quietly exiting the room. Within minutes, the sea shook the ship from side to side as they sailed into a heavy storm. Carter aimed to get into his temporary bedroom before falling to the ground. Once he walked in, he couldn't believe that his room looked remarkable. The comforter was fresh, the nightstand was clean, and the room had a flowery scent. He didn't understand how she did it, but his room was nearly spotless. Carter happily snuggled into the bed and covered himself in blankets up to his chin. Maybe a nap was a good idea since his time here was quite stressful.

Drifting in and out of sleep, memories of his mother greeted him. From laughs at parties to snuggling in front of the fireplace on chilly nights, his entire understanding of her was that she was a warm, fun person. Now all of that might change if she is, in fact, an angry creature. Either way, every inch of his intuition said that he must try to find her. He would give anything to see her again.

As he traveled in his dream, he came across a castle covered in ice and snow. The closer he got to the castle, the more he felt spiders crawling on his skin, from his neck to his toes. Despite knowing he was in danger, he persevered through the deep snow. The sky swirled into a dark orange-pink above the Gothic winter castle. Randomly splattered across the snow-covered castle were dark patches of something. The contrast of the colors made it quick to detect, but Carter couldn't see close enough to decipher if the dark patches were mud or dirt. All the weight of his body sank to his feet, making each step nearly impossible.

A noise suddenly emerged from behind him. The thumping matched that of his heartbeat. Immediately, Carter whipped his head behind to see a dark horse headed in his direction. Carter started running as fast as he could, which felt increasingly slower. His body was straining to make it to safety, but what was safety? Carter didn't know where he was running to, but he knew if he stopped, it would be the end of him. As he turned his head around to face the castle, he stopped dead in his tracks. He fell to his knees as he finally saw the dark patches were turning into bloodstains, dripping all over the castle. It was then that he noticed something slumped in front of the castle. He slowly crawled over to the body that lay motionless.

As he observed the body, his lungs ceased to inhale air. Shock set in as he recognized the pile of blood-soaked, blonde hair neatly draped over the snow.

"Mom," Carter quietly cried.

When he spoke, the body appeared to twitch. He looked closely but saw nothing. Carter wondered if she was still alive. Looking closer at her body, he attempted to see if she was breathing as the thumping grew louder.

There it was again! Her hand twitched!

"Mom!" Carter yelled out of desperation.

Fingers tapped on the ground to the thumping, before lunging forward and gripping Carter's neck. He tried screaming for help as he felt her hand squeezing tighter and tighter around his throat. The pressure was so severe that she cut off his airway. While prying her hands from him, Carter rolled over on his back and tried to kick her off. As he felt himself losing consciousness, he looked up to see his mother's rotting face staring back at him.

The horse's thumping was just mere feet away as she slowly brought her mutilated face closer to his. Right as Carter thought he was a goner, she screamed in a shrilling voice, "Wake up!"

Carter immediately sat up, drenched in sweat. His heart felt like it would burst through his rib cage as he tried to catch his breath. Once he looked up from his bed, he saw a pair of ethereal eyes peering at him through the doorway. Qita sat at the table facing the connecting bedroom, just observing Carter.

"How long have you been sitting there?" Carter asked, spooked by her presence.

"Well, I found out Linx visited you. I wanted to make sure she wasn't causing any problems," Qita said while looking deep into Carter's eyes.

"No, she was fine." Carter rolled over in the bed, avoiding eye contact.

"You seem very tense. You okay?" Qita bluntly asked.

"Yeah, I'll be fine. The chaos of my journey has left me feeling a little tired. Not to mention, I just had a bad dream. I'll be okay though," he nonchalantly replied.

"Well, what'd she say to you anyway?" Qita pressed.

"Not much. She just cleaned up my room, so I could go to sleep. Is there anything that I should know?" Carter asked inconspicuously.

"Linx has just been known to tell tales. You know, tell stories to get her way. I just wanted to make sure she wasn't bothering you," Qita instigated, slowly standing up from the chair.

"Thanks for looking out for me." Carter smiled at Qita as she left.

The bright morning sun started peering into the room coating the bare wooden table, and Carter's stomach began mimicking sounds of a pot boiling stew, as it desperately begged for food. He noticed nothing was on the table at all. He wondered when they'd bring in food. Not wanting to be rude, he attempted to think of ways to ask. Sliding out of bed, he adjusted his clothing and hair.

Despite being awake, the traumatic dream stuck with him like glue. The blood, the thumping, and the scream from his decaying mother were too hard to forget. Even his throat still ached from the thought of being strangled. What did it mean? Did she want me to wake up since Qita was there? There were so many red flags, but one stuck out. Where was Linx? She said she'd return, but she never did. He wondered if Qita was right about her.

Walking out of the eating area and into the hallway, something to the side caught his eye. It was Linx, poking her head out of a small room. She waved her hand impatiently to call him over. Carter quickly ran towards her to see what she needed. She dove into the dark room and quietly shut the door behind him. He noticed a bunch of shelves lining the walls. It seemed like the tiny room housed cleaning supplies or non-perishable foods. Since the light was minimal, he could barely see anything.

"Hey, what happened? I thought you'd come and find me last night?" Carter persisted.

"Aye, I know. It wasn't safe. Somehow, someone saw me going in there and told Qita. That's all she needed to immediately question me. She hates me on a normal day, and I, her, but she is relentless if she has any ammunition. I figured it'd be safer to wait until the morning. I saw she visited you. Is everything ok? Does she suspect anything?" Linx nervously asked.

"I don't think she suspects anything, but she asked a few questions about you. She was there when I woke up from a terrifying dream about my mother," Carter confided, rubbing his neck.

"Good. We cannot afford for her to suspect anything suspicious is going on. As for your mother, that's interesting! That means she is reaching out to you! She knows you're here," insisted Linx quietly.

"Uh, is that a good thing?" Carter asked.

"I don't know," she said. "What I know, though, is that we have an excellent shot at getting off this wretched ship when the sun goes down tonight. Normally we wouldn't want to rush anything, but if we wait until we get closer to my island, they might get paranoid and ruin our plans to escape."

"All right, just let me know what to do."

"Okay. I'll go on the main deck and do my normal work. When you come up, keep an eye on me discreetly. I'll start wrapping a rope around my arm, and that'll be your cue to jump in the water. Jump in the water on the exact opposite side of where I'll be standing. That way, Elena won't suspect anything. Anyway, swim straight down until you see a blue light—that's my wand. Grab it, and I'll meet you when you come up for air. I'll jump down to you, and then we'll finally be free!" Linx cheered at the thought.

"That's all I have to do? Just grab it?"

"Yes, I'll take it from there. But, if something happens to me, you need to save yourself," Linx divulged.

"Well, we don't need to worry about that. We'll both get out of here!"

Grabbing his hand, she articulated, "Look, I really hope so! However, I want to make sure you're safe too, especially after risking everything for me."

As he imagined something bad happening to her, sadness swept over him.

"Don't worry, we just need a backup plan. Once you have my wand, you need to close your eyes and imagine a purple forest filled with fairies. The wand will transport you there. If this happens, remember to ask for the elder. Tell them *everything*, and they'll help you. Let's just hope that it doesn't come to that," Linx explained with dark eyes.

Carter let out a heavy sigh. "Okay, I understand. I won't focus on that, but I'll keep it in mind, just in case."

With a slight smile, Linx nodded. "Okay, good."

Sadly, Carter's heart sank a little when she looked at him with giant doe eyes. The emotional tension explained so much more than what was said. There was pain, excitement, and fear that lingered in her heart and in her mind. Was he now able to read minds, or was she just allowing herself to be an open book so he could trust her? Either way, her vulnerability made it easy for him to sympathize with her, so the thought of something happening to Linx was heartbreaking.

While they stood in the darkness, Carter felt something gently tickling his neck. He went to brush it off of his skin with his hand. As his hand moved across his neck, the creature ran down his back. Carter shook his shirt violently and stepped backward onto a broomstick, which fell to the floor with a loud smack. Both Linx and Carter looked at each other. Nervous someone heard the broom fall on the ground, Linx held her finger over Carter's lips to keep him quiet.

"What was that?" an unrecognizable voice boomed.

"Probably that smelly rat living in your room!" cackled another voice, walking past the closet.

Looking at each other with a smile, Linx and Carter breathed a sigh of relief. With a wink, she slowly opened the door to check and see if anyone was there, before sliding into the hall. Carter's heart started pounding when he thought about how he would have to get through the next several hours without being questioned and then dive off of a ship in the dark. He planned to sneak back into his room. Hoping he could play off motion sickness, this idea was probably one of the best shots at avoiding unnecessary conversations. A few hours passed with no visitors, but then he heard a knock on the door.

"Hello?" he grunted, lying under the covers of the bed.

"Are you okay in there?" asked Elena's sweet voice.

"Oh, yes. I'll be okay. Just a little motion sick from the sea," he mumbled.

"Well, okay. I'll be up on the deck. I can send someone to check on you soon. Would you like me to send someone to make you food?"

"No, I'll be okay. Thank you very much," he insisted, despite the severe hunger pains rolling in his stomach.

Unfortunately, he had to take the chance of not eating for now. Carter couldn't risk being outed. Hopefully, Linx could help him later. As he rested, swaying with the ship, he quickly drifted off into a dream again.

Chapter 6

Strolling towards the deck, Carter gazed at the sky. Streaks of navy blue and black painted the canvas above him as bright stars delicately scattered from left to right. Suffocating gusts of wind whipped around the main deck of the ship, nearly toppling Carter. As he started looking for Linx, Carter noticed he was being watched from afar. When he finally spotted Linx near the ropes, Qita walked out of the darkness and blocked him. Her eyes were flaming red and looked deep into his mind. Terrified she would find out the plan, he immediately looked away and tried making his way towards Linx. He thought he was scot-free when Elena appeared from the shadows.

"Carter, where are you going?" she asked, with a giant smile on her face. The edges of her lips curled up freakishly. The thoughts of Linx describing the women as sirens ran through Carter's mind. What if all the niceties were just a façade to gain Carter's trust? Were they really going to send him to Donem?

"Uh, nowhere. I just wanted to look around," he nervously replied. Carter noticed Linx starting to wrap the rope around her arm.

"My cue!" he shouted. The sky darkened with a distant island growing larger in the distance.

She slowly transformed into a sea serpent right in front of his eyes. "Your cue? I knew you were up to something!"

Carter fell to the floor as he looked up to meet her eyes. The body of the sea serpent could swallow a walrus whole. She stretched as tall as the mainmast and whipped her tail towards Carter. He rolled over swiftly to avoid being smashed by the large tail. Quickly glancing over at Linx, he noticed that she almost finished rolling up the rope on her arm. Carter slid around the sea serpent and ran straight to the edge of the ship.

As he looked down towards the water, it appeared he was hundreds of feet in the air. Despite swimming in the past, he wasn't a high diver. The thought of diving into the water instantly made him nauseous, but he had to do it. How could he possibly leave Linx as a prisoner on a ship?

Looking behind his back, he witnessed the sea serpent heading towards Linx. As she continued to loop the rope around her arm, Carter noticed shackles resting on her ankles. If he didn't help Linx, the serpent might consume her. He knew that he had to jump now; otherwise, they would lose their chance of escaping. Carter and Linx would be stuck on the ship forever until the sirens disposed of them.

As Linx neared the end of wrapping the rope, she yelled out of desperation, "Jump!"

Carter took a deep breath and dove into the water. His knees were weak and his internal organs felt as if they were floating within him. Suddenly—SPLASH—he hit the water. Fully submerged by cold liquid, the feeling was overwhelmingly scary as he couldn't feel or see anything beneath him. Carter hopelessly tried searching for the blue light from the wand. Where was it? Everything was dark around the anchored ship, and he had no idea where to look from here. His heart was beating fiercely until he felt a latch on the ship. *Yes,* he thought to himself. As he flipped the latch on the ship, a tiny compartment door opened up to reveal a brightly shining wand.

Reaching in cautiously, he gripped the wand and removed it from the ship. The light grew brighter as he brought it closer to his face. He floated to the top to see if Linx could jump down to him. As he waited for her, he heard nothing. Where was everyone? Was she okay? Was the sea serpent still aboard the ship? He didn't know what to do. Slowly inhaling a deep breath, he counted to ten in hopes of Linx's late arrival. When nothing happened, he held the wand close and thought about saving Linx.

Slowly opening his eyes, he looked around to see if he transported himself to her. Carter did not understand what happened. The environment was a bright orange from flames that erupted from the ground. His body temperature was increasing at an alarming rate. Where was he? His feet crunched onto the dry grounds as he made his way through some brush. Once he reached a short stone wall, he looked into the secluded patio to see some muscular, beastly guy dressed in a cutoff gray shirt. Surrounded by severed heads, he was rocking back and forth on a chair while singing an inaudible song. A putrid and nauseating smell filled the air, violating Carter's nostrils. He glanced through several tumbleweeds to see a pile of rotting corpses. Dread seeped from his chest through his stomach and bled into his knees. Knowing he was in danger, Carter attempted to figure out an escape plan.

Rubbing the sides of his pants, Carter began quietly hyperventilating. Trying to focus, he searched for the wand while avoiding the monster's attention. Where is it? Where is it?! He took a step back to turn around, and the singing ceased.

A deep voice in a southern-like accent calmly asked, "Leaving so soon? I think you were looking for this."

Carter looked up to see the figure, still rocking in the chair, hold out his hand. Like a magic trick, he produced the wand right out of thin air in the palm of his hand. Sadly, he was so far away, Carter had no way to grab it. As quickly as the wand appeared, the figure closed his hand to dispose of it.

"No," whispered Carter.

"There's no need to whisper. You're in *my* land! Speak your mind, boy! It may be the only time anyone will hear your voice," said the giant, standing up to face Carter.

A significant chunk of his right cheek was missing, displaying several dark teeth when he closed his mouth. Blood had splattered his cutoff gray shirt and trailed down to his carpenter pants and work boots. His biceps were unbelievably huge, more than half the size of Carter's body. Terrified, Carter stood frozen in his place.

With a booming yell, he shouted, "Well, come on in! Don't be shy, boy!"

Frozen in fear, Carter heard low growls lurking behind him. He peered over his shoulder to see four massive dog-like demons walking in his direction. They formed a deadly wall, pushing Carter forward.

"What is this place?" Carter asked quietly.

"Speak up, boy!" the giant shouted.

Carter swallowed a hard ball in his throat as he softly asked, "Where am I?"

"Son, you're in the Inferno. The most beau-ti-ful place you'll ever see." His devilish smile grew. "I'm Donem. You must be . . . the queen's son."

"I—uh, how did I get here?" Carter lightly stuttered, changing the subject.

"Ha! Well, it was partly because of me, but part of it was you. Good job on finding the wand! Rumor had it, Linx would be on that ship forever! Now, we don't have to worry about that anymore since Elena ate her." Donem chuckled with a demented smile.

"Wha—" Carter's face sank as he asked. "Are you serious?"

Donem released a high-pitched laugh while slapping his thigh. "No! You are in a dream, my friend! Lighten up a bit!"

"This is a dream? So, this isn't real. This isn't real. This isn't real," Carter began repeating to wake himself.

"Na—ah—ah. Before you get yourself too comfortable, I still have the wand, the real wand," Donem warned.

"Really? How does that work if this is just a dream?" he asked, perplexed by the rules of magic in this world.

"They never had the wand. I helped Elena find that fairy, but the contract she signed had this little itty-bitty clause forfeiting any wands or pixie dust over to me."

"So, this whole time—"

"They never had it." Donem gave a full-bellied laugh.

"Is there anything I can give you or do to get the wand?" Carter asked nervously.

"Hmm." Donem pondered for a moment. "Yes, why yes you can!"

"What can I do?" Carter asked, trying to settle the chaos in his stomach.

"Bring her here. Bring Elena here, and the wand is yours," he said matter-of-factly.

Confused, Carter asked, "Bring her here? Why? How?"

"It's none of your business why I want her here. But she tried to stiff me. No one stiffs me. Now, we must remind people what happens when you do." He grinned.

"You won't hurt her, right? I don't want to be a part of that."

"Son, you were involved before you even got here. Let me tell you that you shouldn't feel so bad for someone who was using you as a cash cow. When they found out you were the queen's son, they got scared your momma would kill 'em. So what do they do? They try selling you to me," Donem explained, while veins bulged from his face. "They still get paid, and the queen comes after me. Idiots! They are done."

"They were going to sell me to you? What for?" Carter inquired, taking a step back.

Donem grunted with a deranged smile. "I buy creatures. You name it—big, small, bumpy, and even them fuzzy, weird ones. I eat 'em, hunt 'em, train my dogs with 'em, make 'em cook for me, and so on. Minions . . . food . . . same thing."

"How do I know you won't break the agreement?" Carter wondered.

"Let me say this: if I wanted you dead, you'd be dead. There's no reason I wouldn't give you the wand. I really don't have any use for it. I just didn't want Elena to have it," he declared with his strong twang.

Carter shook his head. "But to get here, I can't go with Linx to her home island. Am I able to confide in her, so she knows that I'm not turning on her?"

"No! No one can know about anything. If anyone finds out, you'll never get Elena here. You cannot tell 'em what the plan is! You cannot chance it," he hollered.

"Okay, fine, but you have to help me with something. Teach me how to prevent people from reading my mind. I can't stand it. That's all they do there," he begged out of concern.

Donem snapped his fingers and said, "There. Problem fixed."

Carter looked at him as if he was playing a joke, "What are you talking about? How is it fixed? Nothing happened!"

"Maybe you can't tell the difference, but everyone else can. One of the most annoying characteristics of those siren wenches is their ability to read minds. Only some can deflect their powers, and now you're one of the few. Your mind is a sealed box, so take care of it. This way no one will know anything about our plan or the wand unless you tell 'em—which you won't."

"Really? This will protect my thoughts when I wake up?" Carter exclaimed.

"That's right."

"Well, thank you," Carter muttered. Despite the current predicament, he was grateful for the ability to think without others listening.

Donem walked up to Carter and brought his singed face close. "No, boy, thank you. Now . . . wake up!"

Like a bat out of hell, Carter jumped up out of bed. This world has been producing some strange and intense dreams. Despite the smell of burning flesh still inhabiting his nose, he knew there was no way his dream had any influence over real life. Right? He didn't know what to think. What was real life at this point, anyway? What if Carter ignored something very important and wound up getting himself killed? He wondered if he should test out whether the women could still read his mind. He came out of the room for a bit. The deep orange sun was sinking down into the sea. He had some time before he was to retrieve Linx's wand, so he wanted to walk around the deck to familiarize himself with the jump.

The deep blue water swirled and viciously splashed against the ship. It was then that he thought about whether his dream had influence over his current reality. If Donem truly was aware of his existence and had the wand, then Carter would risk everything for nothing.

"Feeling better?" Elena asked as she approached Carter.

Carter almost jumped out of his skin. "Uh, yes. Sometimes my stomach doesn't handle the movement well," he replied, shrugging his shoulders, conscious of not making too much eye contact.

"Is everything okay? You seem a little tense. I hope no one made you feel uncomfortable." She tilted her head to the side.

A giant gust of wind temporarily suffocated him as he thought of a response. "Seriously, don't worry. I'll be fine. It was just overwhelming waking up in a new place."

Looking deep into his eyes, she whispered, "Something is different about you."

"I don't know what you mean, but I hope that's a good thing." Carter chuckled. Slowly trying to walk away, he hoped it wouldn't create additional suspicion.

Elena intently monitored Carter as he left her side. She wondered if it was just a coincidence that he stood near where the wand was stashed, but she couldn't read his mind. Perplexed by the chain of events, she wanted to see if he would go near Linx. They truly had no reason to speak, unless there was something going on. Elena tried to act busy with another task, so Carter wouldn't notice her. Right before her eyes, she saw him snake his way over to her without trying to draw any attention. Rage surged through her and darkness filled her soul as she acknowledged the defiance growing on her ship. She needed to find Qita. She was right, and now they had to separate them until she disposed of Carter.

Unaware Elena had noticed him, Carter quickly walked over to Linx. He needed to at least tell her the plan was off. If she could still read his mind, she could see why and then ridicule him for being an idiot. However, if Linx couldn't read his mind, at least he knew he saved her from potentially killing herself.

Stacking boxes, Linx whispered, "What are you doing?"

"We can't do the plan," Carter said before anyone walked by.

"What are you talking about? We are just minutes away before doing this! I knew I couldn't count on you." Linx angrily turned away from him.

"Linx, I'm sorry. I can't explain why right now. But I can't, and you can't either!"

"Look, I'll figure out what I need to do *without* your help. Don't worry about me," Linx argued.

"I'll worry because I care about you. I don't want to see you get hurt. The wand isn't there. That's all I can say," Carter nervously articulated, looking around where they were standing. He hoped that what he said wouldn't anger Donem.

Linx sarcastically laughed while her eyes twinkled with rage. "What? How would you know where anything is? You had no idea about the wand until I told you. Unless you're working with Elena?"

"I can't say anything else. I just can't chance it," he insisted.

"I'm right. I'm right! You are working with Elena now! I cannot read your mind at all. She must have wrapped you into some crazy plan and blocked your mind from me. Look, I'm done with this place, and I'm done with you. I'm out of here," she concluded, turning and walking away.

"Linx!" he whispered, hoping no one heard him.

Although he attempted to gain her attention, she refused to acknowledge him and disappeared into the darkness. Carter knew he needed to protect her and look out for himself, so he was going to have to play dumb for the plan to work. If Elena suspected anything, she would refuse to go on the island. Carter didn't understand what Donem would do to her, but he immediately thought about Linx's kidnapping. If she could kidnap a fairy and sell others to a monster for money, her fate wasn't his problem.

Defeated, Carter shuffled his way over towards the side of the ship. Looking out over the railing, he became hypnotized by the fluid movement of the sparkling water. Time passed as no one spoke to him. Nevertheless, he wasn't complaining that he was alone. He wanted to savor the beautiful sights of the sea and sounds of the waves crashing against the ship. It was an unanticipated therapeutic moment that he desperately needed. Exhaling a sigh, Carter was about to turn around as someone approached him.

"For your safety, I have to ask you to rest in your room until we get to our destination," Elena demanded from behind him.

Carter jumped into the air, unaware if she had heard his thoughts. Wanting to stay on her good side, he complied, although he didn't understand the urgency to contain him. Surprised, he noticed a few of the pirates were going towards their rooms as well.

"Avast, me hearties! Time to batten down the hatches!" Elena shouted out to the crew, while bringing the spyglass down from her eye.

Carter noticed a woman walking down the stairs beside him. "What's happening?"

"Ah, you're that new boy. Almost at the Inferno. Preparing to pass through the spouts," she replied with concern.

"Spouts? What are spouts?"

"Lad, you need to find a safe spot. The sea is fierce over this way. Don't go on deck, savvy?" she muttered, passing Carter's room.

Carter's mind started racing as he dashed to his bedroom. Not knowing what to expect, he grew nervous about these spouts she had mentioned. If the pirates are concerned about the active sea, it must be dangerous. As he sat on the bed thinking about what was to come, he heard wind whistling through some boards on the ship.

"Where's that fairy?" shouted Qita from a distance. The wind began picking up speed and screamed through minor holes in the wall.

"I haven't seen her," yelled one woman.

"If I find she's up to something, she'll be feeding the fishes—along with anyone else found to be helping her! We don't have room for mutiny on this ship!" Qita boomed out of anger.

"Where could Linx be?" Carter said aloud to himself.

Rushing to the door, Carter almost tripped over his feet trying to find her. The ship was erratically rocking from side to side, making it difficult to navigate. He darted through the door and ran up the stairs to the deck. When he scanned the surrounding area, two giant cylinders of water connecting the sea to the sky caught his attention. The eerie sight shook Carter to his bones.

Searching the deck, he couldn't see anyone who resembled Linx. He quickly checked a stack of wooden boxes, hoping he would find her. Where could she be?

"Well, well," Qita uttered, appearing from the shadows of the stairs.

Startled, Carter yelled, "Qita! I didn't know you were there."

"What are you doing up here? Oh, let me guess. Hmm, looking for the fairy?"

"Well, I, uh . . . yes," Carter admitted. "Someone said it was poor weather, and I would feel awful if something happened to her."

"Why would you feel responsible if she didn't listen to the cap'n?"

"We got into a disagreement right before Elena made the announcement, and she might not have heard—" Carter mumbled, before Qita interrupted.

"Cap'n, not Elena. She is your cap'n, so show some respect. What were you fighting about? Do tell!" Qita openly pried.

"Oh, it was really nothing. I just—" Carter tried to avoid Qita's question.

"I know what's going on. I knew since you got here. You came to rescue the fairy to bring her home. I had my doubts when you let me read your mind, but now—nothing. I can see nothing. That must be the work of the fairies. You only let me see what you want. Well, it won't work. You're not going anywhere. I'd rather sell your meat to Donem than send you alive," Qita warned.

Donem was right! He was right! Despite Elena's previous statements, they intended on selling him to a massive, demonic giant. Carter saw Qita grabbing the sword from her hip beneath her jacket, so he quickly glanced around to find something useful for protection. Luckily, there was a metal rod tied to the wall. In a split second, he bolted over towards the rod and tore it off the wall. Qita wasn't far behind. As she went to slash the back of his knees, Carter turned around and deflected the hit. He had no interest in harming her; Carter just wanted to protect himself against her attacks.

"Luck won't stand with you for long. We'll be rid of you, and you shall be tossed overboard as bait!" Qita swung her sword towards Carter's shoulder.

Carter couldn't believe how strong she was as she slammed her sword down, clanking against the metal rod.

"I didn't do anything! And I wasn't working with the fairies," he yelled, blocking a hit. "I don't remember how I got here. I kept trying to remember what happened, and it was blurry. I was fighting with my father after my mother died, and I ran away. When I got into the forest, I slipped. That's all I remember before waking up here in the water. It wasn't because of the fairies."

"Liar!" she screamed. Qita pinned him on the floor.

As the wind howled, the ship sailed close to an approaching water spout. Swiftly, she lifted her sword and went to slash Carter across the neck. Taking all the energy he had, he kicked Qita off of his body. With a scream and a clink from her sword falling to the deck, she flew overboard into the water below. Carter jumped up to see if she was okay. As he looked down, he witnessed her shifting into a sea serpent right before his eyes! Her legs stretched and fused while her body was being covered in a myriad of scales. Although Linx had briefly mentioned the pirates being close with the serpents, she never explained that some pirates turned into serpents! Qita raised her serpent head up out of the water and towered over Carter, attempting to bite him. Her head was massive with teeth that were as long as Carter's arms. He instantaneously rolled away from Qita's attack to grab her sword.

Out of nowhere, Elena and two other pirates ran over towards Carter.

"What's going here?" Elena yelled at Carter, standing ready for Qita's attack.

"She is trying to kill me! She followed me up here and tried cutting off my head!" Carter screamed, using every ounce of his breath to be louder than the howling wind.

Standing in between Carter and Qita, Elena yelled, "Qita! Qita! Stand down!"

The sea serpent screeched a loud, ear bleeding cry, pulling back from the ship. The amount of control that Elena had over Qita amazed Carter. Unfortunately, no one noticed how close the waterspout was until it was too late. The spinning cylinder of water viciously sucked in Qita's tail and whipped her into the middle with ease. As everyone watched from a distance, her head turned and quickly spun into the waterspout. Like a whip cracking, it effortlessly broke her neck. Elena dropped her head out of shock and sorrow. Her right-hand woman of years perished in an instant. Heartbroken, she ordered Nira, another pirate, to accompany Carter to his room until they passed the waterspouts. At that point, she would figure out what she would want to do with him.

"Elena—" Carter begged.

She turned to him without uttering a word.

Carter pleaded wholeheartedly, "I'm sorry this happened! She followed me up here and accused me of working with Linx. When I denied her accusations, she attacked me with her sword. I never wanted to hurt anyone or see anything happen to any of your ladies."

Elena turned away, "I saw you approach Linx earlier, and one of my ladies overheard the talk of a plan. Qita was trying to find out the truth! When she saw you approach the deck, she figured you were attempting to find Linx. So, tell me, were you?"

Carter stared at Elena, not knowing what to do. If he said nothing, then no one would know anything, and Elena's fate rested with Donem. Nevertheless, if he told the truth, he risked everyone's life. The decision would seem clear; however, he didn't feel right about lying to her. Something about her made him feel like he could trust her, but then he questioned if that was because she was a siren.

"I came up here because I heard Qita yell that Linx was missing," Carter explained. "I spoke with Linx earlier, but it was of nothing important."

"Oh?" Elena asked, very unamused.

"Elena, can I speak to you in private, please?" Carter inquired, looking down to the ground.

"Come with me."

As Carter followed her, he had no idea where she was headed. They proceeded toward a set of intricately designed double doors. Elena opened one of the doors and ushered Carter in to sit at the wooden table inside. As he glanced around the room, Carter noticed a very cushy bed against the distant wall along with an elegant red chair in the corner. This must be the captain's quarters. It possessed an aroma similar to a sweet garden. He gently slid onto an ornately carved chair at the table.

Rapidly, she closed the door and walked over to a tiny table. Elena slowly poured a drink into her mug. As she sat at the table, a thick whiff of alcohol splashed Carter in the face. Instantly, he thought about the last time he had spoken with his father. For the most part, he almost forgot about his father and that last interaction. Right away, a devastating mix of anger, sadness, and guilt consumed him. Despite their last fight, he wondered if Richard was okay. Was he even looking for Carter?

Elena let out a heavy sigh. "What did you want to speak about?"

"Well—" Carter took a deep breath. " . . . were you going to sell me? To Donem?"

Those simple questions ignited Elena's dead eyes into raging fires. Alarmed by the reaction, Carter refused to break eye contact.

Staring back at him, Elena demanded, "That's ridiculous! Who told you that?"

"I'm not trying to get anyone in trouble," he confided. "I just didn't understand what was going on. Someone told me you were going to sell me to Donem since my mother was a queen here. They said you didn't want to take the risk of her killing you."

Increasing the volume of her voice, she repeated, "Who told you that?"

Carter sat quietly, refusing to mention any names.

After a moment of no cooperation, Elena looked deep into Carter's eyes. "I don't know who told you that, but it seems like they are trying to start trouble by stirring the pot. Now, I need you to tell me who said that. I cannot have that behavior on this ship. I hope you understand. It is too dangerous to allow people to gang up behind my back and spread lies."

His mind flashed back to when he was with Donem, and he felt very grateful for him now. He took a deep breath to try calming his wild nerves. Hoping that everything would play out smoothly, he shut his eyes before answering her, "Qita."

Elena raised an eyebrow as she studied his face, "Qita?"

"Qita said you were going to sell me to Donem, and she didn't care if I was alive or dead. That's what happened minutes before you came over when she tried to kill me," Carter thoroughly explained.

"Well—" Elena cleared the lump from her throat, "I guess we'll just call this one a wash then. There'll be no need to discuss this with anyone else on this ship. Ya hear? If any of my ladies give you a hard time, just let me know. I'll handle it accordingly. Is that clear?"

Without breaking eye contact, Carter agreed. "Definitely. I won't say anything. I understand why you wouldn't want anyone else to know that Qita betrayed you. Thank you for speaking with me, Captain."

Grimly, her eyes looked Carter up and down before she uttered, "You may go now."

Appreciative he would get to keep his head and go back to bed for a while, Carter promptly got up from his chair to walk towards the doors. He tried not to appear too happy due to the severity of the previous hour. His hand was on the doorknob when he heard Elena ask one more question.

"Carter, I was meaning to ask you, what were you and Linx talking about earlier?"

"Um, nothing. I just made an off-color comment about fairies. It made her mad, and she stormed off. Is she okay though? I know Qita said she couldn't find her," Carter nonchalantly inserted into his reply.

"She's fine. I just saw her moments before."

"Oh, good. Those waterspouts are wicked," he said. Realizing he should just leave before getting himself into trouble, Carter walked out the door.

"Please send Nira in," Elena ordered, removing her captain's hat.

When walking back to the main stairs, Carter passed by some women and looked at Nira. "Nira, Captain Elena requested to speak with you."

He admitted to himself that maybe he looked a little too happy walking around. However, knowing Linx was okay had brightened his spirits. Nevertheless, not everyone was happy aboard the ship. Several women sulked in a group once they found out about Qita. He could feel their burning glares singe his skin. Guilt instantly rushed through Carter's body. Anxiety sunk into his knees while his stomach performed somersaults. Why did he feel this way, despite Qita trying to kill him?

Once Nira finished speaking with Elena, she promptly exited the captain's quarters and descended the main stairs. Carter could only wonder what they had spoken about. It didn't seem like he did anything else suspicious that needed to worry him. Waiting a few minutes, Carter decided to flee the staring eyes and go back into his room for the night. This moment was one of the few times he truly felt grateful to escape into his hole of a room.

Chapter 7

Once Carter entered his room, he dove for his mattress and buried his face into the pillow. How he would give anything to hide in the comfort of his own bed. He thought about how each time he woke up in this room, a sinking feeling of terror would blanket him. No matter how much time passed, he couldn't escape this musky bubble. As he analyzed his current reality, a light knock on the door interrupted his thoughts. Linx slowly walked in with wide eyes and rosy cheeks. Although she appeared distressed, her eyes soon softened when she spotted Carter. She approached his bed and let out a sigh.

"Linx! Where were you?" Carter joyfully bumbled.

Wringing her hands together, she whispered, "Some of the girls blocked me in the storage room. They said we were up to something, and that they would find out what. They harassed me, hoping I would say something."

"I'm so sorr—"

"Then Qita showed up. I thought she was going to help, but she threatened to kill us both. She pressured me to talk, even saying they would sell me to Donem next," Linx disclosed as she sat near Carter, wiping her eyes. "I said nothing, hoping to protect you."

In disbelief, Carter asked, "They blocked you in a room? What made them think we were planning anything?"

Hanging her head, she explained, "Someone overheard us talking. They thought we were trying to overthrow Elena. Why would I care to overthrow her? I just want to go home."

"I'm so sorry that happened to you."

"I'm used to it. They hate me here. I'm surprised they kept me alive as long as they have."

Carter looked at the ground as his heart broke for Linx.

Without breaking eye contact, she asked, "By the way, I heard what you did. How did you get away with it?"

Confused, Carter questioned, "How'd I get away with what?"

"Killing Qita," Linx blurted out in a whisper.

"I didn't kill her! The water did. It was an accident," he defensively yelled.

Nervously smirking, Linx shook her head. "Sure, keep telling yourself that. The women believe differently."

"Linx, she tried killing me when we were passing the spouts. She tried slicing my neck with her sword. When I kicked her off of me, she flew into the water. It was an accident!" Carter defended himself.

She genuinely apologized, "Look, I'm sorry they put you in that situation. My question is, though, how did you get away with it? Qita has been Elena's most trusted woman for a very long time. Not to mention, the women here always looked up to her. She was seen as the fearless warrior Elena needed by her side."

"Well, I explained everything to Elena, including being sold to Donem," he began.

Linx's mouth dropped, and her eyebrows rose. "You told her what I said? I thought I could trust you?"

Shaking his head no, Carter explained, "I only said Qita told me, which she did. Elena denied it. She said not to talk about it with anyone else or there'll be consequences, so can we change the subject?" He started rubbing the back of his neck.

"Since when do you care about your relationship with Elena? Or are you afraid of her?" Linx shook her head. "You know this changes nothing. She will still want to sell you off to Donem. You are a risk, and despite whatever she told you, you're a danger to her ship—inside and out. Don't fall for the siren."

After dealing with all the stressful activities earlier, Carter didn't have the energy to walk on eggshells. It would be a matter of time before he let something slip about Donem's plan. He couldn't afford to let her find out, so he closed his eyes. "Look, I'm sorry you feel that way. If you don't mind, I wanted to take advantage of the silence and get some rest for the night. A serpent almost ate me—again. That's enough fun for now."

Linx laughed out loud while rolling her eyes. "You think that's bad? Wait until you're stuck on an island as you're being chased by monsters as big as this ship. You scream for mercy, but Donem laughs as he sends three more snarling creatures your way. All of it a game to see which one takes your head first. If you can't handle this pirate ship, how well do you think you'll do in hell?"

Immediately, Linx spun towards the door and left Carter alone with his thoughts. His mind began racing through the events spanning from his demented dreams to his surreal reality. What if all of this was for nothing? Who could he trust? Questions ran through his mind while the wind continued to whistle. The sound was like a teapot of boiling water, yet it was soothing enough to allow him to drift off to sleep.

His mind began recounting his fight with Qita as he descended into unconsciousness. The sheer terror rushing through his body as her enormous mouth approached the ship. Although being terrified, he knew Elena would come to save him. He took a deep breath, just waiting for her to intervene as she did before, but she never came. The serpent let out a scream as it dove towards Carter. He tried to run away, but the serpent swallowed him in one gulp.

When he opened his eyes, he found himself in an eerily familiar place. The scorching heat, the repulsive smell, and the singing; he was in Donem's lair.

No, no, no. Get me out of here, he thought to himself.

"Nice work, my friend! You are darker than I thought!" Donem's deep twang boomed.

With both hands holding his head, he shouted, "Why am I here again?"

Shaking his head with a chuckle, Donem laughed. "Oh stop! You're here to tell me all the details about breaking that serpent's neck!"

"I had no intention of killing her!" Carter adamantly defended himself.

"Whatever you say." He laughed. "There's no reason to say that. She was going to kill you if you didn't get her first."

Feeling tense, Carter snapped, "Look, I take no pleasure from someone dying."

"Well, it's all about perspective. Kill or be killed. You should be proud that you survived. You're better off than where she's at now. Oh, by the way, I look forward to seeing you soon! If you stay on my good side, maybe I'll let that little fairy live too. No promises, though." Donem chuckled into a sigh.

"I thought you only wanted Elena? What are you going to do with the rest of them?" Carter anxiously demanded.

"Son, that's none of your business. You'll have your wand and fairy, and then you'll be on your way. If you don't hold up your end, well—let's not worry about that. Now, it's time to wake up. I'll be seeing you soon!" Donem grinned as the intensity of the Inferno faded away.

With a sharp breath, Carter awoke from yelling in the distance. The women were on edge. "We have passed the waterspouts! Captain said to prepare yourselves for the Inferno. We shall be there by tomorrow morning!"

Carter's heart sank to the pit of his stomach as he thought about the future of everyone on the ship. When Donem holds Elena captive, what was he going to do? Did Carter really want to do this? Did he have a choice? He felt absolutely alone. Not one person could know anything about his agreement with Donem, but he wished he could consult with a soul—especially Linx. The last thing he wanted was for someone to get hurt, and there were so many people to consider. Then his mind wandered to deeper, darker places.

He needed to talk to someone—now. Jumping out of bed, he went to search for Linx. Why did he have to snap at her? Maybe she was right about Elena. Maybe Elena's siren powers had a hold on him. He began searching the ship while dismissing the vengeful looks being received. He couldn't find Linx anywhere. The mid-morning sun rose as its bright reflection bounced off the rippling water. Suddenly, he heard a scream come from the side of the deck. He ran over to see Linx swinging upside down with a rope around her ankles. Carter sprinted over and pushed a few women out of the way.

As the group dispersed, a pirate shouted, "You better hope Elena is dropping you off at Donem's because you won't survive here. We'll make sure of it!"

Carter yanked the rope, pulling Linx to safety. "Linx, Linx! Are you okay? What happened?" Carter screamed.

Coughing up water, she whispered, "They tried drowning me."

"What?" he shouted out of disbelief.

"A few of the sirens . . . they thought I had involvement with Qita's death. They don't understand I have minimal powers without my wand. Someone went into the water to grab the wand to force me to bring her back. When they reached the compartment, they said it wasn't there. They tossed me into the water to die."

"Oh my goodness, I'm so sorry no one tried to save you before I got here!"

"You got here just in time. Once fairy wings get wet, they become a heavy mess. It can kill us if we fall into deep water."

"That's ridiculous. I can't believe it! Are you okay?"

"I'll be fine now. I thought I was going to die down there. Thank you!" she gratefully exclaimed, looking into his eyes.

"Yeah, of course. You're welcome. I can talk to Elena to let her know what was going on—" he mumbled.

"No! Please don't!" she pleaded. "That'll give them more ammunition to come back after me when no one is looking. Plus, I wouldn't be surprised if she already knew. She cursed Donem's name and holed herself in her room when she found out my wand was missing."

"The least I can do is accompany you while we're still on the ship."

"At some point, we'll part ways, if what everyone says is true. They'll sell you to Donem, if that's Elena's plan. Then these sirens will torment me until they kill me." Linx hung her head out of defeat.

"Well, Elena denied that she'll be sending me to Donem, but regardless, you'll come with me!"

"Um, this isn't a vacation spot we are talking about. He is a monster that takes pleasure by brutally torturing souls. I would take being pushed around by the pathetic sirens for the rest of my life instead of risking one minute near Donem," she refused.

"What if I say that you won't get hurt?" he offered.

"There is absolutely no way you can promise that. Look, it's been said that he killed both of his parents because he grew tired of them. What reasonable person does that?"

"I don't need you to trust him. I need you to trust me. Come with me, so we can find our families," Carter begged with his hands.

Dumbfounded, she shook her head in disbelief. "Um, I don't know. I'll have to think about it."

"That's fine," he agreed, looking to see if anyone could hear them.

"I better go. I need to rearrange and stack boxes over there before Elena sees the mess." She sighed.

"Let me help you!" Carter suggested with a smile.

"Are you sure? You can go rest and feast, but you want to help me with labor?" Linx blushed.

Without blinking his eyes, he immediately stated, "Yes, I would love to help you!"

"But what will you say when everyone sees you with me? I'm sure that will cause even more of a stir."

Looking into her eyes, Carter reached his hand for hers. "That I'm helping a friend."

Her heart fluttered with happiness as she never experienced a healthy friendship while on-board. Although Linx was still suspicious of him, how could she turn down help? No one has ever offered to lend a hand.

"All right. We need to stack these crates of spices over there," she accepted, pointing across the deck.

Over the next few hours, they worked side by side, neatly stacking materials while discussing random topics to pass the time. Linx found herself elated to have a friend working with her, something she envied about the other girls. An outcast on the ship, she missed her life inside the Violet Woods and having that connection to others. The pure joy was incomparable to anything she had ever felt, that was until now. Carter had her laughing so hard the pirates whispered amongst themselves. The women eventually dispersed, going to their bunks for the night.

Carter's eyes scanned her bright face as she giggled from silly stories of his past. In a way, he felt accomplished to have made her laugh. There was so much sadness in her before, but to see her face now was priceless. As Linx turned to pick up another box, Carter's attention dropped to the silver chain wrapped tightly around her back. He knew that he needed to help her find the key to release her wings.

She looked at him with a weird smile. "What? What are you looking at?"

As he sorted the last box, he stated, "Nothing. Seems like we finished all the chores. I guess we should rest before the morning comes."

"Carter?" Linx called as he began walking towards his room.

He turned around. "Yes?"

"Thank you . . . for everything. My chores weren't nearly as boring as they normally are," she said.

"No problem at all." He chuckled.

"Oh, um, one more thing."

"Yeah?"

"I'll go with you."

He didn't understand what she was talking about. "What?"

"I'll go with you to the Inferno," she insisted. The thought intimidated Linx, but she knew they needed to work together to escape Elena.

Shocked, Carter smiled. "That's great! I promise, we'll figure out your way back home."

"I hope so," she mumbled. "Now, go get some rest. You'll need it."

He nodded his head towards her. "Goodnight, Linx."

"Goodnight."

Carter slowly made his way back to his room, savoring each step as he recounted his interesting night with Linx. It thrilled him to see that she appreciated his help. It was the least he could do to make her life easier. As he entered his room, he let out a sigh. Crawling into his bed, he wondered what the morning would bring. His fears tried to control his thoughts. What if something happened to Linx? Was she really safer with him than with the sirens? Closing his eyes, he pictured Linx happy with her family. He needed to help her.

Not too long after he shut his eyes to fall asleep, the morning sun shone into his room. Carter's gut twisted as he thought about what they faced today. Guilt seeped into his shaky bones as he thought about the situation he was pushing Elena into. Although he wasn't happy about doing it, Carter reminded himself of all the horrible things she did. Maybe she deserved this fate.

Making his way to the main deck, Carter scanned around to see if Linx was there. Unable to find her, he grew nervous. What if something happened to her again? Carter turned to see a bunch of women congregated in the center of the deck. Looking through the crowd of several pirates, he spotted her leaning up against a railing as she stared off into the distance.

"Hey. I hope you got some sleep," Carter commented, trying to not to spook Linx.

"I got a little," she responded slightly distracted.

Turning his head back, Carter noticed a dim, orange light in the distance. Black smoke puffed and soon covered the sky. It was alarming to see how quickly it overwhelmed the horizon. Even the air felt heavy and dirty.

"Is that a forest fire? That's crazy!" Carter said.

"No—" Linx replied quietly.

"No?"

Linx threaded her fingers through her hair. "Are you still confident that I won't be ripped to shreds by one of his beasts?"

The closer they sailed, the darker the sky became. Repulsive smells of decaying flesh infiltrated Carter's nose. A choir of screams echoed in the distance, begging for mercy. Carter noticed that the heat radiating off of the island was almost intolerable.

His nerves betrayed him. Carter feared that he pushed Linx into something he no longer felt comfortable with. If they don't leave this island together, he could never forgive himself.

"What's Elena's plan?" Carter asked Linx. He looked over at Elena, wondering if she had any idea.

"I don't know. But she was very upset the wand wasn't there. I am too. Truly, I'm lost without my wand. I don't want to be on this ship with these awful sirens forever."

"Me hearties, as we approach land, stand your ground and be ready to fight. These little flying devils almost capsized us last time," Elena directed, gazing into the eyes of her fellow women.

The women of the ship prepped themselves with swords, daggers, and other weapons. It was clear they trusted Elena's lead, but they feared the worst with the Inferno.

As the ship got close to the swampy shore, five reddish, thin imps flew down from a charred tree and dove for the ship.

"Ready!" Elena yelled. Right when the first one dove to bomb the ship, Elena swung her sword in the direction of the flying creature. "Kill 'em all!"

A few of the sirens stood their ground with swords at-hand, while others prepared to man the cannons. Without hesitation, Elena slashed the first one across its chest and kicked it into the green, swampy water. The next two swooped down together and attacked one of the siren's faces. She screamed as it made a giant gash across her cheek. Another siren came to her aid and stabbed the imp through its stomach. Nira's sword impaled the third imp and sliced off its wing.

Carter and Linx stayed hidden within the stairs of the ship to avoid being seen by the little demons. They watched as Elena turned to help a fallen siren. The fourth imp dove towards the back of her head with both claws sticking out. Carter didn't know if he should say anything. He held his breath, but then Nira yelled, "Behind you, Captain!"

Elena swiftly spun around, wielding her sword high in the sky as she struck the imp in the head. As she got close to finishing him, the imp took off heading toward the flames.

"He's off to warn Donem. We need to make fast work ladies! Stay here to guard our ship. You two ladies come with me," Elena shouted to the crew. "Carter and Linx, you're coming too."

Carter and Linx looked at each other in shock as they slowly followed Elena and two other pirates off of the ship. Everyone appeared eager to get off of the island, but they knew they couldn't until they located the wand. When they descended the ladder on the side of the ship, their shoes began sinking in the sewage-like mud that outlined the island. Rushing to the land, they coughed as their lungs attempted to adapt to the high smog.

"Elena, what's your plan to get the wand back? How can we help you?" Carter asked in between coughs.

"Oh, you're more important than you'll ever know," Elena responded with a raised eyebrow.

Linx looked at Carter with sad eyes. Despite Carter displaying confidence in his plan, she knew that sirens were unpredictable, and Donem was no one to be trusted either. He was known to cause pain and mayhem with no regrets, no compassion, and no repercussions. To think Carter could just wake up in this world and walk into the Inferno with minimum fear was astounding. The bones in her legs transformed into weak tree branches, shaking without effort. As they walked over the malnourished soil, one could almost hear them screaming to just taste a drop of water.

They trudged up a giant mountain of hot sand, making the trek all the more grueling. Until this point, everyone was silent since no one knew what Elena had planned. From the journey to the thick heat, tension rose within the group. Linx feared for Carter and did not trust Elena. Meanwhile, the two siren pirates were frustrated that the other women stayed on the ship.

Once they reached the top of the mountain, they noticed a giant pad in the middle of chaos. It was Donem's lair. There he sat, right in the middle of it all, just serenely rocking on his chair while someone in the distance was screaming bloody murder. Carter couldn't believe how Donem could be so demented that he found this environment entertaining. This island was a living nightmare.

"There he is." Elena pointed out.

"Elena, what's the plan for when we face him? What if it goes wrong? Shouldn't we know what to do or how to help?" Linx asked eagerly.

She ignored the questions again without even acknowledging any of Linx's concerns. Carter shook his head in disbelief that Elena felt she was going to handle this all on her own, but then she spoke.

"I couldn't answer before. It wasn't safe back there. I didn't want to say anything before, in case more creatures tried to get the plan out of the other girls on the boat. You'll have to strap your big kid boots on for this because he is a powerful and scary monster, but we can beat him!" she encouraged. "When we get close enough, I'll disable him, but you need to help me find the wand. I don't know where he'll have it hidden, but we need to look everywhere."

"If he's so powerful, how will you be able to disable him?" Carter asked, rubbing sweat from his forehead.

"Boy, you mustn't be familiar with sirens," Linx said.

"I thought sirens can paralyze victims under their song, but why didn't anyone sing earlier?" Carter inquired.

"You must know your foe," Elena explained. "Those imps can't hear anything."

"Imps are deaf?" he asked.

"No, those imps had their earlobes sealed shut. Donem wanted to prevent us from visiting unannounced and taking over his creatures. Needless to say, he poured scorching liquid in their ears and blamed us. They'll do anything to kill us."

"Oh—" He sighed. "That's so sad he would do that."

"Ha! That was probably one of his kindest interactions." Elena laughed. "And don't try running away. My girls will keep a close eye on you."

Carter shuddered, thinking about the pain those poor creatures suffered at the hands of Donem. He wondered if Elena's plan would work. If it did, then he would have to rethink his own. What if she was stronger than Donem? What would happen if she ended up with the wand and not him?

Although the journey was unbearable with scorching heat and suffocating stenches, they all attempted to contain themselves to prevent Donem from knowing where they were. If the imp got back to him in time, he would expect their arrival. They needed to sneak down towards him to get close enough, so he would hear Elena when she sang. There were a few boulders that sat close to his lair, so they quickly darted behind them before anyone or anything could notice. Carter was instantly hit with heavy déjà vu as he looked across the sandy soil to the stone wall that separated his patio. In the center sat his large rocking chair covered in dried blood, but he was nowhere to be seen.

"Where did he go?" Linx blurted out.

"Shh! I don't know. Just be quiet and wait!" Elena whispered, peering around the boulder. She began impatiently tapping her shoe into the ground. After five minutes passed, Elena suggested they try to get a little closer by running over to a different boulder. It rested right next to the stone wall.

"Can I wait here, please?" begged Linx. "I don't know if I'll be much help."

"You WILL run over there and you WILL help to find my wand!" Elena ordered.

"*Your* wand? You mean my wand?" She asserted.

"We'll discuss that once we get it in our possession," Elena argued with tense eyes.

Linx looked over at Carter with raised eyebrows and concern in her eyes. Neither knew what would happen if Elena got her hands on the wand, but her behavior was growing increasingly aggressive.

"Okay. Ready? Set?" Elena muttered.

"BOO!" yelled Donem from behind. "Oh, I meant GO. Ah, I was never good at playing games."

Chapter 8

Gasping from shock, the group scattered towards the boulder. Donem grabbed the two pirates by their throats and strangled them. Both women kicked for their lives while trying to pry his giant hands from their necks.

"Let them go!" Elena screamed, looking over towards Linx and Carter.

The most beautiful sound came out of Elena's mouth as she swayed back and forth, entrancing everyone around her. Luckily, Linx held her ears and blocked out the hypnotic music. She kicked Carter in the shin and motioned for him to cover his ears before Elena's song got hold of him. Carter looked over to see Donem frozen in his place, staring into Elena's eyes. Within seconds, he dropped both pirates onto the ground. They fell like rag dolls as they heavily wheezed air into their lungs.

Carter and Linx attempted to sprint towards Donem's rocking chair.

"Where are we looking?" Carter asked frantically when he saw Linx finally drop her hands to her side.

"I don't know! I don't know! It could be anywhere! He could have stored it four hundred feet into the ground for all we know," she yelled as they ran towards his lair.

Once they had almost reached the stone wall, a loud ear-bleeding screech dropped from the sky. Carter and Linx turned around to see the last imp dive-bombing from the sky, heading towards Elena. Their mouths dropped as they looked at each other, then back towards Elena and Donem. The imp continued to scream as it slammed its thick claws into her face, knocking her to the ground with a loud thump.

"Ah! Ah! My face! It slashed my face!" Elena screamed in sheer pain and horror. Her hands dripped in blood when she removed them from her disfigured cheeks.

Donem laughed loudly while he raised two rock peaks from the ground, instantly impaling the two pirates in the stomachs. "Nice try! Really, I am impressed! But you think you can outwit me, you poor fool! After shorting me in the past, you now wanted to dump the queen's son on me? Like I wouldn't notice the desperation in your eyes? Funny thing is that you were even willing to trade the fairy for the wand too! Now, I have everything I want and need, right here in front of me!"

"What are you going to do now?" she wept, trying to hold her sleeves up to her face to stop the blood.

"First thing will be to contain that powerful voice of yours." He grabbed her by the face and poured a searing, sticky solution onto her lips to seal them shut. "Now, that's better. I might use you later . . . or not."

Elena's pain melted through Carter as her muffled scream became a transparent window into Donem's tyrannical world. She rolled around on the ground, trying to pry open her mouth with no luck.

"Next thing is to dispose of these *aargh pirates*," he mocked, pulling out a large shard from a broken mirror. Elena watched in fear. She sadly anticipated Donem stabbing or cutting their throats. Instead, he did something much worse. When he walked over to the pirates, their breathing was very shallow due to the heavy blood loss. He grabbed one by her dark hair and forced her to look into the mirror. She let out a high-pitched shriek as her body turned to stone. Carter's mouth dropped as he witnessed Donem walk over to the second pirate and turn her into stone, too. Within seconds, Donem crushed their skulls under the soles of his giant boots. Elena stared at him with pure hatred.

"Really, I'm doing you a favor at this point. My minions completely capsized your ship, but not before crushing every skull of each dirty pirate on there," he articulated, soaking in her misery. Elena hung her head, defeated.

"I feel like we have to help her," Carter admitted, unable to hear Donem's demonic taunting.

"Look, you can help whoever you want, but the last thing I'll ever do—is help her. She dug her grave, Carter! She solely came here for her greediness. She wanted my wand for herself. Not to mention, she'll risk all of us for it! Don't let her sad face fool you. If you were to somehow 'save' her, which I don't think is possible, she'll do this again in a heartbeat! She is not a genuine soul!" Linx aggressively challenged.

"I know. I just feel awful leaving her to die. If that's even his plan with her," Carter mentioned with a shudder.

"What do you think you can do to help her? It's not like you can just overpower him and save her," Linx mocked.

"If we get the wand, can we all leave together?" Carter ruminated aloud.

"Do you really think we'll be able to find the wand? I was thinking about heading back to the ship," Linx eagerly suggested.

"That's not what I asked. Can we all leave together if we get the wand?" he pressed.

"Well, uh, yeah. We can all leave together if *I* have the wand. If someone like you has the wand, we can only leave if we are connected. Fairies harness the wands' full magical abilities. What makes you think we'll not only find the wand but be close enough to Elena to save her?" she curiously demanded.

"Follow me," he urged.

"Wait! What are you doing? Where are you going?" she asked, holding her hips.

"If we want to get out of here, we have a chance, but you need to trust me. Oh, and whoever is closest to Elena needs to grab her."

Linx stared at Carter with her giant doe eyes as she couldn't believe what he was saying.

"Okay?"

"Uh, I—I guess so. I can't believe that we are doing this."

As they started running towards Donem, Carter noticed the tremors rushing through Linx's body. Despite the high temperatures, Linx was white and shivering in fear. He tried pushing his concerns down into his stomach as he walked forward. The only thing keeping Carter's hopes alive was that Donem appeared to not want the queen as an active enemy. He refused to think about the possibility of this not working out. When the thought popped into his mind, it was nauseating.

"When we get close to him, stand in between Elena and me. Try to stand as close to me as possible. We have to make sure this plan doesn't fail."

"Fine, but I wish I knew what the plan was."

"Soon enough you'll find out, and you'll be furious with me. Just know that I had no choice," Carter replied with dimmed eyes.

Linx stared at him before looking to the ground. Carter could risk nothing going wrong from here, so he focused on where Donem was standing. He maneuvered around the boulder to put Linx as close to Elena as possible. Elena looked over once Carter was in sight, but he motioned with his eyes to ignore his presence. She was shocked that he was coming back right into the hellfire.

With a deep breath, Carter prepared to play the hero . . . or the sacrificial lamb. "Donem! It's Carter. I'm going to come out from behind this rock, if that's okay."

"Ah! Boy, yes! Come on out and join the party!" chuckled Donem in his deep voice.

Carter walked out from around the boulder, attempting to block Linx. He was hoping Donem would disregard her presence.

"I did as you asked, do we still have a deal?" he said. Carter felt Elena and Linx's eyes searing a hole in the back of his head.

"Well, one thing I'm not is a liar. Here it is, your beloved wand," he explained, opening the palm of his hand to reveal the light pinkish and silver wand. The wand sparkled and glowed, which was surprising since it wasn't vibrant when he saw it in his dreams.

"What?" Linx whispered.

As Carter reached his hand towards the wand, Donem pulled back his hand. "Ah ah, if you take this, then you can't come back. I mean, it was fun and all, but I don't need you or your mother meddling in my business. If you come back here, I'll kill you."

"Deal," Carter agreed, reaching his other hand towards Linx.

"You wanted me to trust you, so trust me. Throw me the wand," Linx demanded in a very low tone, so Donem wouldn't hear her.

He didn't know what to do. Would she catch it? What choice did he have, though? If she couldn't reach Elena in time or if something went wrong, he wouldn't be able to fix it. He was messing with something he never even knew existed—magic. Glancing into Elena's sad and defeated eyes, he gave a don't-give-up-on-me look, but she shook her head. Elena knew what was about to happen and how it would end. In a matter of seconds, Carter reached for the wand and tossed it behind his back. With grace, it flew over to Linx, and she jumped up to catch it.

As her fingers wrapped around the wand, she screamed, "I'm sorry, Carter!"

With a quick nod, Linx's body transformed into a spark that disintegrated like an imploding star, leaving Carter and Elena defenseless.

Chapter 9

Carter's mouth dropped, and his heart started racing at the thought of being stuck on this hellish island. His eyes darted to Elena, profusely apologizing for what he had done. Trusting Linx over Elena not only destroyed his journey to find his mother, but it also cost many creatures their lives throughout the process.

'Don't worry. I have a plan,' Elena calmly said in his mind. As Carter's eyes widened, she explained, 'You are not going crazy. I'm talking to you. Consciously open your mind, so I can hear your responses. There is a block that I can't force down myself.'

'This is incredible! What should we do?' Carter tried to ask.

'We need to run to the shore as fast as we can—right now!' Without looking back, they both instantly ran back the way they came.

"I always win this game!" Donem bellowed, chasing them across the dry turf.

Elena and Carter's shoes kicked up dirt as they attempted to pick up speed. The mountain was coming up, and there was no way that Donem could catch up to them. They were a fraction of the size of him and gaining a comfortable distance.

"Are we heading for the ship?" Carter asked, barely able to breathe as they ran. He looked into her eyes to hear what she wanted to say.

'I need to grab something from the ship and head for the water. Go to the closest shoreline while avoiding the ship.'

"What about the others? He'll kill them all if we don't get to them!"

'He already did,' she mentally replied, trying to hold back tears.

"What? I—I am so sorry," Carter whispered, thinking how this was all his fault.

'This isn't all your fault. You were pulled into a complicated situation. You're just learning things we've been accustomed to for quite some time. Anyway, get in the water as fast as you can. Donem can't swim.'

Carter quickly glanced over his shoulder to see how far Donem was behind them. *He's gone,* he thought to himself. *Well, that was easier than I thought.*

As he looked forward, he heard a grumble in the distance. He spun his head around to see a terrifying beast with a massive head running full speed towards them. The creature's human-like finger-claws gripped into the ground as it sprung its body forward. Maybe it was because of the speed, but Carter noticed the beast had a massive jaw formed into a smile that could easily tear his thigh right off of his body.

"Elena! Behind us! What is that thing? Can that swim?" Carter yelled.

'I don't think so, but they're fast. We need to hurry!'

The monster created a cloud of dust that sprayed into the sky as it busted through the path like a high-speed train. Before they knew it, the creature was about a hundred feet away and was going to catch up in just a few minutes. Luckily, Carter and

Elena slid down a hill as fast as they could and saw the edge of the shore. Right before they reached the water, Elena looked over and spotted one of the girls bloodied and slumped over a wooden box on the ship. They tore another pirate to shreds as she clutched her sword. Elena was about to turn her head to prevent viewing the trauma sustained by her crew, but then she witnessed something move behind a rock near the ship. Quickly, she darted towards the shadow while being mindful of the approaching beast. If one of her girls was still alive, she had to save them.

"Where are you going?" Carter yelled.

'I saw something move over here. I need to make sure it wasn't one of my girls,' she desperately thought while looking at him.

Elena cautiously proceeded towards the accessible side of the rock near the water. As she peered around the corner, her heart was beating like a drum, unaware of who or what waited beyond the rock. Her eyes glanced up to see that it was one of her girls, Yvette, holding her stomach while thick, red liquid poured over her fingertips. Her face was white from losing a significant amount of blood, and her eyes could barely look up at Elena.

"Oh, no!" Carter saw her slipping away in front of their eyes.

"El—Elena," Yvette whispered. "I—I'm so sorry. We tried to protect your ship, but they were too . . . too strong."

'Never apologize! You are a strong woman and you did everything you could to protect OUR ship!'

"They—" Yvette forced out, choking on blood.

"They who?" Carter demanded.

"The imps—they destroyed everything—" Yvette attempted to explain between heavy gasps for air.

'Relax, let me see what happened.' Elena grabbed Yvette's face and forced her to look into her eyes. She tried looking into her thoughts to see what she was trying to say.

"Elena! We have to hurry! The beast is coming! He's getting close!" Carter shouted.

Transporting herself through Yvette's eyes, Elena saw images of wreckage from the battle and blood being spilled across the ship. Out of nowhere, thieving demons appeared and snuck into the Captain's Quarters to raid whatever they could find. Several women were massacred by larger monsters, and Yvette's mind went dark. Elena was pushed to reality when she realized that Yvette had passed away. Rage filled Elena's blood as she kissed the top of Yvette's head and gently rested her body on the ground.

Immediately, Elena looked over towards Carter. 'Get in and swim as fast as you can.'

"Where are we swimming to?" he panted, beginning to lose his breath.

'The sea serpents are my friends. They'll help us get to a safe place.'

Carter stared at her for an extra second. "You want me to swim towards the monsters that were going to eat me? Don't we have any other option?"

'I don't. Do you?'

Carter looked behind them to see the beast was very close to catching up. "No."

Elena ran into the sea as she grazed the water's surface with her fingers. It was mere feet away when Carter jumped into the water. Thick muck created the perfect suction to slow them down. Once they got far enough so the sludge thinned out, they dove into the water and swam as fast as they could. The beast was snapping his jaws in the water, almost reaching Carter's foot. Carter pumped his legs with more force than ever before. In his mind, he feared it was going to grab his leg and drown him in the water. Carter felt the creature right at his feet. He turned his head around to see the beast open its mouth and lunge for Carter's leg. Right as the beast went to jam his head into the water, a sea serpent flung up from the water and swallowed it in one gulp.

He rolled over in the water, almost choking from swallowing too much liquid as a panic attack almost set in. Noticing what was happening, Elena grabbed him to keep his head afloat. 'Breathe.'

Unable to speak, he looked over at her in shock. She tried to smile through her mutilated mouth and cheek. 'You are okay. You'll be fine.'

Carter took a deep breath, relieved that he was no longer in imminent danger. But what about this serpent? He was terrified it would try to eat him. "So this big guy here won't hurt me? What if it gets hungry?"

'You have nothing to worry about. There's plenty in the sea to eat. Not to mention, that beast will probably fill her for a while. By the way, this beautiful serpent is Pree. She's not a guy.'

"Oh okay, glad I got that straightened out," Carter responded sarcastically.

Like an island rising out of the water, Pree rose from beneath Carter and Elena, bringing them to safety. Carter hugged onto her back, afraid he would slide off at first. When he finally gained enough confidence to sit up properly, he looked back at the Inferno to see Donem standing on a hill looking out towards the group. With a swoop of his hand, he sent out his last imp, trying to prevent at least one of his two guests from leaving. The imp let out a blood-curdling screech as it swooped into the sky.

"What are we going to do?" Carter yelled, ducking low against the serpent. Carter saw how it tore Elena's cheek to shreds with one quick swipe. Since they had no weapons to defend themselves, he feared that both of them would lose their lives. Even Elena looked concerned for a moment, not knowing what to do.

When it got close enough, the devil-like imp let out another ear-popping shriek before diving and stretching out to grab Carter's neck. He immediately rolled into the water, unsure if the imp could swim. As the imp made its way towards the water, Pree swiftly lifted her head and gulped it down while crushing its wings in her mouth. Both Elena and Carter looked at each other, impressed by the speed in which Pree could catch the imp.

'I guess she wasn't full,' Elena joked, reaching down to help Carter climb on Pree's back.

"So, now what?" Carter gasped for air while lying flat on his face.

'We visit Violet Woods.'

Chapter 10

"Violet Woods? Is that a person or a place," he asked, naïve to this world.

Her voice soothingly echoed in his head, 'Place. They can help me open my mouth again and help you find your mother.'

"Really? Why do you want to help me find her now?" he questioned, raising his head.

'Believe it or not, my original plan was to unite you with her—at a price,' she responded bluntly, looking away for a moment. 'I have nothing and no one. Maybe she'll at least spare me if I bring you back alive.'

Furious with her lies, Carter spewed, "Your original plan was to unite me? Do you think I'm a fool? You wanted to sell me to Donem!"

'Before your arrival, the queen sent out her screechers to inform the masses. It stated you were on your way, and anyone who encounters her son must turn him over or face consequences,' she said, smirking her deranged mouth. 'Once you boarded my ship, your thoughts in your unprotected mind connected to the queen clear as day. Who else fancies foxes? That's just repulsive.'

"Well, if that was the case, why were you going to give me to Donem?" His eyebrows scrunched together.

'There was some tension on the ship. The women feared that the queen would punish us. I figured it would settle my girls' nerves if we let you go.'

Appalled by her reasoning, Carter shouted, "You were so concerned about their feelings, so you risked my life? I could've been killed by that psycho!"

Shaking her head with amusement, Elena continued, 'Keeping someone like you is not that easy of a decision when there's the risk of mutiny. My girls and our ship were everything to me.'

"You could've turned me over to my mother!"

'I still needed money to buy my girls a better life. Yes, it was at your expense, but I saw it as an effective way to make money. Once we got away from Donem, I would've turned you over to your mother, unharmed and fed.'

Carter couldn't believe how she described ransoming and selling a person as a logical thing to do. The concept of holding someone in an unfamiliar area away from their parents solely for money was incomprehensible. Shocked by her transparency, he sat in silence. Maybe it made sense to a pirate, but Carter couldn't fathom making those same decisions. Concerned for his safety, Carter looked at Elena wondering if she would turn on him again. Disputing his thoughts, he asked himself, what choice did he have, anyway? She was helping him survive and potentially find his mother. He couldn't do it on his own.

'I'm not going to kill you,' she explained once their eyes met.

"I didn't say anything," Carter refuted.

'You didn't have to. I could tell by the look on your face. According to others, why would you trust me?' Elena said, glancing into the sky.

Carter raised his eyebrows as he turned his head to see what Elena was looking at. Shielding his eyes from the sun, he squinted into the sky, too. A dark creature with silver-tipped wings dipped towards the water, gliding just inches above the ripples. It wasn't alarmingly big, but the creature's shocking yellow eyes scanned the serpent, Elena, and Carter.

"What is that thing?" he shouted.

Elena stared at the flying creature as she ran her hand through her hair. Carter grew nervous, thinking another imp had found them. With remarkable speed, the creature flew towards Carter's face and hovered as its camera-like eyes inspected him.

"Elena, what should I do?" he sharply whispered.

Without moving her body, Elena looked over into Pree's eyes and shifted her eyes back to the slim bird. As if it was right on command, Pree snapped her head back and swallowed the bird whole. Shocked by what happened just inches from his face, Carter stuttered, "Wh—what was that?"

Elena smirked. 'Nothing to worry about now.'

Carter thought to himself that maybe he could trust Elena.

As the hours passed, Carter admired the bright, colorful sky. The wispy hues of vibrant blue and light purple faded into one another. A strange calming feeling swept over Carter as they skimmed through the still waters.

'Beautiful, isn't it?' Elena asked once Carter looked over.

Inhaling a slow breath, Carter whispered, "Yes, I'm surprised by how still the water is. It's very peaceful here."

'Yes, it is. It was Qita's favorite spot to pass through,' Elena responded, turning her head away.

Realizing where the conversation was headed, Carter figured he would attack the issue. "I'm sorry, Elena."

'She was a beautiful creature and unique. She was, like me, a siren. Able to persuade any sailor to let us aboard, her power was limitless. On top of everything else, she had a special power of her own. Something that no one knew was possible. She could transform into a serpent once she would submerge into the water. When we found out, we couldn't believe it. She was the connection between the sirens and the majestic serpents of the sea. It was incredible,' she relayed through teary eyes. 'I loved her so much.'

Carter didn't know what to say. Guilt drenched his heart as he saw the pain in her eyes, but he reminded himself of why she died. Her actions led to her demise.

'I know she tried attacking you. That was her one downfall. It was too hard for her to trust. Luckily, she knew that she could trust us—well, most of us she did. We were the only family we knew. What about you? Is your mother your only family? Or do you have more in your other world?' she asked.

He looked down into the water, thinking about the lack of a relationship he had with his father. It made him wonder if his dad even realized he wasn't home. He couldn't miss Carter if he never spoke to him when he was around. "I have a father back home, but we don't really talk much. Honestly, I don't know if he cares that I'm gone."

'Is he worth going back for?'

Looking away to prevent any tears from forming, Carter clenched his jaw. "I don't know. I really don't know."

They grew quiet with each other once again.

Out of nowhere, they approached an island that Carter had never seen before. The trees, leaves, bushes, and shoreline all had a tinge of shimmering purple coating everything. Even the island somewhat appeared to have a glittery, purple haze floating in the air. What could that be?

'Violet Woods. It's Violet Woods. Looks beautiful, doesn't it?'

"Yeah, why's it covered in glitter and purplish? That's so crazy!" Carter exclaimed in amazement.

'That's magic,' she replied.

"Magic? Is it dangerous? And why's it purple?"

'Dangerous? Yes, it can be. It all depends on who's using magic. The color shows us who the magic is coming from. This one, in particular, is the radiation from fairy magic; so yes, it's dangerous.'

"Fairies? Is this where Linx went?" Carter felt his heart started pounding with anger.

'Yes.'

Carter's eyes widened, glancing from Elena to the Violet Woods. What would happen if they crossed paths with her? Does she know that they are there? Why did Elena bring them here? So many questions ran through his mind, but Elena answered none of them. Carter didn't know if she wasn't reading his mind or because she truly had no idea what the answers were. Slowly glancing up in her direction, Elena stared deep into the woods and began breathing heavily. Carter's heart sank as his eyes inspected her flawless face until his attention hit the giant wound from the imp. He couldn't help but feel responsible for her trauma. How could Linx leave them there to die? The closer Pree swam towards the island, the more intense electrical pulses he felt through his veins.

'I understand you're angry, but you need to know that they're darker than you can imagine. Follow me.' Elena slid off of Pree and into the water.

"So, what's the plan? Do we just swim up to the shore and go find Linx? How does this work?" he nervously questioned, wading in the water.

'Oh, no. See that glowing bubble around the island? It's a force field preventing anyone from entering and stealing pixie dust.'

"They have pixie dust in there?"

'Yes. It's potent. Picture the capability of a hundred wands combined to fit inside a tiny vial. It supplies the wands with their power if something ever goes wrong. On top of everything, you don't need to be a fairy to use it.'

Carter couldn't believe that this was his new reality: fairies, siren pirates, sea serpents, demons, and now pixie dust. He wondered what kind of magic pixie dust held. Based on Elena's description, it was something powerful and potentially dangerous. His mind immediately thought about the possibility of using it to get to his mother.

'Yes, you can find your mother with the pixie dust. You just need to know with this magic comes great danger. If we use it, we put everything at risk due to the possibility of something bad happening. Magic always comes with a price. We just need to figure out—is it worth it?'

Carter looked into her eyes and recapped everything that had happened. What more can go wrong or occur? His mother is dead. He ended up in a different world, watched numerous creatures die, and almost died himself a few times. Somehow, now there was a chance that he could find his mother. Undoubtedly, Carter knew he had to try finding her.

"How do we get in?" he eagerly asked.

'We can do one of two things, both of which are pretty dangerous in their own rights. We can wait for lightning to strike. It creates unsecured waves of energy, allowing us to pass through beneath the water's surface.'

"Um, that seems dangerous! What's the other way to get into the woods? Anything has to be quicker and easier than that!" he exclaimed.

'Quicker, yes. However, easy is not probably the best way to describe it.'

"Well, how?" he demanded.

'If you're invited into the fairy world, you can enter Violet Woods.'

"How'd you get in when you kidnapped Linx?" Carter blurted out.

Sharply batting her eyes, Elena was not prepared for his question. 'Kidnapped? That wouldn't be the term I'd use.'

"What do you mean? Linx said that you kidnapped her and wouldn't let her go back home," he curiously inquired.

'Um, we can say that she was a package deal.'

"A package deal?" Carter's face was twisted.

'I was exiled from my old home, and I soon found many souls similar to myself—beautiful, lonely, and down-and-out on luck. We built a smaller ship to sail the seas, but we found it to be an unreliable contender during brutal storms. We came here out of desperation and needed to find some pixie dust to sell. The prices some would pay were astounding, so how could I not? Some of us waited four days until the lightning finally came. I couldn't make it through, but Qita and another did! They went underwater and swam to the shore. To prevent anyone from seeing them, they crouched and crawled through some bushes until coming across a beautiful patch of pixie mushrooms—'

"Pixie mushrooms? What are pixie mushrooms?" Carter interrupted.

'Pixie mushrooms? You know, they create pixie dust. '

"I kind of picture—well, I don't know what I pictured. I just didn't think that they came from mushrooms," he stated, looking around to see if any fairy or creature saw them.

'I'm not sure what you thought it was, but pixie dust is the crushed-up insides of the pixie mushroom. Very dangerous if you don't know what you're doing. You can kill yourself or worse,' she explained.

"What's worse than killing yourself?" he looked confused.

'Killing everyone else.'

"Oh."

'Anyway, they gathered some in their pouches before someone spotted them. The lead fairy, Phea, approached Qita before she got to the shoreline. Phea originally threatened to kill them, but when Qita waved all the mushrooms in front of her, she about had a heart attack. Trying to find a way for her to give the mushrooms back, Phea explained that it was a danger to everyone. Phea stated there was no way Qita could grind the mushrooms properly without blowing up many islands. Qita agreed to give up the mushrooms for a new ship. How could we say no? Once Qita said yes, she handed over the mushrooms and headed towards the ship. Per her words, they included Linx with the ship,' Elena explained, shrugging her shoulders.

"That doesn't make any sense," Carter said.

'Of course it does. They didn't want her anymore, so they thought she would be of use to us. It was really a kind act on our part if you ask me.'

Carter shook his head in amazement. He couldn't fully trust her. At times, Elena appeared sincere, but then she follows up with something like that. Knowing that he wouldn't get the truth about Linx's story, he focused on how to get inside Violet Woods. He asked, "So, are they going to be happy to see you again? Seems like they gave you their ship to get rid of you."

'No, the fairies nor the trolls will be happy. That's why—'

"Trolls? There are trolls here? When were you going to mention that?" Carter whispered, ducking behind a nearby boulder that jutted from the water.

'Yes, fairies and trolls live here. They coexist kind of as *you scratch my back, I'll scratch yours.* I don't think they even like each other though.' Elena let out a giant sigh from her nostrils.

"Well, it seems like they won't be willing to let you in, I assume?" he lightly mentioned, rubbing the back of his neck.

'No, they won't. They cannot know that I'm here. We need to get in, grab the pixie mushrooms, and leave.'

"Who will turn them into pixie dust?"

'There are a few people who might help.'

Impatient with their current plan, Carter swam towards the coast of the island. He heard Elena quickly swim up next to him. Carter thought he could out-swim her, but she was quick. Elena circled him and grabbed his face as she stared into his eyes.

'What are you doing?! This isn't part of the plan.'

"What kind of plan is this? We wait for maybe days or a week? Then *if* we get in, we look for dangerous mushrooms that can kill an entire population if mishandled. After that, we bring said bomb mushrooms to someone who may or may not help turn them into pixie dust, so I can hopefully go on my way to find my mother? I'm sorry, but no. I don't have the time to wait and see if it happens. I appreciate you bringing me to the Violet

Woods, but I'll take my future in my own hands from here," he bluntly responded.

'What do you plan on doing?!'

"Option two—get invited in," he explained, pushing past her.

Chapter 11

By the time he finally looked behind his back, Elena vanished. He figured she was waiting for her opportune time to enter whenever it stormed, but he thought it was too unpredictable. What if he waited a week before getting to enter the Violet Woods? He swam towards the force field, hoping that someone would see him.

The plan didn't fail him. Almost immediately, a tiny blue sparkle in the air approached him.

"Who are you and what do you want here?" a deep voice growled.

Taken aback by the vicious voice, Carter expected a high-pitched or cheery response, like how fairies are portrayed in the movies.

"Um, I'm Carter. I've come to see Linx. I believe she might be here. I helped her get her wand back," he stuttered.

Instantaneously, the force field broke to reveal a hideous stocky troll standing nose-to-nose with Carter. This must have been who Carter was unknowingly speaking to. Feeling weak in the knees, he tried not to look in its face. His eyes were beady, little pebbles in the middle of crusty, bumpy ridges that formed cheekbones. His nose was like a rotten summer squash adhered to his face. Slightly petrified, Carter didn't know if he should leave or try talking to this horrid creature.

"What did you say?" bellowed the miserable troll.

"I, um, know a fairy named Linx. I was wondering if I can speak to her. Please?" Carter pathetically begged.

"Just because you know a fairy doesn't mean you're allowed in."

"Well, I—we were on the same ship together, and I helped her get her wand back from Donem on the Inferno island. Can I please just speak to her? She said that she was going to help me find my mother," he demanded. At this point, he didn't know what else he could do. It was all or nothing.

With a swift swoosh and grunt, the troll hurled Carter over his shoulder and carried him through the Violet Woods. As he walked with Carter on his left shoulder, he swung a thick, blunt club with his right hand. Carter felt nauseous because of the putrid body odor that peeled off of the troll's body. He had no idea where the troll was headed, but he knew that he couldn't wait to breathe a breath of fresh air.

The troll pushed through the thick bushes covered in bright purple berries. While he continued on his path, he ripped off several giant leaves to chew on during the walk. The tiny dot of light followed at a distance, both curious and alarmed.

As he was getting tossed around, Carter looked down the back of the troll's torn coat to see glitter and gems shining through. For such a terrifying creature, it was peculiar to see him decorated with so many valuable and lustrous items. When they finally arrived at a pond in the middle of the woods, several enormous lily pads lay resting on the water's surface while countless fairies bounced between them. The tiny dot of light traveled towards the group of fairies and blipped herself to the size of the others.

Immediately, the troll swung Carter off of his shoulder and plopped him on the ground with a thud. In an effortless motion, he shoved him inside a cage sealed to the ground. All the fairies stopped their dancing, laughing, and merriment to watch the drama about to unfold. This event was uncommon since they rarely would have anyone near the island, let alone get inside and survive with a troll aware of their presence.

"This thing said he worked on the ship with Linx. Said that he needed to speak with her. Said she promised to help him. I can dispose of him if you'd like," the troll grumbled.

A petite voice yelled from the back of the commotion, "He's fine. You can leave him with me."

The voice sounded familiar, but it was so quiet. Suddenly, the tiny girl popped out of nowhere from behind the others. It was Linx!

"I see you made it here in one piece! Did anyone else make it out?" she inquired with a giggle and clap of hands. It was strange to see her so happy since he only knew the miserable faces associated with her time on board the ship.

"I, um, I'm not too sure. It seems like the majority of everyone was killed near the ship," he nervously answered.

"Hmm, what a shame!" she sarcastically replied. "What about Elena? Is she still alive or did Donem end her?"

"Well, uh, I—" he stuttered as he tried to figure out how to answer her question without outing Elena's whereabouts. "I'm not sure."

"What can you do? You did the best that you could. Luckily, I could send for help in time to rescue you! Hopefully, the screecher found you quickly!" she replied with a gleam in her eye.

Whoa! Carter wondered what she was talking about. "You sent a screecher?"

"Yes! Did you see a dark bird with silver wings flying near you? Those are screechers. They work for the queen. I'm surprised you don't know what I'm talking about. It's been screaming your name whenever it flies by," Linx explained.

In shock, Carter realized what she was talking about. "I did see one, but it was killed before it got too close."

Raising her eyebrows, Linx stammered, "What? It was eaten? Well, whatever killed it will be on the queen's list."

Remaining silent, Carter didn't know what to say. If he alluded to Pree eating the screecher, he would out Elena.

Unsure of the awkwardness radiating from Carter, Linx gleefully stated, "Well, you must be starving! That was a very long and strenuous journey. And you've come just in time for our meal! We have wonderful food here! I can't wait for you to try our berry tarts!"

Linx gracefully levitated off the lily pad and swirled over towards Carter. With a swish of her bright wand, his cage door unlocked and swung open. He hesitated for a moment before slowly stepping outside onto the cushioning, moss-covered ground. Surprisingly, the environment was comfortable and welcoming. Laughter and merriment resumed as fairies began poofing their favorite dishes onto an elegant table, resting in the middle of the woods. Beside the table was a myriad of delicate wooden chairs, appearing fragile enough to break under the weight of the trolls. When Carter looked into the sky, beautiful wooden wind chimes swung from the tree branches while vibrant flowers hung from above. They were strung together carefully to make natural streamers decorating the woods. While the fairies finished prepping for their party, a few grumpy trolls passed by, dropping off kegs of ale in the far corner of the gathering.

Carter shyly walked back towards the table to see everything they had to eat. He passed by two trolls singing while playing an instrument that resembled a banjo. They made it out of a slice of a tree trunk with vines used as strings. Their songs elevated Carter's spirits and made him want to dance, despite knowing that he would make an utter fool of himself. As Carter continued forward, a small group of two trolls and three fairies chatted about snow on the other side of their island. The conversation didn't interest Carter, so he moved on with a smile.

When he finally reached the table, wooden bowls and plates overflowed with various juicy berries, fresh bread, petite berry tarts, pear pies, honey cakes, roasted potatoes, and warm carrots. A large, wild boar cooked over a nearby fire rested in the center of the table. To his surprise, Carter noticed several more dishes further down the table, which he wasn't able to identify. He was so happy to be away from the water and far from the blazing hell island. Carter didn't understand this world one bit, but it excited him to learn more about Violet Woods.

As all the trolls and fairies gathered at the table, Carter stood back in the distance to avoid getting in the way of the others. Although they were all very welcoming, he was nervous to insert himself into their party. They all moved in sync with one another, as if they all had like minds. With such a tight-knit community, it made him wonder how a leader would willingly give away a fairy. On the other side of the table, two younger fairies sat fully pampered by those that surrounded them. They were hugged, coddled, and kissed by all. Smiles and giggles met even the simplest gestures. When he turned to look for

Linx, a tiny fairy flew over to him and handed Carter a petite flower covered in glitter.

"This is for you!" merrily sang the tiny fairy, fluttering back to the group of children.

Carter looked down at the stunning petals delicately attached to the flower. The colors of purple and green swirled down to meet his fingertips. When he brought the flower up to his nose, it exuded a sweet, fruity smell that happily filled his lungs. He looked up to find Linx, when he saw someone standing in the far distance next to a tree. The figure stood eerily still while staring at the party — Elena!

Linx joked, pointing to the open chair next to her. "Hey Carter! You can sit wherever you want! We don't bite! We swear!"

Carter smiled at her and looked back towards Elena.

She was gone! No one was there!

Blinking a few times to see where she went in the darkness, he realized that she wasn't there. Where would she have gone? Carter started walking towards the dark woods when Linx yelled out again.

"Carter! Come on! You have to try these tarts! They are to die for!"

He snapped out of it and turned back around to walk towards his seat.

"Sorry about that," he explained. "I thought I saw something, but then it disappeared. I must have been seeing things."

"Ah, yes. The woods are generally very safe and tranquil, but you have to be wary of the north woods. Dark fairies roam there, and they're very dangerous," she whispered into his ear.

He looked at her with a half-smile. Unable to figure out if the person was the real Elena, or the woods were messing with his mind, Carter's stomach turned. He felt helpless as he couldn't mention Elena was waiting right outside the force field. Carter tried to put it out of his mind for now.

After the meal, Carter was feeling very sleepy. The journey had been more than exhausting, and the food was absolutely delicious. Linx was right, the tarts were exquisite.

"I hope you enjoyed yourself! I'm very glad you made it out alive." She smiled from ear to ear.

At this point, he couldn't play games. This lie could potentially kill more, and all for what? He could barter for Elena to stay with him, if they were able to find her again.

"Um, Linx?" he quietly confided.

"Hmm?" she responded.

"There's something that I have to tell you. Something that I haven't been fully transparent about," he hung his head.

"What are you talking about?" she asked, irritation evident in her voice.

"Well—" he stumbled, "Elena is alive."

Rolling her eyes, she blurted, "Oh, okay. Well, that's good. She got away from Donem. I'm sure she's in pain after that attack."

He whispered under his breath, "I saw her here."

"What do you mean *here*?"

"I just saw her in the woods around the time that we were sitting down for food. I didn't know if my eyes were deceiving me or if she was really there. I'm sorry I didn't say anything sooner."

"Carter, it was your mind playing tricks on you. There's no way that she could get inside our island," Linx said.

"What if there's lightning? I remember her mentioning how lightning disables the force field around Violet Woods."

"Carter, that doesn't make sense." Linx began scrunching her eyebrows.

"What do you mean?" Carter asked.

"For one, lightning doesn't affect the force field. The only way you can enter is if you were born on the island or if we invite you in. There is no other way to enter," she stated matter-of-factly.

"Um, well, I don't know what to say. It's just very weird. Elena said there were two ways to enter: during a lightning storm or by being invited in. I wonder why she said that."

"Maybe she didn't know the rules or someone lied to her. I'm not sure," Linx replied.

"We were talking about you. She explained that you weren't kidnapped. Instead, she stated they gave you to Qita along with a ship in exchange for some pixie mushrooms," he said, looking in a different direction.

"Carter, whatever they're telling you, none of that's true! I was sleeping in the forest with my family and friends. We were practicing how to make pine cones float when it was time to go to sleep. The next thing I remember is waking up on a ship surrounded by sirens. It was absolutely terrifying. They wouldn't bring me home. They said that they couldn't. No matter how much I begged and cried, they wouldn't," she said with sad, glazed eyes.

"I'm so sorry, Linx. I don't know. That's awful."

"Because it is! I was kidnapped and forced to work on a ship. I wasn't traded to thieving pirates. Our clan cherishes our kind more than the fruit that blossoms in the trees. Why would they give away something so precious to monsters?"

"I—I don't know. Elena mentioned that someone named Phea traded you and a ship to Qita, so she would give back pixie mushrooms she harvested."

"Did you say Phea? As in . . . the leader of the clan?" Linx almost jumped out of her skin.

"All I know, according to Elena, was that Phea was the one who traded you. We didn't talk much about Phea, just the interaction that she had with Qita," Carter answered nonchalantly.

"Phea aside, if Qita was on the island, how did she get here?" Linx questioned.

"Well, I don't know. It made sense if she could get in; but if you can only come on the island by invitation or if you were born here, who invited her?" he inquired.

Shaking her head, Linx whispered, "I don't know."

At that moment, a branch broke in the distance and crashed down to the forest floor. Linx and Carter felt their hearts jump out of their chests while looking at each other.

"What was that?" Carter asked.

"I'm not sure," Linx cautiously replied. "We don't go over there. It's forbidden—for our safety, mainly."

"Why is it dangerous? It seems a little creepy there, but it just looks like woods," he naïvely mentioned.

"Carter, that's the Dark Woods over there. We are safe here because of our own force field; but if we cross the stone wall, we are at the mercy of very dark people," Linx advised, staring into Carter's eyes. "I recommend you heed my warning. They'll do whatever they can to lure you in. *Never* go over there."

"Oh, okay. Sure. I won't go over there."

"Good! Now follow me! There is a beautiful waterfall that you must see!"

Zipping through the air, Carter had trouble trying to keep up as Linx fluttered through the trees and bushes. The foliage got so thick that he almost lost her. Luckily, nature eventually opened up to show a stunning view of a large waterfall that gushed over the edge of a mountain, dropping into a deep blue basin. He slowly approached the side of the cliff that overlooked the water spilling into the pool. The sound was almost deafening as the water hissed and chattered.

"Move out of the way!" screamed a little voice quickly approaching the water's edge.

Carter bolted to the side as he witnessed a parade of trolls dart past him and dive into the water. His heart dropped as he saw them cannonball over the side of the cliff. Looking over, he saw them swirling in and out of the water, laughing until they reached the bottom. His eyes widened at the thought of falling off the cliff.

"Ready to fly?" Linx asked with a loud giggle.

"Um, what? No!" he shouted with fear.

"I'm just kidding. It's beautiful, isn't it?"

"Yes, it's so pretty." Carter smiled, looking at the sun setting over another mountain.

"I figured you'd like it! It's one of the most beautiful sights here."

Carter stared off into the mountains while inhaling a full breath of air.

Linx awkwardly added, "I was talking to the elders about your mother. They think they might be able to help you find her."

"How do we find her?"

"We have to travel through the Dark Woods . . . " She hesitated with a deep sigh.

"So, no one can just poof me to my mother?" Carter felt so confused.

"No. Just like the Violet Woods, there are certain protection spells to prevent that. Think about it. If anyone can transport themselves to these islands, who's to say that they don't automatically transport an entire army to overtake them too?"

Linx made a fair point, but it was so frustrating that there was a brick wall at every step of the way. Now they had to enter a dangerous area, according to Linx. For a moment, he wondered if he would ever see his mother or would something happen to him along the way. Before his mind went down a rabbit hole, he attempted to reframe his approach to this alternative plan.

"When do we go? And how long will it take to get there?"

"We can leave tomorrow, but I'm not sure how long it'll take us. I've never gone through the Dark Woods myself. Plus, we've never tried to reach Crystal Woods before."

"Crystal Woods? Is that where my mother is?"

"Yes," she replied while looking over her shoulder.

He inhaled a deep, refreshing breath of air into his lungs as he thought about the possibility of meeting her soon. What was he going to say to her? Did he just say 'Hi, how are you?' or did he ask how she has been? What if she didn't remember him? His heart grew heavy and ached at the thought of his mother not knowing who he was. Part of him wished this was just an exhausting dream that he could wake up from. Carter didn't have the energy to even think about his father either. At this point, he probably buried a picture of Carter right next to his mother and called it a day.

"You okay?" Linx delicately asked.

"Yeah. I just don't know what to make of all of this. To think I'll finally see her, I hope she's happy."

"Let's get back to the site, so you can rest your eyes for a bit."

They stood up and slowly made their way back while Carter focused on the forest ground. He found himself looking for the magical mushrooms Elena had described earlier, but there was nothing that he could see. Throughout the journey, he didn't encounter any different mushrooms that would lead one to believe they could create pixie dust from it.

"Linx," Carter peeped.

"Hmm, yes?"

"I have a question—" he began.

"Ha! I figured," she interrupted, laughing and rolling her eyes.

"Well, I was wondering if you have pixie mushrooms here. I haven't seen any, and it confuses me. How would Qita get so many? Or are there no mushrooms?"

She sighed heavily before answering his question. "There are mushrooms, but they aren't easy to find."

"How would Qita find them?"

Linx continued to flutter. "It looks like they made some yummy food for us to have for dinner!"

"Linx! Did you hear me? How would Qita have found them? Do you think someone helped her?"

"I've been trying to figure that out myself. I don't understand how she got in or how she found the mushrooms," she explained with a frown as they approached the gathering of people.

In his mind, Carter didn't know what to think. Maybe there was a weirder dark side to Qita than what he already felt. She was charming yet felt dangerous. Who was he going to compare her to at the time? For all he knew, that's how everyone was going to act towards him.

By the time they reached the table, Carter's stomach surprisingly grumbled again. He thought he wouldn't be hungry for a long time since he ate so much during their first meal together. Nevertheless, the irresistible sweet aroma of desserts filled the air along with the trolls' potent ale. Carter quickly pushed air out of his nostrils to cleanse the scent from his body.

"You can sit right next to Byren. I'll be right back. I need to go speak with the elders before we eat," she lightly ordered.

"Um, okay. If you need help with anything, let me know."

Linx gave a slight smile when she flew off into the distance towards a huge tree. Carter took the moment to pile his dish high with a variety of foods resembling the colors of the rainbow. Next to him sat a grouchy troll that smelled of dirty armpits and old fish. He couldn't understand how these lovely fairies could handle the stench that permeated the air wherever the trolls traveled. Trying not to be rude, he gagged over on the opposite side of his chair, so the troll wouldn't see him.

"Ugh! What is that smell?" shouted the troll that sat near Carter. With a lumpy scrunched face, the troll glared over at him while squinting one eye.

Carter shrugged, attempting to look unaware of what the troll was referring to. Clearly, they don't realize how much they stink. He ate his food facing away from the troll, trying not to destroy his appetite. The food was so delicious he forgot about the troll altogether.

"Argh! That's disgusting! What's that smell?" The troll looked over at him again.

"Sorry, I don't know what you're talking about." He raised his eyebrows.

"Well, you stink!" bellowed the irritated troll.

"I stink? You're saying that I stink?" Carter shouted back at the grumbling troll.

"Disgusting," he sneered as he stood up and moved to a different chair away from Carter.

"Hey, hey there." Linx laughed, hovering over the chair next to Carter.

"What the heck? That troll said that I stink! I don't stink, if anyone stinks it's—" Carter vented.

"Just let him go," she whispered with a smile. "They have very sensitive noses."

"Sensitive noses? I'd think it would be the opposite! Does he even bathe?" he whispered loudly.

"What stinks to you, doesn't smell to him. What stinks to him might be pleasant for you," she gently educated. "By chance, do you have any flowers or herbs on you?"

Sitting back for a moment, he realized the small fairy gave him a flower earlier in the day. He pulled it out of his pocket, slightly wilted and bent. "This thing? This is the thing he was making a big deal about?"

Linx grabbed the flower and fluttered past the troll. Immediately, he whipped his head around in disgust to see where the horrid smell was coming from. Once he saw that it was Linx passing by, he sloppily jammed food in his mouth while shaking his head. It was so strange for Carter to see such a reaction from such a light, sweet smell. Who would hate the smell of flowers so much that they'd yell in the middle of dinner?

"See what I mean?" Linx laughed once she arrived in her chair.

"I don't understand how he has a problem with a measly flower, but he doesn't have a problem with smelling the way he does," Carter quietly confided.

"A long time ago, the trolls used to live deep underground. They would harvest different crystals and rarely came up to the surface. When they did, it was to gather a bunch of food and trudge back underground again. Since they're in such close proximity to each other for so long, either they get used to their smells or they just don't smell it. However, the sweet smells up here would trigger them to be aware of their surroundings," she explained while Carter stared at her. "Think about it, though. You are in the dark tunnels underground for so long that your eyes get used to the darkness. Then you come up here in the bright lights, I'm sure it's hard to see and process."

"I guess, but what made them come up here, anyway? Why didn't they stay underground?" he blurted in between ripping a piece of bread.

"Here, I'll show you," Linx said with a straight face, reaching to touch his forehead.

Chapter 12

Images and motion pictures, not of Carter's memory, popped into his mind. He was slightly uncomfortable until he realized Linx was showing him something. As he rested his mind, Carter saw several trolls mining beautiful crystals in a deep cave.

Randomly at night, a troll would climb out from the depths of the tunnels, squinting his eyes to retrieve some leaves or vegetables to eat. As he hobbled back underground, the environment was astounding. Blue crystals covered the walls while green and purple gems were scattered on the ground. A constant ping rang through the distance along with grumbling and groaning. The trolls were splitting the crystals and gems with a pickaxe and tossing them out onto the floor.

A nearby group of very young trolls ran by and scooped up some gems. They giggled as they tossed some into their mouths and stored the rest in their pockets. Time started to fast forward as the young trolls grew into adolescents, developing immaculate capes covered in gems. It was just like the one he saw on the troll who carried him from the shoreline! As he observed the visions, he noticed these were not normal capes after all! They were thick jeweled skins growing from the trolls' backs.

Carter couldn't believe the trolls would eat gems, and then they would develop into a cape for them. This concept appeared strange but fascinating. As he watched, he noticed instances where the trolls would encounter other creatures attempting to hurt them. While wielding only a sword, they defeated every opponent. But how? Sure, they were strong and well-versed in sword fighting; but how did they never lose a fight without a shield? It was then that he noticed their capes.

These incredible capes would swoosh in front of the trolls' faces or chests to absorb any hits from the attackers. The trolls were truly incredible creatures! Mixing their regular capabilities with the energy, strength, and protection from the gems and crystals; they were unstoppable. But how does this unstoppable community of underground-dwelling trolls end up partnering with tiny, flower-scented fairies of the forest?

Being on top of the food chain brought the trolls confidence. This strength soon became a weakness. In their minds, they truly were unstoppable. One night, a troll named Ekun came up from a tunnel to gather some random surface foods. During his travels throughout the forest, he saw the sparkle of the seawater through the breaks between the trees. Ekun sloshed through a mild swamp to appease his curiosity.

When he finally pushed through the last bush, he saw a beautiful woman playing in the waters of the sea. She dove under the sea and rose, dripping water from every inch of her body. Despite being naturally attracted to the bumpy and large build of trolls, this woman intrigued him. Her skin flawless and smooth, her eyes bright, and her smile resembled the pearliest gem he'd ever seen. As he approached, she turned her head to look at him. Her smile and laugh created a weird feeling in his stomach. She gracefully swam over towards him. When she stood herself up before him, he looked at this woman in amazement.

"I hope I'm not a bother. My ship went down, and I was looking for a safe place to rest until I figured out what to do. Is it okay if I stay here with you?" the beautiful sing-song voice asked.

He slowly shook his head yes as he turned around and led her into the woods. As they walked, she asked for one more thing—anonymity. She didn't want to meet anyone else; she didn't want anyone else to know of her whereabouts. The goddess-like woman explained that she feared for her life and did not want her location to be known. The woman only wanted to be his friend, no one else's. Little did he know that she was a parasite who would destroy the trolls' world and way of living.

Once she was "invited in", she used the crystals to blow a hole inside of the underground world, leaking in water from the outside. In a couple of hours, the trolls had to evacuate their underground world and flee to the main surface. A passing fairy shockingly noticed the huge congregation of trolls and flew back to the elders to inform them of her discovery. An elder fairy went to offer assistance in exchange for protection. They both agreed to help each other, and the alliance became fruitful for each party. The fairies soon allowed the trolls to dig their new home within a different section of the island, even though they knew the original construction had taken hundreds of years.

To expedite the progress, the fairies used their powers to transform the underground. Busting rocks down, digging holes and tunnels, and designing the most efficient layout to incorporate a new underground waterfall became the new focus. The process took so long that they placed all of their attention on this new section of the island. The old tunnels were abandoned and forgotten.

When a group of fairies flew through the forest, they noticed the old tunnel waters were rippling and swirling. They immediately told the others, and they rushed over to investigate. Noting the fairies couldn't swim, two brave trolls, Raza and Poba, slowly slipped into the water. They held their breath until they could see what was there. Right before his eyes, Poba saw one woman harvesting gems while another was retrieving crystals in a distant air pocket within the flooded cave.

Due to the water's darkness, the trolls couldn't confront them without drowning. They both swam up to the surface to go tell the others what they saw. As they walked in the forest, Poba's ego grew larger than he could control. He explained to Raza that he needed to do something quick, and he'd meet up with him at the campsite.

He never showed up.

Speculation had it that Poba went back into the water to confront the women himself, or because they lured him in by their beauty. Over time, the first troll, Ekun, discussed his encounter with the goddess-like woman. Everyone attempted to compare the women from each story to see if any were the same ones. After deep discussion, no one could confirm the identity of the women, but it was apparent, the women knew what they were after.

The fairies placed a larger spell on the island, one that went over and under the ground. This spell was powerful, using an excessive amount of energy from the crystals and the pixie mushrooms combined. When it finally sealed, it prevented anyone from entering or leaving until they were verified by both a fairy and a troll. This clause was to help protect the island from other manipulative creatures wanting to enter.

Little did they know, they had sealed the women inside the underground world, unable to escape. Once night fell, the women stealthily exited the tunnels.

As they walked through the woods, they encountered a patch of pixie mushrooms, of which they stole bagfuls. Right before they made the turn towards the shoreline, the other woman noticed a clan of fairies sleeping in their pods. Since the fairies shrunk down to a tiny size while sleeping, it seemed like the perfect size to fit in her vial. She carefully slid a sleeping fairy into the vial, sealed it shut, and placed it in her pocket. Although the women were very mindful of being quiet during each step, one of the women turned around to see four fairies and seven trolls searching for Poba.

"Who are you?" shouted a fairy, pointing their wand towards the woman.

"Leaving," whispered one of the hooded women, running in a different direction.

"You aren't going anywhere," another fairy said, stepping in front of the women.

"How do you plan on stopping us?" the first woman asked, tilting her head with a smirk.

"There's absolutely no way for you to get off of this island. You have nowhere to go, so give us back what you have stolen and tell us where Poba is!" Phea stepped forward, spinning her wand to create a bright blue bubble.

"I'll blow this island up if you don't let us leave," the second woman threatened.

"We can't let you do that. We won't let you leave with the crystals and mushrooms," Phea yelled while enclosing the four fairies, five trolls, and the women inside the giant bubble.

"Maybe we can come to a deal, but you cannot leave with the crystals and mushrooms. What do you want?"

"A ship and food," the woman replied, knowing the others weren't aware of the fairy in her back pocket.

"Fine. There will be a ship fully stocked with food sitting alongside the shore. We'll escort you to the shoreline, and you're to leave immediately. Deal?"

"Deal," the hooded women sneered, dumping out their bag filled with crystals and mushrooms.

As Phea and two trolls herded the women off of the island, the trolls noticed something was strange about the second woman's demeanor. She had a powerful aura surrounding her. When she began sloshing through the swamp to get to the ship, a troll noticed her hooded cape fluttered in the wind, revealing what she wore beneath. A glimmering gem and bumpy skin cape rested beneath her own.

"Stop her!" yelled a troll. "She's wearing Poba's cape!"

Phea transported herself onto the ship in front of where the women stood. Her wand lit up with energy about to restrain the women when the first woman pushed Phea into the water. Torn between saving Phea or stopping them, the trolls split up to attempt both. Unfortunately, the hooded women set sail before the troll approached the ship. Although the others tried to save Phea, the trolls moved so slowly in the swamp that Phea's lungs filled with brown water. She had passed away before they could bring her body back to the land. That same day, they buried Phea in the Garden of Roses.

The visions faded from Carter's mind as the fairies placed Phea's body in a beautifully decorated gravesite. He had so many questions, but he didn't know where to start. Not to mention, Carter couldn't talk about this topic at the table with others nearby.

"Can we go for a quick walk?" he pleaded, looking into Linx's eyes.

"Sure."

They both excused themselves from the table and walked through a nearby trail. Fading orange sunset rays peered through the trees as they walked in silence. The warmth of the day was still very present, but the nighttime chill was slowly creeping in.

"Okay, I really don't know where to start. I'm so sorry your clan went through all of that! Watching that was horrific." He heavily sighed.

"Thank you for the kind words, Carter. I haven't been completely candid with you. Honestly, I didn't know if I could fully trust you since you seemed somewhat close to Elena," Linx analyzed his reaction to her words.

"I really have no loyalty to anyone, Linx. I came here out of nowhere, and I only know what I saw. Plus, I just wanted to find my mother. It's definitely self-serving, but I would never intentionally hurt someone out of an evil heart," he confided.

"Well, you might change your mind about having an alliance. I was the fairy in the vial. No one knew until it was too late."

"Linx! Are you serious?" Carter's mouth dropped.

"Yes. Every night, fairies shrink to prevent any passing enemy from noticing us. Most cannot see us, but they did. She saw me sleeping and put me in the vial. I had no clue what was going on. I couldn't hear anything. Next thing I know, I was on the deck of the ship, and my wings would no longer work. They chained me and took away everything. I had no way to contact my clan," she wept into her hands.

"Linx, I—I'm so sorry that happened to you. I had no idea."

"Carter, I told you I was kidnapped. I guess you didn't believe me." She looked away.

"It wasn't that I didn't want to believe you. You and I had such an odd relationship when I first came aboard the ship. You were very distant, for good reason, but I didn't know how to process that. Clearly, I can understand now why you were distant."

"Not only was I unhappy about being in an unknown group of sirens, but fairies *need* their island. When we are away from our island for a long time, our energy and power drain. We lose our magic if we don't recharge," she admitted, sitting in a patch of grass.

"So you were dying when you were on the ship?" Carter sat next to her.

"In a sense."

Carter took a deep breath and sighed. "Did they ever figure out who the women were?"

"I always thought one was at least Qita," she guessed, shrugging her shoulders. "But she never admitted to it. Based on your story on the ship, it seems like she didn't care who she had to take down for the sirens."

"That's unbelievable she would do something like that."

"They mentioned another suspect, but they were not confirmed," she added with a shake of her head.

"Who do you think could've done that?"

Linx looked Carter deep into the eyes and said, "I don't know if I can tell you."

"What are you talking about? Do you think I won't believe you?"

"If you didn't believe me before, why would you believe me now?" she said matter-of-factly.

"Linx! I believe everything you said! I may have had a harder time with it earlier, but it was because I didn't understand everything that went on," he pleaded while holding her hand.

Peering over her shoulder, then looking around to make sure no one was listening, Linx started shaking. "I—I don't know how I can even find the words to say it."

"You have to tell me!"

"Your mother. Some trolls and fairies believe your mother could be the other hooded woman," she uttered, stepping away to bring distance between them.

"*What?* What are you talking about? You think my mom came here and terrorized your land? This doesn't make sense to me. She was always the sweetest person I ever knew!" he yelled at Linx.

"See! What did I tell you? You can't handle the thought of your mother potentially wiping out the trolls' homes, murdering Phea, and kidnapping me, huh?" she argued. Her cheeks turned a bright shade of pink.

"No! Actually no, I cannot handle that thought! It's absurd to me!" Carter shouted.

"Well, who did you think I was going to say?"

"I don't know, Linx! I thought you'd say another pirate on the ship, maybe someone sent by Donem, or even that you felt Elena was responsible! Why can't you suspect that it was Elena?"

"Because it couldn't have been her."

"Why not? It would make sense since she's waiting right outside your island," he admitted to Linx out of rage and embarrassment.

"What? Elena is here? You said that you *thought* you saw her. You didn't say you knew that she was here! See, I knew it. I can't trust you!" Linx screamed, beginning to fly away.

"Linx!" He chased after her.

"What Carter? What do you want? I don't have time to talk since we have another threat outside *my home!*"

"I didn't tell you that because I thought she was going to help me! She said fairies are evil, and I needed to be careful! What was I supposed to do?" he questioned.

"What were you supposed to do? How about not be an awful soul and tell me she was waiting to pounce?" Linx whispered.

"I figured I would talk to you and see for myself. Which I can see you're the most caring fairy that I could ever imagine."

"Well, that means nothing now, doesn't it?"

"I'll help you! Please, though. Tell me why you would think it was my mother and not someone like Elena?"

"I don't have proof yet, but—" she explained.

"But what?"

"Poba's body was found. He was floating in the tunnel—with his cape sawed off from his back. One thing that only a few know is that they can remove a troll's cape, and it'll adhere to another's body if they put it on."

"That is crazy and awful! But what does that have to do with my mother?"

"While aboard the ship, I have been in close enough proximity to see that neither Qita nor Elena had the cape attached to their bodies. Despite the possibility someone would try to cover it, they wore such skintight gear, there would be no way it could hide the cape. Not to mention, the cape can never be removed from the new owner unless they cut it off again," Linx disclosed.

Confused, Carter asked, "Okay, so that might clear Elena, but why would that incriminate my mother?"

Linx shrugged and replied, "This all happened right before your mother took over the kingdom. After the attack, they announced her as the new queen of Crystal Woods. Although no one saw the cape on her, it's very interesting that she challenged and defeated the previous queen. She was a mature and respected mage for many years. How could someone so new to the area defeat her?"

Speechless, Carter ran his fingers through his hair. "Do you really believe the women were Qita and my mother?"

"I'm not sure, but it seems like they probably were."

"Well, let's find Elena. Maybe she can help us figure this out too, especially if she was the one who looked at this hooded woman in the face," Carter proposed, still hoping that it wouldn't lead to his mother.

Frowning and shaking with rage, Linx said, "Fine, let's go."

Chapter 13

By the time they searched for Elena, darkness had fallen within the forest. As moonlight bounced off of random trees, the tension during the walk was thick. Carter didn't want to believe his mother was responsible for all the pain so many people and creatures endured. How was she capable of something so deep and dark? There must be a mistake. Elena can explain what truly happened when they find her.

"Before we go any further, I need to let the elders know what you had said about Elena," Linx said, aiming towards a huge tree.

"Okay, should I go in with you?" he inquired.

"No. Stay here while I go into the Elder Tree," she uttered, flying inside a doorway carved into a tree.

Carter felt awful about everything. His gut was torn between keeping Elena's secret and making sure that Linx and her clan in Violet Woods were safe. Nevertheless, he wondered what Linx was discussing with the elders. If only he could enter, he would be able to explain himself.

After a few minutes, she returned while accompanied by a different troll, unfamiliar to Carter. They were both covered in dark cloaks that draped to the ground. As they approached,

Carter didn't know what to expect. Why was he with her? She didn't mention someone else coming with them.

"Here's the deal," Linx whispered, walking up to Carter. "We find Elena to see what she has to say. If it makes sense, then we'll go find your mother."

"Sounds great, but who is your friend?" he insisted.

"Oh, sorry. This is Raza. He is coming to help us in case anything goes wrong. It's always best for fairies and trolls to work together if there's a possibility of danger. That means at night or if someone wants to leave our force field. Not to mention, he might be able to identify whoever the women were if he sees them again."

"That makes sense. Let's see if we can find Elena," he stated, walking towards where he saw her last.

They wandered through the woods, anxious about what would come. Carter noticed the bushes and the general area looked familiar from when he arrived with Elena.

"Are you sure this is where you came from?" Linx impatiently questioned.

"Yes, this has to be where we came from. I just don't see where the swamp—" he said, sinking into the swampy water.

"Keep your eyes open for anything weird, Carter. I know you feel that you can trust her," she warned, "but we need to remember what they're capable of."

Carter finally arrived at the edge where he recalled talking to the troll. As he walked toward the familiar rock in the distance, a zap threw him on the ground. The force field shot him back beyond where Linx and Raza stood.

"I guess I should have warned you. We are close to the edge." Linx lightly giggled.

"Yeah, that would've been good." Carter debated whether it was an accident or not. Either way, he hoped her anger towards him had dissipated.

"You can call out to her if you want. She'll only see you and me though. Raza's cloak makes him invisible through the bubble," she whispered.

"Okay," Carter replied with a nervous sigh.

Walking along the edge of the bubble again, he shouted, "Elena! It's Carter. Are you still there?"

Nothing. It was completely silent. There was no response, and the water remained still. Carter looked over at Linx. She stared out into the water, waiting.

After they stood for what seemed to be an hour, Carter blurted out, "Maybe she left. I don't know where she would go, but I guess she isn't here anymore."

"She's here. She's just not coming out," Raza grumbled.

"Are you sure?" Carter asked, slightly shocked Raza came to that conclusion.

"Of course, I'm sure. I could smell her as soon as we came to the water," he matter-of-factly responded.

"Well, what do I do?" Carter demanded.

"I'm not sure," Linx whispered, looking at Raza.

"Can you open the force field? I can go over there. She might be hesitant to reveal herself," Carter suggested.

"Absolutely not. We're not chancing an ambush for a shot at finding Elena!" she declined with a huff.

"What if she has the answers you're looking for? How about this? You open the force field, and I go to check on her. In the meantime, you close the force field behind me. That way, if anything happens, it'll only happen to me," he offered, gazing out toward the rock.

"How noble of you," she mocked with a light chuckle.

Carter adamantly defended himself, "Look, I'm offering because I benefit from this too. I want to find my mother and see if she was involved. It doesn't sound like her, but if it was, I need to know. That is why I said I'll go."

Linx looked over at Raza and their eyes met. "Fine, you win. We'll open the force field, but you better hope you can trust her. We won't open this up to save you."

Scrunching his forehead in amazement, he uttered, "Fine."

Linx waved her wand and touched it to a gem on Raza's cape. As he stuck out his hand, the solid clear force field became wavy and blurry. A hint of a light blue ring formed with a tinge of green, and Raza looked over at Carter. "Go now."

Carter's eyes widened, and he darted through the vague hole in the wall. He, too, hoped he could trust Elena. The thought of not getting back inside made his stomach turn, but he pushed through. One foot after another, Carter sloshed through the thick murky liquid. Once the ground level sunk beneath his feet, he dove into the water and swam out toward the recognizable rock. With heavy thumps, he swore that he felt his heartbeat ripple into the water. As he came to the side of the rock, he shouted one more time, "Elena!"

When he didn't hear anything back, he took a deep breath and swam around the corner. What he encountered was both devastating and gruesome. Elena's body was floating lifelessly before Carter. Half of her arm poked out of the water.

Once he got closer, he was frightened to see Elena's decapitated body with her head missing. His face turned white as he quickly backed away from her body and swam as fast as he could toward Linx and Raza. His heart was beating painfully fast as he pushed himself to swim faster. Whatever happened to

Elena could happen to him. Like a child running up the stairs at night before the boogie man could get him, he yelled to Linx, "Please open the force field! Please! Hurry!"

"What? Why? What happened? We said we won't put everyone in jeopardy, Carter!" Linx shouted.

"Please! Open it up! Elena is dead!" Carter panted as he stood himself up to push through the swampy water.

"Elena is dead?" Linx asked, confused.

"Linx, please!" he demanded, approaching her quickly.

"Okay, hold on."

Linx swirled her wand in the air and immediately connected the wand to the blue gem on Raza's cape. Raza stuck out his hand to break through the force field. Without hesitation, Carter flung himself through the hole and fell to his knees. Unable to breathe, he held his breath to calm himself.

"Elena is dead? Was she there? Did you see her?" Linx blurted out.

"Yes, yes, yes," Carter panted, shaking his head from the thoughts in his mind.

"What—I don't understand what or who would have killed her," she speculated.

"I don't know who would have known she was there, but her head was cut off," he slowly recalled.

"Well, I have a few ideas, but I'll keep them to myself," she explained, turning her head away from Carter.

Glaring at her, he thought about some possibilities himself, one of which he quickly pushed from his mind. It couldn't be, could it?

"She had many enemies," Linx attempted to comfort Carter, knowing he feared it could be his mother. "It could be someone associated with Donem."

Attacking the elephant in the room, Carter blurted out, "I know you think it was my mother. You're just trying to be nice."

Heavily sighing, Linx walked up to him. "Look, I don't want to believe someone you care about did this. I really don't. At this point, I still promised to help you find your mother, and I will."

"Are you sure?" He looked up with sad eyes.

Her heart empathized with his pain. "Yes, I promise. Let's see if we can go now, if you're up for it!"

"Yes, I'm ready to go! Don't you need sleep?" he politely asked Linx.

"Honestly, this was enough activity to prevent me from sleeping for days." She laughed. "Let me see if Raza will join us."

"Okay. Sounds good." Carter sighed.

"Uh, Raza!" she began. "We need to check in with the elders first, but would you join us on a journey to go find the queen?"

"Only if the danger is high," Raza responded with a smile.

"Those are the only journeys we take." Linx twirled.

"Thank you," Carter whispered to Raza.

Walking through the woods, Carter replayed the assumed vision of Elena's head being brutally ripped off of her beautiful neck. The fear that must have run through Elena's veins transported inside Carter. His heart grew sad and dark with the possible thoughts of his own mother being vicious enough to end a life.

Thinking of several points, he remembered Linx explaining that she might not be her same self. What if this was her? An angry, murderous queen that has no remorse. Trying to stop his mind from racing through pitch-black allies, he focused on what he knew. Whoever had prompted this chaos in the first place, now has the cape, and that's something which cannot be removed. His primary focus was to find his mother, and then he could determine if she was innocent. They quickly approached the massive tree. Linx asked for him to wait outside again for safety of the elders.

Once she came back outside, she looked up at him, "They want to see you."

"Um, okay," he shockingly stuttered. "Why would they want to meet me now?"

"I don't know. Just go in," she persistently demanded.

Passing under the carved archway inside the Elder Tree, he descended tiny wooden stairs that were met with iron bars, locking the room from unwanted visitors.

"Hold on," Linx directed. She waved her wand with her right hand while placing her left hand on the center of the lock. The gate popped open and swung forward, directing them where to go.

Carter shyly walked towards a table of three cloaked creatures. He stopped a couple of feet directly in front of them.

A whispering, aged voice lightly articulated, "Welcome, Carter. We've been anticipating your arrival. Forgive us for the delay in meeting you. It seems as though your travels will begin sooner than expected. Despite our complicated relationship, we were alarmed to hear about your friend. Linx has informed us about the details of your journey. We have come to an agreement. We'll send you with Linx, Raza, and Udin. We know you're familiar with Raza, but Udin is one of our prestigious warriors amongst our clan members. We hope you find the resolution that heals your soul."

"I appreciate everything that everyone has done for me here. It means so much to me," Carter expressed.

"Before you leave, we have also put together armor and a sword that should serve you well. Good luck with your journey, Carter," a cloaked elder explained, laying pieces on the table for him to take.

Looking at the table, Carter couldn't believe the quality of weaponry they gave him. He was very grateful for the consideration of his safety, "Thank you so much for everything! This is amazing. I hope to see you soon!"

"Carter, there's one more thing. Let me prepare you for what you'll be encountering. When traveling through the Dark Woods, be sure to stay close to Linx and the trolls. The Dark Woods are very dangerous. Sadly, it's the quickest route to take. They'll use your fears to torment you, so try to stay focused on the group and your destination. Do what you can to block out the madness. You'll be protected by a magic force field bubble that cannot be penetrated, so their magic and tricks will be useless—as long as you ignore it," warned a hooded elder.

"Okay, I'll try my best. Thank you," Carter quietly replied. He began to visualize what the elder was describing while thinking about how Elena was found. Carter didn't know if he would ever get the image out of his head.

Linx peered into the room, "Are you ready, Carter? We're good to go."

"Yeah, I'm good, but I did have one more question. Do you know who would have killed Elena—especially like that? Do you have any clues or hints or even ideas?" Carter asked the elder, rubbing his elbow to prevent tears from streaming down his face. Despite having an odd relationship, the sight of her would not leave Carter's mind.

"I'm sorry, Carter. We have no leads on who could have done this. Sure, we have our own speculations, but that's all they are—just speculations. Alas, no one has come forward as a witness to the death of Elena. We'll be having some fairies and trolls look further into it," an elder genuinely explained.

"Thank you."

Carter hung his head, feeling like he was responsible for her death. He thought by swimming to the shore, he could do the logical thing. Only if he realized how impulsive and selfish his actions were, maybe she would be here now—alive.

"It's not your fault," Linx said warmly.

"What? What are you talking about?"

"It's not your fault that Elena died," she repeated.

Embarrassed, he turned his head. "How'd you know what I was thinking? I thought no one could read my mind anymore."

"Carter! Carter, look at me," Linx commanded with a boom.

"What?"

Stopping in front of him, she looked Carter in the eyes. "Listen to me. I cannot read your mind, but your facial reactions and aura say something you'll never be able to hide. Don't ever be ashamed of being a compassionate person, but don't try taking accountability for her own actions and reputation. I see you as sad, guilty, and regretful. It's okay to be sad. Everyone gets sad when someone they care about dies. *However*—it's not your fault she died."

"Linx, you're right. I feel guilty. It's because I'm guilty, though. No, I didn't physically kill her, but I may as well have. Had I not left her behind, had I waited with her, she might still be here today."

"First of all, yes—might. She might be here today, but you might not be. Whatever killed her could have killed you too. Consider yourself lucky you weren't there. Secondly, I don't think you were the only reason she came to Violet Woods. If you learned anything about Elena while working with her, you would know that she always had her own agenda. No matter who she said she was helping, she always cared about herself first," Linx carefully articulated.

Thinking about what Linx said, Carter couldn't figure out Elena's motives. His mind immediately thought about the screecher Pree had killed. Carter asked, "Linx?"

"Yes?"

"I wanted to ask something before you knew Elena was here," he continued.

Linx stared at Carter with her eyebrows raised, waiting for him to get to the point.

"Well, it was about the screecher. You said the screecher worked for the queen?"

Nodding her head, Linx said, "Yes, they work for the queen. What are you getting at?"

"Does everyone know that? Like would Elena know that?" he curiously asked.

"Of course, she knew what screechers were. That's how she knew you were missing when you first arrived. They flew around screaming, 'By order of the queen of Crystal Woods, any creature who finds her son, Carter, should notify the kingdom immediately.' Not to be rude, it became annoying." Linx laughed. "We didn't think for a second that you would crawl up on our ship."

Forcing out a half-smile, Carter stated, "That's interesting."

"Well, at least the torteen made it before the screecher died," Linx added.

Confused, Carter looked at her. "Torteen?"

"Yeah, the giant creature that brought you to Violet Woods. You know, the one with a giant neck and enormous shell to ride on?" she described.

He shook his head. "Ugh, that's not what brought me to Violet Woods."

"What are you talking about?" Linx demanded.

"I didn't ride here on a giant shelled creature. Elena summoned a serpent named Pree who carried us from the Inferno to Violet Woods," Carter confessed.

"You rode a serpent? But that doesn't make sense. Why didn't the torteen show up? It was supposed to help bring you to safety."

Carter shook his head again. "The only thing that showed up was what you described as the screecher, and Pree ate it once it was close enough."

"Oh my, Carter. I thought it was killed after guiding the torteen to your location! You are so lucky to be alive! Those slimy serpents!" Linx shouted.

"Honestly, I had no idea what it was. Pree ate it, and Elena smiled. I thought Pree did us a favor!"

"See? You cannot trust a siren! This is ridiculous. Let's focus on what we can do now, which is to figure out the safest path through the Dark Woods."

"O—okay," Carter stammered, trying to snap out of the thick cloud suffocating his mind.

Looking him in the eyes, she asked, "Are you ready?"

"Yeah," he mumbled.

"Carter, I need you one hundred percent invested in this. If anything goes wrong, it can be catastrophic."

Rubbing his face aggressively, he shouted, "Yes! Yes! Let's do this now."

Chapter 14

Walking out from the Elder Tree, the group of four headed towards a rock wall, lining the edge of Violet Woods. Distant birds fluttered and chirped as they woke up at the crack of dawn. Carter couldn't believe that they didn't have a chance to sleep. Surprisingly, he felt restless anyway. He wouldn't be able to sleep, even given the chance.

For a split second, Carter was reminded of home. A nearby brook was loudly babbling as it poured over countless smooth stones. He remembered how much it soothed him to sit on the large boulder next to the creek behind his house. Heavy breezes carrying the fragrance of pine swooshed around Carter's body, giving him a much-needed hug. Passing fairies were giggling as they prepared for their morning. Every aspect of Violet Woods was serene and perfect. Carter wondered if he really wanted to leave. In his mind, he wondered if maybe this could be his new home.

"Linx, I'm having second thoughts about this. I don't know if I can put everyone at risk for me to find my mother. I wonder if I can go myself or if there's a safer route for us to travel," he expressed with heavy concern.

"Carter, stop. No offense, but you can die without our help. Plus, you aren't forcing us to go. Not only did we volunteer for you, but we volunteered for ourselves too. There are so many questions revolving around your mother that make us want to go too!" Linx excitedly reaffirmed.

"Are you sure?" He glanced at her with an uneasy gaze.

"Yes, I'm sure! Also, this will be the perfect opportunity for you to learn about some magic and fighting. I mean, who am I kidding? I heard the stories about you taking down Qita with no problem!" She chuckled.

"With no problem, eh?" He smirked, looking behind him at the trolls. "Do I smell that bad they can't walk near us?"

"Ha! No. They're probably gathering themselves before we cross the wall. It takes a lot of strength and magic to protect us from what we are about to walk into." She laughed, waving to Raza and Udin.

"I feel like I have to ask, but what are we walking into? Everyone is talking about the danger within Dark Woods, but no one has talked about what we'll actually encounter once we are in there."

Linx sighed. "Well, I'm sure that everyone has different motives and goals. Some will try to scare us, some will attack us, and some may even try to kill us. That's why it's very important we try to stick together. If we split up, we'll be easy pickings."

Carter and Linx stopped only feet from the crumbling stone wall to wait for the trolls to catch up. He stared into the Dark Woods, wondering if he would see anything, but all he could see were shades of gray, black, brown, and deep green. Darkness engulfed brown and gray trees while displaying no sight of budding flowers, fruits, or even leaves. The woods looked like everything was dying or dead. At that moment, Carter's knees began faintly shaking.

"Are you okay?" Linx looked over with sympathy.

"Yeah." Carter nervously chuckled.

"Linx, you and the boy will walk ahead of us as we guard the back of the force field. If we take on anything too strong, our capes should absorb any unexpected hits. Are your spells up to par for this trip?" groaned Udin.

"Sounds good. They're as good as they ever will be!" She laughed at him. "Stand back a second!"

As Linx swirled her wand in the air, blue sparks and smoke accumulated above their heads. The trolls stood on the other side of Carter as the magical bubble bled down around the group. Within a moment, the bubble was almost closed when they heard a tiny voice yell, "Wait!"

The group looked into the distance to see a tiny hooded elder blipping towards them with another troll. Linx released her wand from the sky to see why the elder and troll needed them. The magical force field immediately evaporated into thin air. In a matter of half of a second, the elder and a troll dressed in a dapper overcoat appeared before the group.

"Elder." Linx bowed towards the elder fairy and then troll. "Teshi."

"Hello, Linx." The elder looked over towards the other troll to join the group. "Carter, this is Teshi. He is another strong warrior and has some experience going through the Dark Woods."

"Hello, Teshi." Carter awkwardly waved. He noticed that the trolls behind him were bent on their knees with their heads bowing to both Teshi and the elder fairy.

The elder stepped forward while yielding their wand. "Another surprise is that I'll be joining you on your journey as well."

Linx stood speechless with a kind smile. She was unsure why one of the elders would risk their own life for this journey. Regardless, it was a humbling move. "Are you sure? We don't want to risk your safety."

"I've been around long enough that if anything happened, I have lived a good life. Now, it is time for me to make sure others have the same opportunity. Not to mention, it would probably help to have an old experienced fairy around just in case." The elder fairy chuckled.

The elder made a point, but Carter was now wondering who this elder was. It was strange that someone offered to join a mission, risking their own life, but didn't introduce themselves or show their face. He wondered if everyone was content knowing them solely as an elder. Looking over at Linx, she appeared honored to have the elder fairy offer their skills.

"We are grateful for your presence. We were going to form a square to move forward with the trolls behind us. Do you have any new suggestions for our updated group?" Linx inquired with shining eyes.

The elder turned to Teshi and asked two questions quietly before responding to Linx. "We should form a large pentagon to protect Carter. Although he has a sword, the less the Dark Woods has access to the better. Therefore, Teshi will guide us through the Dark Woods as the peak of our pentagon, followed by Linx and myself as the next points, then we'll have Raza and Udin protect the rear of the group." The elder looked at Carter. "Carter, you will stay in the center of the pentagon. You'll have the most protection within our force field."

Not knowing what else to say, he nodded. "Okay."

"All right. Ready, Linx?" the elder shouted as they swirled their wand, creating a green smoke that sparkled where the light kissed the vapor. Linx also started swirling her wand again to recreate the impressive blue cloud that she had started earlier.

All three trolls stood in formation as the fairies were combining their powers to form a massive, beautiful cyan cloud. Once almost finished, the cloud created a shell around the group which bent around the corners of the five exterior members. Carter looked around at the giant bubble in amazement. He couldn't believe that he was surrounded by such power and support.

"As I mentioned before, we have a few simple yet important rules we must follow the moment we cross the stone wall. Eyes on the prize, so keep the goal destination in mind. This is important because when things get crazy, you don't want to get lost in there. Do not—do not—separate yourself from the group. Your presence is invaluable, plus it is the safest way to move through the woods. Lastly, keep your mind in a happy place. Yes, this is easier said than done. However, they feed off of fear, so give them no bait. Any questions or comments before we start?" the elder articulated with a deep, rejuvenating sigh.

All the trolls stood silent with nothing to add. Carter had a shy and uneasy smile, nodding along with the elder's rules, and then he firmly shook his head no to the question. He glanced over at talkative Linx to see what else she would contribute to the group. Surprisingly, she shook her head no. Fear, tension, and anxiety electrified the group. No one knew what to expect, even those that had traveled through the woods before.

"Good. Everyone, take a deep breath. I'm lighting a tracking bubble that will show us the route to take through the Dark

Woods," the elder explained, using their other hand to create a bright green bubble which floated just above their heads. "Now let's go!"

With a collective exhale, the group proceeded onward. Teshi stepped his right foot on the crumbling stone wall, and then he swung his other inside the Dark Woods. One by one, each member entered the shadows. It was apparent that everyone tried to heed the elder's warnings, but their curiosity drew them deeper into the woods.

Almost instantly, the elder whispered, "Keep your gaze forward. Stay quiet."

For a moment, the group continued through the woods and cautiously observed what the Dark Woods was like inside. Not many experienced what the woods offered; and for those that did, many never came home to tell their tale. No one made reference to the Dark Woods out of fear of what could happen.

Luckily, nothing happened for the first half-mile of the journey. Carter grew comfortable with the thought that maybe people embellished the stories to have creepy tales to tell. It was just a regular forest, like the one he frequented behind his house. He started thinking about how much he missed what once was. From Mom's home cooking to even his dad's leather office chair, the once familiar smells seemed so distant now.

"I'm sorry, son," rang a deep, eerily familiar voice. Carter did not initially respond out of fear. "Carter, come back home."

He looked up to see his father sitting on a rock, holding a glass of scotch. Carter felt his heart swell. "Dad?"

"No, it isn't your father," the elder snapped. "Don't look into their eyes, Carter!"

With a tight squeeze to his chest, he looked back down at the ground to avoid the image of his father. Who was he kidding anyway? Like his father would actually care that Carter left. Similar to the image, he was probably sitting at his work desk talking on the phone to a client and drinking. Carter never understood what he did to deserve the hatred he felt from his father. Despite the feelings that overwhelmed his body, he thought about the elder's instructions to think about happy things.

"Poba?" shouted Raza, panicking with a heartfelt shriek.

"Raza, it isn't him," the elder repeated.

"The hell it's not!" Raza shouted.

"Raza, that can't be him. He's dead," Linx confirmed.

"I know Poba, and he's right there! He's even missing his cape." He hung his head. "I'm so sorry, buddy."

"It isn't him," Teshi chimed in.

"What would you know, Teshi?" Raza argued. "We have been partners for the past twenty years. Working side by side—"

"What would I know? I'll let you know what I know. I know that I just saw my dead son crying for me to pick him up about five minutes ago when we passed that pile of rubble," he mumbled, stepping over a rotting log.

"How can you be so nonchalant about that?" Raza demanded, throwing up his arm.

"Because, Raza. Because I have walked through this disgusting forest before, and I know that it wasn't him. Was it heartbreaking to see? Of course. But it wasn't him. You need to remind yourself of that, or you'll never make it out."

They quietly continued following the green bubble down a gravel walkway with moss trim on the edges. The path was painted over a large hill in the woods. Sadly, throughout the walk, Raza thought about everything Teshi described. He couldn't handle seeing a dead friend, so Raza couldn't fathom seeing a deceased child crying for his affection. This place was pure mental hell.

Once they crossed over the hill, the group encountered a pathetically lit campfire. Everyone snapped their focus forward while acknowledging the eerie prickle of eyes on their skin. Someone or something was there—watching, waiting. Carter tried his best to keep his gaze on the back of Teshi's cape. He thought he was fine until he noticed something run in front of the group. Strangely enough, no one responded to the sudden movement. No one flinched a muscle except Carter.

"You okay?" Raza whispered with a low grumble.

The elder spun their head toward Carter. "Did you see something? If so, don't respond. They are testing your fear."

It was easier said than done. Immediately, Carter's eyes glanced over to an image of a woman standing up against a tree. She crossed her arms, staring with a giant grin that pushed through his body. Her eyes, hollow yet piercing, made Carter's stomach sink. Trying to avoid maintaining eye contact, he looked back at Teshi's cape. Carter counted the gems from left to right in his mind.

One, two, three, he started.

"Nice try, but you can never ignore me," her voice yelled aloud.

"Four, five, six, seven, eight—" Carter sped up to drown out the noise of her voice. At this point, he didn't realize that he shouted the numbers out loud.

Raza revisited his initial question. "Carter, are you okay? Do you see anything?"

"No, I see *nothing*," he shouted, looking up at the treetops.

The group looked at each other, not knowing what advice to give. Carter was mentally battling something, but they had no idea what. Carter remained quiet for a moment.

"Despite all that I've told you, I see you're close friends with that wretched fairy. Isn't that cute? I try to help you, but you decided to join her side. Not only that, but you killed me over it too!" Qita accused with a sarcastic laugh.

"I didn't kill you! You attacked me and tried killing me! I was only protecting myself," he snapped in a huff.

Everyone jumped at the volume of Carter's voice. Unsure of who or what he was talking to, the elder looked over at Linx to see if she knew what he was referring to. To the elder's surprise, Linx had an idea who Carter was screaming at. Her eyes locked on Carter's every facial twitch.

"Well, well. Hello there," Qita mocked with a deeper grin. "Did I strike a nerve?"

"You are not real. I don't even know why I'm arguing with you."

"I'm as real as you."

"You are dead."

"Death is subjective."

Carter just looked at her for a moment, baffled by what she was getting at. What did she mean that being dead was subjective? She's dead, she died. What was subjective about that? He thought in his mind about how manipulative she was on the ship, and her personality was consistent—dead or alive. Qita thrived off of being in control and manipulating to get what she wanted.

"Let's just say this will be the kindest interaction you'll receive here," she blurted out, turning to walk away with a chuckle. "Oh. By the way, Elena is waiting for you. Unlike how you didn't wait for her."

Carter's heart sank to his feet. Qita always gets the last jab. Nevertheless, there was something she said that made him nervous. Carter was now awaiting an encounter with Elena, something he never thought would happen again. What would she say to him? Would she hurt him? Was that possible?

Each step they took through the woods made Carter that much more uncomfortable. At this point, his journey had run out of gas, and his car was about to stop. Now it wasn't a matter of if, just when and where. Linx picked up on his uneasy energy. Unsure if she should address it, she made a quick hiss and mouthed 'are you okay' when he looked over. When he shook his head no, she grew concerned. By no surprise, they expected to be taunted and scared, but Carter appeared fully traumatized. She had no idea what had occurred.

"Want to talk? It'll make the time go by." She smiled warmly, hoping he would bite on the offer.

"Qita."

"What? I'm sorry, did you say Qita?" she attempted to clarify.

"I just saw Qita back there."

"Oh, my! What did she say?"

"She blamed me for her death," he slowly recapped. "Then she said Elena was waiting for me, despite me not waiting for her."

Realizing she was holding her breath, Linx let go of the stress that had built in her chest. "Carter, I'm sorry she was bothering you. First of all, you know her death was of her doing. It wasn't your fault. Second, they aren't real. Elena is only waiting for you in your mind. This forest knows that, and it uses it against you."

"That's the strange thing, though. Qita said that she was as real as me. As you probably heard, I told her that she was dead. She looked at me and creepily smiled; then she said that death was subjective. What does that even mean? Is she not dead?"

Once Linx became too spooked to reply, the elder quickly responded with a vague attempt to soothe everyone's nerves. "They like to play tricks here. You mustn't pay too much attention to the context of their words. Take it at face value and move on. Better yet, don't let their words enter your ears."

"Elder, can I ask you something?" Carter genuinely inquired.

"Of course, Carter."

"What's creating these images? Is it the trees? Is it our minds? Is it another magical creature responsible? If I reach out to touch the person, will anyone be there or will my hand go through them?"

Surprised by everything Carter spit out at once, the elder was quiet for a moment. "Honestly, no one knows what creates the images that we see when we walk through the Dark Woods. Many have speculated, but there hasn't been a definitive answer. Maybe it's the wind or trees, maybe it's our mind getting the best of us, or maybe it's a combination of both. It, also, can be the effects of a strong magical spell cast by a dark creature. As for your question regarding if people are there, no one has ever attempted to touch them. If they did, they never came back to tell their tale."

As thoughts flooded his mind, Carter remained silent and overwhelmed by the complex mystery surrounding the Dark Woods. If no one knows what these images are or where they came from, who's to say they aren't real? From Carter's perspective, anything is possible. When you think it would be impossible, it happens.

"Udin, has anything bothered you up until this point?" Carter pried out of curiosity.

"No."

Unsure if he wasn't talkative or if he was angry, Carter looked over at Linx to see what she was thinking. Her eyes were wide and on alert. Instantly, Carter felt guilty for bringing everyone on this journey. It was apparent that no one enjoyed being here. Who would?

Another ten minutes of mental anguish persisted as the group followed the bubble through the woods. It was unknown what was more unsettling, seeing eerie things harass the group or waiting to see what was going to happen next. He felt as though they were walking through the woods just waiting to be attacked. Right as Carter was thinking about this, the clock struck and it was his turn. As they were approaching a stream, Carter saw a woman standing behind a tree. She was standing in a shadow watching them walk towards her. As he looked closer, she had disheveled hair and a giant gash around her neck.

Carter's knees buckled when he realized who the woman was—Elena! Once she had his attention, she reached down to grab a sharp rock from the forest floor. As she bent forward, her head fell off of her neck, but her fingers grabbed her long hair, preventing her head from rolling away. Standing up, Elena tossed her head back on her neck. With one hand, she held her cheeks firmly in place. With the other, she grabbed the sharp rock and dug into her mouth as hard as she could—tearing a jagged opening from one side of her face to the other.

With the final audible tear to her face, Carter bent over and violently puked on the forest floor. Linx, the elder, and the trolls looked at him in utter disbelief and surprise. Carter stood up and took a deep breath as he continued to walk. No one in the group noticed her standing there, so they stopped out of concern for Carter alongside the tree that Elena was leaning against.

"Aww. You okay, babe? Didn't mean to upset you. It's just been so frustrating since I had my mouth sealed shut. I've been waiting and waiting to find someone to help me. I thought you would help me, but then you abandoned me. Someone else said that they would help me, and then they took a sword and cut my head off," she rapidly spat out. Humoring herself as she saw Carter's face turn white, Elena's eyes focused on him. "Sorry, babe. Cat got your tongue?"

He gasped for air and blurted out, "YOU—AREN'T—REAL."

"Whatever makes you feel better about abandoning me—after I saved you." She theatrically sighed. "Oh, and for your information, I remember who killed me. They are in your little group now."

"What?"

"But that's as much as I'll give you. I really want to see how this will play out! This will be so much fun!" She laughed with a clap of her hands. "Word of advice, keep the details of my death to yourself. It will help narrow down who did it."

He kept blinking, attempting to make her image go away in his mind. She was still very visible as she walked away. Right when he thought she would finally go away, she turned around and yelled, "Oh, and Carter?"

He looked up towards the direction of her eyes.

"If you don't figure it out by the time you reach the end of the woods, I'll help you out." She laughed. "Because I'll kill 'em myself."

"Carter, Carter!" Linx yelled at him. "Is it Elena?"

He shook his head yes, motioning to stay quiet. Luckily, the other group members stood far enough away that they didn't see his gestures.

"What did she say?" she whispered, almost letting go of the force field.

Not knowing how to verbalize this crazy message, he stuttered, "Sh-she . . . "

"She what, Carter?! Say it!" she whispered loudly.

"She said someone in our group killed her."

Chapter 15

Linx's couldn't believe the thought of someone in their group being responsible for the gruesome death of Elena. "Do you think it's true? Do you think someone here could've done it?"

With a solemn face, Carter whispered, "I really don't know what to think. She seemed to get great pleasure out of watching me figure it out, though."

"That's so strange."

Taking a deep breath, he quietly whispered, "The scariest part was that she threatened to kill whoever did it, if I didn't find out by the time we left the Dark Woods."

"How's that possible?" she asked. "I understand there are threats here which could easily harm us, but I didn't think images of dead people had any chance of doing damage."

"I didn't think so either," Carter replied. "This is creepy, and I don't know what to do."

"What do you mean?"

"Well, I feel awful not telling the others," he whispered.

"You're not going to say anything? You are going to risk their lives over this? What if we have the chance to prepare for an attack? You have to tell them, Carter!" she persisted.

"Look, I want to! Think of it from my perspective, though. What if no one owns up to it—"

"Your perspective?" Linx interrupted him. "You have risked countless lives on this journey to find your mother. Even now, you're willing to put our lives at risk for your own agenda. If you aren't telling them, I will!" she impulsively hissed.

"Linx! You can't!"

With a condescending roll of her eyes, she said, "It'll be good if we do! Maybe it's not true, anyway. If it's true, who knows, I'm sure they had a good reason."

"Good reason? She came to help me! If it wasn't for me, she wouldn't have been there," he defended.

"Carter, I don't think you know the true Elena. I think you might have a skewed view of her. You only saw her as being nice. She was going to ransom you so your mother would pay. Not to mention, she was going to sell you to Donem! What kind of friend is that?"

Carter thought to himself that she had a point, but there was something that held him back from wanting to tell everyone. Linx disregarded any opinion Carter had on what they just found out.

Believing that no one would have killed Elena on purpose, Linx piped up when the Elder looked over. "Carter just stated that Elena appeared to him."

"Oh?" the elder responded.

"Um, yes. She mentioned someone here murdered her," Linx threw out into the open, just hoping that someone would bite on it. When no one said anything, she asked, "Is that true?"

Again, no one responded, nor acknowledged what she was talking about for a moment. Soon the elder took a breath and responded with, "Carter, do you feel that someone here killed your friend?"

"I, uh," he stumbled, unsure of how to respond without everyone turning against him.

"See? Even Carter does not know what to believe. We need to stay mindful that some of this dark magic will try to break us apart. It'll be easier to devour us while we're alone rather than together."

Afraid to pursue the issue further, Linx stayed quiet as they continued to walk behind the green bubble. Sadly, she didn't know why the elder was avoiding the possibility that someone within their group had murdered the siren. Was anyone there capable of committing such a violent act? It'd be understandable if Elena had threatened their clan, but her body was still in the same place Carter remembered. It appeared she truly was waiting for Carter to come back and find her. All these thoughts flooded Linx's head as she tried to swallow the uncomfortable interactions for now.

When Carter witnessed Linx's vibrant gaze dimly drop to the ground, he knew something was bothering her. She knew something, or she had a hunch about what was going on. He needed to talk to her alone at some point, but where? He didn't know if they would take any breaks. Spur-of-the-moment, Carter decided to make time for them. "Are we going to pitch a tent around here at some point? I'm so exhausted. I don't know how long I can go without sleep."

"Well, this is not the best spot to sleep. Maybe we can construct something quick enough that'll hold up against a passing intruder," the elder said, looking around to see where would be the most secure location to seal a force field.

"I would appreciate that. I don't know the last time I slept more than a couple of hours, and now everything is hitting me at once."

"It looks like we can form a secure force field over there against the small cliff." The elder pointed to a secluded area resembling a small cave indented into the side of a hill. "Linx, can you help me, please?"

Looking over without turning her head, Linx answered quietly, "Yeah, sure."

Carter grew worried and slightly impatient thinking about having to wait to talk to her about what was going on. Her normal personality was bubbly and bright, but she had just receded into herself and wouldn't look anywhere near the other members of the group. She knew something.

As the group crunched over dead branches and leaves, something small and dark hobbled by and hid in a neighboring bush. Carter's heart sank and the rest of the group slightly jumped to see some creature appear out of nowhere. "You guys saw that too?"

"Yes, we're not alone." Teshi stepped out beyond the force field, swinging his spiked club.

Since everyone else saw the creature too, it brought a little ease to his nerves knowing that the images wouldn't haunt him alone. Unfortunately, this also meant whatever lurked in the woods could harm them if it wanted to.

Wondering who their uninvited guest was, the remaining group members slowly walked toward the bush together. While still casting the protective cloud around the others, Linx and the elder formed a flame in each empty palm in order to brighten the darkness. As Teshi's hand grazed the protruding branch covering the creature, he firmly ripped the branch out of the way. Two bright yellow eyes, furry tipped ears, and a pointed beak-like mouth lined with dagger teeth lunged forward onto Teshi's chest.

Flying backward, Teshi attempted to swat the goblin from his face as two ravenous claws dug into his neck. The elder let down half of the force field, while Linx held up the other half, as they conjured a spell to blast the goblin off Teshi. Right as the elder was about to throw a purple orb at the goblin, the elder clunked their head off of a large rock thrown from the darkness. Udin and Raza looked around and attempted to secure the other directions, making sure no one would ambush them.

Carter's eyes darted to the elder and back to Teshi, seeing four more goblins spring out from the bush as they leapt onto his shoulders and head. He tumbled down a rock hill, yelling as the goblins viciously attempted to pluck the gems and crystals from his cape. When the goblins realized they couldn't remove the gems, they screeched to each other before trying to tear the cape from Teshi's flesh. Blood spewed from Teshi's back as another goblin used one of his nails to saw the full cape off. Before leaving Teshi to die, the first goblin quickly slit his throat and escaped with the others.

Carter froze with fear after what he just witnessed. Stunned, he realized that he did absolutely nothing to stop the attack. Why? Why didn't he try to help Teshi? Why couldn't he move? Even while mentally interrogating himself, he noticed that he couldn't move. What was going on? His breathing deepened as he attempted to calm his heart before he went into a panic mode.

"Nice work."

It took a moment for the words to register in Carter's mind. Once the words entered his ears and slapped his brain, he recognized the eerie familiar voice again.

"There's no way. Was this her doing?" Carter whispered aloud. "You were behind this?"

"Who are you talking to?" Linx looked over with raised eyebrows and teary eyes, unable to hear what he said.

Carter shook his head towards her in a 'never mind' kind of way. Linx and the trolls surrounded Teshi to see if they could revive him.

"Shh! You better be careful. You don't want too many people to know you can summon goblins now, do you?" the voice said.

Confused, Carter looked behind the closest tree, "What are you talking about? Did you do that?"

Elena sat with her outstretched crossed legs, resting her head against the tree trunk. "No, my dear. I only gave you the little push you needed."

"What are you talking about? Did you have him killed?" Carter demanded furiously.

"You summoned the goblins. I only told them who you needed them to attack," she explained in a matter-of-fact tone.

Laughing, Carter repeated, "I summoned goblins? How can I summon goblins?"

"Every being in this world has strengths, weaknesses, and specialized traits," Elena revealed.

"Mine is summoning killer goblins?" Carter asked with a scrunched face.

She shrugged her shoulders with her arms sticking out. Elena continued with a laugh. "I mean, we don't get to choose who we are. I would've been happy if you summoned those little demon babies when Donem and his puppy chased us. What can you do?"

Carter fell to his knees and cradled his body onto the ground. "How—why would I do that?"

"It's not that hard to see. You missed me, which was cute, and you were concerned about your precious Linx. Combining those feelings and whatever thoughts were going through your head, probably were the perfect combination to attract the goblins. Who knows? I don't know where you got any of your powers from, but maybe it had something to do with that too." She glared with an accusatory stare.

Carter stepped back as he deeply thought about what she said. That would make sense. Who else thrives off of terror and mayhem? Donem. If these guys can take down a massive troll like Teshi, maybe he can use this superpower to his advantage especially in the Dark Woods.

"Anyway, don't be so down. Teshi or the elder would have tried going to kill your beloved fairy if you didn't off Teshi," she said with a laugh.

"Why would they kill Linx?" he asked, shocked from what he heard.

"Because she was about to tell you what she overheard between the elder and Teshi. I think the elder sensed it because they brought it up to Teshi. They said that they could murder her and blame me, due to the whole 'find my killer' comment." She laughed. "Funny thing, they didn't know all of us lurked around the woods. Just because you don't see us, doesn't mean we aren't here."

Carter's gut sank, knowing these creepy figures were watching their every move. Nowhere was safe until they got out of these woods. Suddenly, a thought popped into his mind. "Elena, what's this place?"

"From what I have learned so far, it's a bunch of dark magic and dark creatures that pull in dark souls or those who have unfinished business. They can be from other areas or even different worlds. Seems like we cannot leave until our business is finished—which may never happen," she said with a sad roll of her eyes. A tear formed in the edge of her eye that she quickly brushed away.

"Why did you come here? I can imagine being a pirate came with its problems, but you never came off as an evil person to me. What is your unfinished business?"

"Well, thank you, sweetie. I have done my fair share of awful things, but there was one awful thing that stuck with me. That was another reason I came to Violet Woods." Elena's voice dove from strong to shaky. "During one of our raids on a local ship, we jumped on their deck to just take their jewels or anything valuable. We were out at sea for so long that we were desperate for any kind of money or food. As I fought off one of the sailors, I ran over to check a chest. When I turned around from a noise behind me, I accidentally slammed my sword into a small child's chest, thinking it would've been someone who had a chance of killing me."

Carter's jaw dropped, and his stomach turned as horrible visualizations popped into his head while she spoke.

"I couldn't believe it. My mind darted from trying to save the kid to throwing him overboard, so no one could trace it back to me. As I went to stop the bleeding, one of my ladies yelled over that we had to go because another ship was approaching. Fearful the child would rat us out, Qita dumped them overboard. Eventually, the body washed up, and they were looking for whoever stabbed the boy. I had a feeling that someone ratted me out. Luckily, we are always at sea, so no one could ever get to us for questioning. I never forgot about that kid. It bothered me so much that I wanted to find the child's parent, to apologize and see if there was anything I could do. A few hours after you left, someone must have seen me in the water. When he arrived, he didn't take kindly to seeing me; and since Donem sealed my mouth shut, he didn't give me the time to connect telepathically to him. In a matter of seconds, he grabbed his sword and sliced my head off. Now, here I am."

Speaking slowly, Carter asked, "Elena, was Teshi the parent?"

"Yes."

"I'm so sorry you went through all of that. If you wanted to apologize to him, why did you tell me to figure out who killed you? You made it seem unjust."

"I was irritated, but I wanted to annoy him too since he was ignoring me," she admitted, rubbing her face.

"He was able to see you? He said he saw his child but didn't mention you!"

"Oh, he saw me. His child isn't here. His child has no reason to be here. The poor kid was not evil, nor did they have enough unfinished business that would get them sucked into this bleak hell."

Carter returned to his original thought. "Elena—"

"Yes?"

"Are you aware of all the creatures or people that are here?"

"I have come across a lot. I can't say if I know them all. Why do you ask?"

"Well, I saw someone who I thought was a fake image until all of this happened, and now I'm concerned," Carter asked, kicking his foot into the dirt.

"Your father?" she asked, looking him dead in the eye.

Carter took a deep breath, and before he realized he was speaking, he said, "Yes."

Chapter 16

"Carter, I'm sorry. I don't know, but there is one thing I have to tell you," Elena advised, standing up while holding onto the tree for support.

"Okay. What do you have to tell me?" he impatiently inquired, thinking about if his dad was truly in the forest.

"I need to apologize," she admitted.

Shocked by her words, Carter questioned, "For what?"

Elena began, "I kept you from your mother for my own personal gain. When we first found out, my ladies and I needed resources desperately. I thought this was the perfect way to receive payment, and then we would deliver you safely to your mother. Plus, you were such great company. Well, as you know, that never happened, and I risked everyone's lives to attack Donem. If it wasn't for me, you would've been with your mother a long time ago. Now you have to go through this journey and risk everything again. I'm so sorry. Because of my choices, so many people have died."

"You kept me from my mother on purpose? I did nothing but trust you, and you kept me from my mother all this time? How could you, Elena?"

"Carter, if you walked in my shoes, you'd understand, but here we are. I'm dead, you're stuck in the Dark Woods, and you've a long way to go now. You need to stay safe," she cautioned.

"How can I trust anything you say now? I don't know whether you are you—or some other creature trying to screw with my mind."

"There's more that I need to tell you, but I can't right now. I'll find you soon."

"Please, Elena. Do you know anything about my dad?" Carter desperately begged, lunging forward towards her.

"I have to go and so do you, but I'll see if I can find someone to answer your questions. Take care, Carter." Elena hastily vanished into the air.

Head spinning, Carter turned to walk around the tree to find Linx and the trolls. It was an intense way to die and sad for the others that witnessed it. Linx looked over her shoulder to see if Carter was near her to help. "Did you see where those things went?"

"No, I couldn't see what direction they traveled once they passed those bushes," he responded, pointing to distant brown bushes barely clinging to the ground.

"Where did the elder go? They were over there a moment ago." Linx frantically searched around while holding a blood-soaked cloth on Teshi's neck.

"I thought the elder was over here, but I don't see anything." Carter ran over to the spot where the elder fell after getting hit on the head. No one was there. "Linx, they were right here the last time that I saw them."

"He's gone. Linx, he's gone," Raza sorrowfully mumbled, pulling her hands away from Teshi's body.

"What are we going to do with him? Do we carry him with us or take him back? I mean, we can't leave him here." Linx scanned the dark, lonely corner in the woods.

"I think we should bury him. We can always come back if we can. However, we don't know what we'll be walking into, and carrying a dead body won't help us," Udin suggested, kicking around the ground to find the best place to bury Teshi.

Despite leaving Teshi's body in the creepy woods, Linx brought up another question that stuck in Carter's mind. Where was the elder? Where'd they go? One moment they were standing right there, and then they disappeared after getting hit on the head. There was nothing left behind. I didn't see blood either. Carter wondered if they were still alive or if something took them away.

"Do you see anything?" Linx asked.

Carter looked around for a trace of evidence leading to the elder. "No, I can't find anything. How did they just disappear?"

"I don't know."

"I can't imagine they can still be alive though. If they overpowered someone like Teshi in a matter of seconds, how could the elder survive?" Carter asked.

"I'm hoping they did, but it's not looking good," Linx replied, sulking.

Carter noticed Linx couldn't look up from Teshi's body. "Linx, are you okay?"

"When we figure out a spot to rest for the night, we need to talk," she whispered, so the trolls didn't hear her.

Carter nodded his head. "Sure. Yeah. That would be good."

Linx, Carter, and the trolls agreed upon the most ideal spot to bury Teshi's body. Udin made a valid point. How would they be able to travel through the rest of the Dark Woods and into the next world while carrying a decaying body? It was sad they would have to leave him behind, but there was only so much that they could do. Under the most appealing tree in the dying forest, there was a quaint, quiet spot that seemed like the perfect place to rest. The trolls began digging into the ground with their hands. They slugged through heavy soil, bugs, and rock to create a deep spot for Teshi. Linx brought out her wand to push away the remaining dirt.

"Thanks, Linx." Raza panted, wiping sweat from his forehead.

Distracted by her own aggressive thoughts, she mumbled, "You're welcome."

Immediately, Linx created a force field to protect them from other enemies. Her shield was lighter in color than when she paired with the elder. Carter hoped it would withstand another savage attack by whatever lurked in the woods.

Once they secured the force field, they agreed to bury Teshi and say a few words in his honor. The trolls lowered the body into the ground as Linx and Carter gathered whatever weeds, flower remnants, and sticks to create a makeshift grave for Teshi. Although Carter didn't know Teshi at all, he found himself traumatized by what had happened. He kept glancing at the spot where the demonic goblins flung Teshi to the ground and ravaged him. How was it possible that Carter summoned them? In his other life, he couldn't even kill a fly—maybe a mosquito, but here he is summoning miniature killers out of feelings of sadness and anger? It was hard to fathom.

"Teshi was a loyal soldier and a proud father. May he happily find his son, wherever they are now," Udin boomed, tossing the last scoop of dirt over Teshi's grave.

Afterward, Carter walked over to Udin, who was sitting next to a tree forcefully sharpening his dagger. "Udin, can I ask you something?"

"Hmm?" Udin looked up with a touch of sadness in his eyes.

"What happened to Teshi's son? How did he die?" Carter asked cautiously. He didn't want to seem insensitive. "You mentioned when burying him that you hoped he would find his son."

Udin could see the concern in Carter's eyes. "We had a ship everyone used when we needed time for ourselves. It allowed the trolls to experience the serenity of being surrounded by water. Anyway, Teshi's son boarded the ship to enjoy himself. He recently lost his mother and had been going through a rough time. Poor kid was only there a little while when passing pirates attacked. They ransacked everything they could, but only left some food on the ship. He hid, along with some others, because they didn't know what to do. When he realized they were looking for money, he thought he could help save others by letting the pirates know they were on a recreational ship, not a merchant ship. A few others warned against him confronting the pirates, but he thought he was doing the right thing. He wanted to protect everyone else that was trapped with him. Once he stood up from where he had been hiding, one of the pirates turned around and sliced him right through the chest. To make matters worse, they dumped him over the side of the ship. The only reason we knew what happened was because of some others that were there. I don't think the pirates were aware of it. Had they not watched what happened, his body would've been lost forever. Teshi was never the same after that day. He vowed to avenge his son."

Tears filled Carter's eyes, and a tickle overcame his throat as it tightened. "His son died because he was trying to protect others. That seems like such a—"

"He was six years old. If you want to say how sad, sick, and awful it was, you'd be right. Barely able to carry a sword, and his life was stolen from him." Udin groaned, continuing to sharpen his blade.

Carter spewed rage and sadness as his mind replayed what Udin had described. Despite trying to fight it, Linx was right. This whole time she was right about Elena. All she cared about was herself, and maybe—just maybe, those that supported her. Elena had no interest in other creatures, people, and apparently not even children. She was a murderous thief who was only trying to play with Carter's feelings as a way to get out of the Dark Woods.

Now stuck alone in the terrifying realm of uncertainty, she has poorly tried to redeem herself by justifying her despicable actions. He couldn't swallow the intense electrical shocks that surged through his heart and chest. With his mind racing and his body heating up, it took a moment to hear a string of shrieking screams echo through the forest. Thinking it was another poor soul who ran into the beasts that solicited the woods, he darted down around the side of the hill to see something he never would have imagined.

A giant roaring fire engulfed a significant portion of the local trees and brush. The flames rose with every passing second, so Carter sprung down towards the fire to see who needed help. As he quickly scanned the forest floor, he couldn't see anyone. Repetitively and meticulously, his eyes looked a second time, studying every nook and cranny in his line of sight. It wasn't until a gust of wind shot the flames over to the side that he noticed a round object appearing to be a head.

Following closely behind, Linx shouted for his attention. "Carter! Carter! Where are you going?"

"There's someone in there!"

"What? Where? I don't see anyone! Get away from there! You'll kill yourself!" Linx screamed through the cry of the trees igniting.

"Linx, help if you can!"

Unsure if it would work, she attempted to funnel water from a nearby stream to douse the flames. First attempt . . . fail, second attempt . . . fail, third attempt . . . fail. She never knew why she always had issues with water, but no matter what she tried, she couldn't gain the momentum to suck the water from the stream towards the fire.

Once close, Carter observed a female head lying within the bright orange flames. "Linx, please!"

"I'm trying!" she hollered back, putting all of her effort into forcing the water over.

Finally, she jumped with joy as she overcame a milestone that always held her magic back. Instantly, water shot over towards Carter and sprayed the flames until they ceased to thrive. Carter stepped back as the water covered the forest floor and then dove to get a closer look. Not able to believe his eyes, he dropped to his knees in the mud. Elena's head lay charcoaled next to bundled herbs and a crystal.

Unsure of how to interpret what he saw, Carter just looked over at her in horror. He couldn't understand how it got there and what they were doing with it. Once Linx appeared next to Carter, she gasped.

Refusing to look closely at the head, she said, "Oh my. Someone was doing some dark stuff here. Whoever did this was banning this soul from relocating to another realm."

"What do you mean?" Carter asked, trying to hide the fact that he knew the head was Elena's.

"Well, whenever anyone dies anywhere, you're sent to a new world, as you know—"

"What? What do you mean, as I know?" Carter shouted.

"Um, I thought you knew that you died in your other life to get here?" she said, confused with a red hue tinting her cheeks.

"Linx! I had no idea how or why I got here! I'm dead?" Carter cried, sitting back on his muddied shoes.

"Well, here you're not, but wherever you came from, you are. I'm sorry. I thought you knew, and that's why you wanted to find your mother here. It's not common to be linked in a new life."

Unable to gasp a full breath, he turned to her. "How do you know this?"

"With great power comes great knowledge." She shook her head with sorrow. "It's a sad reality, knowing that when they leave one realm, they won't see other loved ones. There is always a bright side, though. It gives you a chance to start over again. Do better, or for some like Donem, do worse. But for this woman, she no longer has the opportunity to continue into a new journey. Whoever did this completely ended her existence anywhere. It is an intense and dark spell that is almost unheard of."

"Are you serious? That is so extreme." Carter's stomach turned, still thinking about the fact that he was dead.

"Yes, it is. She really must have upset someone so much that they wanted her gone forever."

Carter began sinking into himself. How could he really be dead? What if what happened to Elena was his fault? He didn't know what to do. If Elena was right, how could he trust that this wouldn't happen again? He thought about the pain and torment felt by those who he apparently harmed. How would he know that he wouldn't hurt the others like Linx or the trolls? Dread oozed over his body as he thought deeper. Was he responsible for the disappearance of the elder too?

Observing guilt in his demeanor, Linx attempted to comfort him. "Carter, are you okay? I mean, you don't seem okay. There was nothing you could do to stop it. Whoever was responsible for this was very powerful. Not to mention, look at the rest of us. If this forest can rip a group of people to shreds in front of each other, how do you expect to help a complete stranger?"

"That's the thing, though. This person wasn't a complete stranger," he said.

Linx squinted her green eyes and furrowed her eyebrows. "Huh?"

Releasing a heavy sigh, Carter said, "It was Elena."

Her eyes widened.

"I can't believe it either."

"I wonder what she did or who she had wronged." She shook her head in disbelief.

"Linx!"

"What?" She shrugged. "I'm not saying she deserved it. I can only wonder who else she's angered or hurt along the way. Clearly, this time it was a very dark person with no patience for games."

Attempting to ease the pain of the guilt that swarmed Carter's mind, he wondered if it was of his doing or merely a coincidence. If he potentially had the capability of destroying Teshi, what else could he do? He needed to either take a leap of faith by confiding in Linx or allow the guilt to consume him alive. Nervously contemplating what to do, he reviewed the pros and cons of each decision. Would Linx be understanding and try to help? What if she tried to kill him or told someone else who would?

Slowly inhaling while he closed his eyes, he forced his voice out of his mouth. "Linx."

"Yeah?" She turned back around towards him.

"I need to talk to you about something."

"I do too, so let me see if I can get us away from the trolls. I can't have them hear what I'm about to tell you."

"Okay," he sighed.

Pondering what to say, Linx walked over to Raza and Udin sitting beneath a rotting tree next to a campfire they created. "We need to split up to find the elder. I have no idea what happened, but they've completely vanished. I'm hoping they're alive and unharmed, but it doesn't seem likely if the Dark Woods treats everyone like they treated Teshi."

"Are you sure we should split up?" Udin addressed with concern. "What are you going to do if you encounter a pack of creatures?"

Willy-nilly off the top of her head, Linx replied, "I'll just throw a protection spell up, so they can't touch us."

"Well, what about us? What if someone with magic tries to ambush us?" Raza questioned with a nervous face. Clearly, the trolls were as nervous as the others.

"I'll conjure a protection bubble for you guys as well. Before we split up, I'll have you covered. It should last an hour or so before we need to meet together again."

"Where are you guys going to look? Don't go too far. We don't want to lose the tracking bubble. This place is very dangerous. You don't know who you'll run into," Udin suggested, looking over his shoulder into the woods.

"We'll just look over the hill there." She pointed to where the goblins ran off with Teshi's cape. "I just want to see if there are any clues that help us find the elder."

"All right. We'll backtrack where we came from," Udin explained with a head nod, motioning behind where they were sitting.

Swirling her wand in the air, Linx stretched a protective bubble around the trolls as she gave them a warm smile. "This should be sufficient until we meet again. When we gather later, I can form one strong force field around everyone. We'll yell if we need you."

"Good luck."

"Thank you. You too."

Chapter 17

Carter paced a few feet away as he saw Linx covering the trolls with a protective bubble before returning to him. With her face tense, she appeared bothered by something. "Ready to go?"

"Yeah. What did you tell them?" Carter asked, rubbing the side of his face.

"Well, I explained that we'd look for the elder down that way. It's not a complete lie, but I didn't feel comfortable with them knowing what I have to tell you," she whispered, walking together down the hill.

"Did you find something out?" Carter attempted to hide that he had something very important to discuss himself.

"Kind of. Hold on. I'll explain once we get down there," she revealed.

They slid down a hill covered in decomposing leaves while they held onto weak tree limbs for support. Once they reached the base of the hill, Linx looked behind her back to make sure no one had followed them. Carter did not know what to expect when his eyes met hers, and he saw fear screaming through her pupils.

"What's the matter? Can you tell me now?" he begged, grabbing her shoulders.

Taking a deep breath, Linx resisted the waterfall of tears, begging to roll down her cheeks, "If I tell you something, can you please never—never—repeat it?"

"Uh, yeah. Of course," he agreed with widened gray eyes.

"The elder is not missing," she confided, wringing her hands together.

"What do you mean? Do you know where they are? I haven't seen the elder since Teshi's attack," Carter curiously mentioned.

"I-I cursed the elder to Donem's lair," she confessed as she ran her hands through her hair.

Confused, he shook his head to understand the point. "Why'd you do that?"

"I-I-I had to."

"What's the matter? Why did you send the elder to Donem's lair? Won't he hurt them?" he asked while looking into her eyes.

Rubbing her face aggressively with her hands, she whispered, "Look, I have no proof. That's the biggest problem, but I have a feeling that the elder or Teshi had something to do with Elena's murder in the Violet Woods. On top of that, I think they knew that I knew. I stumbled upon them talking about Elena's neck being slashed when no one besides you had seen her dead. Either they did it themselves or they knew someone who did."

"Are you serious? Wow. That would make sense."

"What do you mean?"

"You know how I saw Elena earlier?"

"Yeah."

"I saw her again around the time that Teshi died. Elena said she wanted to apologize to Teshi for killing his son," Carter elaborated.

"Seriously? I can imagine wanting to kill her, but I didn't think he would do it. I didn't believe it when I heard them talking—like it was no big deal. I wonder if that was the reason they joined us. To throw us off their tracks or worse," Linx explained.

Bewildered, Carter mumbled, "That's crazy."

"Yeah, and the worst part of it was that a vision came when we were walking. Once they found out Elena threatened to kill whoever murdered her, I saw that they were going to kill me. After I died, they would make it look like it was revenge for Elena's death," she articulated as her knees shook. "Carter, I didn't kill Elena."

"I believe you. I believe you. I saw your face when I discovered her. It's also believable that maybe Teshi had a role to play in it, whether it was only him or with someone else. But you felt threatened by the elder too?" Carter questioned, thankful he wasn't alone.

"Yes. Like I said, they had no intention of coming with us at all, but then I walked by when they were discussing something that the siren's head was cut off. Clearly, they knew I would soon put the two together. It all makes sense now. If anyone ever got hurt in the Dark Woods, it was just attributed to the dark fairies or demonic creatures that lurk in the woods." She sat down as the gears turned in her mind.

Grabbing Linx's hand, Carter blurted out, "Wow, Linx, that is crazy. I can't believe they would kill you because you overheard them!"

"Me neither, but now I sent the elder to Donem's lair to buy time. It was a poorly thought-out decision, and I understand that. What if I was wrong? What if the elder had nothing to do with Elena's murder, nor were they going to hurt me? Carter, any vision I had always came true. I've never been wrong, but what if I was this time? No one would forgive that. They would excommunicate and exile me to . . . " she shrieked while looking around the Dark Woods. " . . . to this place. There is no way I could survive. "

Trying to absorb the chaotic story that Linx described, Carter wanted to help calm her nerves before anything else went wrong on their trip. "Just like you said, if something happened to someone here during the trip, others expect us to get attacked. No one has any way to say that you did that. I don't know if Donem cares enough to keep the elder alive. I would think not. With that being said, I don't think anyone would ever find out. You did what many would do if they thought they were going to be killed."

Massaging her forehead gently, Linx nodded her head in agreement with Carter. "I just can't believe they attacked Teshi. The goblins made it the perfect opportunity for me to save myself. If the goblins didn't ambush Teshi, I don't know if I would've been able to do anything. I don't know if I'd still be here now."

"I'm glad you are." Carter smiled. "You said that coming down here looking for the elder wasn't a complete lie, but if you sent them to Donem, how isn't it a lie?"

"I wanted to make sure they left." Linx gave a slight smile before asking, "So what did you have to tell me?"

Carter parted his lips to speak when they heard a deep scream. It must've been one of the trolls, but how could anything happen? Linx gave them a protective bubble. "Udin and Raza!"

"Let's go!" Linx yelled.

They attempted to run up the hill but kept sliding on slippery leaves covered in mud. As they finally found their footing, they could only see Udin standing over a giant hole in the ground. He was desperately looking around, trying to find something. Linx grabbed Carter's hand and zapped them over near Udin. Carter felt uneasy transporting for the first time. "Why didn't you do that before?"

"We have to conserve our magic when we're away from the Violet Woods," Linx said. "Udin, what happened?"

"We were walking and Raza fell into this trapping pit!" he shouted.

Everyone looked down to see that Raza had snapped both legs. He rolled and writhed in pain, unable to gather himself. Linx attempted to assess the scene as she debated on using magic to bring him up.

"Well, what are you waiting for!" Udin boomed, throwing his hands in the air.

"Udin, please! I'm trying to see if there's any trace of dark magic here," Linx asserted, touching the soil surrounding the pit.

"What are you going to do? Leave him there?" he yelled.

"I might have to, Udin! If there's dark magic here—" Linx sadly explained. "Yes, just like I feared. There's not much I can do!"

"Useless fairy!"

"Look, Udin, why don't you do something then! I don't know what you expect me to do when the pit is swarming in spells. They're not only preventing us from getting him, but it could make things worse," Linx articulated.

Blood-curdling echoes bounced up from the hole. "Ahh! Help me! Help me! I can't move my legs! Help!"

"Hang in there, Raza! I'm trying to figure out what to do!" Linx shouted, trying to convince herself she could help.

"What do we do?" Udin demanded with a grumble.

"I—" she started, trying to think about what she could do. She knew there was no way to break this, or at least she couldn't think of one. It was now that she regretted sending the elder to Donem's lair. Maybe they could have helped.

"Look, we don't have time to wait to get him out! We'll either have to kill him or get him out. We can't afford to attract demonic spirits here."

Shocked by the level of ridiculousness of his statement, Carter looked over to Linx. She was no less stunned than Carter, but she didn't want to provoke any irrational or irreversible actions. "Udin! Just because I haven't figured out how to get him out, doesn't mean that we kill him!"

"What do you propose we do if we can't get him out? Leave him down there to starve? Just let him sit there, waiting for someone or something to come back for him? What's worse, Linx? At least here, we can make it as humane as possible. If someone's coming back for him, there's no telling what they'll do to him. How terrifying is that?" he argued, flailing his arms in the air.

He had a point. They had no clue who was behind the trap, and what they would do with their prize. If they couldn't get him out, they might have to consider something a little unorthodox.

"Why can't we go down there and pull him up? I don't understand," Carter revisited the idea.

"Because whoever created this trap intended for no one to make it out. They have spells that block us from going in, him coming out, and me even using magic. Look!" Linx shouted as her wand turned black.

"What the—" Carter mouthed.

"The only option we have, besides what Udin mentioned, is for someone to walk back to Violet Woods to get help," Linx suggested, looking over at Carter.

"We just spent hours walking through the forest to get where we are now. There's no way we could make it in time before he bleeds out," Udin shot down Linx. "Not to mention, we haven't even survived our first night. We'll have to find a spot to sleep soon."

"Look, I don't know what you want us to do. Do you have any suggestions?" she pressed.

"Kill 'em and move on."

Shocked at his response, she judged him. "How can you be so cold even among your own?"

"I have my reasons, but you can do whatever you want. Once you figure out what you want to do, let me know," he mumbled while walking away.

Linx rubbed her face with her hands, thinking about what to do. Feeling there was no right answer, she looked over at Carter to see if he had any helpful suggestions. "Do you have any ideas? I don't know what to do. We can't take him, but leaving him behind is cruel. Even the hike back to the Violet Woods is very long and dangerous."

"Well, the way I see it, we leave him with a few weapons and some food until we can locate help as we go forward. That way, he's protected and has food while we see if someone can help us."

Pacing back and forth, Linx thought about what Carter said while assessing other options. "All right. Fine. Let's do it. Let's put some food, a canteen, and a blade in one of the bags. We can drop the bag in before we go."

Carter and Udin agreed as they grabbed some supplies to load into a thicker bag that would withstand the fall. As soon as they bagged everything for Raza, Udin tightened the strap, sealing the bag shut. He looked down at his fallen friend howling in pain, rocking from one side of his hip to the other.

Despite recommending to kill Raza, it was truly because he was a loyal friend and an even more incredible warrior. Udin felt that leaving him there to suffer was disrespectful and distasteful for the image Raza had established for himself. Although the clans had the protection treaty, Raza always acted out of the goodness of his heart.

While Udin began reminiscing about the unforgettable moments Raza had created, he noticed something alarming as Raza moved in the pit. When Raza rocked back to his right side, Udin saw there was a wooden shard stuck through the artery inside Raza's leg. Blood slowly seeped out around the plugged hole. Shocked and concerned, Udin was about to yell down to Raza. As Udin opened his mouth, Raza rocked to his other side, ripping the shard of wood from his leg.

Blood instantly spewed from the hole as Raza tried covering it with his hand. Udin felt compelled to do the right thing. He searched around for something so he could devise a makeshift tourniquet. He looked down at his clothing and approached the trapping pit.

Linx looked over and darted for him before he descended. "Udin! Don't! You can't—"

"The hell I can't! He'll bleed out within minutes if I don't help him!" Udin shouted, turning himself around to descend the pit wall.

"He's not the only one in danger! You can kill yourself if you go down there! Very dark magic created this, some of which would seep into any creature that attempts to intervene," Linx warned.

Without a second thought, Udin grabbed onto a thick vine secured into the ground, and he stepped into the pit to save Raza. With a thud, he slid down and slammed his foot into the wall of the pit. As he went to re-adjust his stance, he noticed a burning sensation flaring from his foot. It tricked into his ankle and climbed up his calf. Udin looked down to see that his leg was turning to ash. Pain and fear consumed Udin. He hollered while attempting to claw his way back onto the ground above. Carter and Linx rushed to hoist him back to safety.

With the weight of Udin pulling on the vine, the dry ground crumbled where the vine had once held strong. Udin slid down into the trapping pit. Carter snatched one of Udin's hands while Linx grabbed the other. Each pulled with as much strength as they could muster, but their effort was to no avail. With a snap, the thick vine broke, sending Udin to the bottom of the pit. Following a deep thud, Udin's skull was floating in his own blood.

Flying backwards, Linx held her mouth as she tried muffling her cry. Diving to his knees next to her, Carter hugged her shoulders as he buried his head in her hair. Nothing could prepare them for what was happening or what was to come. What started as an innocent trip to find his mother, has led down a path that left them with just two. If they lost three powerful members this easily and sent one to an eternal life of damnation, how were they going to make it through? Should they continue through this path, or should they reconsider going back to the Violet Woods? Carter felt helpless.

"You okay?" rang a familiar voice, causing both Linx and Carter to jump a mile in the air.

As they turned around, they couldn't believe their eyes. How could this be?

Chapter 18

"I-I can't believe it!" shrieked Linx. "Raza, is that you?"

"Uh, I think so. Am I not me? Have I turned into something strange?" He initially laughed, looking down at his feet because of the reaction he received.

"How-how did you get out of the pit?" Carter yelled. "And how are you standing?"

With a confused look, Raza shouted, "What are you talking about?"

"Raza, you were just in the trapping pit. How did you get up here?" Linx cried with tears of joy.

"I wasn't in any pit. I don't know what you're talking about. I saw something running away, and I went to chase it. I heard Udin yelling my name, but I thought he would catch up. When I eventually turned around, no one was there. It turned out to be a white fox that got away from me, so I figured I would come back to find you guys. Where is Udin?"

With tear-filled eyes, Linx pointed to the trapping pit. As they moved towards the hole in the ground, no one could speak. Raza looked down to see the body of his friend that lay lifeless at the bottom of the pit. "Oh, no."

"He was trying to save you—or at least he thought he was," Linx said, cupping her face. "It must've been a curse, but we all saw you at the base of the pit with two broken legs. You started bleeding out because a sharp branch had impaled you. Although dark magic coated the pit, Udin couldn't let you suffer and attempted to save you. Once he went down, he quickly turned to ash. We tried to save him . . . but he fell when the vine snapped."

"Well, that wasn't me." He solemnly shook his head. "Why'd someone do this?"

Instantly, they noticed the ground crumbling beneath their feet. Raza shouted, "Sinkhole! Run!"

They all scrambled far enough away to safety, watching the ground swallow their friend. Raza shook his head in disappointment for what had happened. Knowing that his friend passed away in such a gruesome way brought more sadness into Raza's heart. "Who would've done this? Who could've done this?"

"I'm not sure, Raza. I know one thing, though. I'm so happy to see you!" Linx gushed, flying over into his arms. "We thought we lost you too."

"They'll have to try a lot harder than that to get rid of me," he blurted out, trying to save whatever happiness was left within their group. "That's so strange it convinced you I was in the hole. Could you see me? Did it really look like me?"

"Yes, it looked identical to you. Even the voice, the scream, was the same. It must have been a mirage pool, but it really appeared to be you in danger. If only Udin knew."

Walking away from the sinkhole, Carter questioned, "What is a mirage pool?"

"A mirage pool is a magical spell that's used to manipulate people into thinking they see something that isn't true. They hid the spell well enough that I couldn't detect it until it was too late." Linx hung her head with guilt.

"Linx, none of us knew what was going on. Clearly, this tragedy wasn't your fault. However, it means that we shouldn't let each other out of our sights. Raza said he saw a white fox. Is that normal around here?" asked Carter.

"Well, since none of us ever went into the Dark Woods before, it's hard to say what's normal. It's strange to see such a vulnerable, bright animal running through these woods, though. It makes it so easy to spot and track. The only reason I stopped chasing it was because I couldn't see anyone else behind me. Figuring it would be a trap, I turned around to find everyone. Maybe it was a trap," Raza pondered aloud.

"Would you be able to bring us to where you last remember seeing it? The white fox could be something important for me to follow," Carter said calmly.

Surprised by the request, Raza responded with a silent shake of his head up and down. He turned around to trudge his way through the brush. Raza's boots crushed dead branches as he climbed a hill, leading them up the mountain. Carter glanced behind at Linx. He noticed she looked behind her one last time, quietly saying goodbye to Udin. Carter found the bond between the fairies and trolls to be unique and interesting. Their differences aside, they worked well together.

After ten minutes of travel, Raza looked at Carter. "So, what about the fox caught your interest?"

"I, um, had an encounter with a fox that led me to believe it was associated with my mother," he said with a slight shrug.

"I believe it," Raza agreed.

Surprised by the support, Carter asked, "Really? You do? As much as I would've loved to see her again, I kind of felt like I was going crazy or others might interpret it that way. I didn't know if there was a way her spirit could live on through the fox."

"Actually, it was said that foxes had transporting abilities amongst the realms, but it's never been confirmed. Foxes are very elusive and are rarely seen."

"That's very interesting. In my previous life, there was a white arctic fox that just sat and stared at me when my mother died. It appeared several times after that. Now that I think of it, the fox was the last thing I saw before I woke up here," Carter recalled.

"Well, I'm sure you'll find what you've been searching for. We are getting closer to the Crystal Woods. We just need to get through one more area."

"Really? That's great. Are you familiar with the next world? Is it better than this one? Safer or more uplifting than this one?" Carter asked, scratching the back of his neck.

"I know very little of what we'll be walking into. The elders have mentioned the connecting region is an underground cave. I'm sure there will be many beasts and creatures we've never heard of, but anything is better than the Dark Woods," Raza bluntly admitted.

"I guess you've never been to the Inferno then," Carter interjected with a shudder. "Donem is the bane of everyone's existence. He thrives off of pain and misfortune. If I never go back there, then it'll be too soon."

As the words left his mouth, Carter realized how poorly it came off since he knew about Linx's recent decision to send the elder there. He cautiously glanced over to see if she was upset by his remark, but to his surprise, the comment didn't faze her at all. Strangely, it appeared as if Linx had come to peace with her fateful decision. She was walking, observing the dark tinge to the sky.

"No, I haven't been to the Inferno. How did you get there?" he inquired with a raised eyebrow.

"When we were traveling with Elena, she brought us there," Carter explained, lowering his eyes. He was unsure how much detail Linx wanted anyone to know.

"Oh, that evil siren. It must've been scary to be kidnapped and held hostage by the sirens," Raza mumbled, looking over at Linx. "Were you kidnapped too? I know our village was going through such a rough time after Linx was suddenly taken."

Waiting a moment to answer, Carter thought back to his first interaction with the sirens. With lungs almost filled with water, Carter somehow made his way onto their ship. He couldn't figure out what was creepier though—when no one showed themselves or when they did. "I kind of found them. Nevertheless, my fate was in their hands when I met them. I had nowhere to go and was forced to go wherever they went. Unknowingly, I was going to be sold to Donem, once they decided that ransoming me to my mother wouldn't be a good idea," he confided.

"Interesting. Who is your mother?"

Linx butted in. "The queen."

Raza looked over while doing a double-take. "Wait, you're the queen's son? I'm confused. Linx, why didn't you tell me that? You only said you were going to find his mother, but you didn't say it was the queen."

Giggling, Linx uttered, "Well, I figured you needed an adventure. You've had your head buried in the tunnels for so long. It seemed like the perfect opportunity. Not to mention, I knew you didn't hear that last screecher go by."

Giving a heavy sigh towards Linx, Raza asked Carter, "What happened? Why are you here with us?"

"I wish I knew all the answers myself. I still haven't come to terms with dying in my normal life. I thought this was all a dream."

"You saw the fox in your other life?"

Carter nodded. "Yes."

"And the fox appeared after your mother died, but before you did?"

"Yeah."

"Have you seen her since waking up here?" asked Raza.

"No, I haven't seen my mother here." Carter sadly shook his head.

"Well, it would make sense that she's in this world then. I wonder if the fox appeared to you so you could follow your mother here."

Shocked, Carter asked, "Do you think she knew I was going to die?"

"I'm not sure what her powers are. I've only been told the myths about foxes." Raza continued walking.

"So, will everyone I know come here?"

"Not necessarily. Some souls funnel into this one, but there are many worlds they can funnel into. I'm wondering if she wanted to make sure you could follow her here, and then she could protect you. I don't know. I'm only speculating," Raza suggested, crossing a very thin stream.

Carter's head spun as the knowledge of this new world overwhelmed him. How does this even make sense? Not only are there multiple worlds besides Earth, but there are multiple afterlife worlds where you can end up. He hoped he could locate his mother because he needed some normalcy.

"How do you know all of this? It seems like a lot of detailed knowledge for everyone to understand," asked Carter.

"Well, most of it is common knowledge. The elders have access to magic that runs deep into the workings of life. They teach the knowledge to the fairies. If your mother is truly the queen, then she should be able to explain more. Anyone who can overthrow the previous queen must be nearly unstoppable."

"I'm confused though. If the queen, possibly my mother, is so powerful, why is she not able to find me now?" Carter wondered aloud.

"She's very powerful, but she's not an eternal navigation system for everyone. That would simply be too much to handle. This world is enormous. You've only seen a small portion of the Violet Woods; and apparently, the Dark Woods are even bigger," Raza explained.

"It appears the white fox was leading you in the right direction! There's the tracking bubble," Linx said.

Raising his eyebrows, Raza admitted, "Yeah, that's interesting."

As they continued to follow the bubble, the ground became slightly damp. They sunk into the soil as water hugged the exterior soles of their shoes. Although moving onward to another area brought some hope, they were apprehensive for what was about to come. The only ones who had any experience with traveling through different lands were no longer with them. They looked at each other as the green bubble dipped inside a dark cavern with icicles protruding from the ceiling, making the cave resemble the mouth of a shark. Once they entered the dark chamber, intimidation and fear surged through their bodies, creating an everlasting tickle in their stomachs.

Whatever lived within this cave never wanted to be found, so Carter soon became concerned when the bubble continued to descend deeper into the ground. "Are we sure that this will be safe? Sure, the bubble is telling us to go this way, but—"

"Do you want to find your mother? We were only doing this for you. Now, I kind of have some interest vested into this journey," Raza explained with an uplifting chuckle.

Thinking about everything he went through here and his last moments on Earth, he responded firmly, "Yes, I want to finish this journey, too. Linx are you in?"

"Yes, definitely. I have plenty of my own questions that I need answered. Let's just hope we aren't too far away," she agreed with a shudder.

Raza smiled. "Me too. Now, be careful as you step down onto those rocks. They're very slippery. Everything is damp or covered in water."

Looking into the dark tunnel, Carter saw an extensive set of stone steps leading down an unknown path. Thick moss lined the top three stones, thriving in the moist environment. Slowly, he went to take a step down while bracing himself with one hand on the cold, slimy wall. Raza wasn't joking when he said to be careful. As Carter went to take his second step, he slid forward far enough that Raza straightened out his arm to catch Carter before he fell. Fortunately, Carter gathered himself before crashing into Linx. As they continued, Linx slowly followed behind with only a stream of daylight, and the dim shine from the tracking bubble lighting the way. When they followed the green orb down the stairway, an overpowering musky smell penetrated their nostrils.

"Do you see the bottom, Raza? I'm definitely going to fall. I might have to fly down if we don't get off of these stairs soon," Linx complained.

"No, but there's something you'll want to see," he slowly uttered in amazement.

"What? What is it?" she demanded impatiently.

"Linx, look!" Carter shouted.

When Linx made it down the next step, the wall on her right opened up to a beautifully secluded waterfall, pouring into a deep basin. The pond glowed from tiny vibrant flowers as they gently sat on the water's surface. Walking over, she scooped up one of the coral flowers in her hand while staring deep into its light. "I can't believe it."

"What?" Carter blurted out. "You can't believe what? The flower?"

"Yes, you fool!" Linx mocked with a smile. "You have no idea how special this flower is, do you?"

"No. I mean it's pretty, but I have no clue what kind it is," he admitted.

"This flower is a waterbloom. It's a very powerful healing flower. Fatigue, wounds, and even if you have a broken spirit; this flower can cure it all," she described with pure admiration dripping from her eyes.

"But I thought you have magical powers, can't you do all of that stuff?" Carter shrugged his shoulders.

"Carter, I'm flattered you have that much faith in me. We, as fairies, are limited by how much power we can access. Depending on where we are or how much strength we have; along with other factors, we can use all the help we can get. Nevertheless, these flowers can travel well and withstand a bit before they get damaged."

"Seriously? That is very interesting! Should we take a bunch?" he wondered, slowly dipping his hand into the water.

"Despite traveling just fine, they need to have a constant supply of water. Do we have a spare canteen?" Linx asked her group.

While digging through his bag, Raza offered, "We can use this jar."

"Great! That'll be perfect!" She cheered, snatching the glass jar from Raza. "Let me just see how many we can comfortably squeeze in here."

With a quick, smooth scoop, Linx gathered a generous amount of water into the canister. Lightly plucking four waterblooms, Linx gently placed them inside the jar before sealing it shut. Proud as a parent, she handed the jar over to Carter with extreme caution.

Carter fumbled his words, "Um, should I be holding this? What if I drop it?"

"You won't drop it. You better not drop it. There are four flowers inside. One for each of us with an extra in case *someone* ruins one," she emphasized, looking into Carter's eyes with a smirk.

"Ha! Hilarious. I'm not clumsy, just a little nervous about carrying something so important." He laughed as his trembling hands reached out for the jar.

"Carter, can I ask you something?" She switched to a serious face.

"Uh, yeah! Sure."

"It's becoming harder to read minds lately, hasn't it?" Linx stared as her eyes grew fierce.

Baffled, Carter looked like Linx just read his mind without reading it, "Uh, yeah. I didn't really put much thought into it.

Since Donem gave me some powers before, I figured it might have been a temporary power to help him out."

"Although that may be true, there's a way to test out your theory. I have one of my own, too."

"And what's that?" he asked.

"Just like the rest of us, we all have full access to our powers when we're on the land where it originates from. For me, I was born in the Violet Woods. As you know, all of my power stems from there. Being a fairy, I can harness more than an average being, but it can fizzle out. When I was on that ship, I was so afraid I would never feel normal again. I felt so drained and not myself, but once I returned to Violet Woods, it was an instant burst of energy. Like an immediate jolt of life," she explained with animated hands.

"How can I test whether I still have any kind of superpower or extra ability?"

"Simple. Pick your poison and eat it." She smiled.

"What do you mean poison? Surely, they aren't poisonous. Are they?"

Linx tilted her head and widened her eyes in a 'try it to find out' gesture.

"Linx, it isn't worth me risking my life—dying again—to see whether I can read minds. As nice as it is to see what others are saying, it doesn't seem that the benefits outweigh the risks. I want to find my mother. That's my main priority," he firmly responded.

With a quick raise of her eyebrows, she laughed. "I was only kidding! It isn't poison! The flower only revives you, but it creates nothing. If there aren't any magical powers there afterwards, then you can probably skip your next snack because you just ate a huge coral flower for nothing."

With a reluctant look, Carter asked, "There's no risk in eating this?"

"There's always a risk with magic," Raza inserted himself.

"Don't be ridiculous. What can be so risky about eating a flower, Raza?" she snapped back at him.

"Ah, I have no intention to fight about it. I merely was just pointing out the obvious rule that magic always comes with a price. It may be small, but it's always there." Raza tossed his hands into the air.

"Raza, I never heard anyone saying that waterblooms created any issues. Carter has nothing to worry about. The worst thing that can happen will be another pimple on his face. Right— over—there." Linx cheekily tapped his nose with her finger.

Slapping Linx's hand away, Carter shouted, "Look, I'll try it, but just knock it off already."

With a big grin, she clapped her hands together in amusement. For a moment, Carter didn't know if she was just excited or knew something else was about to happen. He bent down to skim the water's surface with his hands until the web between his fingers locked onto the flower's stem. With this stunning and vibrant plant resting so peacefully in his palm, he cupped the full flower and plucked it out of the water. Droplets dripped from the petals as he brought it closer to his face, so he could observe and smell the flower before placing it in his mouth.

"Do I eat the whole thing?" he quietly whined with a disgusted face.

"Yes! Come on, Carter! We haven't got all day," Linx said.

To avoid looking like more of a fool, he jammed the flower in his mouth and began chewing. His ego was telling him one thing, but his body said something else. Instantly, his gag reflex kicked into hyper-drive as tears formed. His stomach and chest forced him into several progressive convulsions, each worse than the previous. In his mind, Carter begged his body to breathe and focus on chewing and swallowing. Just as he thought he might have a shot at safely consuming the flower, his forehead broke out in a hot-sweat. Was this supposed to happen, or was he potentially allergic to this radioactive plant? Either way, he didn't know if he could calm himself enough to finish it.

As he was about to spit it out, Linx stepped in front of his face laughing. "Can't handle it, champ?"

Knowing that she loved his reaction, his eyes fumed with a competitive spark. With four final chews, he finally swallowed the lump of a flower. The large mass slowly pushed down his throat as the bump scraped deeply into the lining of his esophagus. "Ah! What did I just eat? That was awful! Looks prettier than it tastes."

"In a few moments, you'll recognize the effects of the flower." She gathered herself. It was apparent she was nervous and hoped there'd be some progress in regaining Carter's abilities.

As he sat in silence for a moment, he felt his heart pounding through his chest like an aggressive gorilla rattling a fragile cage. Luckily, the burning soon faded down to a mild tingling sensation cascading throughout his body. To his surprise, he was feeling like he could run a marathon despite not sleeping. Looking into his eyes, Linx desperately searched for the possibility that Carter had gained his ability back. Carter looked over towards Raza, "That wasn't funny, by the way."

"What are you talking about? I didn't say anything," he defended himself.

"I know," Carter said with a grin.

"Yay! It worked?" Linx smiled while clapping her hands.

"This is crazy! How long does it last for?" he asked, rubbing his hands over his face.

"Um," Linx thought while scratching her head. "I really don't know."

"What do you mean that you don't know? Has anyone else tried it before?" Carter screamed.

"Well, uh, yeah," she stammered. "It's been said that several fairies and trolls have used the flower before when they were in a world that wasn't their own. They ate it and regained their powers back. It was never said if it was conditional or eternal."

"So, you just had me eat a random flower. What if it poisoned me?" Carter boomed.

"But it didn't," Linx confirmed with a laugh.

Not amused by the bantering, Raza started sloshing through the crystal-clear water to get back on the path. "As much as I'd love to see where this goes, we still have quite a distance to travel. Not to mention, we need to construct a safe spot to sleep. Linx, are you able to set up a protection spell to keep away unknown visitors? I don't know who uses this cave, but we don't want to find out when it is too late."

"Yes, definitely. Now that I know the flower is safe, I can use that to boost my magic," she explained, taking a side step away from Carter.

"Seriously?" Carter whispered with a crumpled frown on his face.

Poking his head near a shadowy corner, Raza ordered, "Okay, good. Let's see where the best spot would be. One that would gain minimal attention."

"How about back here?" Carter suggested, walking behind the falls.

Quickly, Raza and Linx made their way behind the roaring falls and into a dome inside the cavern wall. Carter continued, "It sits just far enough away from the water that we won't get wet, but we can see everyone and remain unseen at the same time."

"Looks good to me. What about you, Linx?" Raza nodded his head in agreement.

"This is perfect! Let me get up a solid force field to attach to the wall." Linx pulled out her wand and swirled it precisely in the air. A bright flame shot from her wand as a dark wall slowly formed around them. The dark wall connected from one side of the group to the other, sealing up to the ceiling and down to the ground. Once the wall fully formed, Linx gently pushed against it to feel its strength. "Go ahead, boys. Someone give it a whack."

"Are you sure?" Carter asked, genuinely concerned about ruining her project.

"Well, if it doesn't stand up to you. How will it withstand a head butt from a Cerberus?" He laughed.

With shoulders falling to the ground, Carter whined, "A Cerberus? What's that?"

"You've never heard of a Cerberus?" She mocked with a shifty eye roll. "A Cerberus is a three-headed monster that will tear you to shreds."

"Those three-headed dogs are real? I thought it was just a myth?" He panicked.

"They are rare, but they exist. Trust me, you don't want them catching you off guard," Linx warned, ushering someone to attack the wall.

With broad shoulders, Raza stepped forward to give the force field a whack with his hammer. He looked over to Linx with a raised eyebrow. Carter imagined the force field shattering right in front of them.

With a swift swing, he slammed the hammer forward again, and it bounced back, nearly slugging Carter in the face. Impressed by the quality, he sat down in the dome and rested his head against the wall. "Now, let's rest."

Finding a comfy spot to call their own, Linx and Carter snuggled up close to each other as a matter of staying warm. They joked and laughed for a little while before agreeing to get rest. Slowly, Carter realized Linx had fallen asleep on his shoulder. He turned to look at her and smiled when he noticed how comfortable she appeared. Despite everything he went through in this new world, he was very grateful for their developing friendship. Although he had a few questions about the decisions she made, he knew she didn't have an ill bone in her body. She calculated every decision, and she did everything for the good of her people. Nevertheless, he still didn't understand her choice to leave everyone at the Inferno. Yes, her magic was running low, but it does not match her current character to leave someone behind, knowing they would die.

One thought led to another, and soon Carter found himself analyzing his own baggage. There was one issue that stood out in particular, the reaction to his feelings. Every time extreme emotions overcame him, something occurred on a severe level. Why was this happening? Would consuming this flower make it worse?

Carter began freaking himself out by thinking about the random swarm of goblins overtaking and destroying Teshi. Would they come back? If they did, could he stop or control them? Realizing he needed to take advantage of this quiet moment, Carter closed his eyes. Within that moment, Carter had drifted off to sleep against the cold, rocky wall.

Chapter 19

BOOM. BOOM. BOOM.

A loud banging on their force field wall abruptly woke the group. No one knew what to think as they looked at each other in shock. Who was banging on the wall and why? Should they open it or wait for them? Would they leave? Each rapid thump grew more irritatingly impatient.

Linx looked over to Raza, "Should I bring down the force field?"

He glanced over towards the wall and back at Linx, "Wait."

BOOM—BOOM—BOOM.

Silence.

Everyone slowly looked at each other in confusion. Whatever was out there, was it still there? Did it leave? Raza looked over towards the others and whispered, "Let's try to get some more rest. We don't know what's out there, but it seems like they can't get through. No point in bringing down the force field for doing what it was intended to do."

"All right, makes sense," Carter agreed.

"I'll stay awake for a while in case the bubble needs any repairs." Linx nervously scanned the wall.

"Get some sleep if you can." Raza grumbled, sitting back down against the wall.

Right as Raza went to shut his eyes . . .

BOOM.

Instantly, his eyes shot open and his hand wrapped around the thick handle of his battle hammer. Carter's stomach sank as he saw Raza's veins bursting from his neck, traveling up to his forehead. He was ready to fight, but Carter wasn't ready to see what was beyond the wall. Raza is a trained fighter, Linx has impressive magical skills, but Carter only considered himself lucky until this point.

What will I do if it's a Cerberus? He thought, *How will I be able to help them? I'll be the reason we all die here.*

As his mind panicked, Linx and Raza prepared themselves for whatever was on the other side. She raised her hand, and the dark wall melted in front of them, "Let's do this, friends!"

"I can't—" Carter tried to argue, but the wall came down faster than his words.

A large growling shadow loomed over them. The monstrous body blocked the distant light. It was clear this beast would not be easy to overcome. Carter sunk towards the ground as he felt like he was going to meet his fate—again. Where would he go after he dies here? Was there a path of worlds you travel when you die in this world? What if someone burned him, like Elena, and he ceased to exist? Is that how it works? Would he never see his mother again? His blood boiled as his heart rapidly pounded.

The beast slowly approached the group, with its massive spit strings dripping from its three mouths. Each paw was the size of an elephant foot, which could easily crush Carter, Linx, or Raza should they fall on the ground. The fur was a slick black, and it circled the creature's bright yellow eyes.

This is it! This is the end, Carter thought to himself.

A tingling sensation overcame his body as he froze in front of the Cerberus. Within seconds, the beast lunged forward, trying to bite the first adventurer it could grab. Carter flew back and fell on the floor as fear coated his body.

As Carter fell, Raza went to stab the beast's one head, and Linx tried to launch explosive balls of electricity at its heart. Carter sat back in fear, ashamed that he was going to watch his friends die right in front of his face. An eerily familiar feeling surged through his body. One that reminded him of—Teshi!

When he recognized what was about to happen, it was too late. The congregation of high-pitched screams began racing down the tunnels. A thunderous stampede of chaos was hurling toward their location. Linx and Raza turned and looked at Carter as the Cerberus backed away from the group. Even the giant beast felt something, darker than itself, had been triggered.

Within a couple of moments, dozens of goblins sprang out from the darkness and covered the Cerberus from paws up to its heads. It squealed and whined as the goblins unmercifully dug their claws into its eyes and blinded one of the heads. The view was so repulsive that Linx began dry heaving while she watched the beastly Cerberus turn into a victim.

These goblins weren't protectors. They were sadistic, savage demons, amused by tormenting creatures. They laughed, screeched, and jumped up and down like children while the Cerberus howled in pain. Once the Cerberus could turn around, it ran off whining and darted down a cavern tunnel.

Terrified for her life, Linx began shaking, unaware of what was to come. Even Raza's eyes scanned the countless miniature demons that stood in front of them. For a moment, several of the goblins bounced up and down, laughing as another threw himself up into a backflip. Carter stood paralyzed, observing the chaos.

Unable to move, he stared at these horrid little creatures. When one caught his eye, he backed up against the wall. The goblin turned his head and released the most skin-crawling laugh, displaying a myriad of tiny, sharp teeth that resembled miniature razor blades. With grace and confidence, it tumbled toward Carter and stood up just mere inches from his feet. Its piercing eyes looked deep into Carter's. With a grumbling voice, Carter heard it mutter in its mind, "Master." With a swift bow, it confirmed that all of this demonic destruction was tied to Carter.

As quickly as the tornado of goblins stormed in, they charged out down a tunnel, screaming and laughing as they destroyed a path wherever they went. In shock, without flinching a muscle, Linx and Raza slowly slid their eyes over to look at Carter.

Linx was the first to vocalize her thoughts. "What-what was that, Carter? Did you do that on purpose?"

"I, uh, I don't know what to think," Carter slowly fumbled, standing to his feet.

"Well, you were clearly someone they respected, and I'm very thankful for that. We could've easily been ripped to shreds like Teshi. Not to mention, those demonic goblins completely mauled the Cerberus. I've never seen such savagery." Linx shook her head.

"What did you do to summon them?" Raza looked over.

"Nothing that I know of!" Carter adamantly defended. "I felt overwhelmed and nervous that I couldn't help you guys. When I got scared, they appeared. I don't know how or why they came."

"Well, somehow, you have control over them or can persuade them to not hurt us! They had no interest in attacking us, which they easily could have. I mean, Raza holds the same gems in his cape as Teshi, but they didn't even glance at him!" Linx pointed out.

"Woah! Linx, let's not bring that up. It makes me ill thinking about Teshi going through that. I-I have seen many deaths, but that was just pure torture. Just like what they put that Cerberus through." Raza turned away.

"I don't know why they did that, honest." Carter hung his head.

"But did you notice something else, though?" Linx pondered.

"No," Carter said, quickly dismissing her conversation.

Linx speculated, "The first time, there were several goblins that attacked Teshi. I didn't try counting them, but it was a smaller number compared to now. There were so many that I wasn't able to keep track of where they were. I was afraid they were going to sneak behind us and kill us all. I wonder since you're responsible for them if the flower had anything to do with it. You regained some magic and energy, so it's a possibility the flower had recovered more of your abilities than you know."

"I have no idea, and I really don't want to think about having any association with them."

"Carter, there are things that haunt us all, but that makes us who we are. Some powers might terrify you, but it's because you don't understand them. I have something to tell you. Yes, you know me as a fairy. Long ago, I found out I was a little more different from the rest of my clan. I could conjure exotic spells and see into the future. Carter, I'm a seer. That is something not too many creatures know about me. I'm afraid people will judge me or threaten to kill me, but I have to tell you something. From the very beginning, I could see a prosperous future for you. Yes, it may be laden with heartbreak and trials of strength, but you're rewarded in the end. I already knew this. This is why I have made it a point to assist you until the end. I'm your friend, and we'll make it through this."

"Linx, that's incredible! Is it something you control or does it just happen?" Carter asked.

"A little of both. Some things I can access, but others just occur without notice," she confided.

"Did the elders know?" Raza whispered, slightly alarmed.

"No." She looked Raza in the eyes. "I've only explained this to both of you and one other creature."

"I'm afraid to know what they'll think of me once they find out. I don't trust anyone else finding out, so please don't say anything," she pleaded.

"I, uh, I," Raza muttered as he thought about everything.

"Raza, please!"

"I promise, I won't tell a soul. You have my word," he agreed, bowing his head in her direction.

"Thank you, Raza." Appreciative of the confidentiality, Linx suggested, "Now, it's time we move forward. Let's gather our supplies."

The trio looked around to assess the recent madness. They quickly stuffed the items into their traveling bags. When they walked past the waterfall, Raza opened up a canteen and generously filled it with fresh, cold water.

Once he placed the canteen into his bag, he pointed to climb a steep trail which led to streams of light breaking through the cavern ceiling. The rocks shifted beneath their feet as they pulled themselves up the daunting incline. One step after another, they could ascend the dangerous hill. At one point, Carter looked behind, and his knees grew weak once he saw how high they had climbed. Any misstep could send one, or all of them, tumbling down the rocky slide.

Carter brought his head back as he sent his right foot up the hill, but when he put pressure to move forward, the rock gave way beneath him. His heart dropped to his stomach as his hands braced for a painful fall. As he fell forward and slid down the hill, a strong arm grabbed his wrist, jolting Carter's body. Luckily, Raza was close enough to help Carter regain his composure.

"Thank you!" Carter gratefully shouted.

Quickly giving a comforting smirk, Raza turned back around to continue hiking up the mountain of rocks. "Almost there! I see a plateau ahead!"

"Thank goodness!" Linx sighed with relief.

They desperately pulled themselves to the safe, flat ground and flung their bags into a pile. Taking a seat near each other, Carter curiously asked, "Linx, not to be rude, but why can't we use your powers to go up a ridiculous hike like that? I know that you mentioned not wanting to drain your supply of magic, but I thought that would change now that we have the flowers."

"It was different when we were in the Violet Woods. We were surrounded by very powerful fairies that had access to an endless supply of magic. We have to be careful, Carter. We don't know what we'll encounter along the way. It's best if we have a stash because we need all the help we can get. Not to mention, magic can attract unknown and unwanted attention. We use it when we have to, but refrain if possible," she lectured, holding her wand.

"She's right. You'll want to save as much magic as you can." Raza motioned towards an opening in the cave wall.

A burst of cold air shot through the tunnel and pushed through Carter's hair. It was an eerily cold feeling, like one he had felt before, at home. They made their way towards the narrow walkway when Carter noticed something. "Where did the bubble go?"

"I'm not sure," Raza admitted, looking around.

"Well, are you sure we should go this way then? That would be awful if we went the wrong way," Carter disputed.

"There's no need to worry. This is the right way. I know it," Raza assertively persisted. "I saw the bubble come up here before, but it's gone now."

Unsure of what else to say, Carter looked at Linx. She stared at Raza for a moment. When she didn't hesitate, he muttered, "Oh, okay."

Raza swiftly turned back around and led the group through the tunnel. As they walked forward, the temperature dropped. The ground that was once so soft soon cracked beneath them and felt like a slick, icy pond. The water that streamed from the cave ceiling formed solid icicles, covering the rock walls with a translucent shimmer. When they finally made the turn around the bend, a blinding light burst through the tunnel. Carter's hand covered his eyes, peering through his fingers to see where they were heading.

"Brace yourselves!" Raza boomed as a sheet of snow slapped his face.

"I-I, uh," Linx stammered, attempting to force her thoughts into words. The deep temperature suffocated her mind. The cold was so shocking that she froze in place. Luckily, Linx reached for her wand and changed her wardrobe in time. "There. Argh. This weather is not fairy-friendly. Are you okay, Carter?"

"Yeah, I should be okay for now," he said, hoping she wouldn't notice he was lying.

Either she read his mind or she realized that he was just being difficult, but she waved her wand towards him. "How about I just bulk up your outfit? Can't hurt, right?"

Thankful, Carter smiled. "Sure. Thanks!"

Before Linx spoke with Raza, he began crunching into the fluffy snow. The vibrant sunlight was refreshing, yet overwhelming, as it bounced off the powdery ground. The winds picked up speed once they exited the safety of the dark cavern tunnel. Linx and Carter blindly followed Raza, trekking through the arctic valley.

"Raza! Where are we going?" Linx shouted through the swirling breeze.

"We're getting close to our destination," he stopped and turned to face them. His eyes were fiery with excitement as he pointed to a partial view of a distant stone castle, which was resting on the peak of a mountain.

"Is that—is that where my mother is?" Carter stumbled with a breathy whisper.

"Yes, we are in the Crystal Woods. If it gets unbearable, we might need to find shelter with any locals."

Elated, Carter shouted, "I can't believe it. I can't believe we're this close!"

"I hope we find a community nearby first! If we travel through this blizzard too long, it might kill us!" Linx shouted, trudging through another mound of ice and snow.

"I see some tracks ahead. Let's hope they'll lead us to a village." Raza motioned to several unknown foot tracks, trailing between two lines of dark, tall trees.

Carter held his breath to retain heat within his body. Despite being surrounded in wintry conditions, the actual temperature was quite tolerable. However, the high winds were so overwhelming that he longed to find shelter. Once the group reached the tree line, the wind finally let out a big sigh.

In between the dying gusts of wind, Linx said, "This is absolutely beautiful."

With his heart hopeful, Carter agreed as he glanced up towards the castle. "It is beautiful."

The majestic castle sat firmly on a snowy plateau, topping the colossal mountain. Elegant steeples, dusted with snow, overlooked the land and icicles hung from each architectural dip. As the sun fell, the stained glass sparkled like gems throughout the stone.

"I can't believe my mom is there. After all of this time, we are almost there!" Carter smiled ear to ear.

"I'm very happy too! We just need to be careful, though. I'm not familiar with this land or the creatures that inhabit it. Hopefully, we encounter someone that can help us find food and shelter through the night," Linx said with a warm grin, tightening her snow-sprinkled cape.

"We're almost to the tracks. I wonder what came through here," Raza said, bewildered by their size and shape.

Once he reached the paw prints, his face dropped from the shock of how large they truly were. The prints from the pads were larger than the size of his fist, with four giant toes that pressed firmly into the snow. As he looked around, Raza noticed that the cluster of prints parted ways around a nearby tree.

"What do you think it is?" Carter asked.

"Whatever it is, it isn't alone."

Chapter 20

A chilly gust of wind crept up on the group as they looked around at each other. Despite being prepared for battle, it was unnerving to think about running into something of this size. Without a second thought, Raza pulled out his hammer and scanned the surroundings for any trace of movement. Each burst of wind forcefully shook the tree branches.

Unsure if she should move, Linx stood still while her eyes looked around each tree line. Her attention bounced from one dark tree trunk to the next, hoping that nothing would spring out. "I don't see anything. Let's go before that changes."

"All right. Carter, stay in the middle. I'll grab this side and Linx can cover the other side. Stay alert! We don't know what is out there," Raza ordered, pointing his hammer into the dark unknown.

As they continued on their way, the moonlight bounced off of the snow-covered path between the trees. When their feet pressed on the ground, it created a crunch that echoed into the distance. The night was still, and eyes were watching their every move.

Three more trees before the valley of snow opened up into a field. Beyond the fields lay a rocky trail, leading up the mountain. Their destination was in sight, so close yet so far. Counting down the trees until they hit the field, they were picking up the pace to escape the dark shadows. The last trees were close.

Crack.

A branch snapped behind them, crashing to the ground. All but Raza jumped as they spun around to face two giant cats pacing close by. As the cats circled the group, it was apparent that they were responsible for the tracks at the valley's entrance. Their paws were massive and had thick nails prepared to strike. Bright eyes locked onto the trio as long fangs jutted from beneath their lips.

"Uh, are those saber-tooth tigers?" Carter fumbled, trying to find the handle to his sword.

"They are jaks. Backs together! Form a circle now!" Raza yelled with a deep howl.

The mammoth cats stealthily tiptoed closer, despite being spotted. Carter didn't know what to think. What were they planning to do? Why were they drawing out their attack?

"They thrive off of the chase. Don't try to escape. You can't outrun them. We need to fight them head-on," Raza ordered. The group slowly spun in a circle with their backs sealed together.

The jaks were within a few feet when both creatures split up and surrounded the group. The length of the cats appeared as if a full human body could comfortably rest in there, and the cats would still have room for a snack. Carter's throat prickled as if he had swallowed a spiked ball while he internally cowered in fear. How were they going to defeat two of these beasts? Sadness overcame Carter as he thought about being so close to finding his mother and dying such a short distance away. The low growls shook the group to their bones.

Linx whimpered and quickly conjured a temporary force field. "This won't last for long! I need more time for a stable bubble! Prepare yourselves to fight!"

When the sparks flew off of her wand, the jaks launched toward the group. Flying in the air, they were inches away when the force field finally solidified, ejecting the jaks back into nearby trees. Their screams were of mild pain, but mainly anger, as they rushed the group again. One beast attempted to slash the bubble while the other pounced toward the top. Ducking to the ground, Carter tried to gather any strength to prepare for a battle he never thought would happen. These cats were monstrous, agile, and by the looks of things, very hungry.

"The force field is melting away! Be careful, everyone!" Linx shouted with a shriek, making Carter's hair stand up on the back of his neck.

Grasping the sword so tightly that his knuckles split, Carter pushed his sword straight up to where the bubble separated into shards of magical bits. Not knowing if he would be successful, he closed his eyes tightly as he shot up from the ground. As his knees attempted to straighten, Carter's body jolted from the impact of his sword slicing into the belly of a jak. A high-pitched yelp alerted its partner to come over and help with the fight.

"Nice, my friend!" Raza yelled in amazement. "Be careful! The other one is on its way back."

Carter spun around to see the second jak gripping the ground as it launched itself forward at an alarming speed. As each of its paws connected to the earth, the sound was so subtle that Carter barely heard it coming his way. His legs trembled as its jaws dripped with saliva, and its eyes locked on Carter. "Linx! Help me!"

Within seconds, Linx sent a shot of condensed power towards the creature. As the ball of magic struck the second jak, it flew back into a large tree and fell to the ground. Raza attempted to combine his strength with the others to help defeat the jaks. The outcome was looking more in their favor as the first one fussed to stand up. Carter grew optimistic as he looked towards the second jak, which refused to rush back over towards their group.

"Just keep your eye on the injured one while I kill this one here," Raza shouted, sprinting towards the cat under the tree.

When Linx and Carter turned their attention towards the other beast, it had vanished. Nothing remained in its place except a small puddle of blood and a human-like footprint. Shocked by what had happened, Carter ran over to where the jak was last seen. As he stood next to the footprint, it was roughly the size of his own. He noticed it came from behind the tree. Cautiously, Carter looked over towards Linx, and then slowly peered around the dark tree. His gut was telling him to look no further. He knew it, but something inside him pushed past his intuition. Maybe it was curiosity, or maybe for reassurance that the animal had left, but something urged him to look around the tree.

As the beast lunged for his neck, Linx shouted, "Raza, be careful!"

Spooked by Linx's shriek, Carter jumped out of his skin and turned to see what was going on. Raza had fallen to the ground, but he still managed to crack the side of the jak with his hammer. With a sigh of relief, Carter quickly turned to check behind the tree before returning to Linx's side. As he turned his head back, he came face-to-face with an odd, thin face with elfish ears poking out of a brown, hooded cape. This being wasn't a fairy, but what was he? His face sagged with wrinkly folds, hanging over so much that he could barely see out of his eyes.

Slowly stepping backwards, Carter cautiously mumbled, "Hi, um, I was only looking for—"

"This?" said the gurgling voice.

Carter looked towards the ground and saw one jak dead next to the tree. Carter couldn't believe this being had the strength to carry the beast as far as he did. He appeared frail underneath his outfit, almost as if he was in his last years. As Carter's eyes looked over the old man, he shockingly noticed a scythe in his right hand. Deep red blood lightly glazed the blade as it dripped off the point.

"I, um, yeah," he began to back away from the being. "I was just searching for the jak. I wanted to make sure it wouldn't come back and attack us. I'll leave you be and get back to my group."

"You are going nowhere," he threatened, pointing his scythe towards Carter.

"What? What do you mean?" he fumbled his words, stepping back.

The decaying man pointed his scythe towards Carter's face. "You. You are the queen's boy."

Without answering his accusation, Carter's eyes gazed down at the shining blade, the wooden staff, and then onto the old wrinkly hand of this strange man. His long, yellow fingernails had dirt stuck underneath and along the cuticles. Who was this man, and how could he possibly know who Carter was? As the man's eyes met his, Carter felt a weird connection, creating a sense of comfort within his skin.

"You've come from a far land. Heed my warning. Someone you trust isn't who they say they are," he vaguely gurgled. "There is deception underneath the mask they wear."

"What does this mean?" he whispered back to the man.

The old man transformed his scythe into a staff, gracefully cupping a crystal ball on the top. "Trust no one."

"How do I survive here if I trust no one?" Carter questioned. "If it wasn't for these friends, I don't know if I would be alive now. Who are you?"

"I'm a wanderer," he sharply responded, wrapping up the jak in a blanket. When finished, he turned back to Carter. "Consider my warning. I'm taking this as my pay. It's a delicacy."

"Carter!" Linx yelled. "Are you okay? Did you find anything?"

Looking up towards the old man, Carter saw him fade into thin air while taking the jak with him. "Yeah. I'm okay. The jak is gone."

"Gone? Where did it go? That's strange," Linx nervously speculated.

Carter shook his head. "It's gone. I really don't think we have anything to worry about. I don't think it can hurt anyone anymore."

"Well, let's keep going," Linx suggested. "We don't want to take a chance of it coming back. After Raza hit the other one, it ran off in the other direction. It's a matter of time before we get ambushed again."

"Linx, have you ever heard of a wanderer?" he abruptly asked.

"Um, I have," she said, glaring at him for a moment. "Why do you ask?"

Unsure if he should say anything, he just nodded his head from side to side.

"You have to be careful around them. They're strong and mischievous creatures," she warned.

Thinking to himself about his recent encounter, he was confused. Maybe the old man was just a random magical soul that wanted to steal the jak. After all, he did say that it was valuable. If that was the case, why would he go out of his way to tell Carter about the potential threat in his group? As Carter thought more, he wondered if maybe the man truly was a wanderer, warning him about Linx. Their relationship was fine, but he never forgot when she left him at the Inferno. What if she had an ulterior motive for helping him?

Distracted by Raza's yell to keep moving towards the trail, Linx temporarily dropped the conversation. The tension the jaks had created was a stressful addition to a fierce journey. They moved quickly, gaining more distance from the cats by the time they reached the field. Carter began to breathe heavily as he looked around, hoping not to encounter any more surprises. Just when he thought everything would be okay, he looked into the distance, beyond a tree, and saw a sly smirk reflecting the moonlight off of jagged teeth. The image was enough to send a chill down his spine and remind him that he was still being watched. As he inhaled deeply, the smile slowly faded into the night's air. Turning his focus forward, he noticed a vast field that collided with a dark, rocky mountain.

"So, Carter," Linx interrogated.

"Yes?"

"Why were you asking about wanderers before? It was a very random question."

"Someone appeared when I went behind the tree," he partially confessed. "He said he was a wanderer and took the jak."

"That is strange," Linx mumbled, turning to see if Raza was nearby. "What did it say to you?"

"Well, the wanderer looked like an old man. Very frail and said that he was going to take the jak since it was valuable," he explained.

"That's interesting."

Considering the experiences the group had lived through so far, he asked, "Yeah, are they dangerous?"

"They have a significant amount of power. Will they try to use their power against you? I don't know. Probably not. Speaking from personal experience, I have never encountered one though. Only heard they're very spirited in a mischievous kind of way," she admitted, crunching over frozen blades of grass.

"A wanderer? You saw a wanderer?" Raza asked with raised eyebrows.

"Yeah."

"Watch out. Those things are dangerous," Raza ordered with a stern tone.

"Really? I didn't know they were dangerous. I thought they were more into causing mild chaos for the humor, but not anything detrimental," Linx questioned.

"Turning his head to scan the open field from side to side," Raza said. "Why would something with great power just want to play games?"

The snow speckled the sky and lightly fell into place with a low hush. Although tiny flakes spotted the air, only a few stuck to the ground. A blotch of deep magenta seeping into the distant sky proved there was an end to the everlasting field. The tiny moment of serenity between worlds of disarray lifted Carter's heart.

Despite being surrounded by beauty, Carter's mind instantly jumped back to the strange man in the woods. What did he want? Was he dangerous? He hoped Linx did not ask any more questions because he felt awful lying to her, but he was too far into the journey to risk being naïve.

After what felt like a lifetime of walking through the snow, the group got closer to the trail that scaled the steep mountain. Carter desperately hoped this mountain was the last obstacle between him and his mother. How he longed for her embrace, along with her gentle and caring smile. Time was no longer a method to track moments, so Carter's mind swirled, thinking about how much might have changed since he last saw her. Would she recognize him? He seemed like himself through his own eyes. But what if she sees something different? What if she doesn't want him here? His brain was flooding with questions, none of which he could answer on his own.

As a heavy wind swooshed around the mountain, and through the trio, Raza looked over. "Well, we can either find a safe space to rest or break into your stash of flowers. We'll be out of energy before we get to the top."

With deep thought, Carter and Linx weighed out their options. Yes, those who needed them could use the flowers to get over the mountain, but at what cost? They still didn't know how long the rejuvenating power lasted and what else waited ahead. Nevertheless, the group was leaning toward using them. Figuring they had extra, maybe it would be useful to get them over the mountain.

"Might as well use them now," Linx agreed with Raza.

Right as Carter was about to agree with the both of them, the eerily jagged smile appeared behind Linx and Raza. The wanderer emerged from the shadow of a boulder which the group was passing by. Dread molded Carter's face to a permanent frown as he saw the wanderer shaking his head from side to side.

"Be warned, the flower holds a great power that you don't want your enemy to have during the final hour," the wanderer sang in a high-pitched tone.

"What do you mean?" Carter questioned, not realizing that the others would hear him.

Instantly, the wanderer slammed his staff onto the ground, causing a loud ting which visibly resonated throughout the land. While using his staff for support, he feebly approached Carter without grabbing Linx or Raza's attention. Carter was confused about how he could kill and transport the jak, yet could barely walk without support. "How did you do that? They can't see you?"

"They are frozen," the voice grumbled. "They are unable to hear, see, or smell. Paralyzed until I release them."

"That's unbelievable," Carter uttered as he looked over towards his immobile friends. "I didn't understand what you said before. What did you mean about the final hour?"

"There will soon come a time when a final battle will occur before you reach your goal. When you need to battle your hidden foe, do you want them at their peak energy level?" His smile straightened to a solemn line.

"Well, no, but this journey is so arduous. We just figured it could help us get to my mother. How do you know there will be another battle?" Carter curiously inquired. His stomach turned slightly on its side.

"There'll always be a battle. It's not just one. Nevertheless, there is one that can crumble your journey before you reach your objective. If your friends and enemies consume the flower, they will pose a threat. Do what you can to avoid this mistake."

"Okay. I understand. I'll do what I can to prevent them from using the flowers, but how can I find you? Will you always follow me? Are you good? Does your insight cost me anything?" Carter blasted questions, afraid he would lose the wanderer's attention.

"Good or evil, you mean? It's all based on interpretation. An angel can be seen as a devil amongst those with opposing views. If you want to summon me, use this," the wanderer articulated, pointing his glowing staff towards Carter.

Lifting his wrist, Carter felt warmth tingling on his skin as a glowing object appeared in front of his eyes. A brown vine tightly wrapped around his wrist and knotted at the ends. As his eyes grew with amazement, three gems appeared over the top of the vines. One ocean-blue gem appeared, followed by a green, and then a blood-red gem emerged from the vines.

"What do I do with this? How do I use it?" Carter whispered in disbelief.

"If you need guidance, pluck a crystal from your wrist and smash it on the ground. Beware, though, with every good comes a bad."

Looking down at his wrist, Carter asked, "Do I just choose any color?"

"Blue will calm your nerves with its tranquil message, but can soon bring sorrow or depression. Green will bring rebirth and growth, but never doubt the power of envy. Lastly, the fiery red will bring elevated levels of energy and confidence, yet blood-red rage and danger linger. Use these with caution. Only when necessary," the wanderer warned with a dip of his head.

"Can anyone else see you?"

"Only those who consume the waterbloom will see my existence. That is another reason I warn against letting another absorb the power from the waterbloom. Once one can identify a wanderer, they have access to the same magic you do."

"Can you tell me if I'll make it to my mother?" Carter pleaded while rubbing the studded vine bracelet.

"Everything comes at a price, Carter. If you're willing to pay a price, I'm willing to talk. Otherwise, you'll just have to wait to find out," the wanderer stated with an eerie grin.

Unsure of what the price would be, Carter took his fate into his own hands and avoided asking any more questions. For all he knew, this could have been a trick played upon him. Any ties to magic could lead to his plan backfiring, if good and evil are woven together.

"Thank you. I must go now," Carter quickly replied to the wanderer.

"Before you go, there was one more thing you must know," the wanderer teased with a twist of his staff.

Reluctantly, Carter spun around to face him.

"One of you must die before your goal can be reached," he whispered, tilting his frail head to the side. With a swift motion, his staff made another high-pitched ting during impact against the ground. Instantaneously, Linx and Raza looked over towards Carter.

Remembering what Raza and Linx heard, Carter quickly changed the subject. "What do you think if we find a safer spot to stay and sleep for the night? I'm getting tired, and who knows what we'll encounter beyond the mountaintop."

With furrowed brows, Raza pushed back, "This is one of the most dangerous spots we have encountered, and now you want to sleep instead of using the flowers? The flowers we brought along for this very situation . . . "

Unsure of whose side to stand on, Linx looked from Raza over to Carter. If Carter wanted to make sure no one else consumed a flower, he needed to be very convincing.

"I stand with my opinion of waiting here for the night. If I'm already experiencing some lag, who's not to say these flowers will only get us to the top and then will cease to work? Not to mention, we have no idea who or what is waiting for us. What if all we needed was the extra boost from the flower to defeat an enemy, but instead, we used it to climb? We should be smart and take our time," Carter tried persuading the others.

Irritated by the additional time added to the journey, Raza rubbed his hand over his eyes and forehead. With a deeply loud sigh, he looked over toward Linx for some support. Interestingly enough, Linx shook her head in agreement with Carter. Raza's face grew heavy with defeat as he knew he was outvoted.

"We just need to find a safe space to hide while we rest. Luckily, the area seems quiet now that the jaks are gone. Let's check out what it looks like behind those rocks there." Linx pointed over towards an edge on the mountain.

"All right. Fine. But we are leaving early, so we can keep moving," Raza argued, walking past them.

Unprepared for Raza's level of aggression, Linx raised her eyebrows in shock. She watched him closely as he grumbled up the side of the mountain. "I know you're exhausted, Raza. As are we. Maybe we should wait to continue the journey."

"Fine," he responded with a short breath.

Elated with the thought of swaying the group from using the flowers, Carter let out a sigh of relief. Knowing that Raza was on the verge of starting a riot, he thought about sleeping in shifts to lessen the level of stress. "If you want, we can sleep in shifts to watch out for predators. This way we can minimize the amount of magic we use. I can even stay up the first shift. You guys can get some sleep."

"All right. Fine," Raza agreed.

The trio found a secluded area that had a sharp view of the field below, along with a trail leading up the mountain. Carter positioned himself in a way that he could have his back guarded while looking out for his group. Linx used a spurt of magic to create some warm blankets for the group to lie on.

Once Raza and Linx fell asleep, Carter found himself falling into a deep, meditative state as his breath became shallow and quiet. The wind was barely existent, and the sky was clear while the stars beamed brightly above Carter's head. This night was the first moment in a long time he could sit back and fully digest what had happened since waking up in the sea. This world was so bizarre, yet so real as they progressed throughout their journey.

Sometimes the adventures felt like a dream, but the pain he encountered was undeniable. Thoughts sailed across his mind like passing ships in the night. He wondered about his father. Carter hoped his dad could find some happiness amongst the pain. Maybe a new friend or an old, but someone to confide in. Carter also hoped his father could take a moment for himself, something he had never done before.

Consumed with guilt, Carter thought about all his father had sacrificed for the family. Carter always interpreted his father's actions as abandonments, but now he observed his past life through a different lens. Unfortunately, it was too late. He could never go back and hug his dad, and he could never just sit next to him on the couch again. This entire journey had Carter focused on the end, but now he had the ability to reflect on what he had lost from his past.

Silently, he wished to himself that he could meet with his father again. Deep inside, he knew the man he confronted in the dark woods wasn't his father. It must've been something or someone trying to break him. Sadness sank his heart even lower.

Shifting rocks woke Carter from his daydream, and his eyes darted towards the dark trail lightly dusted with snow. Blood started pulsing quickly through his body as his heart rate picked up speed. Fearing that something was going to pop out from the shadows, he clutched his sword tightly. His eyes zoomed to a rock that had bounced from above. Nothing moved. Breathing slowly, he waited patiently. Carter jumped out of his skin when he heard the eerie grumbles of his familiar friend.

"What are you looking at?" the wanderer asked quietly, perched next to Carter.

"How? Where did you come from?" Carter whispered loudly.

"Oh, me? I'm always around. It's just a matter of whether I feel like talking." The wanderer laughed. "I see you convinced them not to use the flowers. Good job."

"How come you can't tell me who my enemy is?" Carter impatiently boomed. "Realistically, it could be either. The only thing is, why would they waste so much time to help me if they were my enemy?"

"They have a lot to gain when you reach your destination. The sooner you identify them, the less likely they can cause damage. The longer they help you, though, the further you can go on your journey."

"What? That doesn't make sense," Carter argued.

"It's illogically logical."

"I hate this," Carter impulsively grunted.

"You hate what? My company? Because I can go if you want," the wanderer suggested with disappointment.

Carter questioned his sporadic friend's mental stability.

"No, I don't like the riddles, the games. I'm tired and sad and confused. I just want to find my mother." Carter threw in the towel.

"I tell you what, I'll help you understand this riddle a little more. Don't worry about who is your enemy for now. When you see an old, familiar face, one that brings you joy, judge your friend's actions then. You have time for now. Rest."

"Thank you," Carter said with a genuine smile. Hearing that he'll soon see a familiar face brought so much joy to his depressed heart.

"It's time for me to go for now, but remember, should you need anything," the wanderer said, pointing to Carter's wrist.

Instinctively, Carter grabbed his wrist and rubbed the gems roughly. Unable to tell if it was his imagination or not, the gems felt like they were heating up. As if they knew that they'd be summoned upon shortly, they let Carter know that they were waiting for his call.

Within a matter of moments, Raza turned over and woke up. Linx tossed around a bit before opening her eyes as well. Carter wasn't sleepy one bit, and his heart was racing. He was hoping they were ready to proceed on their journey up the mountain.

"Thanks for standing guard. You can rest now if you like," Raza mumbled in an upbeat tone. Clearly, resting had done him well, as his spirits seemed better.

"Honestly, I'm okay. We can just get going if you guys are ready."

"Carter, you should really rest up!" Linx piped in as she made her way towards him.

"Seriously, I'm fine. I think I'm just ready to get this trip over and done with. No offense," he explained, gathering his items.

"Well, okay. If you're really fine with no rest, I guess we can start our day. It seems like it'll be a long one though," she sighed, looking up at the vicious mountain.

Once all ready, they climbed the daunting trail, spiraling and zigzagging up the rocks and lightly snow-covered dirt. The path looked like it went on for days as it faded off into a thin line at the top. Raza slung everything over his back as he led the group.

"How was it throughout the night? Was it creepy, did you hear any animals or anything?" Linx asked out of curiosity.

"No, it was actually quite peaceful. It's been a while since I could sit back and think to myself. This new world has been very full, and something is always happening. It was a good moment to just reflect on . . . everything," Carter thoughtfully responded.

"Wow, that was heartwarming," Linx mocked as she patted his back. "I'm glad you enjoyed a moment to yourself. It has been an active adventure since you came!"

"Were you able to get any sleep?" he asked with a smile.

"Yeah, I was exhausted! Oh, look at the beautiful sky!" Linx pointed out where bright orange and yellow colors kissed the deep blue-violet above them.

"Wow! That is really cool," Carter agreed, climbing up the trail.

Raza glanced up towards the sky and looked back. "Yeah, it's a shame that Udin, Teshi, and the elder aren't here to see it."

Linx and Carter looked at each other, with a silent agreement to keep Linx's secret.

Chapter 21

The wind whistled loudly as they ascended the mountain. One step after another, energy and enthusiasm faded by the time they reached the halfway point of the steep trail. Part of Carter debated on using another flower, but he wanted to avoid influencing the others. What if the wanderer was right? If all the group members used a flower, what would happen once his enemy was revealed?

Dread and fear loomed as he thought about the unimaginable power they might obtain. What if they prevented him from finding his mother? What if they tried to hurt his mother? Trying to reel his thoughts back to a digestible level, Carter remembered that the wanderer stated he would come across a familiar face. That statement brought some excitement into Carter's heart as he wondered who he might see.

"Be careful when you're walking up here. The rocks are sliding everywhere," Raza warned, pointing to piles of small, loose rocks on the trial.

Without a second thought, Carter stepped onto the rocks, bearing all of his weight on his foot. Once he picked up his second foot, the rock beneath his first shoe had shifted enough that Carter lost his balance. His heart dropped as he fell backwards. Unable to yell, Carter only pictured his immediate death as he saw the cliffs quickly approaching.

Closing his eyes, he accepted his fate. With a jolt, he felt his body hit a whiplash state as he was pulled back to his feet. As he opened his eyes, his face met Raza's wide-open eyes and bumpy nose.

"Thought you were a goner, kid!" Raza exclaimed with a pale face.

"Me, too," Carter heavily panted. "Thank you for a second time."

"Pay attention! This is no place to be daydreaming. You don't want to fall down that." Raza pointed to the jagged rocks that Carter had nearly grazed.

"I, uh," Carter fumbled.

"We made it this far. We've fought beasts I've never seen before, and we've lost more than I ever expected. However, we are warriors. More importantly, we are friends. Let's not lose another soul," he genuinely elaborated, before turning to continue up the trail.

Stunned by what he witnessed, Carter stood still with raised eyebrows, and his jaw dropped. Linx wore a shocked smile, passing Carter on the trail. No one knew how Raza felt about his fellow group members. Once Carter snapped out of it, he followed the others up the trail.

"Ah, Raza! I didn't know you felt that way about us! Honestly, I didn't think you even liked us!" Linx mocked with a giggle. "Would you say that we are more than friends?"

"What are you talking about?" Raza grunted.

"Would you consider us best friends?" Linx laughed, grabbing his arm.

Tugging his arm back towards his body, Raza shouted, "That'll be the last time I talk about my feelings."

"Ah, feelings! I never knew trolls had feelings!" She laughed with a wink.

"Linx, we're about to see how well you can fly," Raza said, looking down the mountain.

With an immediate frown, Linx pouted while looking towards the other side of the trail. Carter noticed her frown shift into a look of horror as she stared ahead. Without blinking, she barely moved another muscle aside from her legs that pushed her forward. Confused by her reaction, Carter followed the direction of Linx's eyes, afraid of what he would find. To his surprise, he couldn't see anything, let alone something dangerous.

"What is it, Linx? You okay? What do you see?" Carter shouted.

Shaking her head to wake up from her sudden daydream, Linx followed Raza up the incline. "Nothing. It was nothing."

What was she looking at? Why was she so scared? Above everything else, why was she lying to him? Carter didn't understand these unfamiliar worlds and why his magic felt weak one moment and energized the next. Maybe she was intentionally blocking his attempts to read her mind. Either way, something was wrong, and he needed to find out what was going on. As he followed her, Carter monitored her eyes closely. Shifting from side to side, he noticed that her attention was drawn towards something in the distance. Something was haunting her, but why was she keeping it a secret? Carter didn't have a good feeling about whatever was going on.

"I can see the top of the trail!" Raza boomed with excitement. "Almost there! Just keep pushing through!"

Like a painfully optimistic second wind, the trio could regulate their breathing and focus on the goal. The more they pushed forward, the smaller the gap became between themselves and the end of the trail. As a boost, Carter tried to hold back his urge to look down the mountain until he had reached the next enormous snow-covered boulder. As he looked down, it amazed him to see how far they had gone on their journey. The bright sky illuminated the field beneath them, which appeared so tiny compared to how intimidating it was when they had started.

"All right! Nice work! I see a small forest. Let's hope the castle lies beyond the woods," Raza exclaimed with a smidgen of joy.

The group admired the shimmering trees gently layered with snow. Sturdy icicles hung from the branches above, sparkling in the light. Although they were surrounded by a winter wonderland, the winds were tolerable, and the forest was enchanting.

Fluttering wings lifted Carter's heart as he noticed his nerves were riding a roller coaster of emotion. Happiness, sadness, and excitement swirled inside of him. He couldn't believe his mother was a queen. Does that make him a prince? What does the castle look like in person? Despite all of these glorifying questions popping into his head, a single unfavorable one still lurked in the back of his mind. Would she remember him?

As they stepped into the forest, Linx smiled. "She will."

"You read my mind? I was having trouble reading yours." Carter sighed with confusion.

"Yes, being around these woods is rejuvenating my powers. It's a miracle. I thought the only way we would get our powers back would be if we ate a flower." She smiled, sparking a bright flame from her wand.

Trying desperately to feel something, Carter noticed that he was drained of both energy and enthusiasm. Considering he had never felt this before, he became concerned that he was ill or in danger. Should he tell his group members? He quickly became paranoid, not knowing who to trust or what to do. It was then that he felt the poking of his vine bracelet on his wrist. Looking down at the glowing gems, he grabbed one and ripped it off of the vines. As his eyes glanced at the palm of his hand, he saw the bright blue orb shimmering.

When Linx and Raza were walking forward, Carter quickly placed the blue gem beneath his shoe and pressed firmly until he heard it crack. Bright blue smoke seeped out and wrapped around his foot. Elegantly dispersing into the sky, he heard whispers darting from one side of the forest to the other.

Looking around to see what he potentially summoned, the whispers grew louder, angrier, and deafening. Carter was unsure what he released from within the gem. Why would the wanderer give him something that was so hostile? His heart was pounding and prickles went up his back. As he turned to find Raza and Linx, they were nowhere to be found. From tree to tree, Carter scanned the forest. He couldn't believe they had disappeared. When he was about to yell, he couldn't let out a sound. Grabbing his throat, he tried to scream, but with no luck. The smoke turned into a thick fog that blanketed the land.

Suddenly, the whispering voices stopped, and the fog dropped to the ground like rain falling from the sky. Carter turned around to see if he could find the group. As he spun around, his eyes locked on a haunting figure standing still beneath a light blue robe, draping down to the forest floor. Carter froze in place as his stomach flipped upside down. Unable to move, he just stared at the human-like figure which stood beneath the robe. Nothing was visible on the being. No face, no hands, no feet; nothing was showing. The only distinguishable feature was a thin head that sat oddly tilted on the being's shoulders.

Every inch of Carter's soul begged for him to run. For some reason, he couldn't convince his muscles to work. Cement poured through his veins and dispersed into his organs. He was stuck and just hoped he would live to see another day. As he studied the creepy figure, it moved! It started gliding towards him while keeping its lower body still. Carter gasped as he saw its head tilt from side to side and in an animatronic sort of way. When it reached Carter, the blue figure stopped at his feet while continuing to tilt its head, observing Carter.

"What do you desire?" a whisper pushed through the trees.

His eyes widened as he looked around to see where the voices had come from.

"What do you desire?" the voice repeated, before walking through Carter's body.

Feeling weak and defeated, there was only one thing running through his mind. He wanted to feel powerful and energized again. There was an ominous cloud hovering above Carter's head, and it sucked out every ounce of his being. Despite wanting to say this, Carter couldn't find the ability to speak, and the being passed through Carter's body for a second time. It was an intrusive feeling that left Carter uneasy. He looked around to see where the figure went, but they were gone. Without a trace, the blue figure was nonexistent and normal life resumed.

"Come on, Carter! We need to keep moving," Linx shouted back at him.

As he went to walk forward, it felt easier to breathe and function. He lifted his foot without stress and proceeded forward as if he stood on a self-propelled pad. Unable to believe the difference, Carter felt on top of the world. His movements were effortless, and he felt alive with power. Why didn't he use this earlier? Carter felt like he could have carried Linx and Raza both up the mountain without even breaking a sweat. It suddenly dawned on him why he hadn't. He heard rustling in the nearby bushes, and his heart dropped.

"What was that?" Linx asked with a confused look. "Did you hear that? Something is in the bushes."

Opening his mouth to warn Linx, a snickering sound distracted Carter. As he turned around, the wanderer sat on a rock, twisting his staff in his hand. "Feel better? I bet you do!"

"What was I to do? If I used the waterbloom, they would've, too," he defended himself.

"I'm not judging you! Heck, I would have used a gem when I got that bracelet. That is—I would've used one if I were you."

"What does that mean?"

"Well—" he started as he slowly stood up, showing his age. "I would've used one, if I didn't know the power of the gems. Being that I do, I would think twice before using them."

"What's behind the bushes?" Carter desperately begged.

Raising his arms in the air, almost mocking Carter, the wanderer shouted, "You asked to be energized and rejuvenated! Well, you are! All of your powers are fully charged! Maybe even some you forgot about."

Carter's face dropped in horror as he now realized what was lurking in the bushes. His fear and desperation were calling to them, but he had no power to release them. Once he cracked the blue gem, he opened the cage holding in the little demon beasts that will shred the most innocent flower just for fun.

"There is some silver lining, though," the wanderer added briefly.

"What- what could be good about this? I summoned them without realizing it. And there is no enemy here!"

"Ah, ah!" the wanderer warned, shaking his old, thin finger. "You indeed have an enemy here. Remember? Unfortunately, the time to uncover your true friend and true foe was expedited quite a bit."

"What do I do?" Carter's face sank.

Nonchalantly shrugging, the wanderer began walking away from Carter. "Do nothing."

"Do nothing? What do you mean, do nothing? What if someone gets hurt or dies because of my selfishness?"

"What do you expect to do? You can do nothing and let your demons decide, or choose yourself." He motioned towards Linx and Raza. "If that's your option, who are you going to choose?"

Conflicted, Carter rubbed his face vigorously. He didn't know how to fix this situation. The moment the wanderer unfroze the land, Carter's goblins would tear through anyone in their way. He deeply thought about what to do and stumbled across a deplorable solution. He looked over towards the wanderer with wide eyes.

"Do you think you could trick me?" the wanderer laughed while slamming his staff into the ground. "After what I have done for you, the choice you would make is sacrifice me?"

"What do you mean? I didn't—" Carter shouted, backtracking in his mind.

"No, no!" The wanderer spun around, creating a smoke tornado. "You were drained of magic because another while was purposely draining you! I gave you everything that you needed to survive, but you were going to kill me? You are now on your own!"

"But I'm sorry! I didn't know what to do!"

"You fool. You better choose quickly," the wanderer warned as he disappeared.

A tear streamed down his face as he knew what he had to do. The choice was made in his head for who he was going to sacrifice. Who could drain him of magic? Who was the only one that had betrayed him in the past?

The wanderer slammed his staff into the ground, releasing everyone from their paralyzed state. Carter heard the community of grumbling and savage snarls building from behind the bush. His heart sank to the pit of his stomach as he watched Linx inching closer towards the bush with her wand pointed forward. Carter knew she was falsely protected. There were too many waiting for her. They were waiting for her to come close enough for them to pounce. It was a game to them. It always was.

Why did Carter feel so guilty? She had abandoned him regardless of her reasoning, and she was the only one with magic that could be used against him. With these chunks of evidence, the pain in his heart reminded Carter that his good morals were fading into the darkness in this world.

Nevertheless, Carter felt compelled to reach out to her one more time. He quickly shouted, "Linx!"

Nearly jumping out of her skin, Linx snapped her head towards Carter. "What?"

"I just wanted to say that despite everything we have been through, I love you."

"Carter," Linx whispered with a smile, "you are ridiculous. You scared the daylights out of me! Watch my back."

Her words dug a blade into his stomach and turned it sharply. She held her finger up to her lips as she peered around the bush. Carter didn't know what she thought was there, but he knew whatever she had in her mind, it was incomparable. Wanting to dive for her, he planted his heels into the ground as she pulled back the branch. Almost instantly, the goblins dove over the bush and gripped onto her face as she fell to the ground.

Screaming bloodcurdling sounds, Linx tried pounding the ground, searching for her wand. With the other arm, she attempted to rip the goblins off of her chest. The attack was mere seconds, but it felt like a lifetime of trauma as Carter watched his friend be torn apart by his own inner demons. Her fingers dug into the dirt, clinging to her last form of support, before the tension released from her body. Her lifeless body lay limp as the goblins ransacked her belongings and scrambled away with her wand.

"Linx!" Raza shouted, diving towards her body. He swung his giant hammer, slamming one of the few remaining goblins off her body.

The other two goblins bounced on Raza's back and slashed the back of his cape. He twisted around with a yell and flung them into the bushes. Surprisingly, to Carter's amazement, they sped off to find the others, leaving Carter and Raza to clean up their mess.

Panting with fear and exhaustion, Raza looked up towards Carter with a defeated gaze. "W-what happened? I-I think she's dead."

"I-I don't know. Everything happened so fast!" Carter shouted. A sinking feeling grew in his gut. "She's dead?"

Raza sunk his face into her hair while closing her eyes with his hand. "Yes."

Tears started streaming down his face as Carter ran over to Linx's body. What had he done? He kept reminding himself that he had to. He was being threatened, his journey was threatened, and his mother was in danger because of a lurking foe—or so what was said by the wanderer. What if she wasn't a foe? What if no one was in genuine danger? Carter didn't know what to think, and he dared not say anything to Raza, yet. So, he kept his loud thoughts quietly locked in his mind, only allowing them to torture himself with the replaying of Linx's death—over and over again.

"I'm so sorry, Linx," Carter sobbed above her. He could barely look at her mutilated body, so he quickly turned away. "What should we do with her, Raza? We can't just leave her here."

"We can wrap her up and burn her near the opening of the forest. That way we can pay our respects and make sure no one bothers her remains," Raza suggested, wiping his forehead and eye.

"No!"

Raza spun his head in shock as he looked at Carter's face turning red with anger. "What?"

"We're not going to burn her!" Carter's mind replayed when he came across Elena's charred body. "We can wrap her and bury her, but we're not going to burn her."

"Oh, okay," Raza quietly replied, reaching for their bag stuffed with the thick blanket. Pulling out a blade, he tore the blanket into strips and wrapped her body tightly together.

"I'll dig her grave over here near this beautiful tree. I can picture her sitting here, enjoying the life that it brings," he wept with a forced smile, thinking of her appreciation for her warm resting place.

Carter picked up a sharp rock and dug it into the dirt. Using this moment to disconnect from his reality, he focused on finishing the task. He *needed* to give her the perfect resting place. With each swipe, Carter loosened more dirt and scooped it out of the way.

"All right. She's done." Raza stood up, walking towards Carter to see if the grave was complete. Once at her grave, he crouched next to Carter.

"I think this should be deep enough. What do you think?" Carter sniffled as he tossed one last rock out of the grave.

"It's fine," Raza agreed, laying his hand on Carter's shoulder.

Inhaling a deep breath and slowly exhaling the air, he crawled out of the grave to help Raza. They trudged over towards Linx's wrapped body and gently lifted her above the ground. Carefully walking toward the grave, Carter struggled with the thought of telling Raza the truth. They tenderly set her body in the ground and sprinkled the dirt over Linx. After they finished, both men bowed their heads for a moment to pay their respects. Raza raised his head and began to head towards a different tree to wait for Carter.

"You ready to continue this crazy journey?" Raza smirked.

With a sigh, Carter replied with a solemn face, "Yes. I guess we have to keep moving. I certainly don't want to go back now."

"Don't let everyone's energy and dedication be for nothing. We are so close, I can almost taste it." He squinted through the light pouring between the trees.

Crunching through the forest, they saw a break in the trees quickly approaching. They looked at each other with bright eyes, hoping that this was the last bump in their road. When the trees finally cleared, they stepped out to see the giant castle dominating the land. It was magnificent, yet intimidating. They nervously gulped as they inched forward, taking everything in. A beautifully flat, large front lawn spanned a few acres from where Carter and Raza stood, surrounding the majestic castle. Its light-colored stone mixed with deep-colored windows and roof made the appearance eye-popping while it stood above the winter's snow.

"There it is, Carter! We made it. You made it!" Raza shouted with joy, patting him on the back. "The heart of the Crystal Woods."

A bittersweet, broken smile formed on his face. No matter how hard he tried to justify it, he couldn't shake the guilt of Linx's death from his mind. The weight was heavy, and it didn't seem to be going anywhere, anytime soon. Nevertheless, he forced himself to appreciate the thought of finally finding his mother. After all of this time, heartache, and traveling; he was so close to reuniting with her.

"Are you ready?" Raza asked with a light smile.

"I don't know—" Carter whispered, "I mean, yes. Yes, I'm ready. I just don't know what I'll say once I see her."

"Well, let's get going! I'm starving! Hopefully, they have good food, music, and ale. Oh, and a bed! It's been quite a journey!"

Carter looked over at him with a poor smile. Despite everything, he pictured Linx's face drop in amazement as she absorbed the stunning view that Carter experienced now. He could hear her adorable voice going on and on about how big the castle was, or Linx teasing Carter about the possibility of him living there and leaving her behind. As his thoughts raced, his eyes glanced over at Raza and saw blood coming from the back of his cape. Carter didn't understand. He thought the skin of their capes were nearly impenetrable. "Are you hurt? It looks like you're bleeding!"

"Oh, I'll be fine."

Carter's chest rose with each breath that he took. It nearly kissed the bottom of his jaw when he inhaled.

"You okay? You look troubled," Raza wondered innocently.

Letting out a tremendous sigh, Carter looked him in the eyes. This was the first time he looked into Raza's eyes since he saved him from falling down the cliff. "I feel guilty."

"Guilty about what?"

"For Linx's death."

"What can you do? It's not like you intentionally killed her. We knew those beasts were uncontrollable."

Looking away, Carter muttered, "Well, it wasn't a complete accident."

"What do you mean?"

"Well, the wanderer came to me a while ago. It said someone would betray me. I didn't know if it was a good or bad creature, so I kind of ignored it for the time being," he admitted.

"Betray you?"

"Yes."

"But we all came to assist you! Who would risk their lives and waste all of their resources to betray you? Not to be rude, but what would they have to gain?"

Carter shrugged. "I don't know. I didn't really believe it at first, but then things happened. The more I thought about everything, the more I recalled and realized that maybe the wanderer was right."

"What are you talking about?"

"For starters, Linx was never friendly with me in the beginning. She was standoffish and didn't show any compassion towards me for quite a while. She befriended me once she knew I could help her find her wand. When we were at Donem's lair with Elena, she abandoned me at the worst time possible. It was so bad that I could have gotten killed. To make matters worse, she made me promise I wouldn't tell anyone about her sending the elder to the Inferno."

Stunned, Raza asked, "She did what?"

"Linx said she had to because the elder and others were out to get her. It made sense at the time, but looking back now, it was just another way to gain control of the situation. Why else would she do that the moment Teshi was mauled to death?" Carter questioned.

"Wow, I had no idea."

"What put me over the edge was just recently when we got to the top of the mountain. I felt awful! Like garbage! The wanderer came to me and said someone was draining my energy on purpose. As the only fairy or person with the magical ability to do that, it all made sense that she was the one," Carter continued.

"That's when you summoned the goblins?"

"Well, that was the unintentional part. I had no agenda to kill her, especially not here or now. The wanderer helped me regain my energy, but in doing so, it re-energized my connection to the goblins. Since my body was calling for help, it immediately summoned them when the wanderer helped me," Carter admitted hanging his head down.

"That's awful, but at least you figured out she wasn't who you thought she was, especially before reaching the castle. I can only imagine what kind of damage she would have caused," Raza sincerely added. "Don't get me wrong, I'll miss the girl. At the end of it all, though, remember why you're doing this."

"Yeah, you're right. It's just hard to accept what had to be done." Carter lowered his head.

"I get it. Knowing you're responsible for someone's death is never easy, but it brings satisfaction knowing you have helped the greater good."

Understandably, Carter knew what Raza was getting at, but he didn't agree. Whether he helped the greater good or not, betraying a friend was an awful feeling. No longer wanting to talk about Linx, Carter made his way across the edge of the castle lawn. Raza followed closely behind without uttering another word.

As they got closer to the castle, Carter lost his breath as he had a feeling that he had been here before. Something was oddly familiar about the angle the snow fell and the way the sun bounced off of the castle. How would this make any sense? He was never here before, but every inch of his body said he was. Glancing around the front lawn, no one was outside, and the drawbridge was closed. Carter was slightly surprised since he thought his mother would have waited outside for him, like when he used to come home from school. It was strange to think about the past.

"Carter!" Raza shouted from behind.

Spinning around, Carter nodded his head towards Raza.

"I'm going to take a walk down the edge of the forest here. I thought I saw something that looked like a jak."

"Do you want me to come with you? They are dangerous! I can always wait to meet up with my mother later," Carter offered.

Shaking his head side to side, a small smile curled up his face. "No! Enjoy yourself."

Carter waved to Raza, and then he continued walking toward the castle.

Chapter 22

With his destination in sight, Carter felt a rush go through his body, realizing where he had seen this castle before. It was in his dream when he was on Elena's ship. He remembered running through the field while hooves pounded on the ground, nearly tripping on his own feet until he stopped in his tracks. The bloody pile hunched over on the ground, waiting patiently for Carter's arrival. He shuddered as he recalled the woman resembling his mother springing up and grabbing his neck. Shaking his head to snap out of his daydream, he reminded himself that he was in a safe place, for now. Carter stretched out his fingers and then tightened his fist, thinking about what he would say to her. His nerves pulsated electrical shocks as he made his way to the front of the castle.

"State your business," yelled a guard from above.

Swallowing a lump in his throat, Carter fumbled, "Well—I, uh, don't know. I was hoping to meet the queen."

The guard let out a high-pitched laugh. "You can't just meet the queen! What is your purpose here?"

He took a deep breath before saying, "This will sound ridiculous, but here goes. I woke up in the sea, and some pirates took me in. When I told others what I could remember from my past, some have stated that my mother was the queen. I really didn't know what to make of it because she died, to my knowledge. My name is Carter."

Without uttering another word to Carter, the man whispered something to a second guard standing near him. The other guard walked off for a moment. When he returned, he whispered something back to the first guard, taking him by surprise. Instantly, they lowered the drawbridge and raised the portcullis. Carter paused a moment, not knowing whether to enter or wait.

"Her majesty will meet you in a moment."

Taking a deep breath, his knees grew weak, and he felt a sweat break over his forehead and across his mid-back. *What if this was a mistake? What if the pirates and Linx were setting him up? What if the guards cut off his head for making a fool of the queen?* Carter ran his hand through his hair. His mind flew through so many questions. *Maybe he should leave while he can. Where would he go now that everyone he knew was dead? Raza! He could follow Raza and start a new life wherever he ends up going. Speaking of Raza, where did he go?*

Clicking of shoes over the drawbridge brought Carter's attention back to his current reality. Glancing up, Carter lost his breath as a radiant queen with glowing blonde hair stood facing him. Holding back tears, he whispered, "Mom."

"My son." Her eyes beamed with joy.

They stood for a moment processing this unthinkable reunion, and then she opened her arms, inviting Carter to embrace her. Rushing over, he nuzzled his head into her shoulder, wrapping his arms around her. Carter couldn't believe he had finally found her. It was unbelievable. In his mind, he thought that would never see her again. "I missed you so much, Mom."

"I missed you too, honey," her voice lightly sang.

Wiping streams of tears from his face, Carter sobbed. "This feels like a miracle. I can't believe I get to see you again. I thought you were gone forever. After our accident, you were—"

"This is definitely a miracle. I'm so happy to see you!" she quickly interrupted, saving him from reliving the heartache.

"How long have you been in this new land? I can't believe you're a queen. That's crazy, Mom!" he exclaimed with a giant smile.

Gently holding his face with her hand, she caressed his cheek as tears filled her eyes. "I've been here for what seems to be a lifetime. Yes, it's a change of pace compared to my life before this. Come in, let me show you around after you get something to eat. You must be starving."

Looking at her for a moment, he couldn't believe she was standing in front of him. Her hair glowed in the sunlight as a regal, gold crown rested on her head. "That sounds great, Mom."

As they began strolling inside the castle, she asked, "Did you travel alone?"

Letting out a slow, deep sigh, Carter looked to the ground. "I had a very long journey, Mom. I encountered a lot of people and creatures. Some were bad, but many were wonderful. Regrettably, only one has survived my search to find you."

"Oh? I'm so sorry to hear that, Carter. You've had significant loss recently, but you're safe now with me. Everything will be okay," she explained, looking deep into his eyes.

Despite the brightness shining within her, he sensed sadness seeping through. He couldn't fully understand since he had expected her to be eternally happy. "Is everything okay, Mom?"

"Yes, I'm fine." Queen Alison smiled with a nod.

Knowing he shouldn't question her in front of others, Carter gave a slight smile as they continued into the castle. Once inside, he spun around, admiring the ornate castle. To think this spectacular masterpiece was where his mother lived brought him so much joy and comfort. He instantly felt his heart melt, knowing that this was her haven all along. The guards and servants were extraordinarily kind and helpful once they realized that he was the queen's son.

The first guard came forward and bowed in front of Carter. "My apologies. I didn't intend on being disrespectful. We have had quite a bit of unusual activity recently, and our priority is keeping our queen safe."

With a shy smile, Carter laughed. "Oh, don't worry about it! This is all so strange. Trust me, I know."

"You said all but one individual had survived. Did they return to their homeland, or did they stay with you?" his mother genuinely inquired. "Because we have quite a feast ready, if they were hungry."

"Well—" Carter looked around for Raza. "I really don't know where he went. He was outside, but he said he was going for a walk."

"That's all right. We'll make sure to have hot food delivered to his room whenever he comes in. What does he look like, so my guards can keep an eye out for him?"

"He's a big troll wearing a cape."

"A troll, huh?" Queen Alison questioned out of confusion.

"Uh, y-yes," he stuttered. "He was one of three originally."

"You don't say?" she curiously inquired.

Bowing his head in sorrow, he explained, "Yes. On our journey from the Violet Woods, we originally started out with three trolls, one fairy, and an elder fairy."

"An elder fairy came with you?" she asked with raising concern on her face.

Carter didn't know why his mother was on high alert. Honestly, he was surprised how she dismissed the others who passed away. "Yes, but they're no longer with us."

"No longer with you, as in dead?"

"Well, I-I don't know exactly if the elder fairy is dead for sure. What I can say is that the elder fairy was sent to the Inferno by the younger fairy. After being at the Inferno, I can't really see that Donem would let the fairy escape. At first, the younger fairy, Linx, convinced me it was for the best. Unfortunately, I realized too late that she was in fact the problem within our group."

Concerned, Queen Alison asked, "Have you seen the elder since?"

"No, not at all."

The queen spun around, whispering to a guard while motioning for Carter to come closer.

Dumbfounded, Carter blurted out, "Is everything okay?"

"If you see anyone that resembles the elder, you must let me know," she ordered.

"Oh, I will for sure," Carter agreed with an uneasy look on his face. "But I want you to know, the elder was sent away a long time ago. We were in the Dark Woods when it happened. Throughout our journey, the elder fairy never came back."

A relieved look overcame the queen. "Good, I'm glad to hear that."

"Is the elder fairy evil? They appeared to be very helpful and knowledgeable. I wouldn't have known they were associated with darkness, if it wasn't for Linx."

"Yes, they're powerful and dark creatures. They look for any way to obtain more power and control of this world. If we are lucky, Donem took care of the elder fairy once they arrived," the queen elaborated near the Great Hall.

Surprised to hear his mother talk like that, he mumbled, "I had no idea."

"I can imagine the elder eventually got their revenge on the fairy that sent them away."

"I-I don't know," Carter fumbled while lowering his head.

"Well, let's ease your spirits a bit," Queen Alison said with a smile. "This is our Great Hall! Anything you see that you would like? Help yourself! My dear, you're the guest of honor, so don't be shy!"

Giving a partial smile, he followed one of the servants over to a chair. By the look of things, Carter's seat was right next to his mother's. He laughed to himself. It was a strange way to think of things now. He was *her son*, but he was honored to sit so close to her. After all, she was the queen. He thought that it felt different, but not in a good way or bad—just different.

He hoped that he would get time to be alone with her. There was so much to talk about, and it felt awkward trying to talk with her now. Guards and other people in her court constantly followed her. They all sought her attention. Carter wondered where these other people came from. They appeared similar to himself and his mother. He wondered if they had died on Earth too. *Did they have other families that they left behind?*

Sitting down, he drowned in guilt. Carter thought about Linx, and how his mother made it seem like she was innocent. It was interesting and convenient how the wanderer was never seen again after Linx died. Maybe Carter's mother was right. The elder wanted to be the one with the last jab. Sadly, all of his thinking about Linx's passing had Carter's stomach in knots. He excused himself to get a breath of fresh air. Walking out of the castle and onto the front lawn, he wondered how much Linx would have loved walking inside a castle. After being kidnapped for so long on the ship, he couldn't imagine how she felt about not being home. All she probably wanted was to be home, yet she still accompanied Carter on a ridiculous journey through the most dangerous areas of this world. She gave him everything, and he killed her.

The breeze picked up speed as the night quickly crept in. After dinner, Carter stepped outside in a second attempt to clear his mind. The temperature was comfortable, and it was refreshing to get away from the commotion of the castle congregation. This journey was mentally and physically exhausting, so the last thing Carter wanted to do was chitchat with unfamiliar people.

"I figured I would find you out here," his mother's warm voice uttered from behind Carter.

He turned around to see his mother standing with a bright smile, wearing a different white gown. She looked beautiful and elegant. "Yeah, I just needed a moment. It was kind of overwhelming in there."

"Would you like a moment alone? We can talk whenever you're comfortable," she kindly offered.

"Oh, no. Not at all," he begged. "Please stay."

"How was your father? Clearly, he is going to be hurt. I hoped he was doing okay."

His smile dropped to a solemn face. "I'd love to tell you that everything worked itself out, but that wasn't the case. We barely spoke. He ignored me at the hospital, and he left me by myself at the house. I was alone, scared, and I had no idea where he was. When he finally got home, Dad was drunk, and we got into a fight. I couldn't be alone with him, so I ran away to the woods."

As Queen Alison sighed, she grabbed her son and held him close. "I'm so sorry, Carter."

"There's no need for you to say sorry, Mom. You did nothing wrong. It just felt like no matter what I did, trouble always lurked near. Now, I have so many deaths on my mind, including my own. I didn't know what happened until we were in the Dark Woods, and Linx told me that I had died too. This is crazy. How were you able to digest all of this and still become a queen?" he asked, perplexed by the odds against her.

"It's a long story, honey. Someday I'll tell you, but for now, I just want to hear about you. I have missed you so much. Did you ever put together the model ship we got?"

"No," he uttered as his shoulders dropped. "The time before my accident was filled with hatred, confusion, and mainly sadness. Why did dad always avoid me? Did he hate me? Did I ever do something to him that he was never able to forgive?"

"Honey, no!" she shouted. His mother's eyes teared up, pouring down her cheeks. "No, no, no! Your father loved you. He loved you so much. The problem he had was that he never knew how to have a father-son relationship, but he wanted the best for you. It's just a damn shame this happened. I was trying my hardest to help, but I think he just felt that you would be better off without him."

"What does that even mean, though? What child would be better off without their father?" Carter disputed with a flushed face.

"Well, that was the problem I had with him," she confessed in a low tone. "As time went on, he became completely uninvolved with parenting."

Carter turned his head away from her. A deep red color surged across his face from the conversation.

"The more I thought about it as I was here, the more it makes sense. He just didn't know how to let himself love. After years of fearing that he would become a disconnected, miserable father, he became the parent he never wanted to be."

Carter turned back with tears in his eyes. "Why would he think that to begin with?"

"Because his father was an abusive alcoholic. He forced your father into a life that he resented. When your father needed him most, he was uninvolved or just busy drinking to drown his own problems. It's just a shame that your father turned to his work to silence the noise, rather than dealing with his own problems. Had he gotten help, he could have enjoyed his family while he had it. I just hope he can somehow find some silver lining to see light in the life he has now.

"He deserves more than what he gives himself. I'm sorry we never told you any of this before. Both of us loved you so much and still do. We always felt it was best to not expose you to that." She grabbed his hands and held them tight.

"I love you, Mom. I just wish I could tell Dad how much I loved him too. I really thought that he hated me. I never could understand why he would never make an attempt to be a dad." Carter sobbed, wiping tears from his eyes.

"Maybe, someday, you can. Until that day arrives, the least you can do is allow yourself the time to digest the truth without your mind trying to guess," she whispered.

Pausing a moment, Carter looked at the ground as he confessed, "I killed someone. Technically, I killed a few beings while I was here. There is one that really stands out. I cannot get her out of my mind."

"Oh?" She looked at him, shocked.

"I'm sorry, Mom. I never thought this is what would come of me, but situations have led me to doing the unthinkable."

"Accidents happen, honey. Just try to rest."

"It wasn't an accident. In a way, it could be considered a misunderstanding of my motive, but I killed someone I really cared for," he continued.

Seeing he needed to get this off of his chest, she inquired, "Who did you kill?"

"Before I tell you who, I need to explain something."

"Go ahead. I'm listening. We've got time," she said sympathetically.

"I mentioned I was at the Inferno. Well, before I was there in person, I was there in my dream. Donem was there, and I had never met him until that point. It was strange and eerie."

Her eyes grew as she listened intently. "That *is* interesting."

"The craziest part was that he gave me powers. Some seemed very helpful. Others were very dangerous. On top of that, I didn't know how to control them," he began.

Studying his face, she didn't utter another word as he continued with his story. Although he paused, she waited patiently for him. Carter couldn't tell if it was because she was speechless.

"On our journey here, I encountered a wanderer that no one else could see. After I ate this strange flower from a cave, he followed me wherever we went."

"You ate a flower from a cave?"

"Yes. Linx told me it was a healing flower," he blushed, shrugging his shoulders. "When I came across the wanderer, he explained someone in my group was a danger to me. Now that I think of it, I heard that before from someone else. Anyway, he ended up giving me this bracelet. He said it holds powers that could help me in times of need."

She looked at his wrist.

He explained passionately, "The time of need came just when we got up over that distant cliff. I felt so drained of energy that it was making me sick. I thought I could use one of the gems to feel better, so I could make my way to you. The wanderer appeared to me again. According to him, someone was intentionally draining me of energy."

The queen quietly watched while he slowly incriminated himself.

"Why would someone take everything away from me? It didn't make sense. One thing I noticed—Linx was stronger than ever," he expressed, feeling silly. "I cracked the gem, begging for something to help. Sadly, the surge of energy not only replenished my good magic, but my dark as well. They took a life. I took a life—or at the very least, I didn't stop them from taking a life."

Confused and shocked, the queen calmly asked, "Are you saying you killed—"

"I killed the person I was threatened by the most. I killed Linx," he interrupted, taking a moment to breathe. "I watched as they ripped her apart."

"They?" his mother shrieked with terror, holding her heart.

"They—" Carter sadistically laughed, rubbing his face with his hands. "*They* are demonic goblins that come in a swarm. I try to subdue them, but they come when I feel powerless or severely threatened. I-I just can't control them."

Staring him dead in the eye, Carter could tell his mother wanted to blurt out, 'So, you ate a strange flower, causing you to see a wandering man. Then you climbed a mountain, got tired, and killed your friend?' Surprisingly, she didn't.

"So you have two gems left?" she asked, looking at his wrist.

"Um, yeah," he answered with a confused look on his face.

"Did anyone burn her?"

"No," Carter recounted. He thought about how Raza wanted to burn her body. "Raza!"

"What?"

"Raza! The other traveler that was with me. He was a troll named Raza. He wanted to burn her body, trying to convince me it was a respectful thing to do. I knew it wasn't, so I forced him to bury her with me," he panted with anxiety. "But—but he went for a walk a while ago and never came back. What if he went back to burn her, thinking he was doing the right thing?"

"Everyone knows that when a body is burned in this world, it disrupts the soul's flow from one world to another. It essentially kills their spark within their soul."

"Linx kind of mentioned that when we stumbled upon a charred body, surrounded by herbs and a crystal," Carter said.

"Hmm. Interesting. That sounds like *very* dark magic, but I would need to see what type of herbs and crystal they used. Can you use a gem to resurrect her? They are extraordinarily powerful. Maybe you can get her in time," suggested Queen Alison.

Running his hand through his hair, he contemplated what he should do. "Yes, but something bad happens when you use them. I don't know if I can control the outcome."

"Well, that is something only you can figure out, my dear," she said with a warming smile.

Ripping the red gem from his wrist, he gently placed it on the ground before crushing it beneath his foot. Red smoke flooded the front lawn as Carter focused his thoughts on Linx. Squeezing his eyes shut, he hoped that there was some way she could be saved. All he wanted was for her to be back with him again. When he opened his eyes, a wraith wearing a deep red robe lingered before him.

Carter's heart sank as he feared what would come next. "Please save her."

A deep, savage growl uttered, "One heart for a heart."

Chapter 23

The wraith looped backwards and broke into smoke once it hit the forest. Carter felt in his mind that he was sacrificing his own life for hers, but she didn't deserve to die. He only hoped the wraith would get to her in time. Turning to look at his mother, he mouthed 'I love you' before turning back to watch the woods. When would he know if it worked? Would he still die if it couldn't resurrect her? He looked at the ground, thinking about how awful he would feel if this couldn't work. As he slowly looked back up, he couldn't believe his eyes. Linx stood covered in blood and dirt with her wand in hand.

"L-Linx!" Carter shouted with waterfalls of tears rushing down his face. "You're alive! I'm so sorry! It was all my fault."

"Carter!" She ran into his arms. "It wasn't your fault. I knew you couldn't control them. I just don't know why they attacked me. When I woke up, I was buried in the ground. The goblins dug me out and dropped my wand in front of me. It was so strange. Raza was in front of me—"

"Raza, was there?" he interrupted. As she was about to continue, he touched his chest and realized that he hadn't died yet! Thrilled, he looked back to smile at his mother when he saw her drop to her knees. "Mom!"

"Guards! The queen! The queen has fallen! She's in danger!" yelled another guard in the distance.

Pandemonium broke out in the court. Her people rushed around, not knowing what to do with impending doom.

Like a throbbing migraine, loud hooves pounded behind him. Each clomp on the ground created a jolt that spidered inside of Carter's head. The electric shocks physically pulled him to the ground and brought him back to his dream.

"Carter!" Linx's voice echoed in his head.

Unable to decipher if Linx's voice was from his dream, he painfully looked back as he saw someone riding a horse-like beast towards the castle. When he focused on the rider, Carter could see it was Raza! He was headed in Linx's direction with his hammer. Carter slid on the ground, attempting to propel himself toward Linx. Everything was happening too fast, and Carter couldn't find words to warn her. Linx finally turned around to Raza, who was raising his arm with his hammer. Barely enough time to react, she lifted her wand in the air and a spark formed. Carter knew she didn't have enough time to save herself, but he would be damned if he let her die again. As Raza went to swing his hammer, Carter dove on top of Linx. With both of them falling to the ground, Raza narrowly missed Linx's head. Pulling himself up from the ground, Carter saw Raza was aiming for the queen next.

"No!" Carter yelled out with all of his might. He knew there was no way he could reach his mother in time.

Beginning to suffocate in his emotional chaos, he heard screeches and grunts approaching. Linx held onto Carter tightly, fearing for her life once again. With a powerful focus, he told them exactly what he wanted. Holding his breath, they watched as the group of goblins bypassed Carter and Linx to aim for Raza. Carter was relieved they had survived the encounter, but he feared his newfound friends wouldn't get to Raza in time. A cloud of mixed snow and dust formed behind the goblins.

With loud screams quickly approaching Raza, he looked back to see the little demons focused on him. Swiftly deciding between attacking the queen or defending himself, he pulled the reins on the horse-like creature to turn around and fight the demons. Swinging his hammer from one side to the other, Raza flung several goblins across the lawn. It was odd, but Carter's heart broke to see the little monsters get pulverized by Raza's hammer. Maybe it was because Carter realized he had control over them, or it could have been that he understood they were a part of him. Regardless, he knew that he had to help.

"Linx, I need you to transport me over there to help my demons."

"Are you sure?" she asked.

"Yes. Now!"

"Okay," Linx agreed, picking up her wand.

"Stay here, though. I don't know what will happen, and I cannot afford to let you get hurt," he begged with sad eyes.

"Carter, I'll be okay. To ease your mind, I can help from here," she agreed. "But Carter—"

He looked up at her, wondering what she needed to tell him.

"There's something you should know," she blurted out.

"What is it?"

"There's something strange about Raza's aura. I don't know what it is, but be careful."

He smiled at her. "Okay. I will."

With a graceful wave, Linx transported Carter behind Raza. Luckily, he was too busy fighting the goblins to see that Carter was near. He focused on hitting them despite more flooding towards him. Some had the opportunity to jump on Raza's back and began ripping at the cape. Carter watched for a split second as his cloth cape tore open a bit. What he saw ended up surprising him more than he thought. Beneath the cloth cape appeared to be a troll cape, but something was different. The gems didn't look like the gems he had seen on the trolls before. Even Raza's gems looked different when they started the journey. How could that be? Instantly, he noticed that they weren't gems at all. It was a glittery substance clumped up to give the appearance of gems. Carter didn't know what to make of this. As he continued to watch, he took note of the amount of blood that gushed from the cape as well. From what he understood, it was very difficult to damage a cape. Even Teshi had to be fully subdued by the goblins compared to Raza just getting scratched.

Right when three goblins ambushed Raza, Carter pulled out his sword and darted towards him. With a bit of a struggle, Raza threw one goblin off and then another. Once he turned around, he saw Carter. By that time, it was too late. Holding his sword firmly, Carter drove the sword up into Raza's throat. In a savage rage, the goblins pulled Raza's head backwards until it ripped off. Tipping on its side, Raza's body slid off of the beast and landed on the ground with a thud. Staring at Raza's body, Carter's adrenalin was pulsating too quickly for him to focus, and he temporarily forgot that his mother was injured. Before turning to look at Linx, he noticed Raza's body was mutating.

"Is she going to be okay?" Linx approached, pointing towards the queen.

"I don't know! Look closely at his body while I check on her. Be careful though! You're right. Something seems different," he warned, sprinting towards his mother.

Unsettled by being left alone with Raza, Linx carefully walked around his body. She didn't get the chance to explain to Carter that she had seen Raza standing above her when she awoke in her grave. Slowly, his skin melted off. Despite wanting to vomit, she couldn't look away. It was eerie to watch whatever was happening to Raza. Within a matter of seconds, his secret was revealed.

"Carter! You won't believe this!" she yelled. Her mouth hung open with amazement, standing above the body now lying on the front lawn. Without thinking twice, Linx set the body on fire and transported herself to Carter.

As he was running towards his mother, Linx appeared next to him. "Carter!"

"What happened, Linx?" he asked, shocked that she had popped up.

"Raza—" she uttered quickly.

"What about him?"

"When I was watching him, his skin melted off."

"That's disgusting, really?"

Looking back to make sure the body was still on fire, she slowly said, "Yes, but that isn't the weirdest part."

"Linx, what are you talking about?" he probed, turning to see that she had set the body on fire. "W-why did you do that?"

She tried to find words, but she couldn't digest this news herself. "Carter, that wasn't Raza!"

"Huh?"

"That wasn't Raza. It was the elder."

Stricken with fear, they both stopped and looked at each other. Neither could believe the elder had returned.

"How did the elder know we were here? What did they do with Raza?"

Linx's eyes opened wide. "I'll be right back."

"Okay, meet me over by my mother!" he exclaimed, holding back tears.

As his gaze drifted back towards his mother, he observed her body lying heaped on the lawn. His heart sank to the pit of his stomach. Despite knowing the risks with the gems, he didn't know why this had to happen. Everything inside him wished he could sacrifice himself. After losing his mother once and now losing her again, Carter honestly felt broken. For a split second, he noticed her body twitched. "She isn't dead!"

Chapter 24

Crouched on the ground, Carter held his mother on his lap as she coughed and gurgled blood. A burst of dark magic had hit her in the chest. It appeared to be some poisonous spell as it spread across her chest and up her neck. In denial that he was going to lose her again, he tried lifting her head and talking to her quietly. Thinking she could heal, he asked, "Is there anything I can get to help you?"

"No, honey," she struggled to say. "I just want you to know that I love you so much. I was so grateful when I was able to see you, even if it was from a distance."

Tears washed over his cheeks. "The fox was you."

"I could see through its eyes. I had to make sure you were okay."

As his world was crumbling again, he saw the life fading from her eyes. "I have one more gem! I can heal you!"

"No, my son. Save it."

"Save it for what? An emergency? Like this one?" he boomed as his hand grazed his wrist. His only concern was what would happen afterwards. What would be the price of saving his mother?

"Hello, friend," sang an eerie voice behind Carter. "Just so you know, you have nothing to worry about."

"What do you mean? My mother is dying. What do you mean I have nothing to worry about?" Carter snapped back.

"Testy, testy, aren't we? I was talking about the gem. Lucky for you, it's the pure one with the honest heart. It seeks no price, for your choice is a price in itself."

"What choice do I have?" Carter asked, baffled by the new information.

"You can save her, or you can let her go."

"Let her die? Let my mother die?" Carter disputed.

"I just have to give you your options. If she dies, you become king." He raised his arms, suggesting that it wasn't a bad option. "I mean, how else do you think your mother became queen? It wasn't by saving the last one."

Carter's mouth dropped at the thought of his mother allowing someone to die.

"Your real choice, though, is your mother or your father. You can use the last gem to see him, if you wanted to," the wanderer swiftly added.

"I could see my dad again?"

"Yep. Just crack it, and you can see him in a matter of moments," he explained, raising his eyebrows.

"I would love to see my dad again, but I can't leave her like this. This is the second time she ended up dying—*because of me!*"

"Well, suit yourself. By the way, good job figuring out your enemy." He nodded over towards the dead body slumped in the snow-covered grass.

"It took a second chance to figure that one out," he lamented, pulling the gem off from the bracelet. "I need to save my mother."

"Goodbye, Carter."

He promptly ripped the remaining gem from the bracelet, causing the vine to break in half and fall on the ground. Knowing what he had to do, Carter set his mother gently on the ground. "Hang in there, Momma. Everything will be okay soon."

Gathering himself and his thoughts for a moment, he carefully set the white gem on the ground. With a solid stomp, it shattered under his foot as a white cloudy fog covered the land. He looked around and saw nothing. Nervous about what could pop out, he continued to spin around looking for any sign of wraiths or ghosts. Despite his searching, a sense of peace settled on the land as the fog expanded with an inhale and dissipated.

"My son," a light voice chimed behind him.

Running over to her, he yelled with a giant smile stretched from ear to ear, "Mom! It worked!"

"Yes, it worked!" she warmly smiled as she hugged him tightly. "Thank you, baby. I love you so much."

"I love you, too, Mom."

Confused by seeing Carter's mother alive and well, Linx approached while looking around. She whispered, "Carter! She's alive?"

"Yes! Yes! The wanderer gave me three special powers to use for emergencies. I had one left, and it worked on healing her!"

"That is incredible, Carter! How long does it last for?"

Shrugging his shoulders, he replied, "I would think she's back to normal. How do you feel?"

"What do you mean?" she inquired with a confused look on her face.

"Well, my second was used to bring you back."

"Bring me back from what? The forest?"

Thinking she knew what had happened, he looked her in the eyes. Linx immediately turned away from him, watching everything unfold within his mind.

"Linx, I-I can explain," he shouted as she walked away into the castle.

Wanting to chase her, Carter rushed back to his mother to see if she was still feeling well.

"My dear, I'll be fine. Now, go! You have a lot of explaining to do, but you have a genuine, kind heart. She'll forgive you," his mother sympathized, looking him in the eyes.

"Thank you, Mom. Will I see you soon?"

"Yes. I must rest for a bit, but I'll have the cooks prepare a feast for dinner later on tonight. It's a good day, and I want us all to celebrate." She smiled.

"That sounds wonderful! I would love that. I'm just happy that you're safe now," he said with a concerned smile. "Now, I need to fix this with Linx."

"Okay. Be patient."

Carter ran off to look for her inside the castle. As he walked around the courtyard, he saw Linx hidden in a corner near flowers. She was sipping on a drink, staring off into her own world. He didn't know if he should say anything before he reached her. Knowing how mad she was, it would probably cause her to walk off. When he got close enough to her, he jumped right in, headfirst.

"Linx, please let me explain something to you," he begged, lightly cupping her arm as she tried to storm off. When she didn't resist, he regretfully confessed, "I'm sorry I didn't stop the goblins from attacking you. I didn't know if I could control them or not. Even if I could've, I wasn't going to save you."

There was a moment of silence as Linx soaked in Carter's candid apology. She was somewhat surprised. Part of her expected him to lie or skew what really happened. After all, who could outright admit that they intentionally killed their friend?

"I know that's not what you wanted to hear. If you give me a chance, I can explain what led me to that awful decision that I regret so much."

With tears in her eyes, she sat back. "Go ahead. I can't go anywhere else anyway."

"Thank you," he exhaled slowly. "Remember the wanderer I mentioned so long ago?"

Remaining silent, her fiery eyes glared at him.

"Well, he came to me after I ate that strange flower in the cave. When we were fighting the jaks, he came to me, explaining someone within our group was a danger to me. After Elena warned me, I was getting concerned since we were getting closer to seeing my mother."

Continuing through his story, Carter couldn't believe how much Linx listened. He thought she would have walked off or said something about how much of an awful person he was. Surprisingly, she was very understanding as he reached the end.

Playing with her hair and rubbing her leg, she bluntly admitted, "It's going to take a long time before I can forgive you for what happened. Nevertheless, I appreciate that you had the courage to explain everything."

"I completely understand if you never forgive me. I can never forgive myself for what I did. Deep inside, I just hope someday you can somehow find it in your heart to not hate me. You mean so much to me. Needless to say, I let my fears and ignorance of a new world pressure me into making the worst decision of my life," he confessed. "I-I love you."

Putting herself in his shoes, Linx's heart fluttered. "I don't hate you, Carter. I just thought I could trust you, and you trusted me. This changes things, at least for now."

"I understand, and I'm willing to do whatever I need to."

"But I want to say thank you."

Confused, he asked, "For what? Killing you?"

"No, you fool. Thank you for remaining completely transparent," she explained, tapping on his head. "I expected you to hide your thoughts, but you didn't."

An authentic smile grew on his face. "I have nothing to hide."

"Well, there's something that I have to tell you. Something I have yet to grasp, more so than you—killing me," she whispered, looking around.

Shaking his head from side to side, he asked, "What could be worse or more confusing than that?"

"You'd be surprised," she started to say, checking one more time if anyone else was near. "It's about Raza."

"You mean the elder?"

"Well, yes. After I went to the elder's body, I was able to hold my hand on its creepy face to read some information."

"And?" he anxiously probed.

"The real Raza died when we saw him perish in that trapping pit with Udin. When we saw Raza after that, it wasn't him. The elder made some deal with Donem to come back. Honestly, it probably had something to do with your mother because why else would Donem let the elder go? Anyway, they disguised themselves as Raza from that point on," she said, shaking her head.

"What? Are you serious? Why do you think it had anything to do with my mother?" he interrogated.

"I'm dead serious. It appears the elder wanted revenge on your mother for killing Poba. They believed she was the other woman from the attack."

Slamming his hand down, he aggressively whispered, "This makes no sense. They didn't know for sure, and they were willing to kill her?"

"There's more. Of what I could see, the elder created the trapping pit that killed Udin and Raza." Linx hung her head in sadness.

He couldn't believe what he was hearing.

Tearing up, she sobbed. "They didn't have to die. It's so sad. I couldn't really see too much more."

"Should we send word to everyone else in Violet Woods?"

Shrugging her shoulders, she looked around. "Honestly, I don't know if it's worth dealing with right now. I'm not sure who was in on the plan. It's a shame they suffered so much."

"Yeah, you're right. At least this elder is dead and can no longer hurt anyone else. That's so disturbing to think all this time, we were confiding in the elder," Carter mumbled.

"I know. It's crazy to think about everything we went through together with the elder and not Raza. Nevertheless, it makes sense why the wanderer told you to be wary. If only he could see who it was. It would have saved so much time, heartache, pain, and—death," she insisted while staring at Carter.

"Look, I said I was sorry! Please don't. I need to make it up to you."

Linx cynically laughed and said, "Hmm, I'll have to see what you can do that would make death not too bad."

Hanging his head in defeat, Carter had no idea what to say at this point. He knew that explaining everything was the right thing to do, but now he figured she needed some time to herself. Carter stood up and walked towards the inside of the castle.

When he bumped into a servant, he asked if there was an extra room where he could rest. They led him to a giant bedroom on the other end of the castle. Once he entered, Carter couldn't believe his eyes. In sheer amazement, he gazed at the beautiful and intricate artwork boarding the room. There were magnificent ships sailing high seas across his room while bright skies lit the way.

Wondering if it was a coincidence that he received a room with a nautical theme, he asked, "Do all the castle rooms look like this?"

"No, sir," the servant quickly responded with a warm smile. "Just yours."

"Oh! Well, it's incredible."

"I'm glad you think so," the queen's powerful voice interjected from behind them. "I painted it for you."

"You painted this?" Carter asked, admiring the artwork once again.

"Yes."

"This is so beautiful, Mom."

"Thank you, honey. I had you on my mind, and I wanted to make a room for you. I had no clue if I would ever see you again, but if I did, I wanted you to have a space to call your own," she happily expressed, giving him a hug. "I'll let you rest, and I'll visit again soon."

"Okay! That sounds good," he said. "Mom, before you go there is something that I need to tell you."

"Yes?"

"Linx found out the troll riding that creature wasn't a troll after all. Our friend was being impersonated by the elder.

Somehow, the elder escaped the Inferno and impersonated our friend. Linx even said that she could look into the elder's thoughts temporarily. She found out the elder had deliberately caused all of this mayhem."

The queen looked at him in shock. "That is devastating, Carter. I'm glad they aren't with us anymore. I wonder what they gained from it all."

"I don't know. Maybe Linx can be of assistance, but I'm not sure if she'd be willing to talk at all."

"I'll go find her. You can rest, and I'll see you soon, honey."

"Okay, Mom."

Queen Alison turned with a nod and walked down the halls to locate Linx and check on her. She found Linx dazing off against a window, looking deep into the mountains.

"How are you doing, my dear?" asked Queen Alison.

Shaking her head to snap out of the daydream, Linx turned her head and slightly smiled. "I'm okay. The more important question is, how are you?"

"I'm well," Queen Alison said. "I wanted to thank you for everything you have done. Your selflessness and bravery have transformed, not only a couple of lives, but this full court. I'm sure everyone around me could sense my depression as I searched for my son."

"You are very welcome! You were searching for him? Everyone speculated, but since you never showed, I just thought maybe you weren't coming," Linx blurted out with a frown. "I'm not trying to upset you. I hoped you still were."

"It's okay, my dear," the queen began. "It was a devastating time when I could no longer see him."

"What do you mean?"

"When Carter arrived from the sea, I could see snippets of him, like where he was or what he was doing. It brought hope that I was going to see him again. After some time, I was able to see less and less of him. One day, the visions went away. I feared I had lost him again." She exhaled while looking outside, trying to prevent tears from forming.

Surprised, Linx asked, "You couldn't find where he was?"

"No, I couldn't. The visions made it seem like he had died. At that point, what do I do? I had no clue where he was. I was lost," she admitted.

"I had no clue that someone was tampering with your visions. Did Carter tell you about the elder?" she cautiously whispered.

"He did. Are you okay?"

"Yes, I'm fine. I just get concerned thinking someone else is lurking around," Linx quietly admitted.

"You have no reason to worry," the queen reassured. "Everyone here will keep us safe. I also would like to extend our land to you. You are welcome to stay here at court. I don't know what your plans are with Carter after this journey, but I want you both to have a place to call your home."

"Thank you so much! I really appreciate that!" Linx beamed. "I feared going back to Violet Woods. It was a place that I once confidently called my home, but now I don't know what to think. There have been so many corrupt secrets that I don't feel comfortable going back, at least not now."

"Fear not," Queen Alison said, smiling. "You are home."

Linx sighed for a moment of relief. "Thank you. I have a question, if you don't mind. Carter has told me the stories about the arctic fox watching him. How were you able to do it? How did you cross realms?"

"I had the ability to see him. Unfortunately, it came at a high cost," she muttered, looking Linx in the eyes.

Suspicious of the queen's response, she continued, "Well, I ask because of Carter. I didn't know if he could see his father. Even if it was temporary, his thoughts of his father haunt him."

The queen's eyes widened with sorrow. "Thank you for letting me know. I'll see what I can do."

Chapter 25

Knocking on the door, the queen slowly walked into Carter's chamber. It was unbelievable to see his face again, knowing he was safe within the walls of her home. As he turned to face her, Queen Alison's heart felt so full with joy and appreciation. Despite wanting to see Richard again, she knew there was something she had to do. "Carter, can I speak with you for a moment?"

"Of course! I was going to come out anyway," he quickly responded.

"There was something I wanted to do, but it'll be even more meaningful if you do."

Unsure of what she was getting at, Carter looked up with confused eyes. "Um, okay."

"Just like you, I had encountered magical beings who gave me magical boosts. I ended up using them to go see you and to create the fortress you see now. Unfortunately, they came at a price. I went mad and destroyed the reigning queen. With resistant hearts, the people eventually accepted me as their own. Over time, I convinced them that it was safe to trust me. With the last gem I have, there is something that I've craved to do," she confessed, pointing towards the gem in her crown. "I wanted to see your father one more time. But knowing it would be the last, I had a difficult time making that decision. Deep inside, I knew using the gem was my final goodbye to both you and him. I wasn't ready."

Carter's eyes pooled with tears while watching his mother's heart break. He knew what she was going to say before she said it, and it broke his heart even more.

"Despite my yearning to see him again, and to get the chance to tell him I love him one final time, I feel that the most impactful way we can use this gem is for you to take it."

Swallowing a sharp, painful gulp, Carter shook his head no. "Mom, I can't take that from you. Dad misses you so much. His life shattered when you died."

Tears cascaded down the queen's face as she took off her crown to remove the gem. "This is non-negotiable. Please do this for yourself, for me, and for your father. Give him the opportunity to apologize and to see you one more time. Just let him know that I miss him more than anything. I would give anything to have a big bear hug from him again. We built a beautiful life together, and it's a shame things ended the way they did. Tell him I want him to find happiness, wherever that may be."

In the process of rejecting her offer again, Carter realized what he had to do and what she was giving up for him. Tears filled his eyes. "I will, Mom."

"One more thing, tell him to look inside our safe. There's a gift in there for him. I was saving it for him to open on Father's Day."

"What is it?" Carter looked up at his mother.

"I'll explain later. Now it's time for you to see your dad." The queen sobbed, crushing the gem beneath her shoe.

A thick white fog covered the stone floor and slowly filled the room. Carter looked around as it soon became difficult to see his mother. His heart started pumping as he didn't know what to expect. Within a short time, the room became a giant cloud and he could no longer hear the sharp sniffles from his mother's nose. What was happening? He had the hard, grounding feeling of reality as if he was about to wake up from a dream. His body felt heavy and sounds became overwhelming.

"We will meet again," the queen calmly whispered.

Carter turned toward the sound of her voice.

"You can't see me. You are preparing for an interesting journey, but you'll be back soon."

"Am I going to see Dad?"

"In a manner of speaking, you will. Carter, your body has died. I needed to make sure nothing happened to you, so you won't be able to return to see your father in the flesh. You will enter his dream," the queen's voice echoed.

"Will he know it's me?"

"Yes, you will feel as real to him as if you were in front of him."

"Are there any rules or anything that I need to know?"

"No," she answered. "The only rule is that once he wakes up, your visit will end immediately. Once you leave your father's dream, you will return to Crystal Woods."

"Okay. Will I ever get the chance to see him again?"

"Carter, I'm not sure. Just appreciate today. Not many people get the chance that you're getting right now."

"Thank you, Mom."

Closing his eyes, Carter thought about everything he wanted to say to his father during his visit. There was a lifetime of questions and an everlasting craving to redefine his relationship with his dad. His mind questioned what to expect when he arrived. What if his father was disappointed that Carter was there and his mom wasn't? What if his father rejected Carter's attempt to see him? What if he couldn't find his father?

As he finally opened his eyes, his nostrils filled with an overwhelming aseptic smell and a beeping that pierced his eardrums. Carter looked around the room as the fog dissipated. Bright lights piqued his curiosity as life-saving and monitoring machinery surrounded a white bed. Confused, he slowly stepped closer. A nurse could be seen speaking to someone standing beside the bed. When she walked away, the man began weeping. Was this his father? It was hard to tell what was going on. The unusual feeling of his upper body floating while simultaneously wearing concrete shoes made the walk to the bed take forever. Once Carter finally had the opportunity to examine the body, he was intrigued to see that the body was in fact *his*. Surprisingly, only a light wave of sadness washed over him, but nothing more.

As Carter turned towards the man, his chest grew heavy and beads of sweat covered his forehead. He saw his dad heavily weeping into the hospital mattress. Pausing for a moment, he held his breath as he observed his father's pain. Carter reached out his hand to touch Richard's shoulder, but his grip just fell through his father's shirt. Maybe his dad wanted to be left alone during this time in his dream. Carter couldn't understand. He had anticipated being able to communicate with his father one more time.

Standing still, his surroundings morphed into a strange perception of his house. The next thing he knew, Carter was standing in his own bedroom. Everything felt so real. Not like when he was in the hospital. Maybe he was back? Maybe this was all a dream.

When Carter laid his head down on his pillow, his mind drifted and his heart raced, recounting everything that had happened over the last—well, he didn't know how much time had really passed by. His knees grew weak with the thoughts of his beginning on the pirate ship and then nearly dying when he faced Donem. Creatures that were perceived to be myths had not only threatened his life, but they also reunited him with his mother—something he never thought would be a possibility after that tragic winter's night. He'd never forget the fear that rushed through his veins, and the anxiety that pulsated from his heart to his fingertips as he walked through the hospital hallway. He'd never forget her face, her beautiful face.

I love you, momma, Carter whispered in his head.

He knew he had to get to bed. It was going to be a big day ahead of him, and he desperately needed sleep. Burying his face into the soft, cool pillows, he fully covered himself with the over-sized cushy comforter. As he went to close his heavy eyelids, something bright caught his attention. There was no radio or alarm on his dresser, so he couldn't understand where the light was coming from. Perhaps he had something reflective on his dresser, bouncing light from outside. Attempting to ignore it, he yanked the blanket over his head. Although he never slept under the covers, the bed was so inviting he couldn't bring himself to part ways, not even for five seconds. Just as he thought he could fall asleep, the light grew so bright that it burst through the fibers of the blanket and onto his face once again.

"What the heck?" Carter yelled, flinging the covers off of his head and body.

The cool air slapped his skin and the ice-cold floor stung his feet as he stood up from the bed. Irritated from leaving his warm den, he aggressively rubbed his eyes before walking over to his dresser. Carter was confused as he removed his hands to notice the brightness of the light was quite dim. Nevertheless, Carter hobbled over to see what was on his dresser.

Looking down, he muttered in amazement, "No way."

As his heart pounded heavily, he slowly reached his hand down and gracefully swiped a golden key from his dresser. Holding it up to his eyes, he examined it, twisting the key in his hand. Glancing over his shoulder, he saw the keyhole on the door shining brightly. His hope had sunk to his feet, realizing all of this was his father's dream, and he needed to find him before he woke up.

Unlocking the bedroom door, Carter stepped out into his father's interpretation of their front yard. It was a bright and happy vision, with the sun shining down over the neighborhood. Carter was surprised when everything jumped from gloomy to the far extreme. Turning to face the stoop of the house, Carter was surprised when he saw his father. Richard sat with his face in his hands, weeping while wearing an athletic shirt and shorts. Brand new baseball mitts and a baseball accompanied his father, sitting untouched beside him. Carter's heart broke as the pitch of his father's cry grew. Unable to take it anymore, Carter rushed over to him. "Dad?"

The sobbing stopped as Richard turned to look behind him. Wiping his puffy, bloodshot eyes, Richard uttered, "Carter?"

Richard stumbled to stand up as his eyes locked on Carter. Tears cascaded down his cheekbones. He rushed over and grabbed Carter tightly in a warm embrace.

"I missed you so much, Carter." Richard began sobbing into Carter's shoulder.

Trying not to cry, Carter choked and then broke down. "I missed you too, Dad."

Taking a moment to absorb his father's affection, Carter knew his time with him was limited. However, he couldn't rush this moment. Who knows how long his father had waited to see him, let alone hold him.

"Is this real? Is this real? This can't be real. You died." Richard sniffled and cried.

"No, Dad. This is your dream. I'm able to visit you tonight while you sleep. I won't be able to stay long though. Before I forget, Mom wanted me to tell you she loves you so much—" Carter stopped to take a breath.

"You've seen your mother?" His eyes perked up, then dropped to the ground. "I haven't. I always said to myself that I would give anything to see you guys again. This means so much to me!"

"Well, she also said that you need to check the safe when you wake up. I guess there is a present inside that she wanted to give you."

"Oh, really?" His eyes lit up. "She always spoiled us rotten with gifts. I can't wait to see it."

"I don't even know what it is. She said she would tell me when I got back." Carter rolled his eyes with a smile.

"Ah, didn't want her surprise ruined, huh?" Richard laughed. "Look, I know you can't stay long, but can you at least come in and chat for a bit? I can make you a coffee or hot chocolate."

Seeing the desperation and willingness in his father's eyes, Carter couldn't refuse. "Sure! I'd really like that."

Carter followed his dad into the ever-changing house. When they arrived inside, he noticed the ambiance drastically changed to a happier and warm environment. Sitting on the couch reminded Carter of the years playing video games or cuddling with his mom. Honestly, he never really had significant memories with his father. It was a sad reality, but at least they had that now. Carter laughed to himself, acknowledging what had unfolded.

They could never maintain a relationship, but they had this abnormal dream realm to finally communicate. His father walked into the room within a blip and handed him the most extravagant hot chocolate he'd ever seen. On the other hand, his father held a giant platter of chocolate chip cookies and brownies.

"I hope you still have a sweet tooth." His dad laughed, nervously setting the platter on the table. "If not, I can get you something healthier!"

Noticing his father's urge to please him, Carter felt guilty. "Dad, this is perfect. Thank you."

"Great," Richard whispered, sitting near him while holding a big mug of warm coffee.

The euphoric feeling soon faded, and the white elephant was nearly suffocating the air from the room. Carter looked down towards the ground, unsure of what to say. He had unvalidated feelings he wanted to address, but he believed he would drown in guilt by ruining his father's last moments with him.

"Carter," his father gently proceeded. "Say it. Tell me."

"Huh?"

"I know what you're thinking, but you'll never feel better if you don't tell me. You aren't responsible for my feelings, I am. Plus, you're entitled to express your own."

Carter was shocked because this didn't sound like his father. When it came to discussing feelings, Richard was never reasonable. His method was to compartmentalize feelings and never acknowledge them again. Avoidance was key. "I-I don't know. I'm fine."

"What I've learned, after losing your mother, and then you, was that leaving things forgotten caused a lot more pain than if I had addressed them head-on. It gave them time to marinate in the toxic and sad feelings I packaged up long ago. I know I wasn't a good father. In my heart, I hoped I could be. I thought one day it would click, and we'd have this incredible bond, but we didn't. It never happened. I always relied on tomorrow and took today for granted. I kept pushing off the uncomfortable task of allowing myself to just enjoy life. Please Carter, let me allow you to rest in peace, and then I will too," Richard begged, holding Carter's knee.

Taking a deep breath, Carter exhaled tears. "I was angry, but more than anything, I was sad. I thought you hated me. I felt like I was the reason you and Mom grew apart. It was so tense living in our house, and I never knew what to expect. All I wanted was for you to love me. I wished you would have spent time with me—doing anything at all together."

"I'm sorry, Carter. You deserved more than what you got. You are lucky you had your mother to overcompensate for me. She loved you so much, and I know she always will. The reason I was distant was because I always feared turning out like my father. In the process, I became worse. I wish I could make it up to you."

The words rang in Carter's head and caused a tickle on the back of his neck. Fumbling with his hands, he blurted out, "I just wish you took an interest in me. You don't know how much I wished that you would've just randomly snapped out of being unhappy and asked to do something with me. I didn't care whether it was playing ball together or going for a boat ride. I thought, since you always loved fishing as a kid, you'd be thrilled that I became interested in ships. Part of the reason I developed the obsession was because of you. Instead, you would belittle me or ignore me. There were times I would question if anyone loved me besides Mom. When she died—"

Looking Carter in the face, his father emphasized, "My son, I'm sorry. You didn't deserve that, you didn't deserve any of that. You are worth more than someone treating you like you don't matter. Your presence in this world was so special, and I regret every day that I didn't make you feel wanted or appreciated."

"Thanks, Dad. I never knew you cared. To hear that you did—"

"Still do—"

Carter chuckled between streams of tears, "It means the world to me."

"I always will. Please tell me about everything."

"Well, first, tell me what happened to me. The last thing I knew, I fell and hit my head on a rock in the stream," Carter recalled, shaking his head.

Sadly sighing, Richard's lip quivered. "After that awful night, I went searching for you. At first, I wanted to give you time, and myself some time, to digest what had happened to your mother. When you didn't come home, though, I knew something wasn't right. I went searching for you with our neighbors—"

Richard stood up and began pacing on the living room rug. Carter hoped his dad wouldn't wake up soon. After a few moments, Richard finally sat back down next to Carter.

"You okay, Dad?"

"Yes," he explained, breathing deeply every few words. "It's just an image I keep reliving every night, and I know that it's going to pop up again."

"What do you mean *pop up again?*" Carter asked out of concern.

"Every single night, my dreams are looped at the moment that I found you and where I lost you at the hospital. I hate to say it, but some days, I dread the night time. I try my hardest to think of good times to keep my mind off of it, but it's always drowned out by you floating in the stream." He paused as he held in a deep sob. "I don't know if I was in denial or what, but it was so surreal. Multiple times per day, I would go into the hospital to see if you woke. They would always tell me that you had a slim chance, but there was still a chance you would wake. Some nights, I would even fall asleep there hoping you would see a familiar face whenever you woke up. God, if I could go back, I would do better. I would do it all the right way. Baseball games, fishing, camping—you name it. I would do it all for you. And the ships—oh, the ships. If I could do it again, I would build a ship for you with my bloody bare hands, Carter. I don't care if it killed me. I would've hand-carved for you."

Hearing the pain in his voice, Carter knew now that his father loved him. It was a shame that it took this situation to finally prompt the feeling, but he wanted to make the most of it. "Hey, how about we go for a ride on a boat or a ship now? You don't need to have bloody hands. It's completely your dream, so you can create the perfect one."

With a huge smile plastered across his face, Richard asked Carter to cover his eyes until he was done making his surprise. "You won't be disappointed."

"I know I won't be. It's been a while since I have been on a relaxing ride on the water. I'm really looking forward to it!" Carter responded with an equally animated smile across his face.

"Okay. Close your eyes. I want to make this absolutely perfect!"

"All right," Carter agreed, chuckling to himself.

He quickly closed his eyes while beginning to fidget and tap his fingers together. Never did Carter think he would get this chance to laugh or even bond with his father. What if he woke up before the trip occurred? He tried to push it into the back of his mind and not worry about it. Too excited to think, a trickle of guilt formed in his gut as he thought about how badly his mother would have loved to see them connecting. The last conversation between Alison and Richard was about how he never tried to salvage any relationship with Carter. What would have happened if he brought Carter to the store? Where would everyone be now?

Before he got too deep into his thoughts, Richard yelled to Carter, "All right! Open 'em up!"

Immediately, Carter opened his eyes in pure amazement as he marveled over his father's gift to him. "Wow! No way! This is incredible!"

"She's all yours!" his father proudly shouted.

"She is beautiful, Dad! Thank you!" Carter exclaimed with bright eyes, pooling with tears.

"Do you like it?"

"Yes! I can't believe it! This is just like my—"

"Model ship. I know. That's why I wanted to build this for you. I screwed up in a way that I never thought I could change or fix. I still can't, but I-I hope that somehow, someway . . . " He broke down crying. " . . . we can enjoy our time together. I know I will."

While analyzing every inch of the ship, Carter raved, "Dad, this is truly amazing! The details that you remembered, how did you remember them?"

"I know you thought I never paid attention, but I did. I was just a fool," he said, anxiously smiling. "But we can talk more during our trip! Let's not waste more time!"

"Agreed! I can't wait!"

Following his father towards the ship, Carter was over-the-moon as he thought about the wonderful gift his father had given him. Thinking of how he made an identical replica of his destroyed ship, Carter felt a warm feeling crawling up his arms and neck. It was an overwhelmingly happy experience, and one he never thought he could've had with his father.

After they boarded the ship, Richard laughed. "It's a good thing this is a dream because I have no idea how to work this thing."

"This is crazy, Dad! I can't believe it," he ecstatically shouted. "Down to every last detail."

"After you passed away," Richard explained, "I kept your model ship on my work desk, so I could always have a piece of you with me."

Pausing at the thought of how to approach what he wanted to say, Carter blurted out, "Why? What made you so distant from me? There were times I was convinced you hated me. I could never understand why, though. Yes, I could've gotten myself into some small trouble, but nothing bad."

"Man, Carter. I never hated you. I actually loved you more than words could ever say. It's just that I had this ridiculous misconception of how fathers should be. I thought if I was tough on you, it would help you and desensitize you to the world we live in. Never did I realize that I was the problem or I would be the negativity in the world I feared you would encounter," Richard admitted, hanging his head in embarrassment.

Hearing his father confess his faults and true feelings brought Carter a surprising amount of closure. He felt like a heavy stone was lifted off of his shoulders and heart. The feeling was free and intensely cathartic. "Thank you, Dad. It means so much to hear you say that."

"Ah, well, I'm just happy I have the chance to. Now, tell me about your life now! Knowing I can communicate with you, I'm so curious about what you have been doing since leaving here?"

Thinking about all the chaos and stress which the other realm offered, Carter didn't want to upset his father more than he already was. "It's a magical place filled with creatures that we only thought were myths."

"Wow," Richard responded, "That sounds like a fairy tale."

Chuckling out loud, Carter smiled, "Kind of in its own way, but you won't believe what Mom is now."

"Oh, no, don't say a frog or something strange." Richard's face twisted.

"No, no, not like that. She is still a person, sort of," Carter emphasized. "Mom is a queen of the land."

Tearing up, Richard rubbed his eyes. "She was always my queen. Ah, Carter. I miss you guys so much."

"Dad, we miss you too."

As they looked out over the edge of the ship, the water rested calmly and a whale breached in the distance. It was an incredible sight as it turned to dive back down into the water. "Did you see that, Carter? That whale was massive!"

"Yeah, that was awesome!" Carter's eyes lit up with excitement.

While they stood in silence, Carter observed that his father had aged drastically since the last time he saw him. Richard's face sagged a bit under his jaw while his skin seemed looser under his eyes. Wrinkles appeared next to his eyelids and mouth, and two lines were drawn deeply across his forehead. Despite the intense physical change, Carter noticed something else.

There was a significant emotional transcendence his father had experienced since Carter was gone, and it was visible to anyone that knew him. Carter was proud of the man he had become, the man Carter always needed. Accompanying all of those wrinkles was a giant smile, one that couldn't be described. It was beyond a physical movement; it was deep within his soul.

"Speaking of Mom, please don't forget to check the safe when you wake up. Mom will kill me. Er, that's not the best way to phrase it," Carter said. "Anyway, she wanted me to tell you that."

"I won't forget." Richard laughed. "So, what've you been up to since I saw you last?"

Heavily sighing, Carter vaguely mentioned, "When I got there, I had no clue where I was. Soon, I found out that Mom was there, so I went on a long journey to find her."

"Oh, really?"

"Yeah. It was an intense adventure, but it ended well. I found her in a magnificent castle with a room waiting for me. She hand-painted ships all over it. Truly beautiful."

With a warm smile, Richard said softly, "That's wonderful, Carter. It makes me happy to know that you're both together."

"Yeah, it was nice to find her there," Carter agreed.

With a devastating look, Richard said, "Oh, no!"

"What? What happened?" Carter asked, concerned.

"I think I'm waking up." Richard cried, grabbing his son in a tight hug. "I love you so much. I don't want to lose you again."

"You never lost me, Dad! I'll always be with you, just in a different sort of way." Carter smiled, trying to hold back tears. "Dad, we want you to find something or someone that brings joy into your life. Mom and I are okay. We just want you to live out the rest of your life both happy and fulfilled. Please give yourself that."

"Okay, son. I'll try. I love you so much. Please tell your mother that I love her too. Take care of each other. One day, I'll find you guys again." Richard sniffled, fading away.

Chapter 26

Everything turned black. Everything went silent. Within a matter of moments, Carter felt his body move through a wave of pressure. Feeling heavy for a moment, he didn't want to open his eyes again. The transition of emotions throughout this whole journey, since losing his mother, had been severely overwhelming. He didn't know what to expect. Was it all a dream? Would he be standing in his house again as his mom came home from the store and dad from work? Was he going to be in the alternate world, waiting to see if Linx would finally forgive him? Or would he wake up somewhere else? Nevertheless, he stood there, evaluating everything that had just happened.

Despite the inside of his body feeling unbalanced and ready to expel any piece of food in his stomach, he embraced a new, unfamiliar feeling which was hard to describe. Life felt good. In an odd way, life finally felt somewhat easier to maneuver through. Old, deep potholes that darkened his road were at long last filled in. His shoulders stood tall and pulled back while a natural smile rested on his face. Clear thoughts filled his mind, solving problems that were once too difficult to face. At last, he found power within himself—one that was once deeply hidden under baggage. Even if he woke in the alternate world, he was no longer afraid. Donem, demon goblins, and the wanderer be damned. He feared nothing. Since his biggest vulnerability was now disproven, he was unstoppable.

His eyes were ready to open and face his next mission. Peering slowly from under his lids, the white glowing aura of his mother appeared dim, with a hint of darkness. Carter's skin crawled and his intestines twisted as his body acknowledged something was different. Unaware of why he sensed her presence as a threat, he attributed his feelings to guilt, since he was the only one able to see his father one last time.

Softly standing from a distance, the queen looked at Carter in a peculiar way. "Did it work? Did you see your father?"

Smiling brightly, Carter answered with a happy heart, "Yes, I did! At first, it was hard to see what he's been living through since we left. He's constantly being haunted throughout his dreams and just looked awful. However, we talked about things. It was uncomfortable at first, but I'm so happy we did. Before we parted ways, he built me a ship, and we sailed together for the first time. Although I wished we had done that a hundred times before, I'm so grateful that we finally did."

"Aw, honey. I'm so glad you were able to see him. I'm sure it meant so much for you to have a heart-to-heart. Hopefully, it's what you needed for closure," she calmly added with a kind smile.

"Honestly, it really was. It's changed my whole perspective on things. I-I just feel—happy."

"That's amazing, Carter! I wished I was there so badly, but I'm happier knowing this has changed your relationship! Were you able to tell him about the gift?"

"Yes, I did. He was so excited to open it. By the way, what was the gift? I'm just curious, and there is no way I can ruin your surprise now." Carter laughed.

"It was a love note attached to a long-lost video of the two of you when you were little. It was the sweetest moment, so I was saving it for Father's Day. He was having such a rough year, and I knew it would mean the world to him." She sighed with a tear in her eye.

"Aw, Mom. Really? He's going to love that," Carter said, looking down to the ground. "I feel bad that he'll be watching the video alone. Gosh, I wish I was there so badly. Like you said though, at least I was able to see him. To see the way he looked at me, it was nice. He was proud of the man I have become."

"That's wonderful, sweetie. I'm so glad you were able to do this. Now, I'll let you rest after that experience. I'm sure you have a lot on your mind which you'd like to reflect on. Take as much time as you need, I have to go meet with the chef. We're preparing for a party." She nodded her head with a smile, leaving the room. Closing the door behind her, Queen Alison turned down the hallway, wringing her hands together.

"Do you think he knows?" Linx nervously asked, popping out of a corner in the hall.

"I don't think so," the queen muttered quietly. "If he does, his acting is better than mine."

"Well, that was a good touch adding the letter. It makes it more believable. Not to mention, it makes it that much more devastating. Ugh."

Turning toward Linx, the queen whispered, "Oh, the letter wasn't a lie."

"It wasn't?" Linx asked, holding her heart.

Without batting an eye, the queen said, "No, it wasn't. But it also wasn't a sweet letter like I told Carter. It was a letter stating I was filing for divorce."

Linx's face dropped. "Oh-oh, a divorce? I thought you said he was a good person, but he just had problems expressing his emotions?"

"He was a miserable monster. Carter's father would avoid us, yell at us, and only use our presence as good publicity during holiday parties. He even cheated on me with Carter's babysitter. Only when we caught her abusing Carter did he break it off."

"You stayed with his father after he cheated on you? That must have been hard," Linx attempted to sympathize, rubbing her neck.

"When you have a nice house in a safe neighborhood and a comfortable income with both parents living under the same room, it makes it hard to leave. There were too many what-ifs and not enough of me standing up for myself and my worth. I should have left a long time ago, but I felt selfish doing so. Soon came a time when we just maintained a happy façade. That way, no one would question anything. I started believing the lie we were telling everyone else, and I believed that things would change. It didn't."

Looking behind them, Linx whispered, "I'm so sorry. If that's how you felt, do you think this plan was worth it?"

Shaking her head from side-to-side, the queen elaborated, "I feel absolutely awful about lying to him, but it needed to be done. The amount of confidence he had in that room when he woke up was remarkable. It was a complete transformation. At the end of the day, who's it hurting though? He was so happy finally getting the closure he longed for. He obtained what he needed to heal."

"I just don't know. He'll be devastated when he finds out it was all fake. I wonder if he was better off not seeing his father at all. He'll be crushed, completely crushed," Linx regretfully expressed. "If his dad was such a horrible person, I wonder if it would have been helpful just to tell him the truth. It wouldn't have been an ideal story about his father, but maybe it would've been the truth he needed for an honest closure, rather than an ideal one."

"Look, there is no way he'll ever find out. The only way he'll know is if someone tells him. Only two people know about this, so clearly I'll know who told him. Not that I even have to remind you, but he'll be crushed when he finds out that you played a part in it, too," the queen threatened. "Since you have all the answers, I'll make sure to keep that in mind."

Linx's eyes dropped to the floor as they quickly strolled through the halls and towards the kitchen. Guilt was consuming her, and she didn't know how she'd even look at Carter after what they had done. She knew there was no way he would consider forgiving them. "I-I'm sorry. I didn't mean to upset you. I just feel awful."

"Linx, we needed to give Carter the boost in confidence he needed. I won't be around for long, and we need to make sure he isn't weighed down by past burdens. This role is difficult enough," the queen emphasized while lifting her chin up high. "This land cannot afford a vulnerable, young king ruling their land."

Linx's eyebrows furrowed. "What do you mean 'young king'?"

Stopping in her tracks, the queen turned to face Linx eye-to-eye. "I know you have a soft heart, and so do I. Nevertheless, I am in a position that prevents me from being the sweet mother I used to be. Linx, I'm dying. Carter will soon become king of this land, and we need to make sure he is ready for when it happens. If he doubts himself or is distracted by his father, our land and our people will pay for it."

"Dying? You're dying? How are you dying?"

"That's beyond the point right now. I just need you not to refrain from saying anything to him. Right now, he is motivated and happy. Let's not ruin that for him," the queen responded in a snippy tone, before excusing herself.

Resting her back against the cold stone wall, Linx slid to the ground and dropped her head into her hands. Now she is being blackmailed for helping the queen. How was she supposed to say no when Queen Alison herself had requested help?

Poor Carter. The kid goes through so much heartache after having a toxic relationship with his father, and now he thinks that everything is peachy. He'll fall hard when he finds out everything is a lie. Linx just hoped she wouldn't have to be the person to break the scandal to Carter. She wanted to go check on him but was afraid he would see through the lie. One slip-up and their relationship would be destroyed forever. Fleeing the castle, Linx ran outside to get fresh air.

Chapter 27

After processing the emotional experience with his father, Carter pushed aside the fluffy, red covers. Sliding out of the bed, he made his way to the door. Debating on whether to meet up with his mother or to search for Linx, he walked down the halls until he came across one of them. The light was bright, and the air was fragrant. Maybe it was just his perception, but the people and creatures of court appeared to be in happy moods, too.

Was Carter sad that he wouldn't see his father again? Of course, but there was just something light about life, now that he knew the truth. For a moment, he wondered what life would have been like had he known his father cared about him the way he did. Ah! His heart hurt at that thought. He needed to remind himself of how appreciative he was to have seen him one last time. Strangely enough, the more Carter thought about everything surrounding the closure with his father, the stronger he felt and the more he believed in himself. Life in this realm couldn't get any better.

As he rounded a corner, something caught his eye out of the window. It was Linx and Carter's mother talking about something. Linx was rubbing her hands, then her neck. One would think she was crawling with bugs by how fidgety she was. Carter's eyes moved over to his mother. Her once calm and warm body language was now rigid and cold while she glared at Linx. Clearly, they appeared to be at odds with each other, but why? Carter ran outside to find out. Although he quickly walked up towards them, neither noticed him approaching.

"Look, you do what you want. However, I cannot stay and hide this lie. Something about it seems so wrong to me."

"Which you were a part of and had no problem with, when I asked you. Why didn't you say something then?" The queen growled.

"How was I supposed to say no to a queen? Not to mention, the mother of the only good friend that I have here. I gave up everything to help him find you, and then you ask me to do something so intense like that. I had no way to tell you no," she asserted herself as much as she could.

Unable to sit back and listen to more, Carter shouted, "Hey! What's going on here?"

Uncrossing her arms, Linx turned around and walked away. "You can talk to your mother. I'm leaving."

"You're leaving? Where are you going?" Carter demanded.

Turning to face him at a distance, Linx said, "It really doesn't matter where as long as it's not here."

Feeling pieces of his heart rip off the core, he anxiously asked, "Is it safe to be going around by yourself?"

"I should be fine."

"What is going on? Why are you leaving?" Carter shouted with his arms in the air.

"Just let her go, son," The queen responded.

Turning to face his mother, he asked, "What did you do?"

"What did I do?" the queen contested, holding her hand to her heart.

"Good luck getting anything out of her, Carter," Linx shouted from a distance.

"That's fine. If you don't want to tell me, then I will find out some other way. It'll just be a shame if my own mother won't be truthful with me," Carter said, shaking his head in disappointment.

Looking around at the forest bordering the castle, Queen Alison found herself at an interesting fork in the road. Giving a white flag sigh, she turned to face Carter while throwing her hands in the air. "It was all a lie."

"What are you talking about? What was a lie?" Carter questioned with raised eyebrows.

"Everything with your father. You didn't visit him in a dream. It was a vision that I created with the pressured assistance of Linx. It was all magic from a smoke stone I had in my crown, combined with a mix of our powers. Don't be mad at her though, she felt obligated to help me," she confessed.

Carter's heart shattered at her feet. "W-what? Why would you do that to me?"

"There are some reasons, Carter. For one, I wanted to give you the happiness and closure that you desperately needed and deserved. Two, your father wasn't there for us when he should have been."

"You didn't have to lie and make him into someone he wasn't."

"Yes, I did! Look how happy and confident you were. I could see the change, and I'm sure that you could too!" Queen Alison argued with passion.

Carter shook his head, turning away.

Queen Alison lowered her voice. "There is a bigger reason, though."

Interested in the change of her tone, Carter faced her again with curious eyes. "What is that?"

"Carter, I'm dying," she blurted out.

Instantly, his face sunk to the ground. "What are you talking about?"

"This is a long story, Carter."

In shock, Carter demanded, "Mom, it's fine. Just tell me what's going on."

"When I first arrived, I was very angry and lost. My only objective was to make sure you were okay. I didn't know if you survived the car accident or where you were. I became obsessed. It was an awful time." She paused, knowing the story was going to escalate quickly.

Nodding along, Carter muttered, "Yeah."

"Well, I searched near and far for very strong magic. Everywhere I went, no one could help me get to you. I eventually stumbled upon a special siren who could morph into a serpent. She was interested in gathering magical objects, as well," Queen Alison mentioned.

Floored, Carter questioned, "Wait! A siren who could morph into a serpent? What was her name?"

"Huh? Oh, Qita. Why have you heard of her too?" she asked.

"Heard of her? She tried killing me and even kidnapped—" Carter paused as the pieces fell into place.

"Qita tried killing you? I swear I'll hunt her down," the queen shouted with rage.

"No need to worry about her. She's dead. I kind of killed her. And the rest of the siren pirates are dead too."

The queen's asked, "You killed the full ship of sirens?"

Sighing, Carter shook his head. "No, I only killed Qita by accident. Donem killed the majority of the sirens, and Teshi killed Elena. It was really sad. But you were saying?"

With eyes wide, the queen took a breath before continuing. "Um, anyway, Qita and I took an adventure through the Violet Woods, where I acquired some gems and crystals to give to the mages."

Realizing the myths were now true, Carter was terrified to ask the question lurking in his mind. "Mom, I don't mean to interrupt you again, but I have a question."

"Of course, honey. What's your question?"

Pausing for a moment, Carter gathered himself. "Did you kill a troll named Poba?"

"Poba? I heard that name, but no. I never killed a troll. Why do you ask?"

Carter stared at her for a moment, and then asked, "Can I see your back then?"

"See my back? Carter, why are you being silly?"

With a serious face, Carter boomed, "Mom, show me your back."

As Carter waited, his worst nightmare was revealed. She turned around and lifted her delicate hair off of her shoulders. Hidden beneath her hair was a giant scar that stretched across her upper back from one shoulder to the other. He couldn't believe what he was seeing. The gossip was true. "You killed Poba! I don't know how you removed the cape, but you killed Poba!"

"Carter! I did no such thing! How dare you accuse me of that!" she hissed.

"Well, what am I supposed to think? A troll was murdered after going down underground to search for two trespassing women, who were stealing gems and crystals. His cape was cut off, and you have a scar right where it would be. The one thing I don't understand is why Elena never mentioned it. Why did she only say Qita?" he questioned.

"Because we had an agreement."

Carter's eyebrows raised in disbelief.

The queen gently explained, "I was going to tell you everything, if you give me a chance. Qita handed me the cape. She said she found it floating nearby. I wore it only thinking the cape would help protect me. I never knew it would adhere to my skin."

"So, Qita killed Poba and then gave you the cape? She probably did it to make you look guilty." Carter scoffed.

Sighing, the queen speculated, "Maybe, Carter. I didn't see her kill anyone, so I don't know for sure. Once we left, we encountered some trolls and fairies on our way out. They threatened us, but we escaped—"

"After kidnapping Linx and killing Phea?" Carter confronted her.

"Carter, I didn't harm anyone there. Once we were able to sail away, I stayed with the sirens for a while until I found a new route. Seeing if I could find someone that could help me get to you, I went through numerous villages and lands. I ended up in Crystal Woods and asked the queen if she could help me. After she denied my request, a powerful mage approached me with a proposition. They stated that if I helped them, I would be able to see you," she explained, hanging her head.

"What did they need done?" Carter curiously probed.

Queen Alison licked her lips and rolled her neck before answering. "They wanted me to kill the queen."

Running his fingers through his hair, Carter let out a sigh as he paced back and forth. What kind of person was his mother?

Part of him didn't want her to finish the story, but he knew how it ended.

"Carter, I'm trying to be very transparent with you. You deserve to know the truth. The mage agreed to help me see you again and bring you here if I killed her. How could I say no? You are my world."

He looked away from her as she defended her actions. "What does this have to do with the elder, Mom?"

"I explained I would go through with it, if he removed the cape from my back. I needed it to fight her, but I didn't want to be targeted later on. Unbeknownst to me, the mage was from the Dark Woods. When it was time to receive the reward for my service, there was a dark twist when they removed the cape. The mage unintentionally created the elders, and their lives tied themselves to mine," Queen Alison emphasized.

"Oh wow, that is crazy. The elders were created because of you! That's strange. I thought the elders were around for a very long time?"

"No, that's what the magic made everyone think. The elders were written into the fairies' history. Had I known that would be the cost, I would never have gone through with it," she admitted, slightly embarrassed to show her selfish side.

"But what does that have to do with you dying? I don't understand."

"The magic intertwined our lives together. If or when either of us died, the other subsequently follows. I don't know when or how. We were both very powerful, so I don't think either saw any threat great enough that would risk our lives."

"Why would the elder come here to try killing you then?"

"Loophole per se. If they killed me or I killed all of them, then the surviving one would be able to live separately. Keep in mind, they're very powerful. I'm sure the elder thought they could kill me to live free of fear, and then the ruling position would be available. They probably thought that with me out of the way, they could kill you and take over the land." Queen Alison shrugged while holding her stomach.

"I can't believe you withheld that information from me earlier. I wish I knew, and I could have protected you," Carter vented, remembering that his mother was still dying. "Are you okay? I'm sorry, I'm very confused. Is there anything I can do?"

"I'm sorry, honey. It's hard to concentrate and get through everything. Whatever is going on doesn't seem to be going away. The poison spread across my chest and stomach. I don't know how long I'll live for, so I wanted to make sure you were mentally prepared to take on the role as king. Please forgive me for making the wrong decision. I thought it would help you internally, but I was wrong." She panted from the pain. "Also, don't be mad at Linx. You should go find her before she gets herself lost here. I'm going to go rest."

Not knowing if it was the desensitization or burnout from the intense loss he faced, or maybe it was the shock of finding out that he was the next in the line of succession for the land, but Carter's mind was too busy to process what she was saying. One thing he knew was that he needed to find Linx as soon as possible. For all he knew, she would try going home by herself all because of his mother's actions. Rushing towards the last direction he saw her walk, Carter began to panic.

Chapter 28

"Linx!" Carter shouted, cupping his mouth with his hands. "Linx! Where are you?"

Picking up speed, Carter sprinted to the end of the front lawn to see if he could see her within the forest. Once he reached the end of the grass, he peered into the forest. Hesitating to yell, he took a deep breath.

Shouting with all of his might, Carter yelled, "Linx!"

At first he heard nothing, but he noticed there was a commotion in the distance. Running through the forest, Carter tried his best to remain as silent as possible, trying to reach the noises as quickly as he could. The closer he approached, the louder the noises were. Suddenly, he heard something that sounded like Linx!

"Argh! Ah! Get back!" Linx screamed, slamming a jak with a powerful burst of energy from one hand, holding up an energy shield with the other. Light spewed as she attempted several spells.

At first it was difficult to see, but once Carter got close enough, he realized Linx wasn't using her wand! Bewildered by her power, Carter couldn't believe magic poured from her bare hands. How was this possible? It was an incredible sight to see.

"Linx! I'm here!" he yelled, hoping to attract the attention off of her.

By no surprise, it worked. One of the three jaks turned and leaped towards Carter with a sticky string of saliva dripping from its upper teeth. Although Carter helped as a distraction, it was too late when he realized that he wasn't actually carrying his sword. Sweating profusely, he turned to run away. If anything, this would buy Linx more time to escape.

Carter's heartbeat pulsated viciously through his neck. The pressure was so intense against his esophagus; he thought for a moment that he might suffocate. An acidic sensation coated his internal organs as he tried to suppress his intuition. He knew he was moments away from being mauled by the giant beast.

As he shoved a bush out of his way, an instant wave of deja vu hit Carter. Slightly fearing their power, he contemplated not summoning his deadly secret weapon. If Carter couldn't control the goblins, he knew he could potentially lose Linx again.

Weighing out his options, he realized that doubting his strength to lead the goblins carried an equally devastating risk. How much longer would he be able to run, anyway? Even if he got away, Linx could be mauled by the remaining two she was fighting. With his mind made up, he focused all of his thoughts on his little clan of terror. By keeping his mind open, he allowed them to see where he was located and what was threatening him.

Within a split second, he heard the distant ruffle of leaves accompanied by shrill screams that would've had the trees tearing their bark off if they could. In a way, he felt bad for the jaks knowing their fate. Nevertheless, he had a family to protect. This had to be done.

Feeling the breath of the jak on his neck, Carter knew he had no choice other than to meet the goblins halfway. If he brought the jak close enough, they could destroy it. Condensing his emotions into a singular line within his body, running from his head to his torso.

He focused on controlling his thoughts, so the goblins could understand him thoroughly. Any misstep or misinterpretation of what he needed could be catastrophic. The smoke trail, from their claws gripping the ground, inched closer and closer to Carter's location. Giving his legs everything he had left in his body, Carter flung himself into the goblins' chaotic tornado of dust and debris. A loud whine pierced through the forest as the goblins shredded the jak to nothing.

Pushing himself up off the ground, Carter looked into the eyes of one of the goblins. In his mind, he thanked them for their hard work, but they knew he needed them to do more. Right on cue, Linx shrieked with pain as a jak slashed her arm with its long nails. Carter looked over to see her lying next to a dead jak that she defeated. Nonetheless, the remaining jak pinned her to the ground and repeatedly attempted to bite her face.

"Hold your ground, Linx! I'm sending help!" Carter's voice thundered through the forest.

As thoughts raced in his mind, he focused on his mission, looking over towards the goblins. Telepathically, he explained to the goblins, 'I need you to help Linx. You need to be quicker than you've ever been before. We need to save her!'

The goblins formed their tornado of terror and blasted through the forest, taunting the jak enough to glance their way. Confused by what was approaching, the jak backed off and ran from its impending death. Unfortunately for the jak, the goblins were just moments behind and engulfed the beast inside their whirling claws. Ignoring the jak's cries for help, Carter rushed through numerous bushes and past several trees to get to Linx's side.

Diving to the ground, Carter scooped up Linx and held her close. "Are you okay?"

Linx looked up and saw fear dripping from his eyes. "I'll be fine. My arm just stings now, but it's nothing more than that. Thank you for saving me."

"I didn't save you. You were incredible! How did you learn to use magic without your wand? That was amazing!" Carter gushed while scanning her face.

Swirls of butterflies danced in her stomach as she looked up to see him gazing at her. Linx's cheeks began to heat up as his sweet aroma filled her nostrils. Shaking her head from side to side, she realized the ridiculousness of what was happening. Pushing herself out of his arms and onto the ground, she forced herself up onto her feet.

"Again, thank you for helping me against the pack of jaks, but I've got to go."

"You've got to go? Where are you even going? There's no place safe around here, we both know that. You're willing to kill yourself to run away from my mother? Not to mention without your wand? Where is it?"

"Carter, you don't understand—"

"Yes, I do. She explained everything."

Shocked by what he had said, Linx's eyes opened wide. "She did?"

"Yes. She explained everything about my father's dream."

"No, she didn't. There's no way she did."

"Give me a minute to speak before pushing me away! Seriously, she confessed what she did. I couldn't believe that everything was a lie. I was devastated to find out that I didn't get to sail on a ship with my dad while he told me he cared about me. Trust me, I was heartbroken when she told me that. There was nothing I wanted more than to be validated by my father. My whole life I did things with the pure intent to see if it would bring us closer, but it never happened. She knew it was what I craved so badly, so my mom did what she could to make that come true. Am I disappointed? Yes. Am I mad at her? No. And I'm not mad at you."

"I'm sorry, Carter. I felt stuck and forced into doing something I never wanted to do. Afterwards, I thought you would attribute my involvement as getting back at you—which it wasn't."

"Don't be sorry. Really don't. As I think about it. It was still a cathartic moment, real or not. I finally heard him tell me what I always wanted to hear, that he loved me, and that he was sorry for not showing me how much he cared about my existence. Whether it was the real Richard or the fake one, it made me feel better to hear it in his voice. Honestly, it made me realize how screwed up my mind was," Carter elaborated, running his hands over pebbles on the ground. "My self-worth was always tied to my father and what he thought of me. I tried harder and harder to get his attention, despite never being acknowledged. It doesn't matter what he thinks of me, it never mattered. I'm a good, kind person. Since he didn't care to be a part of my life, then that's his loss."

Linx was speechless at what Carter had to say. She giggled a bit before poking fun. "Wow, since when did you grow up, Carter?"

Ignoring her laughing, Carter responded, "Since I realized the only person I really need validation from was myself."

"I'm really proud of you, Carter. Any person who didn't give you a chance or appreciate you was really missing out on a great guy."

Smiling from ear to ear, Carter said, "Thank you. Now, where is your wand?"

"I don't know," Linx sighed, squatting down to sit on a rock near Carter. "It got knocked out of my hand when I was fighting the jaks. I tried looking, but I couldn't find it."

"Let's try to find it," Carter suggested.

"Okay, I think I dropped it around here." Linx pointed towards a bushy area.

After searching for about an hour, Carter shrugged his shoulders. "I can't find it anywhere."

"Me neither." Linx shook her head, squatting to sit on a rock.

"I wonder if the goblins took it. I'm sorry. I thought I was able to control those things." Carter rubbed his neck. "I don't know where else to look."

Linx sighed, "Now what?"

"I don't know," he replied. "This is just crazy. Nothing can ever remain permanent forever. Every time that I turn my head, my world is falling apart from a different direction. My mom dies, then I die, then you die, we save you, my mom dies again, then we save her, I think I was able to see my father, then that becomes a lie, and now my mother is dying again. My heart cannot handle this stress. I don't know what to do. How am I supposed to rule a land that I've barely been on?"

"You'll do it one day at a time, Carter. Plus, kingdoms will have someone to assist you like an advisor, but that should be something you talk to your mom about. She is a smart woman who cares about you so much. She wouldn't just throw you to the wolves."

"You're right," he mumbled as he stood up from the ground.

Extending his hand to help Linx stand up, he asked, "Are you okay to walk?"

Groaning from the pain in her bicep, she responded, "Yes! I'm fine, Carter! You don't have to worry about me. I only got slashed on my arm from that jak's claws. It will heal. You need to worry about getting back to your mother. She wasn't looking so good the last time I saw her."

Shaking his head in disbelief, Carter uttered quietly, "I just don't understand Linx. I don't understand what happened at all. I thought she was going to be okay."

"I don't know either, Carter. Let's just get back to her," Linx suggested, sprinting back towards the castle.

"I forgot how far this front lawn was," he complained, hoping his mother was still going to be alive.

Looking at him for a moment, Linx thought out loud, "I hope this works."

Within a blink, Carter and Linx were standing at the castle door. They couldn't believe it. Somehow Linx's magic had transformed despite losing her wand. Never had she thought her powers would go beyond her wand and into her actual body. Unable to contain herself, she jumped up and down with joy.

"Linx! How did you do that?" Carter shouted in amazement.

With a giant grin plastered across her face, Linx said, "Isn't it crazy? For so long, I wasn't able to do anything without my wand. It ruled any magical ability I had, but now everything is different! I don't know what had happened to change things."

"That's unbelievable," Carter whispered, nervously walking through the courtyard and into the castle's hallway.

As they approached a servant, Carter asked to be led into his mother's chambers. Although they had been in the castle for a little while now, Carter still found it hard to believe he had reunited with his mother. It made it that much more difficult knowing they were going to be separated again.

"Linx, I wonder if there is anything else we can do to save her. I really thought she was going to be okay."

Linx looked towards the stone floor. "I know. Me, too."

When they reached her chamber door, the servant stated they could only visit for a little while because the queen needed her rest. Suppressing his urge to scream, Carter smiled and walked into her room. Like his room, there were hand-painted walls and ceilings that were so intricate and beautiful. Carter wondered if she had the time to do all of it. The closer he looked into the pictures, the more he realized they were of his childhood with her. From building ships to venturing on the beaches together and even baking cookies, thousands of pictures of Carter's life were scattered within her room. All keeping her company until he came back to her.

Peering through heavy eyes, the queen saw Carter had come to visit. "Sweetie."

Gently grabbing her hand, Carter noticed her vibrant aura was now dim and dark. "Mom, I feel helpless. How could this happen? I used my last gem to save you, but you're still dying!"

"Honey, there was nothing you could have done to save me. Despite all of our efforts, we cannot control everything."

"I can't believe the wanderer lied about the powers of the gems. I'm so sorry, Mom. I thought I could fix everything." Carter's head hung low.

"Honey, you did more than what anyone could expect!" she whispered with audible pressure on her chest. "It seems like the stone wasn't strong enough to overpower the dark spell between me and the elders. It's just a matter of time before I pass, causing the rest of the elders to die as well."

Like a child, he wanted to run away, far away from all of this change and uncertainty. The elder was dead, his mom was dying, and now he was being groomed to rule a land. This dreaded feeling was the same one that surged through his body after his mother had died and his father was being anything but a father.

Sensing his raising anxiety and depression, Queen Alison stared at him. "Carter, look at me."

Raising his eyes to meet hers, it was undeniable that Carter was holding back a waterfall of tears.

"Carter, I'm going to miss you so much. I was waiting what felt like twelve lifetimes, not knowing whether I would get to see you again. We are very lucky to have had this chance that many might not. My spirit will always be tied to you no matter where we end up. However, there are a lot of people who will rely on you here, and you need to figure out what you want to do. By the law of Crystal Woods, you're the next in the line of succession. It's your choice whether you rule this land or not. I suggest taking some time to consider everything before making a quick decision you may regret. This position is very stressful, but it's very rewarding when you see how much you can help other people and creatures alike," she expressed. Suddenly, her eyes collapsed shut as she ran out of energy.

An advisor walked over and ushered Carter and Linx out of the chamber, allowing the queen a moment to rest. Happiness fled his body as he stepped out into the strange castle. No face was familiar, and nothing seemed to bring warmth to his heart.

As they walked down the hallway, Linx gently probed, "What are you thinking, Carter?"

For a moment, he didn't say a word. Walking in silence, millions of thoughts raced through his mind. Finally, he looked over at her. "Linx, I have no idea what to do."

Her soft doe-eyed face looked over at him. "Where are your thoughts right now?"

"Well, I have a kingdom waiting to be dropped right into my hands. What person is ever in that kind of situation? Someone with absolutely no experience, who is on a search for his mother, finds out she is a dying queen, and she asks for him to rule her kingdom. That right there is ridiculous. On one hand, it sounds amazing! I could be a king! I could have servants, a massive castle, and access to almost anything I ever wanted. Sounds great, right?"

"Well—" She smirked, thinking about the luxurious life he could have as a king.

"Maybe. Maybe it can be great. But then, you need to think about all the things that could go wrong. It could be anything from different creatures or people trying to attack the kingdom or me, issues arising at court, and being unable to tell who is being truthful to me or who is using the relationship for some kind of gain. The most important thing that bothers me is that I've come to enjoy our journeys together. Yes, they're insanely dangerous and many people have died alongside of us—"

She laughed as she interrupted him. "Or killed each other."

"Nevertheless . . . " He paused, jokingly ignoring her statement, "I thrived off of our adventures together on the ship, at Donem's lair where you abandoned me, when you introduced me to the Violet Woods, as we traveled through the dangerous Dark Woods, and have now ventured through the Crystal Woods. We are a great team, Linx."

"That we are, Carter. I didn't know you were so fond of our relationship," she teased with a giggle.

"Again, I would be fonder of you if you didn't sacrifice me to Donem and his over-sized dog," he teased back, gaslighting a response out of her.

"Sacrifice you? Please, I would've taken you if I could. I didn't have enough power to transport us all. That's why I told the screecher where you were and sent the torteen," she shouted, rolling her eyes.

Not receiving the explosive reaction he anticipated, he looked over through the window.

Noticing his playfulness had faded, she gave him a little push to set him off balance. "Hey, we can still take adventures like The Great Journey to the Courtyard or Carter and Linx's Adventure to the Great Hall."

Admiring her drive to be positive in the most stressful times, he just shook his head. "Linx, if you were in my shoes, what would you do?"

"Hmm. I would probably choose to become queen and order you to get me things," she joked, shifting her eyes into half-moons.

"Seriously! What would you do?"

Sighing her silliness out, Linx shrugged her shoulders. "Honestly? It's hard to answer. I have lived my life outside of structured walls. Fairies thrive in natural settings and not inside polished stone prisons."

Nodding his head in agreement, Carter was finding the support he was looking for to answer his dilemma.

"On the other hand, I never had a family like you did," she said softly, playing with her hair.

Carter looked up at her.

"All fairies are orphans. We never got the chance to experience what a true blood-related family is like. Don't get me wrong, we love each other! I would've loved to live with my parents," Linx explained with a broken look.

"All fairies are orphans? I never knew that!" Carter added.

"You never knew that? You never knew that fairies were real! How would you know they were orphans?" Linx pressed.

Running his hand through his smooth hair, Carter thought deeply about what she said. "That doesn't make sense though."

"What are you talking about? What doesn't make sense?"

"You said that all fairies are orphans, but there were children, babies even there."

A rush of blue overcame Linx. Her eyes slowly closed as she took a breath. "Just as you came here when you tragically passed, so do others. Trust me, we are all orphans."

Pained by what Linx had divulged, Carter looked down, speechless. What could anyone possibly say at that point? To avoid having to say anything, he continued into the courtyard, looking at the beautiful flowers which were blooming all around.

"Look, I didn't tell you to feel sorry for us. I said that because I never had a legacy to follow. You have the opportunity to follow in the footsteps of not only your mother, but a queen. You'll live in a glamorous castle that has hand-painted artwork created by your mother. There's so much here to walk away from. And all for what? To go on dangerous journeys that you might not survive?" Linx criticized with a glare. "I'm not judging your choice, whatever that may be, but just really think about what you'll be walking away from if you do."

Jokingly, Carter mumbled, "It kind of sounded like you were judging."

"Carter, I'm not. You can stay or you can go. It's your own difficult choice to make. Just remember though, this choice doesn't only impact you. You'll change the lives of thousands with whatever you do."

Instantly, his gut felt like it sucked down a gallon of sour milk. As he looked around at everyone in his line of sight, he knew she was right. Who would the position go to if he didn't accept it? Sure, Carter didn't know anything about ruling a kingdom, but he could learn. What he did know was that he cared deeply for the welfare of people. If someone took over and had skewed motives or morals, many creatures would be directly impacted in devastating ways. Shuddering at the thought, Carter pictured someone similar to Donem walking into the role. He watched the children playing carefree in the distance and thought about how Donem would crush their bones just to hear them scream, and then he would use a broken bone as a toothpick to clean his teeth.

He looked at her in a concerned daze. "You're right."

Linx was shocked at the words that came out of his mouth. "I am?"

"Yes, you're right. Look around," he suggested, motioning his hand towards the countless people and creatures frequenting the courtyard. "Everyone here is happy and safe. How can I take that away from them? I have the opportunity to protect each and every one of them, and I must."

Devilishly smirking, Linx laughed. "Well, you said it. I'm right. I'm not going to deny it. Remember that when you're looking for a new advisor for your royal committee!"

"Just because I said you're right now, don't get used to it," he teased.

Rolling her eyes as she turned around, "Trust me, I won't. Now let's get back to your mother as soon as possible. I'm sure this will be huge for her."

"Yeah, you're right."

"I wonder if they'll have you fitted for your crown right away." She laughed, patting his cheek.

"Linx, will you please stop? I'm really not looking forward to this at all," Carter said, rubbing his eyes and pulling down on his cheeks.

"Relax. I'm sure she'll be able to ease some of your worries. If it's any consolation, I'll stay by your side through all of this," she offered, gently laying her hand on his arm.

"You'll stay with me?" His eyes lit up.

"Of course, I'll stay with you."

"But I thought that you would consider this castle a prison?"

Pushing him forward, she said, "I said a polished prison, and I never said I wouldn't stay."

Chapter 29

As they persuaded the guard to open the queen's chamber door, Linx turned to Carter. "You would think the queen's son, and the heir to the throne, could see his mother. Sheesh."

"I guess everyone is upset about her condition, but I can't believe it either," Carter admitted, shaking his head.

Linx leaned over, whispering into Carter's ear. "I think she'll be excited to hear your decision."

"I'm so nervous, and I don't know why."

"You'll be fine. I'll be right here with you," Linx said, smiling.

Walking up to the queen's elegant bed, Carter's heartbeat resonated through his chest. He thought to himself about what he feared more—losing her again or inheriting a massive, magical kingdom. For some reason, he figured it was more of the latter. He gently touched his mother's hand, letting her know he was there.

"Carter, my son," she whispered in a raspy voice.

"Mother."

She slightly opened her eyes. "I hope you are well. Everyone worried about me so much, have they been taking care of you?"

"Please, Mother, don't worry about us. We'll be okay."

"It's hard not to worry about you. I looked forward to this moment for so long," she whispered, beginning to tear up. "I dreamt of being able to cook you one more breakfast, nuzzle my face in your hair one more time as we watched TV, or just peeking in to see that you were sound asleep in bed. I missed you so much."

"I missed you, too, Mom." Carter silently wept, turning his head.

"If you two wanted to get out for a bit, there is a beautiful creek that snakes through the forest and pools into the most magnificent pond behind the castle," she suggested, trying to raise the corners of her lips into a smile. "That was something I couldn't wait to show you."

"We'll definitely take a walk over there, but first, there is something I needed to talk to you about."

"What's that, honey?" her raspy voice asked.

"I-I was thinking," he stuttered as Linx rubbed his back. "I'll do as you wish and take your place here. As impossible as it seems to fill your shoes, I'll follow in your footsteps and protect the land."

Happily squeezing his hand, she raved, "Carter, that is wonderful! It is a big responsibility, but a rewarding one."

"I just fear I'm inexperienced with everything about this journey," he confessed.

"You'll do just fine. You'll have a good support system that will help you learn the ropes. Lead with your heart because you have a good one. If you made it this far, you'll make it as king. You have traveled far, challenged many enemies, and you have made friends along the way. This journey is no different. There is blood, death, and sacrifice. Don't let the darkness overshadow the beauty and the light which this position offers," she advised, before resting her eyes once again.

Letting go of her hand, he walked Linx outside of the chamber and back down the hall. "I don't know how much longer I'll have with my mother, but I need to step away for a moment. I feel overwhelmed, and the way that she described that pond, it sounds very inviting. Would you like to join me?"

"Yes, that sounds wonderful!" Linx clapped her hands together. "I miss my waterfall so much. This will be so much fun."

As they walked through the hallway, Carter came across a familiar servant's face. "Excuse me?"

"Yes? How may I help you?" A young girl bowed.

"I'm so sorry, but I don't know your name," Carter politely stated.

"Um, Crystal, sir," the girl shyly answered.

Lamely chuckling, he said, "Oh, that's cool. Crystal of Crystal Woods, do you know the fastest way for us to get to the pond? My mother was talking about visiting a pond that connects to a creek."

"Yes, you can follow that hallway. It connects to a rear courtyard. The pond isn't that far from there," she quietly explained.

"Thank you so much. We appreciate it!" he eagerly thanked her as they walked off.

"She didn't think you were funny at all," Linx pointed out, mocking Carter.

Rolling his eyes, he sighed, "Thanks, Linx."

"Ha!" Linx bubbly laughed.

Once they got to the courtyard, Linx shot a look at Carter. Confused, he asked, "Is everything okay?"

Pausing for a moment, she hesitantly responded, "I-I don't know. The more I think about it, something about that girl bothered me."

"The little girl that pulled the bug out of the ground? Good, I'm glad I wasn't the only one. Did you see what she did after that? She ate it! Disgusting —" Carter babbled.

"No! Not that. The girl in the castle that gave us directions. I believe she said that her name was Crystal? I don't know. Something was off about her," she admitted.

"What? The girl in there? Yeah, she didn't chuckle once. Not even a sympathy smile."

"Not that. There was just something about her that seemed strange. I didn't know if you picked up on it too. Apparently not." She pouted, pondering the answer to her question.

"Look, I have no clue what you're talking about, but I need to get to a place of serenity. When we get there, I just need a minute to slowly breathe in the air. I feel so burnt out that I'm making dad jokes now," Carter complained under his breath.

"Sure, Carter. Don't worry about it!" she agreed, battling the issue in her mind.

When they traveled close enough to where the creek was supposed to be, it was apparent the girl had misled them. No pond or creek was visible, and the path led straight into the forest. Wondering if the girl gave out wrong directions, Carter and Linx looked at each other as they stepped forward to peer into the woods. As Carter peeked in beyond the first set of trees, his head pushed through a transparent wave of energy.

"Did you see that?" he asked, pulling his head back.

"No, did I see what?" she asked.

Carter reached his hand out to touch the wavy wall again. "The force field."

"Force field? If it's a force field, you wouldn't be able to get through. Maybe it's just cloaked," Linx suggested, walking over to see Carter's hand enter the transparent wall.

Looking around to see if anyone else was watching him, he asked, "Do you think I should go in?"

Shrugging her shoulders, she cautioned, "What have you got to lose? Maybe you should try your leg first, just in case it gets ripped off. Better than your head."

"Wow, Linx," Carter looked over at her.

"I'm just kidding." She raised her eyebrows. Hoping he wouldn't see her, she said, "When I see that you're okay, I'll follow behind."

"There's something the matter with you," Carter chastised, shooting her a look.

"Hey, fine. I won't then." She laughed, pretending to walk away.

Carter moved into the cloaked area, waving his hand for Linx to follow through. Sighing, she deeply inhaled before hopping through the cloaked wall. Once she opened her eyes on the other side, it was a wonder no one else knew about the pond or was allowed to go there. The area was so peaceful with only a light wind blowing through the trees. The queen probably wanted to preserve the serene oasis for whenever she needed a moment to get away. As Carter and Linx continued walking through the miniature paradise, they noticed that there was in fact a pond in the distance. The rippling water reflected purple specks as the sunlight bounced from wave to wave. Leading up to it was a thin creek which gently dumped water into the pond. Carter slowly walked over to see a tilted, weathered, wooden sign.

It read:

Focus on what you wish to see,
Look in the pond and count to three.

They looked at each other and then looked over towards the water. Carter was unsure of what to make of this pond.

"No way! This is incredible. I never thought I'd ever find one!" Linx shouted with amazement.

"Huh? Find what?" Carter asked, looking around to see what she was talking about.

"The Eternity Pond!" she clarified, pointing at the sparking water.

"What is it? I didn't know we would see a special pond!" he exclaimed with a smile.

"Me neither! Well, legend states that there are two in existence. No one was ever able to find one in the Violet Woods, nor from other areas visited. Ultimately, it was believed that maybe they were more of a myth."

"An Eternity Pond? That sounds interesting. I wonder what it does, though. It seems a little vague. The description said to focus on what we want to see, look in the pond, and count to three. I hope it isn't like wanderer magic with stipulations or toxic consequences attached," Carter hesitantly whispered.

"From what I heard, I don't think there were any bad consequences from using it. Like a magic mirror or crystal ball, it shows you things you wish to see. It doesn't really grant a wish or anything. The only thing is that it's not unlimited. You can only have one vision every moon cycle. Oh, Carter!" Linx shouted with a smile.

"What? That sounds cool, I guess."

"Well, it won't be nearly as impactful as you wished, but maybe you can try seeing your father! Maybe it can at least show you if he is okay!" she hopefully added.

Carter looked down for a moment to think about what to do. Would he want to see his dad? Of course, he wanted to know that he was okay. Nevertheless, what if he wasn't? If that happened, Carter would be stuck here knowing his father was suffering, and there was nothing he could do about it.

"Do it, Carter!"

Licking his lips, he delicately weighed his options. He could see his father, or maybe he could see his own future here. That way, he thought, he would know what to expect if he had any significant traumatic battles approaching. Maybe he could see his own happiness. This was going to be a hard choice. Nonetheless, a choice he had to make. He walked over, standing above the pond as he closed his eyes.

When he opened them up, he saw bright pictures swirling in the water. As the ripples settled, Carter looked deeper into the pond. His eyes filled with tears as he saw the image of his mother's hand dropping from the side of her bed. The next image shifted to show Carter walking up to her grave, decorated in royal garb while setting flowers over the lump of dirt in the ground. It was undeniable. His mother was dying, but that wasn't the question that he asked in his mind. It was then that Carter got the answer to his question when his image turned back around to face a thriving castle.

Flowers were abloom, faces smiled brightly, and his queen approached him. Carter attempted to see who this woman was, but he could only see her silhouette. Instantly the vision was gone. Carter only saw his current reflection desperately staring back at him.

"What did you see?" Linx bombarded her way into his thoughts.

Sighing, he looked over towards her. "I saw my mother dying, but I had a queen standing by my side as we overlooked our thriving kingdom."

"I'm surprised you didn't ask about your father," she admitted, shrugging her shoulders. "That's great about your future kingdom, though."

"Yes, it is."

Impatiently bolting the pond, Linx closed her eyes for a moment. When she looked down into the water, Carter noticed her slight smile had faded to a scowl. One tear dripped from her eye and quickly fell to the ground. With a swipe of her hand, any evidence of the tear's existence was gone. Turning back towards Carter, she looked in another direction and asked if he was ready to go check on his mother.

"Yeah, we can go, but what did you see?" he tried to pry from her.

"Nothing."

"Um what? It didn't work?"

"I saw nothing."

"Oh, okay. I'm sorry you weren't able to see anything helpful or insightful. I guess, let's head back to see my mother. She'll want to know what I thought about the pond. We can just tell her I only looked, so you don't have to worry about talking," he offered.

Without a second glance, she began walking back towards the castle. He followed behind her, maintaining his distance so as to not overwhelm her. Clearly, she was upset, and Carter didn't want to press her about what she saw. Who knows what she wanted to find out, but it was just a shame the results were devastating. Trying to figure out how to make her happy, he remembered all the delicious food the kitchen staff had made.

He jogged up to meet her. "Are you hungry? Would you want to try some amazing pastries that the cooks made?"

Snorting, she responded in a snippy tone. "Isn't it crazy that we've barely been here a few days, yet you've already settled in enough to offer the food as if it is your own?"

Carter was confused and taken aback by her attitude. "What are you talking about? I just figured you'd enjoy a pastry or something."

"You see yourself with a kingdom and a queen, and you offer me a pastry. How kind of you," she scoffed.

"W-what are you talking about?" he shouted. "I'm so confused. Did I do something wrong?"

"No, you did nothing wrong. I did. I gave up too much." She teared up as she transported herself out in a flash.

Frozen in his tracks, he was so flabbergasted by what happened. Trying to replay the events in his mind, he attempted to figure out if he said or did something that could have been misinterpreted. No matter what he thought about, he couldn't see how he would have upset her. The only thing he wondered about was what she could have possibly seen in the pond. Was it truly nothing? Even if it was upsetting, why would she be mad at him? Carter thought that she knew he would give her as much as he could. He wanted to protect and compensate her for what she had invested. After all, he really felt like he loved her.

By the time he reached the castle again, people were screaming and frantically darting around the courtyard like a plague was running rampant. He could barely make out what people were saying as they ran by. Grabbing someone by their arm, he shouted, "What's going on?"

"Queen Alison is dead!" the man screamed, running out of the main castle door.

Hit with dread, Carter tried to make his way through the stampede of people, pushing their way out of the castle. He was upset himself, but he had no idea that her death was going to spark this kind of reaction. After all, everyone had known that she was days or hours from passing. Once he reached her chamber, he finally understood why the kingdom was in mass chaos.

His mother lay soaked in her own blood from a vicious attack, which apparently had occurred while she was resting in her bed. As Carter's eyes made his way up to the source of blood, he saw a wand speared through the chest of his mother. It wasn't any wand; it was Linx's missing wand. In pure shock, Carter finally realized that hovering above his mother was Linx. Her eyes filled with tears, she stared at Carter as three guards held her down to restrain her.

"Carter! I didn't do it! I didn't do it! You have to believe me!" her shrill voice screamed, so loud that it was painful.

"How—" He paused. Falling to the ground on his knees, he held his heart, trying to process everything he had witnessed. Sobbing heavily, he whispered, "Mom."

As the guards pulled Linx through the doorway, she continued to scream for Carter, "I didn't do it, Carter! She was like this when I got here."

Looking away from her, he shook his head in disbelief. He knew she was going to be leaving him, but the gruesome way that her life now ended broke Carter. Once the main guards left, he walked halfway to her bed. Quickly deciding; however, that he could not see his mother in this condition, he turned to leave the room. When he finally reached his own room, he closed the door. Climbing into his bed and surrounded by the painted ships on his walls, he broke down uncontrollably.

Chapter 30

After crying himself to sleep, Carter awoke to a thumping on his chamber door. Prying open his swollen eyes, which had nearly sealed shut, he sat up to see who was there. Almost promptly, a guard yelled through the door to get his attention. "Your Highness! May I enter?"

Taking a deep breath, Carter solemnly responded, "Yes."

The etched door knob spun to the side, and his mother's right-hand guard walked through the doorway. "I'm so sorry, Prince Carter. I'm so sorry for what you're going through. Your mother was a remarkable leader to all of us. She was a wonderful woman, fully transforming this kingdom from ashes to what you see today. We'll avenge her death. We just need your go-ahead to do so."

"You are asking me if it is okay to kill Linx?" Carter nearly stuttered.

"Your Highness, yes."

"I, um, I—" Carter could not formulate one thought to answer the guard's question.

"Your Highness, the fairy is in the dungeon. She was requesting to speak to you, but you don't have to. A woman came running when she said she saw the fairy forcefully stab your mother, the queen, with her wand. Once the guards got to Queen Alison's room, the fairy was still standing above your mother's body," the guard articulated.

Carter teared up as the guard described the scene. The images continued popping into his mind, though he tried his hardest to forget.

"I'm sorry, Your Highness," the guard apologized. "I just figured you'd want to know—"

"There's no need to be sorry. I'm glad you were truthful with me," Carter explained, trying to hold back tears.

"The advisors urge you to move forward with her beheading as retaliation and to deter such animalistic behaviors. I understand this is a very delicate situation. I can escort you to the meeting room now, if you wish," he offered with a bow.

"Yes, can you please do that?" he asked. "Before we meet with the advisors, can you please bring me to see Linx?"

"You wish to meet with the fairy?" the guard questioned, displaying a shocked and fearful look on his face.

"Yes. I need to speak with her immediately," Carter firmly ordered.

"Right this way, Your Highness."

Carter followed the guard through several halls that were dimly lit with wooden torches. Just moments before, elegant curtains, intricate paintings, and thick white candles had decorated the halls. It was clear as day that they were entering the dungeons. Screams traveled from the dungeon chambers, as their howls echoed and bounced off of the stone walls.

His heartbeat pulsated through his veins as his bicep muscles tensed. His emotions were almost indescribable as the urge to murder surged throughout his body. There was no clue what he was going to say to her, but he knew that he needed to see her face. The guard steadily removed a giant ring of keys from within his armor. Carter couldn't identify if he was impatient, or if the guard was moving at a painfully slow pace. His eyes stung as he watched the guard slide the key into the barrel and then turn it on its side. The click of the door unlocking was so intense; it felt nearly deafening to Carter.

The guard held the door handle firmly as he pulled open while whispering, "Be careful, Your Highness. I'll wait just beyond the door. If you wish for me to enter, please let me know."

"I will. Thank you," Carter quickly sputtered.

As Carter walked into the dark, damp chamber, he saw Linx strapped in the corner with a strip of fabric wrapped around her mouth and tied on the back of her head. Carter's heart sank, but he rapidly reminded himself that she was suspected of killing his mother. Treading towards her, he saw Linx's eyes widen. It was hard to tell if she was scared or excited to see him — possibly both.

Untying the fabric and pulling it from her mouth, she spat the residue out before yelling for mercy. "Carter! I'm so happy you're here! I didn't do anything to hurt your mother! I didn't, I promise!"

"But you were there, and she was dead with your wand inside of her," he added with a tense and sorrow-filled face.

"I know! Can you please help me? They twisted my arm. It hurts," she said, insinuating that the straps holding her arms needed to be readjusted.

"I'll only loosen it a tiny bit," he agreed.

"Thank you! It was a setup, Carter! I swear!"

"A setup? Who'd set you up?" he asked with furrowed brows.

"That girl! I told you there was something strange about her!" she shouted.

"What girl? The girl from earlier? The one that gave us directions to the pond?" he questioned almost humorously.

"Yes! I walked into your mother's room and saw your mother dead. When I turned around, that girl was there and told everyone that I killed her!"

"What? You think she killed my mother?"

"Well, I certainly didn't!" Linx boomed, and then she paused. "You don't believe me! After everything we've gone through, you don't believe me one bit!"

"It's not that I don't want to believe you!" Carter shouted. "You got intensely angry while we were at the pond and took off. By the time that I caught up to you, you were standing over my mother's body with your wand in her heart."

"I went to confront her about what I saw in the pond," she argued.

"What did you see?" Carter curiously inquired.

"I asked the pond if I'll be happy here. The first image that appeared was your mother closing a closet door with Poba's cape inside. Honestly, I didn't stay for the rest because I wanted to know the truth. I wanted to know if she killed Poba! When I arrived at her room, she was dead," she explained.

"Why didn't you tell me that's what you saw?" Carter demanded.

"Because the image also showed you two discussing it. I wanted to hear what she had to say."

"Well, she told me that Qita gave her the cape. My mother had no idea what kind of cape it was. She had it removed by a mage, leaving her skin permanently disfigured," he articulated.

Linx glared at Carter, attempting to figure out if the story was believable.

"That aside, you're saying you're being framed by some girl we don't know. Why would she frame you? Where did she get your wand from? Wouldn't we have seen her at some other point?"

Linx screamed at the top of her lungs, "I don't know how she got my wand!"

"Well, we are going to have to figure it out somehow— and soon."

Linx's face dropped. "What do you mean?"

"The advisors are calling for your head as justice. They want to prevent an uprising," he quietly explained.

Linx was silent for a moment as Carter's words processed within her brain. "They want me dead? They want to kill me? Carter, you can't let them! Please help me!"

"I'm going to do what I can. I have to go speak with them now. I'll be back, Linx. If you think of anything, let me know," he sadly muttered, turning to exit the dungeon.

"Carter! Carter! Please don't kill me! I'm innocent!" Linx shrieked as the guard slammed the door between them. Her cries could be heard through the dungeon hallway despite the distance.

"Do you believe her, Your Highness?" the guard questioned.

"I don't know. I really don't know. She has betrayed me in the past, but in no way could I imagine that she would heinously murder my mother. For what it's worth, she sacrificed everything she could to help me—unless she did all of that with a motive," he thought aloud.

"Only you and the advisors can decide, but she seems mighty guilty to me," he whispered, looking down a dark hallway.

"Linx brought up the one servant, Crystal. She felt that Crystal had a part to play in my mother's murder. What are your thoughts about that?" Carter inquired.

"Your Highness, these matters should be discussed with your advisor council," the guard urged.

"I understand, but you see and interact with people whom the advisors might not. Please tell me what you know about Crystal," Carter begged.

"Your Highness, I have never heard of a servant named Crystal."

"The girl who ran out saying my mother was murdered. She is Crystal. What do you know about her?" he pressed.

"I have never seen that girl in my life, nor have I ever heard of a girl in Crystal Woods named Crystal. It would be frowned upon," the guard mentioned candidly.

Carter's gut tied itself in a knot. What if Linx was right? They continued to walk in silence, making their way to the meeting room. Several advisors were waiting to discuss this travesty with Carter. Never in a million years would he think this would be his life, and now he was going to decide if one of his only friends should be sentenced to death for the murder of his mother. As they arrived at the door, he hung his head, breathing slowly and deeply before entering.

"She's escaped! She's escaped!" a voice yelled down the hallway. A second guard came running up to Carter. Barely able to breathe, he panted, "She's escaped, Your Highness. And another body has been found."

"Linx? Linx escaped? How did she escape?" he eagerly questioned, scanning the guard's face.

"I-I went in to retie the fabric around her mouth because she wouldn't shut up, but when I opened the door, she was gone! I saw her through the door window! I don't understand how she disappeared!"

It dawned on him that she had asked for his help to adjust the straps around her arms and wrists. She probably managed to get her hands out and to transport herself. Carter didn't dare say anything. What if they thought he was in on it? He shook his head in disbelief. The first guard opened the door, and Carter started to walk into the massive room.

"You stated another body has been found as well?" Carter questioned, holding onto the doorknob.

Breathing heavily, the guard said, "Yes, our guards stated that the body looked very similar to the one found burnt on the front lawn. It was wearing the clothes of that servant girl that saw the queen's murder."

"An elder," Carter whispered, exhaling every ounce of air from his body. Did an elder murder his mother and then frame Linx?

"I'm sorry, Your Highness?" the guard politely asked.

As guilt seeped through his veins, Carter admitted, "Nothing, it's nothing. I need to speak with the advisors. I made a big mistake. I think Linx was framed."

Stepping inside the monarch's meeting room, Carter was intimidated by the responsibility awaiting his attention. The ceiling was higher than he ever could have imagined, while beautifully carved chairs surrounded an extravagant table. Before he could think of what to say, five men dressed in fine, expensive threads had raised their goblets into the air. "Long Live the King!"

Carter forced a smile and walked towards the table. Barely on the throne, the overwhelming responsibility of ruling a kingdom began to suffocate Carter. As he approached his chair, a knock on the door echoed throughout the room.

"Yes?" shouted a nobleman.

The queen's right-hand guard slid through the open door. Without acknowledging anyone else, he quickly marched over towards Carter.

"Your Highness, we have somewhat of an emergency," the guard whispered in Carter's ear.

Keeping his voice low, Carter asked, "What's the emergency?"

"When our servants were in your mother's chamber, they—"

"Yes? They what?"

The guard hesitated to answer. "They noticed that her . . . closet door was not closed."

Carter took a deep breath as he stared into the guard's eyes.

"Your Highness, the cape is missing."

"The . . . the cape is missing?"

The guard sighed as he covertly slid a note onto Carter's lap. "Yes, and this note was left behind."

Carter's gaze dropped to his lap, unfolding the crème-colored note. Releasing a sigh, his eyes became erratic after reading the paper.

"Um, is everything okay, Your Highness?" asked a nobleman seated near Carter. "Please excuse the forwardness, but what does the note say? We are here to assist you."

Fumbling his hands, Carter attempted to gather himself as the eerie feeling began to sweep over his body.

The nobleman asked again, "Your Highness? What does it say?"

Looking up at all the men seated around him, Carter inhaled slowly and then dropped the note onto the table. Signed in purple ink, the note read:

Prepare for war.

Acknowledgements

Thank you so much to my readers, family, and friends. The outpouring of kindness and excitement throughout this journey has been overwhelming.

To my wonderful husband, Greg Jones, thank you so much for your presence and contributions during this project. You have been my biggest supporter, and I cannot thank you enough for your interest and hard work to help me reach my goals. From your nightly readings to your thoughtful input and patience, I am so grateful to have you by my side. I love you so much.

To my beautiful Scarlett and handsome Elliott, you are my inspiration and motivation to keep writing. I hope that, as you grow, the both of you find something you love doing. Once you find your passion, grab it and never let go. It doesn't matter what age you are, you deserve to be happy. Always remember to embrace your flaws, never stop improving your strengths, and surround yourself with people who appreciate your presence and want to see you succeed. I love you more than you will ever know.

To my parents, Dave and Diana O'Neill, thank you for supporting my writing from childhood throughout adulthood. From writing cards to poetry or stories, you have always shown great enthusiasm with my hobbies. I love you both.

A special shout out to my wonderful readers: Julie Wasilewski, Angela Kern, Sara Nowakowski, Mid Cook, Kerri Stauffer Davis,

Abigail Davis, Dave R. O'Neill, Talia Burgess, Colleen Dori, Mabel McMasters, and Hayley Walker. Your enthusiasm and dedication has been remarkable over the past several months. You have played an invaluable role in helping me to craft the perfect balance for my writing. You brought unique strengths and perspectives to the table, and it has been a pleasure receiving your live feedback. I am so grateful for your time and commitment.

A huge thank you to Filip Zrnzević for the use of his beautiful picture on the cover of my novel. Your talent is remarkable! I encourage anyone to review his breathtaking photography collection. For readers interested in viewing his work, please visit:
www.filipzrnzevic.com

A loving shout out to my beautiful friends, Kimberly Shaheen and Chelsea Collins. No matter what paths our lives may take us down, our friendship is everlasting. Thank you for the zoom meetings, phone calls, texts, and dinner dates (when we are all in the same area). I wish you both the best that life has to offer.

Sabretooth, you're one cool cat. I told you that you'd make it into the book. Thank you for everything.

In loving memory of Elaine Rose O'Neill (Grandma), José Luis Correa (Papito), and my beautiful cousin, Christina Correa. I wish you could be here to celebrate with me. I know how proud you would be of this accomplishment. I love you and miss you so much.

Sammy Jones is a fantasy author, freelance editor, and a Pennsylvania native. She is the wife of a loving husband and a mother of two beautiful children. Sammy obtained her Master of Social Work degree with a specialization in behavioral health from Marywood University. She also has a Bachelor's degree in psychology from Keystone College, with a minor in criminal justice. Sammy is fascinated by the whimsical, strange, and unusual. With a love of music and film, her favorite movies include: Labyrinth, Nightmare Before Christmas, and Alice in Wonderland. Sammy has a never-ending love for animals and enjoys hobbies that include singing, crafting, and baking during her free time.

COMING SOON:

THE SEQUEL TO DARK WOODS

SUBSCRIBE AT:
www.authorsammyjones.com
FOLLOW SAMMY JONES
TO STAY INFORMED!

authorsammyjones

authorsjones

Made in the USA
Columbia, SC
25 April 2021